ON ANOTHER LEVEL

Louise Rought

ON ANOTHER LEVEL

Vanguard Press

VANGUARD PAPERBACK

© Copyright 2011
Louise Rought

A CIP catalogue record for this title is
available from the British Library.

ISBN 978 184386 672 5

Vanguard Press is an imprint of
Pegasus Elliot MacKenzie Publishers Ltd.
www.pegasuspublishers.com

First Published in 2011

Vanguard Press
Sheraton House Castle Park
Cambridge England

Printed & Bound in Great Britain

Disclaimer

This book is a work of fiction, any resemblance to actual persons, living or dead, is purely coincidental.

Chapter 1

Alex woke up feeling rather befuddled, as though she had been partying all night: her eyes were stuck together, and she was scarcely able to open them; her mouth felt dry, leaving her tongue stuck to the roof of her mouth. Lying in darkness, she stretched her hand out to the left side, feeling an empty space, accentuating her confusion further. She lay silent for a few seconds, forcing her eyes open, eventually getting out of bed slowly, staring at the empty space where Matt should be. Thinking that she might have overslept, and that he had forgotten to wake her, she opened the bedroom door and walked along the long landing, shouting for him at the top of the stairs.

'Matt, are you there?' she bellowed.

Silence fell, making her shout louder, without response. Feeling disorientated and extremely groggy, she put her hand on the banister, shaking her head in confusion, creeping down the stairs one foot at a time.

She opened the lounge door and went to the window, peering out, searching for Matt's car, only to see her red, shiny Porsche, making her wonder where his car was. She wandered into the kitchen, took a glass from the cupboard, opened the fridge door and poured herself a glass of ice-cold water, gulping it down before refilling the glass and shutting the door. She leaned her body against the stool in the breakfast bar area.

All of a sudden she yelped out, 'Shit, shit, I've slept in!'

She had noticed the clock on the cooker (1.30 p.m.) In disbelief she raced into the lounge, viewing the clock on the DVD player, which showed the same time. She grabbed the newspaper sitting on the coffee table, realising that it was not the weekend as she had assumed, increasing her panic as she perched her pert bottom on the arm of the leather chair in bewilderment. Suddenly, out of the corner of her eye, she saw a white box on the edge of the table, making her lean across to read the label. It read: '28 Amitriptyline, take 4 a night or as necessary'.

She lowered her head, giving out a huge sigh. Her stomach began to feel tight, as though someone was tying it in knots, as the realisation of why those tablets were necessary came to the fore in her mind, sinking her into the depths of despair as tears flowed down her pale face.

She had lost weight, so much so that her cheeks seemed to have sunk into her jawline, making her look gaunt and withdrawn. She sat holding her head in her hands, startled as the phone rang.

'Hello,' said Alex, shuffling to retrieve the phone.

'Hi, flower. How are you today?' Millie asked.

'I'm not so good.'

'What are you up to today? Do you fancy going for a coffee in town?'

'Oh, Millie, I am not sure I can be bothered. I can't find the energy to do anything. I haven't been sleeping too well so I took those tablets that the doctor gave me and they have made me feel hung-over. I just woke up ten minutes ago.'

'Alex, I know that it's really hard but you have got to snap out of it. We are all worried about you. You have hardly been out of the house for weeks; you need to get out and try to take your mind off things. It's not healthy.'

'Well, I am allowed to feel this way!' she snapped

'I know that, Alex, but if you don't try then you will get worse. We only say it because we care.'

'I know. I know. OK, I will get ready and come out. Just for an hour, though.'

'Great, I will come and pick you up in thirty minutes, so be ready,' Millie said forcefully.

'OK. Bye,' Alex replied, softly spoken.

She quickly went into the kitchen and opened the fridge door, taking another gulp of water, attempting to quench her thirst before going upstairs into the en suite to get washed.

She pulled back the curtains in her bedroom, viewing dark grey rain clouds as she stepped into her wardrobe, finding some attire. She found a pair of blue jeans scrunched up on the top shelf of her wardrobe, a red hooded cotton jumper and heavily worn brown sandals. Searching in the drawers, she pulled out a blue denim bag, throwing in her personal items scattered over her bedside table. She brushed her hair, deciding to tie it back as it was messy, making her face look even more gaunt, emphasising the dark circles and puffy skin around her eyes. She stood glaring out of the bedroom window, waiting for her friend to arrive.

A few moments later Millie pulled up, beeping the horn.

Alex got into the car, raising half a smile, without speaking.

'I thought that we would try the new coffee shop that has just opened in town, Alex, if you like?'

Approving, she nodded, gazing out of the window, dazed, as they drove in silence.

Shortly afterwards, they arrived in town, parking the car, walking the short distance to the coffee shop as Millie scanned her friend from head to toe, frowning.

The coffee shop was very modern with several brown leather couches all around the perimeter, a shiny wooden floor and wooden chairs and tables in the centre.

Alex placed the order while Millie sat on one of the couches near the back of the shop. She ordered a mocha, a bottle of water and a Sprite, which the waitress got, allowing another girl to set out the tray. Quickly Alex felt the water. Discovering it was not cold enough, she asked rather abruptly for a colder one. Scowling, the waitress picked up the bottle and opened the fridge, taking another one out.

Alex felt the second bottle.

'Yes, I suppose it will do,' she commented, shaking her head.

Without comment, the young waitress raised her eyebrows, opening her eyes wide whilst at the same time slightly twisting her face, tightening her lips together, drawing them into her mouth without opening them at all. This strange look of disapproval from the waitress made Alex tutt quite loudly, so much so that the other waitress, who by now had made the mocha, frowned at her, trying to work out what the problem was. Alex remained silent, screwing her lips tight, proceeding to pay for the drinks, glancing at the young waitress, who had moved to the side of the counter. Alex lifted the tray from the counter and slowly walked over to Millie, watched, without her knowledge, by the young waitress, who mumbled something under her breath.

'Stupid bitch,' Alex heard.

Alex turned, glaring, reciprocated by the young waitress with even more distaste, as Alex walked off, banging the tray hard on the edge of the table, spilling some of the mocha, while Millie sat browsing through a magazine that had been left on the table.

'Steady on, flower. You will break the table and have no drink if you bang it that hard. What the hell's the matter?' said Millie.

'Can you believe the cheek of some people?'

'What do you mean?'

'Well, that stupid waitress has got such an attitude problem. I can't believe the arrogance of the little shit!'

'Who the hell are you on about?' Millie asked, searching the room.

'Her,' Alex said, pointing to where the girl was standing.

'Who, that girl? she said, staring.

'Yep.'

'Oh,' Millie replied, raising her eyebrows.

'What are you looking like that for?'

'Well, nothing, I just got a bit of a shock that's all.'

Looking puzzled, Alex sat down, taking off the items, placing them on the table.

Millie began to chuckle (as she often did) and then went on, 'She hasn't half wound you up, hasn't she?'

'No, not really, she is just a stupid idiot with the worst attitude I have ever seen. She called me a stupid bitch under her breath. I heard her as I walked past. I have a good mind to go over there and demand to know what her problem is.'

'God, Alex, calm down, what is the matter with you?'

'I only asked for a colder water than she first gave me. I am the customer, who should always be right, and she gave me this look … well, it was so sarcastic, I got annoyed there and then.'

Flushed from her frustration, so different from the very pale-faced woman that had strolled into the coffee shop, a rather

12

sullen, withdrawn person ten minutes previously, Alex sipped her mocha.

'Maybe she is having a bad day, and took it out on you, Alex,' Millie replied, shrugging her shoulders.

'Mmmm … perhaps. Anyway, let's not think about her. Tell me what happened last night with Benny.'

'Well, he rang me, and we chatted for about thirty minutes, before he had to go. I am not sure I can do it any more. I miss what we had and I miss him so much. He may still ring me, and he tells me how much he regrets what has happened between us, and how much he values my friendship, but I ache for him, and what we had. It's hard. I can't seem to live with him or without him,' Millie commented, shaking her head, placing her hand over her mouth, sighing as she closed her eyes for a few seconds.

'I know it's hard for you, but despite what happened, you did love him, and truly found that forbidden fruit.'

'Forbidden fruit?'

'Yes, the passionate lovers that you were, even if it was short-lived. Not everyone has that.'

'You have that, though, you have just got engaged.'

'Yeah, I guess so,' she commented, unconvinced.

Sipping her drink, she watched the young waitress come to the next table and clear it, glaring once more.

'God, what is her problem?' she said, lifting her hands off the table.

'Yes, I see what you mean, she is staring at you. Do you know her?'

'No, but she is pissing me off now.'

Smiling, Millie shook her head. 'She has beautiful hair, though. Don't you think?' she said, attempting to provoke a reaction.

'What?'

'Well, to be honest, she is really pretty; I was quite shocked when I first saw her. Don't you think?'

Glancing at her, Alex watched her moving to the other side of the shop, leaning over another table to reach for some cups. Her bum was so pert and small. She wore dark blue jeans, and seemed to fit into them as if she had been poured into them from

13

a coffee pot. Her legs were long and thin. Her hips were tiny and her waist very small. She wore high-heeled shoes that could barely be seen, owing to the long length of her jeans, but could be heard, as she clip-clopped across the floor.

'Well, I don't think she is that nice. I think we are just as nice as her,' Alex claimed with confidence.

'You just won't have a thing nice said about the girl because she wouldn't dance to your tune, Alex.'

Alex tutted, shaking her head, as Millie laughed at how stubborn Alex could be.

The girls stayed and chatted in the coffee shop all afternoon, helping to lift Alex's depressed spirits, injecting a faint sparkle into her eyes.

Chapter 2

The next morning Alex woke up early. She had slept better than she had in the previous few weeks. She turned to cuddle into Matt, whose warm and silky skin felt like a pure silk scarf that brushed against your neck.

'Lurve ya,' Alex whispered softly into his ear.

Matt purred like a new kitten tucked up in its basket, all happy and cozy.

'Don't go to work today, stay home with me. We can watch films and lie on the couch all day stuffing our faces,' she muttered.

'What?' Matt replied, both eyes firmly shut.

'Don't go to work today. I don't want you to.'

'I have to, I have things to do.'

'But you aren't that busy at the minute, are you? Anyway, get one of the technicians to do it.'

Finally opening his eyes, he turned, cuddling her.

'But what do you want to do?'

'Well, I thought that we could spend the day together.'

'But we can spend the day together tomorrow as it's the weekend and we will be anyway.'

'I know, but I just felt like having some company today and being with you. It's OK, you go to work, I will just potter around on my own,' she said sharply.

'Oh, Alex, don't be like that. You don't have to be alone, you could come into work and see everyone; they all ask after you. You don't have to do any work; you could just have some company for a bit and take your mind off things.'

'Forget it, Matt. I won't ask you again.'

He sighed, shaking his head.

Sitting up, she attacked him with her words. 'What are you fucking sighing at?'

Jumping up, he attempted to cuddle her. Pulling away, Alex dived off the bedcovers, leading out of bed with her left leg, dragged back by him.

'Alex, please let me help you. I'm so worried about you and how you are being since...' he pausing, red-faced.

'Go on, Matt, say it, fucking say it,' she demanded, pulling away from his clutching.

'Well since...' he stuttered, as Alex cut in.

'Just forget it. I'm fine. I will sort myself out, you don't need to worry about me.'

Matt glared at her, biting his fingernails.

Shaking her head, forcing back the tears, she continued, 'You are unbelievable, you!'

Worried, he walked to the window, placing his hand onto her shoulder, kissing her neck softly.

Flinching, she moved her shoulder, rejecting his advances.

'Alex, don't be like this. I'm here for you. I love you so much and won't let you down.'

Tapping on the window ledge, she yelled, 'How can you be there? Yesterday was the first day in weeks when I felt better; I slept better too, and so today, I come to you and ask you to be off with me, spend some quality time with me, and what do you say? Wait until tomorrow. Has it occurred to you that I need you today, not tomorrow?'

Dropping his head, he advanced towards her, stroking her bony cheeks with his finger, whispering in her ear. 'I'm sorry, baby, I didn't think. I will take the afternoon off with you and we can watch a film, whatever you want.'

Gulping, she wrapped her arms around him, wiping her eyes onto his bare, tanned shoulders, squeezing his muscles tightly.

After a few seconds, he drew away, looking into her dark, hazel eyes, grabbing her hands, holding her close.

'Wow, you have the most beautiful eyes.'

'Quietly, she murmured, 'I look like a woman of forty, instead of twenty-eight, my bags are so bad.'

Gently running his fingers under her puffy eye sockets, he shook his head, smiling. 'No, you don't, you are beautiful and have sparkling eyes.'

Turning away, Alex looked out of the window, fixing on the trees blowing in her garden, swaying from side to side.

Softly pulling her face back towards him, he gently kissed her.

'Why can't you talk to me about what you think and how you feel?'

Alex nodded, swallowing. Realising her sadness, Matt walked off into the en suite. Standing at the window in her short pajamas, she continued to gaze out of the window.

'I will be back for about one if not before. Why don't you go the hairdressers while I'm at work; I notice that you have not been lately.'

Alex nodded, taking a deep breath.

Alex had returned from the hairdresser's feeling better about herself, sauntering up the stairs, deciding to change her clothes. As she came down the stairs some moments later, she caught a glimpse of herself as she glided past the full-length mirror in the hallway. She wore a lighter pair of jeans with a cream leather belt with a large buckle on the front, a cream fitted shirt with letters printed all over in light brown, a beige scarf worn inside her shirt, and tied at the side, and dark brown knee-length boots with a silver buckle at the top left side of each, which tucked inside her jeans. She wore little make-up except for a very fine pink lip gloss with the slightest silver glitter in it, making her lips, although fine, stand out, accentuating her perfect teeth. Her hair rested perfectly above her shoulder as she looked out of the lounge window, waiting for Matt's imminent arrival.

On seeing his car she rushed to open the door. As always he had his suit on, making him look very smart. His big shoulders and bulging arms made his suit jacket look tight, almost as though he was a bouncer. Alex loved him in his suit; he looked so businesslike, she thought, gazing at him.

As he came in, he scanned her from top to toe, smiling broadly. He grabbed her, kissing her.

Alex giggled.

Matt quizzed, 'What are you laughing at?'

'You have lip gloss all over your lips.'

Smiling, he grabbed her once more, nibbling her neck, throwing his jacket onto the floor, as Alex loosened his tie. Panting, he unbuttoned her jeans, touching her inner thighs, biting her neck. She unzipped his trousers, unfastening his belt, tossing it onto the floor. Kissing her, he pressed her against the wall.

'Oh, I'm so hard today, I want to feel myself inside of you,' he teased.

Tugging her jeans off, he slid his fingers inside her pants, licking her ears, pressing himself against her. He tore off her pants, kissing her hard, banging her head off the wall, attempting to make her wetter. He whispered, 'Here, put it inside of you,' placing her hand into his pants.

Alex pulled her hand away.

'No, you put it in.'

Tutting, he spread her legs open, lifting them, shoving their pelvises together, kissing her neck and ears.

Afterwards, they lay on the floor, panting. Matt kissed her softly, wrapping his arms around her.

'I love you.'

'Lurve ya too,' she reciprocated.

'Don't say it like that. Say it properly.'

'Oh, Matt, what are you like? Come on, I'm hungry, let's go out for some lunch.'

'I thought you wanted to stay in and watch TV?'

'I do, but I would like to go out for lunch first.'

Alex and Matt strolled around town hand in hand.

'What about here? This looks new. I haven't seen this place before,' he said, approaching. 'Coffee et al ...'

Alex looked.

'It looks familiar. I think I have been here before.' She paused for a moment before continuing. 'I was here yesterday. It was quite nice. In fact, yes, let's go in. I will see if that very stroppy waitress is in today and I will make her get me another water,' she said with an unpleasant tone.

'What waitress?' he responded as he opened the door, going inside.

Ignoring him, she followed him into the shop, scanning for spare couches.

'Oh, there are no free seats. I am not staying here. Let's go somewhere else less busy,' she demanded as they stood in the middle of the coffee shop.

Just as they were about to leave, he saw a table being vacated.

Hurrying over, he placed his coat on the chair as she followed him, requesting that the table be cleared. Matt looked over to the counter, seeing a very large piece of fudge cake out of the corner of his eye, licking his lips.

'What are you grinning at?' she asked.

'I know what I am having,' he replied.

'I can guess; some sort of cake, either toffee or chocolate fudge cake.'

'Yes, you know me too well. I have had a sandwich at work before I left. What do you want?'

'Erm … a bottle of water and a mocha and … I think I will have a toffee doughnut too as I haven't eaten all day. Will you have half, though, as I can't eat a full one?'

Matt laughed, walking off to go and place the order, not answering her question.

Alex sat down, gathering the dirty cutlery together, placing it to one side ready for it to be cleared. Just as she was doing so, a waitress came over. At first Alex did not recognise her, but then as she approached the table the girl frowned at her, clearing the cluttered table. Eager not to show her keenness, Alex pretended not to look but found herself transfixed by the girl's amazing eyes.

They were green, and so big. Her eyelashes were remarkably long. She wore black eyeliner and mascara, further emphasising those wonderful eyes. Alex took a deep breath, lowering her head, attempting to disguise her gaze. Noticing, the waitress tried to clear the glasses away in a hurry, her cheeks bright red, making her break two of them on the floor, forcing Alex to giggle. With a piercing stare, the girl tutted, prompting Alex to laugh, unmasking the girl's beauty, as she scuttled away, allowing Alex to admire her figure. Matt returned with the cake, doughnut and drinks. Quickly she lifted the water off the table.

'This water isn't cold enough. I will go and change it.'

She leapt off her chair, darting to the counter, standing at the side where the fridge was, content to see that the young waitress had gone back behind the counter.

'Could I have another bottle of water, as this isn't cold enough?' she asked, grinning.

The waitress snatched the bottle from the counter, opening the fridge, pulling the first drink out that she put her hand on, plonking it back in the same place, without speaking or looking at Alex. Alex felt the bottle.

'This isn't cold either. Maybe if you got one from the back of the fridge instead of the front it might be colder,' she insisted.

Once again the girl took the drink, finding Alex another one, this time from the back of the fridge. Once more she banged the bottle back down on the counter with even more force than previously, without speaking, and began serving the next customer. Disgusted with her manner and attitude, Alex remarked angrily,

'Your manner is terrible. I am a paying customer, you know. You should learn how to have manners. I will teach you them if you like!'

Flushed, the girl glared at the floor.

Alex shook her head, walking off, viewing Matt happily eating his cake with it all round his mouth like a child.

Within seconds she had forgotten about how angry she was, smiling at Matt and his chocolate-covered mouth, as she sat opposite him eating her doughnut (giving Matt some), drinking her mocha and cold water.

'It's nice in here. We will have to come again.'

Alex nodded.

As they stood up to leave, Matt's phone rang. Work had asked him to call in, much to Alex's dissatisfaction, wanting to go home and watch a DVD with her fiancé by her side. Compromising, she decided to go and look in the shops while Matt returned to work for a short while, collecting her on his return.

As they made their way to the counter to pay the bill, Alex found herself staring at the waitress in fascination, as she ran her front teeth over her top lip. She noticed that her full lips were beautifully shaped without being too big; in fact they were perfect. Alex admired her model looks, as Matt thanked the waitress, and they exited the shop to go their separate ways.

She perused the shops with drooped shoulders, scanning quickly, the rails full of the autumn season fashions, without picking up a single item, exiting the shops almost as soon as she entered them.

As she strolled by the shops, making her way back into the city centre, she heard her phone beep. Reaching in her bag, she took it out.

'I will be another 30 mins. I will meet u next 2 the entrance 2 the bus stop. CU then!' the text read. Alex smiled, put the phone back into her bag and continued to walk, thinking about something delectable to buy for dinner, en route to the food store. As she sauntered down the high street she noticed a very colourful tie in the window of Matt's favourite designer shop, deciding to go and buy him a present, hoping to cheer herself up. Exiting the shop with her brown bag, she walked briskly towards the food store.

She walked into the store and picked up a basket; she walked up and down almost every aisle. She picked up a pizza, looked on the back of the box, saw how many calories were in it, and put it back down.

As she walked past the sweet aisle her eye moved towards the end of the shelf where she saw liquorice allsorts. Suddenly tears formed as she gently picked them off the hook, holding it in her hand for a few seconds, before putting it back down. Searching in her bag, she took out a tissue, wiping her eyes. Her phone rang; it was her mum.

Preferring not to answer, she placed it back in her bag as she continued to stare at the packets of sweets, quickly wiping away the fallen tears as they soaked her cheeks. Scanning the shop to see if anyone was looking at her in tears, she put down her basket in the middle of the aisle, marching out of the shop, making her way to the bus station.

After a few minutes of what seemed too slow for a walk and was more of a stroll, dragging her feet, she arrived at the bus stop area. She stood with her back against the wall, gazing at the ground. Once again tears slowly trickled down her face; she quickly caught them with a wet tissue that she held in her right hand, swallowing.

'Are you OK?' a voice said softly.

Alex looked up, replying, 'Yes.'

An old lady, waiting for the bus, had noticed that Alex was upset, moving closer to the wall where she stood.

'Are you sure?'

'Yeah, I'm fine. I think that I have just got something in my eye,' she uttered softly.

'Really? They look like tears to me,' replied the old lady in a very comforting voice.

'Yeah, really, I'll be fine. My fiancé will be coming to pick me up soon,' she answered.

The old lady, dressed all in black, lowered her eyes. Picking up Alex's left hand, she said, 'Oh, that is a beautiful ring, my dear. With a ring like that you must have a good man; there is no need to cry, surely?'

Alex smiled at her gratefully, prompting her to stop crying. She had a soft spot for old people. They could always raise a smile whatever they said. The old lady also smiled as she took hold of Alex's hand tightly, quickly letting go as soon as she had grabbed it.

'Here is my bus. Bye,' she said, walking towards the bus.

'Bye,' Alex responded, gazing at her watch.

Boarding the bus, the old lady waved, making her way to a seat near the front.

Lowering her head, Alex stared at the pavement. Suddenly she looked up, sensing that someone was staring at her, seeing a slim girl with light auburn hair blowing in the slight wind. She had noticed Alex, without her knowledge, from the moment she had arrived, transfixed by her beauty. As she stared, Alex did not recognise her, until the girl turned her head sideways, pretending to look away. Immediately then she recognised her: her fabulous eyes gave the game away, they were so big and green and striking. Alex remembered that Millie had commented on how silk-like her hair was as it blew onto her face. Alex noticed how shiny it looked. She watched her put her hands into her pocket, pulling out a tissue, wiping her nose. She had quite a long nose but the exact shape was blocked by her hand and the tissue. She wore a three-quarter-length pink coat, buttoned up right to the top. Noticing this, Alex began to smile. Becoming aware of Alex's staring, the girl glared fiercely at her. Her eyes widened even further, pleasing Alex, who stared in envy at how lovely they were. Eventually, they became locked in a staring competition, halted as the girl was tapped on the shoulder, informing her that the bus had arrived. Sighing, Alex viewed her as she boarded the bus, noticing that she did not seem that tall, looking slightly taller than herself. Gazing at the girl, she had not seen Matt parked on the corner waiting for her. The bus pulled away, and the girl's eyes locked on Alex's as it went past. Neither girl smiled, even though both of their mouths moved, as if they were about to; instead they gazed at each other.

When the girl was no longer in sight, Alex made her way to the car, where Matt was waiting for her.

'Hey, angel, did you have a nice shop? I see you bought something,' he asked, fixing his eyes on the small brown bag.

'Yeah, I bought you a nice new tie.'

Leaning forward, he cuddled her, stroking her face.

'Your eyes look red, have you been crying?'

Ignoring him, she reached in the bag, pulling out the tie.

'Do you like it?'

'Yes, it's really nice. Didn't you get anything for you? You haven't been shopping for ages. Didn't you get any food? I thought that would definitely have attracted you?'

Becoming red-faced, Alex gritted her teeth, drawing in her lips, tapping her hand on her leg.

Gulping, Matt asked, 'What's up, baby, have I upset you? I only asked if you…'

Alex cut in, 'Oh shut up, Matt. You are getting on my nerves!'

Closing his eyes, taking a deep breath, Matt started up the car, driving off. Alex stared out of the window in silence. Matt grabbed her hand, pulled away by Alex.

Rubbing his left hand around the top of the gear stick, Matt drove quicker, pressing his foot on the accelerator pedal.

Staring at him, she uttered, 'Why are you driving so fast?'

Ignoring her, he slowed down.

Biting her bottom lip, she stared out of the window, moving her hand across her face.

Breathing heavy, swallowing as often as possible, Matt stopped at the traffic lights. Pale-faced, he looked at her.

'What the fuck's the matter with you? Stop looking at me,' she screamed.

Shaking his head, he pulled away from the lights, silent.

'What, what are you shaking your head for? I bought you a present, for God's sake, when I couldn't be bothered.'

Sighing, he said quietly, 'I wish you would let me help you. You are just not yourself and it hurts me to see you like this.'

Alex's eyes welled up, placing her hand on top of his, above the gear stick, as they drove without speaking.

Chapter 3

'Hope, are you getting out of that bed? It's after ten a.m. and you have got to look after your sister as I am going to visit Gran,' bellowed Belle.

Ignoring her, Hope rolled over in her pink bedcovers with her eyes still shut.

'Hope, did you hear me? I said get out of that bed now, right now!'

Hope lay still. Some moments later her mother came bouncing upstairs, bursting into her bedroom, standing at the foot of the bed with her hands on her hips.

'Who do you think you are ignoring? Get out of that bed. I have to go and visit your gran and I need you to look after your sister.'

'Why me? Where is my dad? Why can't he watch her? I mean, she is fourteen, you know, and can look after herself,' replied Hope abruptly.

'Your dad is busy looking for stuff on the computer for our holiday to Florida. She needs help with her homework; I don't want your dad disturbing. You know what he is like.'

'Well, where is our Ben? Can't he watch her?' she commented.

'No. You can so get up and stop moaning!'

Hope pulled back the covers, glaring at her mother.

'He gets away with everything. Why can't he watch her? Because he will be in bed hung-over after a night out with his mates. I went to bed at 1.30 a.m. and he wasn't back then so …'

'Yes, he is in bed. He has a headache.'

'That's crap. He is hung-over. Last week when I was hung over and was sick downstairs, we all know what happened then, don't we, but him…'

'Well, I think the least said about that the better, don't you? Just get up now!'

Hope sat up, putting her feet over the edge of the bed, as if she was about to get up.

'You treat me like a child, you and my dad. I am nineteen. All my other friends can do whatever they want. They go out all the time, and go on holidays with their friends, but I am not allowed, as you say that I am not responsible enough to be in the house with just me and Ben. It's pathetic. But I tell you what, there is no way that I am going on this holiday that he is looking for. I went last year and told you then that it would be the very last time that I was going away with you …'

Belle interrupted, 'You ungrateful cow, you came on holiday because we paid for you. We even gave you your spending money, as you had been told to save up but didn't, so don't start there.'

'I couldn't save up. I didn't have time. You only told me I was going five weeks beforehand.'

'We booked it as a surprise for you.'

'No, you did it so you could get your way and have me come with you. Did Ben have to go? Oh no, and he is younger than me. You treat me like a child and I am sick of it. He gets away with so much and in your eyes can do no wrong, and is spoilt so much, whereas me, I am treated with no respect in this house.'

Raising her arms, mouth agape, Belle retaliated.

'You only get respect if you earn it. You say you are the older one, yet how come you are working in a dead-end job and your brother has got a good job? I am allowing him to sleep in this morning, and asking you to look after Amber, as he gets up early every day, and works hard.'

'And do I not get up early and work hard?' she asked with an offended tone.

'You call that hard work, serving tea and coffee? I don't think so,' Belle scoffed, much to the resentment of her daughter as she pulled the covers back, staring at her tangled hair in the mirror.

'This room is a mess. You can get that tidied as well,' said her mother as she left the room, clashing the door.

Hope sat on the edge of the bed, combing her long, shiny hair as she said out loud, 'Stupid house, I hate living here. Our Ben gets away with everything!'

She made her way to the bathroom in her pink pajamas, before going downstairs to help Amber with her homework.

'Morning, Hope, did I hear Mum shouting at you to get up?' Amber said, sniggering.

'Shut your mouth or I won't help you with your homework, you little brat,' Hope replied.

David overheard Hope from his computer in the dining room, making him comment, 'Hope, don't speak to your sister like that.'

'God, you can't even breathe in this house without getting it wrong,' said Hope under her breath, making her way into the kitchen to do the breakfast.

Belle came into the kitchen before leaving to visit her mother. Hope was happy to see her go, thinking that she would enjoy peace and quiet without her mother giving her chores to do, and nagging at her, as she so frequently did.

'Hope, can you make me some toast, please, if you are putting some in,' shouted a voice from upstairs.

Hope ignored the voice, continuing to eat her cereal.

Again the same voice shouted the same thing minutes later.

Hope again ignored it. Finally the voice got louder until David stood up from his chair, went to the bottom of the stairs and yelled, 'For God's sake, boy, stop screaming and come down and do your own toast, you lazy sod!'

Ben did not see eye to eye with his father, but avoided arguments and confrontations when Belle was not around to defend him; therefore he got out of bed and went downstairs, making his own toast, joining his sisters.

An hour later Belle returned to make the Sunday dinner. The girls went upstairs and got ready, before eating lunch at about 1.30 p.m. After which Hope, as usual, was given the job of doing the dishes while her siblings left, doing as they wished. Every week she protested, but to no avail; she was made to do them anyway. If she really argued about it, Belle would comment on Hope's failure at college, and how they had supported her throughout those three years financially, still providing a roof over her head at only £10 board per week, still paying for her driving lessons, shaming Hope to do them.

After tidying her room (which took ages owing to how messy it was) Hope rang her friend Macy; they chatted about the previous evening, as Macy explained to her about her imminent holiday with her boyfriend, provoking Hope's envy, wishing that she could meet a boy she liked enough to go on holiday with, enabling her to enjoy all the magical moments that relationships can bring.

After speaking to Macy she lay on her bed listening to music, daydreaming about a better life for herself.

She was such a daydreamer.

Chapter 4

As Hope sat on the bus en route to work her eyes began to close; she was barely able to keep them open, dreading the day ahead owing to sheer exhaustion. Suddenly the bus came to a sharp halt as it arrived at the bus terminal, forcing her to exit. She stood up and moved forward, dragging her legs along. She got off, walking the short journey to the coffee shop, mulling over the previous evening.

11.35 a.m.

Alex woke up with a jerk, almost startled, groggy from her sleeping tablets, answering the phone.

'Hello,' she said, her voice muffled in a sleepy daze.

'Hi, baby, I just thought that I would ring to see how you were as you seemed to be whimpering in your sleep last night, and tossing and turning a lot. Did you have a bad dream?' Matt asked.

'I don't know. I can't remember dreaming.'

'Oh, I was just worried about you, that's all. What are you doing today? You know I don't want to nag you but you can't spend all day in bed sleeping for ever. Why don't you come back into work, just for a few days a week?' he asked, softly spoken.

'I'm not ready yet,' she replied sharply, sitting up in bed.

'But it might be good for you. The more time you have to think the sadder you will become. There is stuff to be done here at work. I need you back, even if it is just for a couple of days to start off with.'

Alex sat forward on the bed.

'I can't believe how insensitive you can be. I am not ready to come back yet,' she responded, grabbing the duvet.

'OK. No problem. We can manage without you. You take more time, then.'

'Thanks, baby.'

'What are you going to do with your day today, any plans?'

'I am not sure yet. I had just woken up when you rang me.'

'Why don't you go to that coffee shop that we went to on Friday? It was nice, you liked it there.'

'What, on my own?'

'Well, no, why don't you ask Millie to go, or your mum? She is off today, isn't she?'

'I don't know what I am doing yet. I will see when I get up what I am going to do.'

'All right, well, I am going to have to go back to work now. I will text you later. Lurve ya.'

Alex smiled faintly.

'What time will you be in tonight?'

'I am not sure; sevenish if I get a lot done. I will text you later and let you know.'

'OK, bye-bye.'

'Bye,' he said, hanging up.

Hanging up the phone, she lay back down, pondering her plans for the rest of the day. After thinking for a few moments, she rang Millie, inviting her to the coffee shop, eager to see the waitress again, bemusing herself. Millie explained that she had made other plans with her mother, unmasking Alex's disappointment for some unknown reason.

Determined to see her, she bounced out of bed, searching in her wardrobe among the many items, finally deciding on a short green skirt and a white V-necked jumper with the front part cut out on the chest, choosing tan-coloured shoes with a wedged heel and square front. Her hair was still in good condition from her blow wave the previous Friday; she combed it through and ran her fingers through it, maintaining the style. Walking downstairs, she grabbed her car keys, and left the house for the coffee shop in the town centre.

Alex drove slowly, reasoning with herself about why she wanted to go to a coffee shop all alone, something she rarely did, unable to fathom it, feeling happy none the less.

She arrived at the coffee shop and stood outside for a moment, deliberating with herself again as to whether or not she should do this. She took a large intake of breath and went inside.

The shop was very busy, owing to the lunchtime rush, as she strolled through the door, scanning the room. Luckily a table

30

had just been vacated, near the back of the shop, so she made her way to it. She took her coat off, laying it on the arm of the couch, indicating that the seat was taken, and went to the counter to place her order.

The young waitress had spotted Alex approaching the counter, eager to serve her, as Alex frowned, noticing how tired she looked.

'Hi, can I have a mocha, toffee doughnut and a cold bottle of water,' she said boldly.

The girl nodded, making up the order. She seemed sluggish in her movements, unlike the previous two days, as she put the water on the tray along with the doughnut, while another lady made the mocha.

'Four pounds ninety,' said the girl quietly.

'Haven't you missed something out?'

The girl checked the order again on the till.

'No,' she said quietly.

'Please, perhaps,' snapped Alex.

With a displeasing stare, she took the money, placing the change on the counter, while Alex had opened her hand to receive it, making a grunting noise. Happy to have incited her annoyance, Alex smirked, placing her change in her purse, as they glared at each other for a second. Alex picked up her tray and turned her back, walking away, beaming to herself.

A few moments had passed, and Alex was happily wading through her mocha, had eaten half of her doughnut and drunk some of her water, whilst racking her brains, thinking of a way to catch the girl's attention, when to her surprise she breezed by her table, prompting a beaming smile. She moved slowly towards a table next to Alex that had been vacated only seconds ago, and began to clear it, brushing past her, pretending not to look. Alex noticed this, looking her up and down, viewing her body from head to toe, as she arched her back, clearing the dirty table, rubbing it over and over, carefully taking the items of cutlery off one by one, slotting them into her cutlery tray, and catching a quick glimpse of Alex at the same time, making her go red. Alex sipped her mocha, staring at the girl: her hair was tied back in a bun, emphasising her long pointy nose, and highlighting her large eyes with very long eyelashes. They seemed smaller than the previous day, Alex thought to herself: small dark circles protruded under them. She wore a loosely fitting pair of black trousers with two pockets on the backside that sat perfectly on each cheek of her pert bottom. She wore a loose-fitting white shirt that stopped just above the waist and black-heeled shoes and black socks with pink dots on them. Seeing this, Alex began to giggle, making the girl turn round, opening her mouth slightly, placing her front teeth on her bottom lip, shaking her head. Thinking Alex was sniggering at her, the girl turned back, gathering her tray, and walked past her, bowing her head, muttering something under her breath.

'Stupid cow,' she said faintly.

Alex saw her lips move but could not make out what had been muttered, preventing any retaliation as she sipped her water. She sat biting her nails, followed by scratching her head, searching for the girl, finding her back behind the counter. She got up, and went to the counter to order more water. The girl was pouring coffee into two cups without noticing Alex. As Alex approached the counter, standing in the queue, the girl caught sight of her, making her glare. She poured the piping-hot coffee into the first cup and then the second, with an unsteady hand, spilling the coffee onto the floor, catching a glimpse of Alex staring at her. She finished pouring, choosing to go into the kitchen and help out with cutting the onions for the toastie order. Alex stood in the queue, reaching the front. As she stood she heard a loud screaming noise. The waitress serving ran into the kitchen, leaving a long queue of people waiting. Again Alex heard crying noises. Tapping her fingernails onto the counter she stood looking towards the kitchen doors on her right. A few moments later the waitress came out, expressing her apologies, wiping the sweat from her brow.

'Is everything OK?' Alex enquired.

'No, not really. Hope has cut her hand quite badly. It is pouring blood. We have wrapped a towel around it but and needs to go to hospital but we are all too busy to take her. It isn't bad enough to call an ambulance and she says that her mum and dad are at work, and doesn't want me to ask them; we don't know what to do.'

Nodding, Alex listened as the kitchen door opened. Immediately Alex leaned forward, viewing the back of the young waitress. As she turned, she saw her blood-soaked, bandaged hand and bloody white shirt. She looked at her, seeing her red eyes and pale look, and gave a faint smile.

'Sorry, what would you like?'

'Erm... Look, I know you are busy but I have a car outside and can take her to the hospital,' Alex replied, rubbing her mouth.

'Are you sure? Do you know Hope?'

'Yes, of course. No, but I have been here a few times and been served by her. It really isn't a problem, I have no plans,' she insisted.

'OK, great, I will ask her.'

Joined by two other waitresses, the lady went into the kitchen while Alex stood at the side of the counter. Within a few minutes the young girl came out of the kitchen, holding her hand tight, screwing up her face, squeezing her eyes tightly.

Alex advanced towards her, taking out a tissue from her pocket, handing it to Hope.

'Thank you so much for doing this. We really appreciate it; Hope is happy for you to take her. Can you please let us know what the hospital says?'

'Sure. Come on, Hope, you look in pain. Let me get you there as soon as possible,' Alex explained, gently ushering Hope out of the door.

Hope sat in the car silent, whimpering, as Alex drove as fast as she could, looking at Hope over and over again.

At the hospital, Alex jumped out of the car, opening the car door for Hope, leading her quickly into the casualty reception area. Hope gave her name and was taken into the triage room, while Alex sat and waited. Hope was then escorted along the corridor into a treatment room where she sat alone. Alex sat tapping her feet, blowing out over and over, watching the treatment door where Hope was taken. A few moments later a nurse approached her, offering for Alex to accompany her friend in the treatment room while she waited for the doctor to arrive. Alex stood up and quickly walked into the room, viewing Hope sitting up on the bed, holding her lacerated hand with the other, very pale-faced.

'Are you in lots of pain?' Alex asked.

Hope nodded.

'Shall I ring your family and get them to come and be with you?'

'No, please don't. I will be alright. You can stay with me if you want. I don't mind,' she replied faintly.

Alex nodded, smiling, gently touching Hope's arm. They sat silently until the doctor came in. He examined her hand, prompting Hope to cry out, as he opened her hand, looking at the wound, indicating the necessity for an X-ray. Hope was wheeled down the corridor along to the X-ray department, accompanied by Alex who sat by her side.

'Oh, I'm really scared. I am scared of needles and it will need stitching, the nurse said. If I have anything in it, will I need an operation?'

Taking her hand, Alex smiled.

'Don't worry, I won't leave you. They will numb your hand so that you don't feel any pain. I'm sure you won't need an operation, it will be fine. You are in the best place,' she said, softly spoken.

'How do you know for sure? Are you a doctor?'

'Oh God, no, but I wish that I was. No, I just have been where you are now and it is very scary. You are being very brave.'

'What do you mean?'

'Well, let's just say I have had X-rays before and had to have my arm stitched too; it didn't hurt though, and so that's how I know you will be fine. Trust me. And I was a lot younger than you too.'

'Really, what happened?'

'Well, when I was eleven I fell down a big flight of stairs and broke my arm in several places. I cut it quite badly too,' Alex replied, filling up.

'Oh. You look sad. Does it still hurt?'

'No, not really. I guess it is a bit weaker than the other but I can do things fine; it just brings back painful memories of what could have been, that's all. Anyway, here is the nurse,' she said, shutting her eyes, taking a deep breath. Hope gazed at Alex as

34

she was wheeled off. Alex sat back in the chair looking down at the magazines, sighing.

After a short while, Hope returned and they went back to the treatment room side by side. The girls sat, catching a glimpse of each other, attempting not to stare. The doctor entered the room, telling Hope that she had not severed anything, only that she would require stitches, making her exhale. Alex smiled faintly, brushing the back of Hope's hand with her fingertips. The nurse followed the doctor into the room, bringing along the treatment trolley. Gulping, Hope saw the needles, breathing in and out quickly. Alex grabbed her hand, looking at the nurse then Hope.

'She's scared of needles, so I want to stay with her if that's OK.'

The nurse nodded as Hope closed her eyes, squeezing them tightly. Alex squeezed her hand firmly, gazing at Hope.

'You are so brave, I'm so proud of you,' Alex said, as the nurse stitched her hand, cleaning around the wound.

'There you go, all done,' the nurse commented.

Wiping her brow, Hope looked at her clean bandaged hand.

'Thank God for that.'

'See, I told you, didn't I? It doesn't hurt. Didn't I tell you to trust me?'

Smiling, Hope rubbed her eyes as the girls stared at each other.

'Thank you,' Hope muttered.

Nodding, Alex's continued to look into her eyes. Pulling a peculiar face, Hope sat up.

'Oh, I have just thought. You have been here with me through this and I don't even know your name.'

Alex giggled. 'Oh, sorry.'

'Well, what is it?'

'It's Alex, Alex Thomas.'

Chapter 5

Two weeks later

Alex woke up early, deciding to return to the coffee shop for the third time that week.

Hope started work at 11 a.m., but had got up early, ignoring her parents' request to take more time off, making an extra effort to get ready.

She wore her new denim skirt, her denim jacket, her knee-length black boots and her white polo-neck jumper. She had more make-up on than usual. She wore her hair down, straightening it to perfection.

She left the house at 10.30 a.m. to take the short ride into work. Her father commented on her appearance, complimenting her on how nice she looked, puzzled at such an effort made for work. Hope ignored his comments, leaving the house in good spirits for a change, looking forward to her day.

Alex left the hairdresser's and made her way to the coffee shop, parking the car, walking the very short journey.

As she swung the door open, her eyes immediately searched the counter, then all around the room. Sighing, she approached the counter, thinking to herself how pleased she was not to see the same waitress that she had for the past two days. She ordered a mocha and a bottle of water, staring at the cakes in the glass case at the front. She took her drink, stretching her neck forward, glaring at the kitchen door as she saw it opening. Out came a chef bringing sandwiches. Turning her back, Alex found a table in view of the counter, and she sat down facing it. She took out her phone, texting. Looking up, she heard a softly spoken voice, making her go bright red.

'Hi, I thought it was you, Alex. So, you remembered to come back then?'

Pausing for a second, catching a glimpse of Hope's taped hand, she responded, 'Well, yes, I thought I would see how the patient is doing?'

Taking a seat next to Alex on the couch, Hope smiled broadly.

'Are you OK now? How long have you been back?'

Screwing up her face, she said, 'I don't understand, you knew I was coming back today after my two week sick note. And if you remember, I said that I would come back earlier when the stitches had dissolved. I asked if you would come back and see me and you said you would.'

Playing with her eye, going even redder, Alex shuffled away from Hope. Hope looked to the floor, touching her taped hand.

'Is your hand still sore then?'

'Yeah, a bit, but I'm brave,' she commented, chuckling.

Grinning, Alex took a sip from her water, followed by her mocha.

Raising a smile, Hope said, 'I bet that's a mocha. And let me feel that water. I hope its cold enough for you or it will have to go back.'

Giggling, Alex continued to play with her hair as they sat chatting for a few moments until Hope was called to do some work, reluctantly leaving Alex sitting alone.

As Alex was about to leave, Hope hurried over, handing Alex a piece of paper.

'What's this then?' Alex asked, unfolding it.

Gulping, Hope drew in her lips, staring at the piece of paper.

'Oh, a telephone number,' Alex revealed.

Placing her tongue onto her top lip, rubbing it from side to side, she did not reply. Alex rubbed her nose several times as they both stood in the middle of the floor. A few seconds later, she reached into her bag, taking out a pen and some scrunched up paper, resting on the table, scribing. Hope bit her nails watching Alex.

Handing Hope the crumpled paper she smiled, giving back Hope's mobile number.

'Here, have my email address, and drop me a line sometime. I never text back so it's best to have this instead.'

Nodding, Hope took the paper, watching Alex leave the shop without saying goodbye.

Chapter 6

The following evening

Hope lay on her bed, staring at a piece of paper for a while before going downstairs to spend time watching TV with her family. She sat looking somewhat uninterested, which was commented upon by Belle. Hope dismissed this and picked up a magazine, flicking through the pages. Within minutes she had leapt off the couch and gone upstairs, retrieving the piece of paper from her bedside table, going into the dining room, switching on the computer, staring at the screen, tapping her fingernails on the computer desk. Taking a deep breath, she eventually composed an email.

'Hi. How are you? I enjoyed today. It was great to see you again. What are your plans for the rest of the week? You could come into the coffee shop again to talk to me if you like? I will make you a nice mocha, and if you come in on the afternoon when it is less busy, I will give you it for free when the boss is not looking? Let me know what your plans are?

Love and lollipops

Hope'

She read it back to herself five times before finally sending it, excitedly, hoping to receive a prompt reply. She returned upstairs and ran a bath. Soaking peacefully, she remembered that she had not given Alex her shifts for that week. Jumping out of the bath, dripping wet as she ran downstairs with the towel wrapped around her, she composed another email.

'Hi, it's me again. I forgot to tell you my shifts for the rest of the week as they change from one week to the next –

Tuesday 1-4pm

Wed 1-4pm

Thurs 9-5pm

Fri 10-1pm

Sat 9-5pm (hate that shift lol)
Sun off hooray ☺
Bye'

For the remaining part of the evening she could not settle, deciding to have an early night, as she lay listening to music, thinking of her new friend. She thought about her age, where she lived (Alex had told her that she had a five-bedroomed detached house but not where it was), what her fiancé looked like, and how long they had been going out (she knew that she had a boyfriend as she saw her engagement ring), what job she did and when she would be getting married. As she thought about this, an air of sadness overwhelmed her, making her dismiss these thoughts, concentrating on her features, and how lovely she found her to be. The more she visualised her, the more aroused she became. Desperate to combat her unprecedented desire, she fixed her eyes on the TV.

Chapter 7

For the next few days Hope rigorously checked her email account, provoking her to send another, due to Alex's non-response.

'Hi again, it's just me. I was just wondering if you were OK as I had not heard from you. It was three days ago that I sent you emails but you have not replied. I hope you do soon or I will have to come looking for you lol. You can email me day and night, I will get it, well not unless it is 4am and I will be having my zzzzzzzzs after all I need my beauty sleep lol you don't though ☺

Bye for now

Hope

PS. Email me as soon as you get it.'

Alex had not been avoiding Hope but she had spent the last few days looking after Matt, who had contracted a viral infection, spending the last few days in bed, making her too tired to think of anything.

As the weekend arrived Hope deliberated as to whether she could be bothered to go to a club that evening with her friends. She liked going out: dressing up in her nice clothes, putting all her make-up on, dancing and receiving copious amounts of male attention. Her parents were going out, therefore she had the house to herself, as her brother and sister were also going out, deciding to stay home, checking the computer over and over.

Alex spent Saturday evening, as usual, with Matt. Owing to his illness, although he was feeling a lot better, they decided to stay in and watch a DVD.

Sunday p.m.

Feeling a lot better, Matt had decided to visit his mother, allowing Alex to sit watching TV, thinking about her father, and her nightmare the previous evening, unable to shake the recurring thoughts of his final hours before slipping away.

41

Wiping her left eye with her sleeve, she dismissed these thoughts, prompting Hope to come into her head. Suddenly, she jumped off the couch, hurrying out of the room. As she logged on her face lit up. Viewing her inbox, she strained to decipher the content. She replied after several minutes:

'Hi. Sorry I have not replied sooner but I have been busy. How is your hand? How has work been? Have you been busy?'

She clicked the send button and continued replying to her other emails.

2.53 p.m.

Hope had not long ago checked her email account for the fourth time that day, but now she perused her account again, biting the inside of her left cheek. Beaming, the reply sat waiting to be opened. She quickly read it, immediately replying:

'That's OK I have been busy myself. Work was crap, it always is apart from I got asked out by a really cute boy. But I said no!! What have you been doing?? My hand is fine now but I am keeping the bandage on for the sympathy vote and to save doing the dishes at home lol.

Hope'

Impressed by Hope's quick response, Alex happily emailed back.

'That was quick. Were you waiting? And I am sorry but I cannot understand the font too well. Sorry.'

Hope smiled broadly as she received an email straight back, replying instantly.

'I am sorry about the font. It's my fav. Is this font better? What are you up today? Are you coming to the coffee shop this week? I am in all week coz they are short staffed. I don't mind if nice people come into talk to me lol.'

Reading the screen, Alex chuckled, typing back,

'Yes that font is much better. The other one hurt my eyes and I have good eyesight. You should have said yes to the boy and got him to take you out, especially if he was cute?'

Send …

Hope grinned, barely able to type fast enough.

'No he wasn't that nice, well he was but, I dunno, I said no for some reason. Are you going to come to the coffee shop then next week to see me?

Hope'

'OK Miss Pushy Boots, seeing as you keep asking and asking, not willing to give up, I may have a wander in next week. I am not sure when. I will surprise you when you least expect it. Take care and have a nice day. I've got to go!'

She clicked send, logging straight off, wanting to visit her dad's graveside before Matt got back and insisted on escorting her there, preferring to go alone.

Hope read the email, rapidly replying without receiving any response from Alex, despite sitting there for almost an hour, allowing her to read the short but poignant messages in her inbox, creating the same aroused feeling as before, forcing her to log off forthwith.

Chapter 8

The following week Alex barely made contact with anyone. After a visit to her father's grave (which she had not visited for over a month, and even then it was only the second time since the funeral) she became inconsolable, and a virtual recluse, residing at home. Matt, family and friends were worried that she had begun showing signs of manic depression, trying many things to help her snap out of it, including suggesting the grief therapy recommended by her GP. But despite their attempts, nothing seemed to break Alex's despairing mood. Everyone knew how close she and Ken had been but it was virtually inconceivable how desolating his death had become for her. She rarely watched the TV or indeed spoke. Instead, when Matt returned from work of an evening, trying to converse with her about his day, she would either nod in agreement to whatever he said, let out very short responses or snap at him.

She declined offers to dine with her sister or visit friends, or to accept visits to the house.

Hope had checked her emails every day, sometimes up to five or six times, but to no avail. Alex had not come into the coffee shop as promised. She had awoken each morning in anticipation, believing that today would be the day when Alex would come; she would leave the house hopeful, returning dejected. Each morning she made a special effort to put on her make-up correctly, choosing suitable attire to wear.

This attention to detail seemed to go unnoticed by her family as they seemed too busy finalising their winter trip to Florida.

The following Monday, after upsetting Matt the previous evening, Alex decided to go into town to buy him some new aftershave. She parked her car, walked to the perfume shop, bought Obsession (his favourite) and strolled back. She had not washed her hair for several days, nor had she slept much. As she caught a glimpse of herself in a shop window, she scowled: she was pale and gaunt and her eyes seemed to have sunk into the back of her head whilst dark circles sat around them.

All of a sudden she heard a very upbeat but somehow young-sounding voice say 'hi'. She lifted her head slightly and there stood a very beautiful girl who was delighted to see her, giving the largest and most dazzling smile that Alex had ever witnessed. Alex recognised her immediately, barely able to smile, trying none the less. Hope attempted to strike up a conversation, rambling.

Watching as Alex strolled down the street until she was no longer in sight, Hope sighed loudly. Glancing at her watch she sauntered along the high street, meeting up with some old school friends. They chatted about boys, hair and clothes; Hope turned the pages in the magazine, pretending to listen, slurping her coffee, leaving after a short time.

The bus journey home seemed long and boring (it was only ten minutes), and Hope could not settle, moving seats twice, staring out of the window.

The house was empty when she arrived home. Sitting in front of the TV, she could think of nothing, aside from Alex, and how nice she had looked with her hair tied back, determined to get to know her better.

Alex returned home and for the rest of the afternoon sat thinking of her father's funeral, and her engagement party, transporting her into a world of her own, so much so that she did not realise tears were flowing down her cheeks, and onto her chin, until Matt entered the house. Immediately he comforted her, taking a soft cotton handkerchief out of his pocket, slowly catching her fallen tears. He held her head, pushing it onto his muscle-bound chest as he stroked her forehead, reassuring her that this pain, in time, would abate.

Chapter 9

Alex woke up early the next morning, having slept well. She thought of Hope for a moment, and how distant she had been with her the previous day, somehow rude. She paused for a moment before getting out of bed to take a shower, choosing to email her.

'Hi, Hope. I just wanted to email to apologise for yesterday. I wasn't very chatty and this may have seemed rude but I didn't mean to be. When I have pulled myself together I will come and see you for that free coffee you offered me. Ha ha ☺

Take care, Alex'

Send …

As soon as she had sent the email she went to make her breakfast.

On her return she saw an envelope on the screen.

'Hiya. Are you OK? What's up? You don't have to say sorry to me, silly. I never thought anything of it really.

Love and lollipops

Hope'

Send …

Alex smiled, replying promptly.

'Well … no, not really. I am very sad at the moment, that's all.'

Send …

'Why, what's up? You did look sad I have to admit. I am at work soon. Can you believe it? What are you doing today? What work do you do?'

Send …

'I have my own business with my fiancé but I am off at the moment. My dad has just died recently and so I am taking time off.'

Send …

'Oh. I'm sorry to hear about that. What happened? My grandad died three months ago too. I was really sad.'

Send ...

Alex liked Hope's directness and youthful naivety, making her answer with ease.

'He had a massive heart attack and died. He wasn't ill beforehand.

He just had chest pains one day, collapsed and died the next day in hospital.'

Send ...

'OMG I'm soooooo sorry for you. It must be awful for you. Do you still have a mum and brothers/sisters? I have a brother, what a goon, and a brat of a sis, but she's lovely. I dress her up with all my make-up and do her hair lol.'

Send ...

Alex read the message and grinned, typing,

'I bet they are both really nice. I bet they are younger than you?'

Send ...

'Yes, how did you know? My sister is 14 and my brother is 18. How old are you?'

Send ...

'Just a good guess. Ha ha. I am 29. Shocked eh?? I know what you are thinking, I only look 21? ☺'

Send ...

'Wow, 21. We are almost the same age then lol. Really, you look about 25 at the oldest. I am shocked at that. REALLY!!!'

Send ...

Just as Hope received the email she glanced down at her watch, viewing the time, needing to go to work, as she was now late, shaking her head. Reluctantly, she explained this to Alex, logging off. As Alex perused the Internet, an envelope came onto her screen.

'Hiya, I'm back. I rang in and told them I was bad and that I had been sick lol so I can talk to you all day if you like???'

Send ...

Alex smiled broadly, as somehow Hope took her away from her bereavement, making her laugh with the silly, childlike things she would write. Emailing back and forth, they conversed for hours about Alex and her father, family and friends. Finally, after over four hours, but what seemed like minutes, Millie interrupted, coming to see her about Benny explaining to her what had been happening with him, and as ever seeking her advice and opinion on the matter, which she enjoyed, happily logging off .

The following day they talked online as agreed. Alex told more in-depth stories about her father's death, and even tried to explain how she felt, finding this young girl easy to converse with, prompting her to ask to meet up in the near future.

Chapter 10

The wind howled outside, causing the window to rattle in Hope's bedroom. She lay awake in the pitch-black darkness of her room, tossing and turning for hours, before finally getting up. She had already chosen her outfit the previous evening: a short denim blue skirt with frilled edging, knee-length black boots and a V-necked black jumper with three-quarter-length sleeves. She meticulously got dressed, drying her hair to perfection, applying her make-up carefully, looking at herself in the mirror, checking for imperfections.

Alex woke up with a blinding headache, glancing at the clock on her bedside table several times, willing time to stand still, lacking both energy and enthusiasm, as she deliberated about cancelling her day out. She lay for some time before dragging herself up, taking a shower, choosing suitable attire from her large, crammed wardrobe, finding an outfit within seconds: black jeans, a fitted red shirt (which matched her colouring perfectly) and black cowboy boots.

She chose some black beads and a red bracelet with silver diamonds on it. She brushed her hair, grabbing her bag from inside her wardrobe, transferring the items from the bag she had used the previous day. She looked at her watch, realising she was going to be late, leaving the house in a hurry, without having breakfast.

She arrived at 11.46 a.m. (sixteen minutes later than arranged), got out of the car and knocked on Hope's door. Hope jumped up off her chair, going bright red. As the door opened she saw this very pretty lady standing before her. Her eyes scrutinised every part of Alex: her hair, bag, shoes, clothes, and in particular her teeth, as they stood before each other.

'Hiya,' Hope said.

'Hi. Sorry I'm late. I was late getting up.'

'That's OK. I was late getting up myself.'

Hope turned, reaching for her coat (which was perched on the banister behind her) and put it on, before both girls made their way to the car, walking side by side.

'Wow, this looks like a nice car,' Hope said, sitting down.

'Thanks.'

Alex started up the car and drove off.

'So, what do you want to do today?' Alex asked.

'I don't mind, anything.'

'Well, we could go shopping if you like? Do you like the cinema? We could go there too if we have time later?' Alex suggested.

'Yes, that sounds great. I don't have any plans later so I can go home any time.'

'OK, that sounds like a plan, then. We can have lunch too.'

'Yeah, sure.'

'What kind of music do you like?' Alex asked as she pressed the CD player, switching it on.

'Erm … dunno.'

'Do you like Madonna? She is my favourite. I love her. I've been to three of her concerts.'

Hope nodded in agreement as Alex played her music, posing questions, asking about Hope's knowledge of fashion, explaining to her about the designer stores she frequented. Hope seemed interested but reluctant to indicate where she shopped. Alex noticed this, probing further.

'I guess I just shop at your normal shops,' Hope remarked quietly.

'Normal shops? What do you mean?'

'Like Top Shop and that.'

Alex grinned and said, 'I love there too.'

Smiling at Alex's remark, Hope gazed at her, running her fingers over her teeth.

The girls arrived at the shopping mall and wandered round happily. Hope allowed Alex to dominate their shopping trip, perusing both the shops and the clothing that Alex liked. Hope looked on in awe of her older friend, taking pleasure in discovering Alex's world, a world that she had wondered about for some days. She studied Alex's mannerisms, such as how she always spoke with her hands, and how she rarely blinked. Alex, however, was far more interested in telling her more about her life, as Hope listened attentively, hanging on her every word.

As mid-afternoon approached the girls searched for a suitable restaurant to dine in, finding Alex's favourite Mexican restaurant, Tortillas. Hope followed Alex's lead, sitting down in this stylish restaurant, taking in the colourful menu, glaring at the unfamiliar food, as the smell wafted from the tables around them. Looking at her older friend over the top of the menu, seeing Alex study the menu in detail, she gulped.

'So, what are you having, then?' Alex piped up, continuing to read.

'I don't know, what would you recommend?'

'Have you never been here before, then?'

'No,' she responded, blushing.

'Oh well, then, I'd say have the fajitas. They are great. I'm having the salmon fillet with the chili and lime dressing. It's lovely.'

'OK, I will have that if you recommend it.'

'You won't be disappointed.'

Hope smiled.

'Do you come here often?' she asked.

Alex began to laugh.

'That sounds like a chat-up line,' she replied, roaring with laughter.

Fidgety, Hope's face went bright red, smiling innocently, bowing her head, as Alex noticed what great-shaped lips Hope had, made even more noticeable by the pink shiny lipstick she wore. Taking a deep breath, Hope made eye contact, fixing on Alex's mouth.

'What are you looking at? Do I have something on my chin or something?' Alex quizzed, taking a sip from her diet Coke.

'Nope,' she murmured.

'Anyway, in answer to your question, yes I do.'

'What question?' Hope replied with a puzzled look.

'The one about coming here often,' she joked.

'Oh yes, I forgot. It's nice here, though.'

'Are you sure that you've never been before?'

'Now that sounds like a chat-up line,' Hope said, feeling awkward.

Alex laughed out loud and said, 'I guess I deserve that.'

'Yeah, you did.'

The food arrived with the skillet bathed in steam.

'Wow, that looks nice. What am I going to do with that?' enquired Hope.

'Eat it. What do you think you're going to do with it?' Alex teased.

Hope dropped her head, trying not to show her ignorance. Alex saw this. Taking the tortilla, and placing the chicken, onions, peppers, salsa and a little sour cream on it, she rolled it up.

'Here, try this,' she said, leaning across, putting the fajita into Hope's mouth.

Hope opened her mouth to this unknown taste.

'Mmmm. I like it. It's lush.'

'Glad you like it. Try some more.'

'Thanks.'

As she did so both girls gazed into each other's eyes before Alex turned away, devouring her lunch. Hope began to laugh, prompting Alex to look up, as she tucked into her food. Hope pointed to Alex's arm with sauce (a mixture of salsa and sour cream) running down it, gently wiping away the sauce with her napkin, looking at her at the same time, as Alex continued to eat, clearing her plate, finishing off Hope's meal also.

'Was that nice, then?'

'Yes, I like it in here. You will have to bring me again!'

Alex smiled.

'You are such a breath of fresh air to be with. It takes me away from my problems, I guess.'

Hope grinned from ear to ear.

'Me too. You are dead funny,' she replied.

Alex asked for the bill as Hope hunted around in her bag for her purse. Refusing to let Hope pay half, Alex paid the bill, leaving the restaurant, thanked with gratitude by Hope. They stood outside the restaurant pondering their next activity, deciding on the cinema.

As they reached the cinema, reading the times, discussing which film to see, Matt rang, making Hope visit the toilet, returning to see Alex happily conversing with her fiancé. Walking off, she read the film synopsis, overhearing their conversation.

'Was that your boyfriend?' Hope asked softly.

'Yes. Bless him, he was ringing to see how I am.'

Hope smiled, quickly changing the subject.

'Shall we see *Bring Us to the House*? It's meant to be very funny,' Hope requested, taking out her money.

'Yes, OK, but on your head be it, if it's crap,' Alex joked, taking out her purse, advancing in the queue,

Hope shook her head smiling, getting used to Alex's unusual humour, standing shoulder to shoulder in the queue. Alex lunged forward, handing over the money, insisting on paying.

'You are so kind. I cannot believe I have met someone like you,' Hope said, transfixed on her new friend as they walked into their screening.

As the lights dimmed for the trailers to begin, Hope slouched down in her seat, feeling Alex's arm next to her; it felt warm even through her shirt. Soon after it began Hope started to shuffle, going to the toilet, returning, wriggling around, as Alex sat watching it. As the film played, Hope continued to move from side to side in her seat, visiting the toilet on two more occasions. Alex commented in jest that she had a weak bladder, beginning Hope's giggles.

'Well, what did you think of that? It was good, I thought,' said Hope, as the credits went up.

'How would you know, you spent most of it in the toilet,' Alex scoffed, raising her eyebrows.

'I'm sorry.'

'Never again, you are like a worm. Have you got ants in your pants?' she joked.

Hope laughed, trying hard not to go red, feeling her cheeks getting hot, as they made their way to the car park.

'So what do you want to do now, then? We can go for a coffee for half an hour or so if you like before I take you back, or do you see enough of coffee?'

'Yes, that's sounds good. I don't like coffee but I will have a hot chocolate. I love marshmallows in them too. Yumma,' she responded.

'Yumma. Cool word.'

Hope beamed, sensing Alex enjoying her youthfulness.

The girls made their way to Coffee Beans. Alex ordered a mocha for herself and a hot chocolate for Hope with extra marshmallows, whilst Hope visited the toilet again. Alex took the drinks over to the table and sat down. She sat on the large comfortable couch, leaving a space that Hope filled on her return, perching her bottom as close to Alex as she could get, leaning forward to drink her hot chocolate, picking out the marshmallows. 'Ouch, that's hot,' she shrieked, taking a marshmallow out of her mouth.

Alex grinned.

'Of course it is going to be hot, silly.'

Hope smiled, waiting for it to cool down, looking at this lady, ten years her senior.

'Thanks for a great day. You have paid all day. You are so kind. Next time it will be my treat,' Hope announced.

'Next time? This was just a one-off, especially given how you wriggle about,' she teased, putting her hand over her mouth, preventing her laughter.

Unsure if Alex was being serious or not, Hope paused and swallowed, letting out a huge breath. She sat for a few seconds before sitting forward, sticking out her chest.

'Can I have your mobile number, then? I'll text you some time. Well, if you are lucky, that is.'

Alex glared at this remark, tightening her lips, scrunching up her eyes as she sat making funny sounds. She reached into her bag and took out her phone, writing her number down on the napkin next to her, as Hope played with her hands.

'I'll text you some time but I never have much credit on it so don't expect many.'

Choosing not to respond, Hope took a sip from her cooler cup, sliding the napkin into her bag. They chatted merrily until

Alex insisted on leaving, wanting to spend time with Matt, feeling fatigued.

As Alex drove, Hope looked out of the window, as the music played in the background. Fifteen minutes later, Alex approached her house, leaving the engine running, tapping her hands on the steering wheel.

'Thanks again for a great day. I have had the best time ever. You are so kind too. Thank you,' she said faintly, staring into Alex's eyes.

'Me too. It was nice. But I have got to go now, sorry.'

Moving her body towards Alex as she took off her seat belt, she said, 'I will text you, I promise.'

'OK,' Alex replied, leaning her body away.

'You can have my mobile number if you want?'

'No, it's fine, you text me if you like.'

'I will for sure, don't worry,' she replied, getting out of the car, closing the door.

As she got out of the car she lowered her back, giving Alex a huge smile, reciprocated by her as she sped off. As she drove she began to think of Ken, realising it was the first time she had thought of him all day.

Alex arrived home twenty minutes later, seeing Matt lying on the couch watching TV. She kissed him on the cheek, before taking the hot bath that he had been asked to run for her.

As she lay encased in bubbles, she heard her phone bleep. She chose to ignore it, preferring to soak, as Matt joined her. He sat on the edge of the bath, gazing at her drenched in bubbles, conversing about his day, quizzing her about hers; keen to change the subject, she invited him in. He pulled off his clothes, oozing with muscle, jumping in the bath, draping himself in bubbles, kissing her. Embracing her, he caressed her small, pert breasts, with the bubbles slowly surrounding her neck. He kissed her shoulders, moving towards her neck and ears, biting them. Alex lay, allowing him to take control as he slowly eased her legs apart, gently slipping himself inside her.

Afterwards he gazed into her with devotion, whispering, 'I love you!'

Smiling, she rubbed her hand across his face.

'I know. Lurve ya too. We have to get out now, as I want to watch the film.'

Agreeing, he got out of the bath, draping the towel around her as she exited.

Going into the bedroom, searching for pajamas, she read her message.

'Hi it's just me. I wanted 2 say thanks again 4 2day I loved it. It was gr8. I can't wait 4 us 2 go out again. Love & lollipops Hope.'

She smiled, before placing the phone on top of the chest of drawers, going downstairs to watch the late film with her fiancé, cuddling up on the couch.

Hope lay in her bed, pondering on her day, anxiously awaiting a text, the phone by her side. She mused about Alex as she lay in the darkness; thoughts about every detail of the day. Closing her eyes, she slowly moved her right hand towards the tops of her long slim thighs, swallowing slightly, beginning to breathe more heavily than normal. She put her hand inside her warm shorts, feeling the moisture, knowing that she had to succumb to her aching vagina. She gently stroked herself with her middle finger, stroking harder and faster as her arousal intensified. Her breathing became louder as her soaking wet finger rubbed up and down her clitoris, slipping all over, forcing her pelvis to bounce up and down on the bed as her arousal reached its climax. Gasping in satisfaction, she eased her hand out of her short pajamas. She reached across to her bedside table, taking a tissue, wiping her hand and upper thigh. Going into the toilet she flushed the soaking wet tissue away. She returned to bed and lay for hours, tossing and turning, incapable of escaping those reoccurring thoughts and desires. She finally fell asleep at 4 a.m.

Chapter 11

'Thanks, kind waitress,' Alex teased.

Hope's cheeks flushed, giving a beaming smile.

'Run along now, kind girl; us grown-ups are talking,' Alex said in jest.

Millie began to giggle.

Going scarlet, Hope turned away.

Alex noticed her different hairstyle: she wore her hair in a small ponytail with the rest of her hair flowing past her shoulders.

'What are you like, Alex? You are funny as hell. That poor girl, you give her gyp all the time. She isn't a kid, you know.'

'I'm only playing. I am friends with her ... well, kind of.'

'What do you mean?'

'I thought I told you. I started emailing her, and then we went out shopping, about two weeks ago now, almost.'

'Really? You didn't tell me. How old is she?'

'How old do you think she is?'

'About nineteen.'

'Yes, she is. She's fun, actually. When I was out with her she made me feel young, like I was a teenager again. She takes me away from thinking about stuff.'

'Well then, that's good. You can have a friendship with people younger than you. What does Matt think?'

'I haven't told him yet. He will think I'm daft having teenage friends.'

'Well, ignore him. You have had a hard time and she may be the fun you need. You are back at work now and see him all the time ...'

Alex interrupted, 'Well, not all the time, I have only gone back part-time for now to see how it goes.'

'I know, but all I'm saying is that she may be good for you and if he doesn't approve then, I would still keep in touch with her. I doubt he will, he dotes on you, and is a very easy going-man.'

'Yeah, too easy-going at times.'

Millie agreed, looking over at the counter, viewing Hope, as she made up the orders, catching a glimpse of Alex when she wasn't looking, spied several times by Millie.

'What are you grinning at, Millie?'

Millie took a sip from her drink.

'Tell me then. Who do you keep looking at, Hope?' Alex continued.

'Never mind, Alex. Let me tell you about me and Benny. She does like you though, I can tell. Are you going to go out with her again?'

'I haven't thought about it. I have plenty of friends though, so why do I need another one, especially as she is so young. What will we have in common? She doesn't even have a proper job.'

Scowling, Millie shook her head.

'What are you looking like that for?'

'Oh, Al, it doesn't matter. I don't want to argue with you.'

Frowning, Alex drank her mocha. Millie looked over at Hope as silence fell. Shuffling on the sofa, Alex asked,

'Millie, we have been friends for years; if you have something on your mind, I'd rather you spat it out, as it is making me on edge.'

Taking a large drink, Millie stared at her friend across the table.

'Tell me, for God's sake!'

Sitting forward, Mille nodded.

'Well, it was just the comment you made about her only working here.'

'What do you mean?' Alex replied, rubbing her face.

'Well, to put it bluntly, Alex, you have changed. You are not the same as you were.'

Pulling a face, she responded, 'What are you going on about? You are not making sense.'

'Look, it's just that you shouldn't judge people for not having lots of money.'

'What are you on about? I haven't mentioned money. I merely stated that I wasn't sure if we had anything in common and that was it,' Alex replied, becoming red-faced.

'I know you have had a really hard time with your dad, and what happened, but you shouldn't care what job she does if you like her. She probably is a lovely girl who may need an older friend to talk to. I don't know, but you seem to enjoy her for some reason so go and have time and don't think what Matt will say or your posh business friends because she hasn't got a great job. I bet he doesn't like me as I don't even work right now.'

Shaking her head, going scarlet, Alex sat up, raising her right hand, waving it in the air.

'Millie, this has fuck all to do with her job, I meant her age. We went to school together, we know all about our lives, and so we have that bond, as I have with my other friends, but all I was trying to get at was, why would I need someone so young in my life? Yes if she was at university, I could relate to her, help her even but … or it doesn't matter. I don't know what you are getting at but, well, I don't even want to know. I will see her again if you think I don't see her as being worthy to be in my life. Watch.'

Alex stood up and marched over to the counter, while Millie sighed, rubbing her eyes. Approaching the counter, Alex stood at the side, hoping to catch Hope's attention as she poured hot drinks. As Hope turned, she took a step back, viewing Alex, creating a huge smile.

'Oh, sorry. You gave me a fright; I never saw you standing there. Are you OK? You look all hot and flustered.'

'Yeah, I'm fine. I was just wondering if you wanted to go out again sometime soon as I promised?'

Hope went bright red, nodding, as they stood gazing at each other for a second.

'When do you want to meet? I finish in a couple of hours if you want to meet then.'

'I can't; I need to go food shopping, but I can soon. I am back to work but I am not in the day after tomorrow, so maybe then, if you can?'

Transfixed on Alex, Hope smiled.

'Yes, that's fine,' she replied, quietly, as she got called into the kitchen, walking backwards, unable to take her eyes off Alex.

Alex walked back to the table and sat down.

'There you go, happy now?' Alex demanded.

Sighing, Millie replied, 'Oh Al, you are terrible. I just want the old you to come back, that's all.'

Dismissing Millie's comments, Alex took a drink, changing the subject.

Three hours later

Leaving the unpacked groceries on the floor, Alex heard her phone bleep and checked it.

'Hi it's me. I had just wantd 2 text 2 tell you something that I have felt since that day in the hospital and it has got stronger since.'

Pulling her face, Alex replied immediately.

'What?'

'Ur so wonderful I fink ur so beautiful x'

Alex smiled, replying.

'Thanks that is very kind of you. You are pretty too.'

Again her phone bleeped.

'No it's not just that. I have to tell you something but I am scared you will not see me again.'

Intrigued, Alex continued to text, leaving the frozen groceries on the kitchen floor.

'Don't be silly. U can tell me anything, I'd still like u.'

Hope plucked up the courage to convey what she had wanted to say for weeks, typing quickly, with her stomach in knots.

'I really wanted to kiss u 2 day.'

Flabbergasted, Alex put her hand over her mouth, reading the message again, before replying.

'What kind of a kiss do u mean?'

Feeling sick but desperately wanting to convey her feelings, Hope replied, as her fingers shook.

'A proper kiss.'

Chapter 12

As Matt and Alex lay naked, clenched in each other's arms, Alex thought about Hope. As Matt took his shower she lay curious, inspired to reach for her phone and compose a text.

'Hi Hope. Sory I didn't reply 2 yr text yesterday but I was busy. Wot r yr plans tom? Do you want to cum 2 mine? I will cook u lunch?'

Send.

Hope read her reply, feeling a shiver course through her whole body, overjoyed, until she realised she had to work, suddenly feeling sick to the pit of her stomach. She stood mulling over her shift dilemma for a few seconds, then replied.

'Hi. That's OK I know you are busy. I am at wrk tom frm 10 til 4 & tues the same 2. totally gutted!!!'

Alex read the text, sighing with disappointment, replying:

'No problem. Some other time!!!'

She sent the message and got out of bed, taking a shower before choosing an outfit to wear. She glanced at her phone, viewing a message.

'Sory2 take ages 2 reply. I have been ringing pep at wrk 2 c if I can swap my shifts. Ges wot??? I'm at wrk 9 til 12 tom & that's it so I can come 2 yrs after if u like? I will get the bus there if u tell me which bus 2 get? '

Content, Alex got ready, desirous for the next day.

Chapter 13

Hope woke up early, speculating on the day ahead, smiling.

Alex had not slept too well, waking up extremely early, mulling things over.

She got out of bed, went downstairs and ate some breakfast, sipping her coffee, thinking of her father, and the night of his fatal heart failure. Quickly dismissing these thoughts, she went to her wardrobe, looking for something suitable to wear.

Hope could not keep still at work. Her hands were shaking as she poured hot drinks into cups, mixing up orders, giving out the wrong change on two occasions. Her mouth felt dry, and her stomach felt heavy, as though she had one hundred butterflies inside it, just flying around. She glanced at her watch repeatedly, as she willed for noon to arrive, enabling her to change and re-apply her make-up before meeting Alex at 12.30 p.m.

Alex got ready, returning downstairs, picking up her keys in transit to collect Hope, excited about the day ahead.

Hope stood at the bus stop, playing with her hair, in between repeatedly checking herself out with her pocket mirror.

Alex arrived at 12.29 p.m., seeing Hope walking briskly towards her.

'Hi,' Hope said, softly spoken.

'Hi. How was work?'

'Oh, it was boring, I kept making silly mistakes.'

'Why was that?'

'I don't know. I just couldn't concentrate.'

Alex smiled, looking at Hope.

'Are you hungry?' she asked.

'A bit, but not that much.'

'Me neither.'

Alex drove, watching Hope glaring at her out of the corner of her left eye, moving her hand over and over the gear stick.

The girls arrived at the house some moments later. As they pulled onto the drive Hope commented, 'This really is a cool car. I'm not very good with them, is it a good one?'

'Yes, you could say that. It's a Porsche 911.'

'OK,' Hope replied, as she got out of the car, standing next to Alex at the front door.

Alex opened the door and they made their way into the kitchen. Hope stood with her back against the fridge door, staring at Alex from head to toe. Moving towards her, Alex touched her arm.

'Would you like a drink?' she muttered.

Moving away from the fridge, Hope stood in the middle of the kitchen, leaning on the breakfast bar, tapping her hand on the wood top. Alex opened the fridge, viewing the cans of pop on the middle shelf.

'Do you want some pop or juice?' she asked again.

Staring at Alex's legs and bottom, Hope nodded.

'What kind do you want? I have coke, lemonade, orange juice and apple juice.'

'Any, I'm not bothered really.'

Alex took two cans of coke off the shelf and closed the door with her elbow, catching a glimpse of Hope as she poured them into glasses she took from the cupboard above her head, standing with her back to her. Hope stood transfixed on Alex, continuing to tap on the bench. As soon as Alex turned around, reaching over to Hope with the glass, Hope lowered her head to the floor, taking the glass.

'Oh, I like your flooring, it's very colourful.'

Alex did not reply, sipping her coke. Hope scanned the kitchen, seeing Alex standing looking at her. She took a large breath before speaking.

'This is a massive kitchen. And it is so trendy.'

Alex laughed.

'Shall we go into the lounge where it is more comfortable?'

Hope agreed, following Alex into the lounge, glaring at her tiny waist and shapely legs. Alex took the remote control from the table, placing her glass on it, putting on the TV while Hope sat in the middle of the couch. Alex stood near the TV, biting the inside of her lip, resting her finger on her chin. Hope sat, shuffling her bottom from side to side, as they looked at each other.

'Did you used to be a fitness instructor?' Alex asked.

Taking her hand away from her mouth, Hope giggled.

'Why is that so funny? You have a good body and look like you work out.'

'I don't, I'm just slim and always have been,' Hope snapped.

Advancing towards Hope, leaning across her to the cabinet behind them, Alex took out a photo album, putting it on Hope's lap.

'Take a look at them,' she replied, sitting close to Hope.

Hope opened the album, viewing Alex in a short black dress, with curly hair and make-up, standing next to a tall man with a light coloured suit on, with short dark hair.

'Wow, you look so different. I love that dress. Where are these pictures taken? Is that your boyfriend?'

'Yes, it's Matt. It was at our engagement party.'

'Oh right. Anyway, these are your special pictures, I don't really want to look at them,' Hope responded, closing the album.

Scowling, Alex re-opened the album, flicking through the pages until she found one of a girl with short dark hair. Shaking her head, she muttered, 'That's me.'

Looking puzzled, Hope gazed at Alex, touching her face gently.

'You are joking; she's really, really fat.'

Flinching away, scanning the album, finding a younger photo of a slim girl, smiling, holding a trophy, she commented, 'That's me, too.'

Staring at Alex, Hope shuffled towards her, rubbing her fingers onto the back of Alex's hand, as Alex closed her eyes.

'Are you alright? You look sad. Did you win something?' she said quietly.

Opening her eyes, rubbing them, Alex nodded.

'What did you win?'

'I won lots of things. I was very good too. I could have been...' she paused, staring into Hope's eyes.

Touching knees, Hope continued to touch Alex's hand, advancing to her leg, rubbing gently.

'It's okay, you don't have to tell me.'

'You are so sweet. Anyone else would be pushing me to tell them but I'm not ready to say… Well, it's just that … I get, I get quite downtrodden when I think about how it was and what could have, well, what could have been,' she stuttered.

Gazing at her mouth, Hope touched Alex's lips, brushing herself closer to her.

Alex placed her right hand on Hope's chin, pressing their lips together as they began embracing. Hope pushed her tongue into Alex's mouth, kissing her softly. Alex removed her hand from Hope's chin, allowing them to lock the top half of their bodies together, kissing faster and harder. Hope forced Alex's head back, resting it on the arm; their breasts touched as their jaws locked together. Alex lifted Hope's legs on top of her, making their bodies stretch out, one beneath the other, knocking the album onto the floor. Hope moved her lips away from Alex's mouth and began nibbling her neck. Alex groaned as Hope kissed and licked harder, moving up to her left ear. Hope attempted to take off Alex's jeans. Alex stopped her, pulling her face back towards her lips.

'You are driving me wild, do you know that?' Hope said breathlessly, moving to kiss her right ear.

Alex groaned, putting her hand up Hope's skirt, feeling her wet crotch, while Hope licked Alex's neck and ears, putting her hand in between Alex's legs.

'Let me take them off. I want to feel you,' Hope said.

Moaning, both girls began to caress each other, as Alex grabbed the back of Hope's head, pulling it towards her mouth, kissing her. Once again Hope tried to loosen Alex's jeans, but Alex steered her hand away from the buttons. Hope began to rub herself against Alex's leg, gently moving up and down, kissing her. All of a sudden Alex stopped.

'I think we should stop now. It is getting out of hand,' Alex said firmly, as she moved away from her.

Hope stood up and went to the toilet without speaking. Returning, she took a drink from her coke, which was perched on the glass coffee table in the middle of the floor. Alex began to flick through the channels on the TV, while Hope put the drink back onto the table, biting her nails, as she stared at the TV screen. Standing up, Alex adjusted her jeans, glaring at the engagement photo of herself and Matt near the fireplace. Hope noticed this, biting harder at her fingernails. Shaking her head, placing her hands over her face, Alex stood still. After a few seconds, Hope stood up, placing her hand onto Alex's shoulder. Quietly, she said, 'I have never kissed a girl before but I think I like it.'

Scowling, Alex pulled away, unable to stop looking at the photo.

'Me neither, but I have a fiancé, and so it can't happen again. I'm sorry but you will have to go, I have things to do,' she replied.

Standing in the middle of the lounge, seeing Alex look at the photo, staring at them, Hope sighed, rubbing her hand firmly over her brow. Turning to face Hope, Alex frowned.

'Look, I'm sorry but I'm just not into this kind of thing. I don't mean to hurt you but I'm not gay. I am getting married.'

Glaring at Alex, Hope sighed loudly, before turning her head away, staring out of the window, feeling choked.

Chapter 14

'Could you get me a coffee?' Alex asked Geoff as he went to the coffee machine.

'Sure, Alex, no problem,' he replied.

Alex sat at her desk and stared at the paper sitting on it in a trance.

She had so much work to do but lacked application. She had telephone calls to make as well as Jodie's staff appraisal to do but could not refrain from staring at the papers on her desk.

'There you go, Alex, that might spur you on, a nice coffee. Those papers must be riveting,' Geoff commented.

'What?' she asked, puzzled.

'Well, I mean, all you're doing every time I go past your room is staring at the paperwork on your desk,' he joked.

'Oh yes, it is stimulating stuff; mainly accounts and invoices etc. ...' she explained.

Geoff nodded, going back into his office, which he shared with three other members of staff . Alex began to stare at Matt's empty desk for some moments whilst sipping her coffee, before going into reception, conversing with Jodie about this and that, pretending to show interest, as Jodie explained to her about her latest boyfriend.

'You seem tired today. Are you OK? You haven't come back to work too soon, have you?' Jodie asked.

'I'm fine. I just can't seem to get motivated today at all for some reason. What time did Matt and Bill say that they would be back from Roberts & Co.?' she asked.

'Yes, we all have days like that, I think. It will take time. They didn't say. It could be all day.'

'I have an appointment at 3 p.m. to try and get business from P & D. I won't be back after that. I will do your appraisal tomorrow.'

'OK,' Jodie responded.

Walking back into her office, Alex heard her phone bleep and found two new messages from Hope, asking her why she had not replied, and when she could see her next. Alex ignored the messages, forcing Hope to ring on three occasions, ignored by Alex. She sat gazing out of the window for some time until she went into her bag and took out her phone. She rang Millie, insisting on her advice, arranging to call round after her appointment.

'I'm going to P & D now. I have spoken to Matt and he should be back soon. He had expected to get back after lunch but the software isn't working properly and so they have to stay. I won't be back after so I'll see you tomorrow and, as I said, we will do your appraisal then,' Alex explained to Jodie.

'Fine, I will see you then.'

Alex left the office, heading for the P & D premises.

After successfully securing their future business, she rang, informing Matt, as she headed to Millie's house.

'Hi, flower. How are you? I haven't seen you for a bit,' Millie said, opening the door.

Alex smiled as she entered the house.

'God, am I glad to see you, Mil,' she said, sitting on the armchair.

'What's up? Your texts sounded weird before. I rang you yesterday but you didn't answer.'

'I bet you won't believe me when I tell you.'

'Come on, then, get it off your chest.'

'Well ...' Alex paused as her mobile rang, leaning down into her bag to see who it was. It was her friend Pearl. She chose not to answer, continuing with her story.

'Well, you know Hope?'

'Who?' Millie quizzed.

'The girl from the coffee shop who I went out with for the day?'

'Oh yes, I forgot her name, Al, sorry.'

'Yes, well, she texted me about two weeks ago now and told me that she wanted to kiss me ...'

'You are joking?' Millie interrupted.

68

'No. Well, I thought about it and curiosity got the better of me and ...'

'Well, it would with you,' Millie interrupted again.

'And on Monday she came over. She looked so cute and, well, her lips were so inviting I just couldn't help myself.'

'You are kidding? What was it like?'

'Well, that's just it. It was amazing.'

'You are having me on, though, aren't you?'

'No, I'm not, and it didn't just end there.'

'Oh God, what the hell did you do? Where? At yours? Have you told Matt? You haven't, have you?'

'Yes, at mine. No, I haven't told him. We kissed for ages and it was really intimate.'

'What do you mean?'

'Well, she was on top of me on the couch as we kissed and kissed. She sucked my neck, almost giving me a love bite, until I stopped her.' Shocked, she shook her head, pushing her top teeth past her bottom lip.

'Why did you do that with her? Just for curiosity?'

'To be honest, yes, at first, but it was so passionate. I have never been kissed like that before and I didn't want to stop. Do you think I'm abnormal? I'm not gay or anything like that, am I?'

''Course you aren't, Alex. You were experimenting. I've told you before, your personality is such that every so often you have to go wild and seek thrills. You have just lost your dad and so you want to escape from it all. She is so pretty she'd turn anyone's head so.'

'But what about Matt?'

'It was just a kiss and, yes, you got carried away. He'd love to have been there watching, I bet. You love him, don't you, and want to marry him? You have a great life together but you need fun and thrills; it doesn't mean you don't love him.'

'Really, do you think that?'

'Yes, I do. Have you told Pearl, as I know you are quite close friends with her, and your Emily?'

'No, but Hope keeps texting and ringing me. I texted her yesterday but just because she hounded me all day.'

'She seems to be besotted with you. Be careful, that's all.'

'So you think I should see her again, then? I'm not sure I should.'

'What's stopping you? Didn't you have a good time with her?'

'Yeah.'

'Why don't you think you should? Be honest – I'm one of your best mates.'

Alex paused for a moment, checking her mobile, taking a gulp from the glass of Coke Millie had brought for her.

'Truthfully?'

'Yes. I know what you are going to say.'

'I'm a bit worried it will happen again and that I liked it too much.'

'I knew you were going to say that. I'd say see her again. Lots of people do stuff like this; you read it all the time. It doesn't mean you are gay. You are dealing with your dad's death, and if this is what you need right now to help you, then do it. Just have fun.'

'But don't you think that it's cheating on Matt?'

'Well, not really, it's not the same as with men. You can't have sex, well, not properly – not intercourse, I suppose. She's a younger mate who you are experimenting with.'

'Maybe you are right. I do like her and she makes me feel good about myself. Matt does too but she can take me away from my problems, and I have felt better lately. Maybe that's helped by her?'

'It could be. Why not see her and see how it goes. Just don't get in too deep. Keep her at bay, and remember, Matt is your soul mate.'

'I know. I will. Thanks, Millie. You always know what to say.'

'Well, what are mates for?'

Millie had given Alex a lot to think about as she dined with Matt later that evening; they chatted about work, distracting her from Hope.

After taking her bath, she lay staring at the TV for a while before deciding to compose a text.

'Hi Hope. I'm sorry aint answerd phone nor text bak, been busy.

How ru? Wot ru up2 nxt wk? wanna go4 lunch wif me?'

Hope responded within seconds, agreeing.

Chapter 15

'Angel, could you turn the music up, please? I can't hear it too well in here as the fan on the oven is noisy,' Matt asked.

Alex turned up the TV slightly as she lay on the couch.

'Thanks,' he shouted.

'Something smells nice. I'm so hungry I'm dying to know what you are making,' Alex said loudly.

Matt came into the lounge, poured her a glass of red wine and handed her the glass.

'There you go, try this; it's a Merlot and I have heard that it's very nice,' he said, kissing her on the cheek.

Alex took a sip.

'Mmmmm, that is nice. Tell me what you are cooking.'

'No, it's a surprise. I love cooking for you,' he replied, smiling broadly.

'Me too, I love you cooking for me. It's great, especially as you are so good at it. I hope it's healthy.'

'Oh yes, you know me, I'm the low-calorie king,' he teased.

Alex smiled as Matt moved back into the kitchen, continuing with the preparation of their meal. She scrolled through the music channels, reading her magazine contently.

'How long will it be? I'm starving,' she shouted.

'About twenty minutes or so. You just relax, angel. It will certainly fill you, that's for sure.'

Matt prepared dinner with precision, making sure his presentation was just perfect. He made delicious meals with such flair for detail, almost worthy of a Michelin-starred restaurant. He loved cooking, often making three-course dinners on Saturday evenings if they stayed in.

'The starter is ready.'

Alex shuffled herself off the couch, strolling into the dining room.

'Wow, Matt, that looks amazing.'

'Tuck in,' he replied.

Matt had prepared a delectable ravioli with refried beans served with a chilli sauce and a cheesy crumb topping. She enjoyed it, clearing her plate.

'Mmmmm, that was so tasty,' she commented, licking her lips.

Matt's face brimmed, as they sat facing one another, sipping Merlot.

'Are you ready for your main course?'

'Yes. I expect it to outclass that delicious starter.'

'You have faith in your fella. Do I ever let you down?' he joked.

'No, baby, never.'

Matt smiled and stood up, carrying the plates into the kitchen, leaving Alex to sip her wine. He washed the starter plates before serving the main course.

'*Voilà, mademoiselle*,' he said as he brought the plate to Alex.

Alex looked at the careful artifice of the arrangement of colourful food on her plate.

'Wow, that looks fantastic,' she commented.

Matt smiled once more as he sat down, reaching for his fork.

'What is it?'

'It's pork loin with a cider and apple jus accompanied by chive potato cakes on a bed of roasted veg.'

Alex began eating.

'Oh, baby, this is so wonderful; the presentation is, as ever, fantastic, but the taste …`mmmmmm. I can't get enough of the sauce, it's so tasty,' she enthused.

'Yes, I exceed my own expectations sometimes,' he uttered, smiling.

After both plates were cleared, Alex reached out for Matt's hand, holding it for a moment whilst they chatted.

'Thank you for dinner tonight, it was so nice. You are just so good at everything,' she admitted, looking at him.

'You don't have to thank me, it's always an honour doing things for you.'

'Lurve you, you know?' she said confessed.

Raising a slight smile, he nodded.

'I know, Angel, and I really love you too. I wouldn't know what to do without you. I just wish that you would say it and look at me when you say it.'

'What do you mean?' she asked, scowling.

'Well, I have noticed that you do glance at me, but never stare into my eyes when you say it, and you never say it …' he paused, feeling his flush. 'Oh, it doesn't matter; I don't want you to get angry at me. You go into the sitting room and put your feet up while I go and tidy up the kitchen.'

Alex sat for a moment, letting out a huge breath, before getting out of her seat, glass in hand, and going into the lounge to sit peacefully.

Chapter 16

Alex had arranged to meet Hope at 12.30 p.m. She had thought all weekend about cancelling her but at the last moment decided against it, arriving on time at the bus station.

As she turned the corner she could see Hope waiting. She pulled up alongside her and Hope got into the car. Within seconds they had struck up a conversation; they conversed about their weekends, both very different, and about what they should do today.

Alex expressed her interest in going to lunch. Hope preferred the idea of going to Alex's house, dismissed by Alex, who made an excuse about Matt being off.

After lunch the girls went for a walk along the pier. They stood side by side as they stopped to watch the waves banging against the cliffs. They stood silently watching the waves, as Alex saw an overweight teenager go past them. Immediately her eyes followed the teenager, shaking her head, as she struggled to catch her breath, striding by. Looking puzzled, Hope asked,

'Why are you staring at her? She can't help being overweight.'

Sighing, Alex ignored Hope, choosing to view the girl, waddling along the pier. Wiping her face, Hope went on, 'It's not her fault she is that fat. At least she's making an effort by going for a walk with her dog. Do you have a problem with fat people, then?'

Biting her nails, Alex bowed her head.

'Are you alright? Do you know her? Has she upset you?'

Walking off, Hope followed her. Alex walked along the pier to the very end, closely followed by Hope. She reached the end, holding onto the barrier, transfixed by the waves. Hope stood by her side, dangling her hand.

'I'm sorry, Hope, you must think I'm mad. It's just ...'

Hope cut in, 'I don't think you are mad at all.'

Raising a slight smile, Alex turned, facing her.

'There is so much I want to tell you about me so that you can understand me better. I don't know why, but I feel drawn to want to tell you things about my life.'

Swallowing, Hope took Alex's hand. Alex scanned the vicinity for onlookers. Viewing an older couple, she pulled her hand away. Hope frowned.

'I'm sorry, Hope, it's just ...'

Hope interrupted.

'It's OK, I'm sorry, you just looked sad, and like anyone I care about, if they are upset or sad, I would take their hand. I didn't mean anything by it.'

Glaring into her eyes, Alex moved closer to her, touching her face.

'You are so nice, do you know that? I wish my life had been as easy as yours when I was your age.'

Touching Alex's side, Hope lowered her head.

'My life isn't great, you know. I don't have it easy. I am the oldest but my mum adores my brother and my dad loves my sister. I am the one they wished they hadn't had. No matter what I do, I can never seem to please them,' she said faintly, glaring at the ground, continuing to move her hand up and down Alex's side.

Alex gently lifted Hope's head up, forcing their eyes to lock together.

'Oh, I'm sorry, Hope. I'm sure they did want you and do love you as much as your brother and sister. Don't be sad.'

Shaking her head, Hope glared at Alex, dangling her hand. Alex moved the blowing hair off Hope's face. Hope closed her eyes, feeling Alex's hand touch her skin.

'You are very beautiful, you know.'

Hope smiled, shivering. Alex buttoned up her coat for her, taking out some gloves from her bag, placing them on Hope. She took off her thick scarf and placed it around Hope's neck, gently brushing her fingers against Hope's skin. Leaning forward, Hope cuddled Alex, muttering something into her ear.

'What did you say?' Alex asked.

Continuing to embrace, Hope repeated what she'd said.

'Thank you. You are so kind and thoughtful.'

Pulling away, glaring at her, Alex smiled.

'Are you okay to stay here for a while or is it too cold? I love being here. I find it so calming watching the waves crash against the rocks.'

Laughing, Hope nodded.

'What are you laughing at?'

'You, you are silly. Of course I don't mind being here with you. I have wanted to see you so much since the last time at your house. I don't care how cold it is.'

Alex smiled, ushering Hope away towards her favourite spot. As they sat just off the pier, Alex tightened the scarf around Hope's neck as it sat loosely.

'Your neck looked cold so …'

Hope interrupted, 'It's fine, you don't have to explain, silly. You look cold, though, sit closer to me. Here, give me your hands and I will warm them for you.'

Alex shook her head.

'No, I'm fine, honest. I like sitting here with you. I feel at ease.'

Smiling from ear to ear, Hope shuffled closer to Alex. They sat looking out to sea for some time, watching people go past. An overweight man strolled by, prompting Hope to comment.

'Are you going to comment on how fat he was?' she joked.

Frowning, Alex moved closer to Hope.

'God, what do you think I am? I would like to tell you why I reacted to that girl before. I wasn't calling her, moreover, sympathising and reflecting to when I was like that, and how it was ruining my life.'

Listening, Hope stared at Alex. Alex sat silent, looking at the waves for a few moments; Hope squeezed her hand.

'Carry on if you like, or if you don't want to, we can just sit here until you are ready to go back. I might have hypothermia but you know … it's fine,' she said, putting her hand over her mouth, giggling.

Alex glanced at Hope, shaking her head, smiling at the same time.

'What are you shaking your head for?'

'You, you make me laugh.' Alex replied, pushing away the hair from Hope's face, enabling their eyes to fix on one another.

Alex lifted up her sleeve, forcing her coat up to her elbow, revealing a faint scar. Hope softly ran her fingertips over it before Alex covered it up, dithering. Shuffling closer, Hope asked, 'What happened to your arm?'

Looking forward, Alex replied, feeling Hope's body next to her, 'I mentioned about having stitches when we were at the hospital, can't you remember?'

'No, sorry.'

'Well, anyway, I broke my arm when I was younger and it stopped me from doing things.'

'For how long? How old were you?'

'Well, it was quite a bad break; I was a great tennis player, and used to play all the time. I had my own coach and everything. But then when I broke my arm I could never play the same. I couldn't get the movement I could before. I did try but, well, it just was never the same.'

Silent, Hope sat mesmerised at Alex. Alex stared at the rocks as she went on.

'It was because of this that I put a lot of weight on. I stopped training. I was so gutted. My dad took me to so many specialists and I had operations but I just couldn't bend my elbow like I could before and it was so painful.'

'Were you quite good then? Oh, are you alright now?'

'Well, you could say that. I put lots of weight on and couldn't seem to diet. I would comfort eat and got taunted at school. I hated secondary school. In fact I hated my teenage years. I would diet but could never stick to it. I was so miserable.'

She sighed, rubbing her eyebrows.

'So how did you come to look so good?'

Alex smiled, shaking her head.

'I don't have a good body. I just decided that as I hated my life, I had to do exercise and diet. Eventually, after sheer determination I lost my weight. Not long after I met Matt.'

Hanging on Alex's every word, Hope's eyes widened.

Alex turned to her, continuing, 'What made me worse was that my sister was so slim and pretty. She had so many boyfriends too.'

Lowering her head, she rubbed her eyes.

Hope's hand rested by Alex's side; lifting her hand, she placed it on Alex's knee.

'You are so nice, you know.'

Moving to face Hope, they gazed at each other, shifting the windswept hair from each other's red cheeks, softly touching the other's skin.

Some moments later, they stood up, walking along the deserted pier. Strolling side by side, Hope grabbed Alex's hand. Immediately, Alex took her hand away as they continued to wander back to the car. As they almost reached the car, Hope took off her glove, taking Alex's freezing hand. Feeling Hope's hand trembling, Alex glanced at her and smiled faintly, making it feel warmer, holding it tighter.

Chapter 17

Hope had managed to change her shifts, allowing her to spend the full day with Alex, much to her joy. She had awoken early – in fact she had barely slept – and meticulously got dressed, matching her coat, bag and jumper (all pink) with her grey trousers and black boots.

She arrived at the bus stop early, patiently waiting for her bus to take her to the bus station in the town centre, where Alex would be waiting for her. The journey took fifteen minutes to the station from her house, a journey that she took almost every day to get to work, but today the time seemed to drag. As the bus pulled into the station Hope could just about see the back of Alex's red Porsche as it stood stationary round the corner. Promptly getting off the bus, she ran to the car, pulling open the door, thrilled.

'Hey!'

'Hi. You look very, erm … pink today,' Alex teased, giving her the once-over.

Hope smiled but dropped her head in embarrassment.

'I'm just joking with you. You look as lovely as ever. I like your coat, actually,' Alex said, driving off.

'Really! Thanks,' Hope replied, high-spirited, studying Alex's face out of the corner of her eye.

Alex drove on.

'So what are you cooking for me today, then?'

Alex grinned, choosing not to answer, preferring to sing along to her CD of Madonna.

Hope smiled, absorbing her sweet-sounding voice, which made the hair stand up on the back of her neck.

Finally they arrived at Alex's house and got out of the car. Hope made her way into the lounge and leaned over the coffee table to pick up a magazine, sitting on the couch, in the same place as last time. Alex went into the kitchen and put lunch into the oven. Hope pretended to read the magazine as Alex entered the room to ask if she wanted a drink, which she declined. Alex sat close by Hope, but not close enough, making Hope shuffle herself nearer to her so that they brushed against each other. As Hope did this, Alex beamed.

'Lunch will be about thirty minutes, if that's OK?' Alex said, trying not to make eye contact.

'Yes, sure. I'm not that hungry at the minute.'

'Oh, OK, I can turn it down so it takes longer, if you want? It's only fish and chips.'

'Mmm, I love that. Yes, if you want, turn it down a bit.'

Alex went into the kitchen and turned the oven down, returning to sit next to Hope. Alex picked up the newspaper, turning the pages, without reading anything. Hope read the same sentence over and over from the magazine that sat perched on her lap. As she eventually turned over the page, her fingers trembled. Breathing heavier and heavier, her mouth became dry. As they sat side by side, Alex stared at Hope's hand, resting by her side, noticing her long fingers. Leaning forward, Alex put the newspaper back on the table, relaxing back, brushing Hope's hand. Hope continued to fix on an article, held by her shaking right hand. Slightly twisting her body, Alex looked at Hope, taking a very deep breath. Without lifting her head up, Hope placed her hand on top of Alex's hand, which was resting on her lap; as she did so goose bumps formed on her arms, making her shiver. Alex saw this, prompting her to release her hand; she rubbed Hope's arms and shoulder, and as she did this, their eyes, which had been trying hard to avoid each other, finally met. Alex smiled. Hope leaned forward, closing her magazine.

'Kiss me,' Hope mumbled.

Alex inhaled and breathed out, before drawing her head back to kiss her. As they kissed, Alex's lips trembled and her hands shook. Hope's stomach did somersaults, as they continued for a moment. Trembling, Alex stopped, closing her eyes, blowing in and out. Touching Alex's red cheeks, Hope said quietly, 'What's wrong, do you not like me?'

Ignoring her, Alex rubbed her closed eyes.

Stroking her face, Hope took her shaking hand, locking them together. Clenching Hope's hand tightly, Alex opened her eyes, unlocking her hand, moving it up Hope's body, fondling her breasts. With her other hand, she stroked Hope's face, moving her other hand onto her face, touching every part of it with the tips of her fingers. With their eyes firmly shut their fingertips explored each other's face, breathing heavily. As Alex's shaking fingers skimmed over Hope's lips, they both glared at each other, stimulating them to kiss harder and faster, pushing their tongues deeply into each other's mouths. Hope stopped for a moment.

'You are driving me wild. I'm aching for you and you have no idea how much,' she said, slightly breathless.

Alex beamed as she grabbed Hope's chin, kissing those perfect lips some more. As they kissed, Hope began to moan, arousing Alex, moving her lips towards Hope's neck, causing Hope to groan louder, making Alex bite and lick her neck.

'Why do you want me to have sex with you? Tell me, I want to know,' Alex asked faintly.

As Alex uttered the words Hope pushed her shoulders back and lay on top of her, putting her hands in between her legs.

'I want to because you turn me on so much. I'm soaking wet, I can feel it. Here, feel for yourself,' Hope said as she took Alex's hand, pushing it down inside her trousers, resting it on the outside of her pants. Allowing her hand to be placed in between Hope's legs, she pressed on her vagina through her pants as she moved it slowly around the area several times, getting wetter and wetter.

'God, Hope, how wet are you?'

Hope kissed her neck for a second.

'It's you. I can't get over how much I get turned on when I see you. Please fuck me, I can't stand the pain, my pussy is hurting me, I need you to make me come,' Hope said, panting.

Transfixed on her, she pulled off Hope's grey trousers, which were soaking around the crotch and bottom area, throwing them onto the floor. Hope was wearing pink silky hipster pants that fitted her perfect figure well. Her legs were long and slender as Alex ran her fingers up and down them before pulling off her jumper and bra and tossing them in a heap on the floor. Alex sat up slightly, gazing at this virtually naked body next to her. Her breasts were small but perfectly round; her nipples were pink (due to her fair colouring) but hard. Alex licked her fingers, running them all over Hope's breasts and around the nipples, forming a circling movement. She lowered her head and began kissing them, nibbling them in her mouth. Hope pulled off Alex's jumper, followed by her jeans, as her olive-skinned body lay next to hers, and she rested her hand on Alex's crotch, rubbing her fingers up and down. Alex put her hand back inside Hope's pants, gently touching the top of her vagina as her fingers slid down, placing a finger inside her, pressing it softly in and out, touching her clitoris at the same time with her thumb. Hope groaned loudly as Alex's finger went in and out of her, stimulating Alex to place two fingers inside her, continuing to rub her clitoris gently with her thumb.

'God, you are driving me fucking crazy. I have never felt so horny ever. I will come in seconds if you keep doing that,' Hope spoke, breathlessly.

Alex moved her finger onto her clitoris, gently rubbing in a circular motion before moving it back inside her, pulling in and out, as Hope's wetness ran down both their thighs. Alex yanked off Hope's pants. Hope tugged hers off too, and they lay side by side, resting their legs on each other, their soaking vaginas touching. Alex kept her finger inside Hope as they kissed. Hope moved away, kissing Alex's breasts.

'You are fucking soaking, here, taste it,' Alex said, taking her hand out of Hope's vagina, putting her wet finger into Hope's mouth. Hope sucked her finger, tasting her wet juice, lubricating Alex's mouth. As they kissed, their fingers played around inside each other. Alex moved her finger up and down Hope's clitoris faster and faster, stopping every second or two, making Hope beg for more.

'Don't stop. Keep it there and go faster. I want to come so much,' Hope gasped.

Alex did as Hope requested, rubbing up and down faster and faster, stopping for a second to make her tingle and ache for her finger more, rubbing her breasts with the wet juice from her vagina.

'Lick it off,' Hope gasped.

Alex moved her head forward and began to lick Hope's breasts.

'Don't stop finger-fucking me, though. I want you to make me come and taste my love juices at the same time,' Hope begged.

Both girls became more and more aroused as they kissed firmly with their fingers inside each other, squelching on the leather couch. The more aroused they became the more their bodies moved. Pressed against the couch, Hope's back stuck to it, her bottom and thighs dripping wet, Alex almost reached her climax. Hope tried hard to sustain the rubbing of Alex's pounding clitoris, as both girls lay naked, their fingers touching each other, but as her pleasure magnified, Hope moved her hand away, selfishly.

'I'm going to come any second,' Hope shrieked.

'Good,' Alex replied as she embraced Hope, continuing to touch her clitoris, quick then slow, arousing her even more, before Hope's legs began to judder, holding Alex's arm tightly.

Alex maintained the intensity of her finger movement as Hope screamed excitedly.

'Oh my God, oh my God,' she yelped as her legs and pelvis moved frantically.

They ceased kissing, concentrating on Hope's imminent climax, as she clung harder to Alex's arm, holding her hand as her body moved rapidly up and down.

'I'm coming. Oh God …'

Hope stopped moving, pulling Alex's hand away, gasping for breath. Alex smiled at her, kissing her lips softly, as both girls lay back exhausted.

Hope rested her head in between Alex's breasts as they lay holding hands.

'That was the most amazing experience I have ever had. You were fantastic,' Hope said quietly.

Alex smiled contentedly, gently kissing the top of Hope's head. Both girls lay relaxed as they closed their eyes for a moment with contentment.

'I know that you didn't come, and I am sorry, but I just couldn't do it as I needed all my energy to enjoy it. But there is plenty of time left.'

Alex laughed, marveling at how lovely Hope looked naked, touching her face, raising shivers all over Hope's body.

Transfixed on each other, Hope plucked up the courage to ask, 'Are you at work, tomorrow? Can I see you?'

Grinning, Alex ran her fingers over Hope's eyes.

'Why are you grinning?'

'Well, you make me laugh, you are so forward.'

'What do you mean? I just wanted to know if I can ...'

Alex butted in, 'I know you are just keen to see me,' tickling Hope playfully under the arms, bringing a joyful glow to her face, eventually leading to a passionate kiss, both of them collapsing to the floor.

Chapter 18

The following morning she awoke early, hearing Matt slam the door, leaving for work, as she deliberated about cancelling Hope so that she could accompany Matt to the RW executive meeting, in the hope of securing the contract. As she lay thinking of work, her thoughts wandered, and this very exciting and thrilling young lady came into her mind, raising a smile, as her mobile bleeped.

'Hi angel, I just wanted 2 say that I love you & wished it was the wkend so that we were 2gether in bed having a lie-in & that I hope 2 get the business 2day. Come if u want? X'

Grinning to herself, she replied, 'No I trust u can do it. I'm having a lazy day at home. Lov u 2. Gud luck xx'

As she lay there, pondering, her mobile bleeped again.

'Hi. I'm sittin on the bus goin 2wrk finkin of u & how much I wanna cu 2day. Can't wait. I wanna c that sexy smile & 2 kiss u all over. I'm not bothad bout goin 4 lunch, rather b wif u. cu in few hrs xxxxxxxxx'

Feeling desired, Alex grinned.

Alex arrived on time and Hope ran towards the car.
'Hiya.'
'Hi,' Alex said, driving off, smiling.
'I'm not hungry at all, you know. I ate at work. Sorry.'
'Oh well, as long as you are all right, Jack,' Alex joked.
'No, we can go if you want to,' Hope replied submissively.
Alex shook her head, heading for home, grinning again.
'You look lovely today,' Hope commented, transfixed on Alex.

Alex grinned, ignoring her comment, continuing to head for home, in anticipation of the day ahead.

'You really don't look twenty-nine, you know. You haven't even got any wrinkles.'

'Your skin is so brown, too,' Hope said, transfixed on Alex's features.

Alex beamed, revelling in the compliments, maintaining her concentration on the road.

'You always smell gorgeous, too,' Hope went on, inhaling with pleasure.

As she pulled onto the drive, Hope placed her hand on top of Alex's leg, overcome by her attraction.

'Kiss me,' she said boldly.

'Where, here?' Alex quizzed.

'Yes, go on.'

Alex shook her head, taking the key out of the ignition.

'Come on, get out, you little devil,' she teased, stepping out of the car.

Hope purred, getting out of the car, entering the house, slamming the door behind her, taking off her shoes, before following Alex into the kitchen, where she stood looking uneasy.

'I must go to the toilet,' she confessed, turning to go, as Alex poured a drink.

'I've been thinking about you all night,' Hope blurted on her return.

'You are crazy, you. You are so forward. I hardly know you,' Alex teased.

'Am I shocking you?'

'A bit.'

'Why?'

'I don't know; I guess you are because you are young and so horny. You aren't afraid to go after what you want.'

'Isn't your boyfriend horny? He must be the same with you as me?'

Alex paused, glaring at Hope's perfect, youthful skin; her shiny, pink lip gloss complemented her blusher, emphasising her green eyes.

'Yes, he is, but … well, no, not really. He's quite shy but is very loving.'

Powerless before her overbearing desires, Hope lunged forward, banging Alex against the fridge, kissing her, tearing off her low-cut beige jumper, covering her neck with kisses. Taking off Alex's silk beige bra, Hope began touching Alex's breasts, creating erect nipples, fondling them in her warm hands.

'We can't do it here, people might see,' Alex said with a nervous tone, leading Hope, topless, into the lounge, thrusting her on the couch, kissing her firmly.

Hope reached for Alex's hand, placing it on her left breast, as she forced Alex's legs apart, making room for her own hand.

'I'm going to make you scream with pleasure today when I make you come. Tell me, is your pussy aching for my hand? Or maybe it's my tongue she wants?' Hope said, quietly, her eyes wide open.

'God, you amaze me with your dirty talk. Where do you get this from at your age? I love it.'

Hope grinned, licking Alex's erect breasts, loosening her jeans.

Helpless, Alex lay allowing Hope to take control, as Hope pulled off her jeans, one leg at a time, running her hands up and down Alex's tanned arms and stomach, teasing her. Desperate to feel her naked flesh wrapped around Alex, Hope pulled her jumper over her head, yanking off her bra, as Alex lunged forward, licking her nipples. Hope pushed Alex's head into them, begging her to take control, which Alex refused to do, flabbergasted by Hope's erotic manner, unprecedented in her experience. Hope glared at Alex's skimpy, lacy underwear, placing her hand over her crotch. Electricity surged through both of them, like a bolt of lightning. As Hope's desire magnified, causing her to moan devilishly, she placed her hand into Alex's moist pants, rubbing her fingers up and down Alex's vagina. Alex lay there, allowing her to take control, enjoying the satisfaction of her increased arousal, as Hope rubbed harder and harder, biting her lips, as they kissed more firmly. Sitting up, Alex dragged Hope's shoulders towards her as they kissed, forcing Hope's arms to lock around Alex's naked flesh. Running their nails up and down each other's backs, they kissed harder and faster, pushing their breasts together. Licking and biting each other's necks, they clawed at one another's backs. Hope sucked on Alex's neck as she screamed out. Grabbing her chin, Alex kissed Hope, biting her lips the more aroused she became. Stopping, she slid to Hope's waist, trying to open her button with her teeth. Unable to, she rived it open with her hand, popping it off, forcing her jeans off, throwing them to the floor. Putting her tongue into her pants, Alex licked Hope's clitoris, sucking it harder the more Hope groaned. The more Alex sucked on her clitoris, the more Hope gripped onto the cushion. Alex stopped sucking, licking the side of her clitoris gently, forcing Hope to bite into the cushion. She gently explored Hope's clitoris, letting out huge groans, enjoying every second of Hope's sweet tasting vagina. Alex continued, licking all over, putting her tongue inside of Hope, making her scream out.

Hope finally relaxed her body, wrapping her arms around Alex for a few seconds until she rolled onto the couch, collapsing into it.

'Wow, that was amazing,' Hope said, trying to catch her breath, her mouth agape.

With a tender glance, Alex reached forward, kissing her.

'You know, I think I …'

Alex positioned her finger across Hope's mouth.

'Shh, don't say anything, just kiss me,' she said.

They lay for a few moments virtually naked, locked together, peaceful. Suddenly a car door slammed loudly. Gulping, Alex sat up, panicking. She reached for her clothes on the floor, pulling them on as fast as she could. She leapt off the couch, urging Hope to sit up. Feeling restless, she reached for her clothes, putting them on, and peeped out of the window, hiding behind the curtains.

Breathing a sigh of relief she looked at Hope half dressed.

'What was all that about?' Hope said, puzzled.

Frowning, Alex sighed.

'Why do you think? I heard a car door and thought it might have been Matt. We are in view of half the street. I don't think that we should do this anymore.'

Moving towards Alex, Hope put her arm around her, shrugged off by Alex, as she walked around the room.

'What's up, Alex? Why are you being like this? Please don't say that?'

Shaking her head, she caught a glimpse of their engagement photo next to the fireplace. Rubbing her hand over her face, she paced the room. Hope perched herself on the edge of the couch, transfixed on Alex. Sighing, Alex felt Hope's glare, making her look over. Hope smiled warmly. Alex lowered her head for a second. Looking up, she said, 'I just don't want to be in that position again, Hope. You are so naïve. If that had been Matt, what would we have done? I don't think he would have been overjoyed to see us lying so closely together. I mean, friends don't do that, do they?'

Immediately Hope's eyes became watery as she bowed her head. Faintly she muttered something. Glaring at Hope, Alex sighed and walked towards her. Rubbing her shoulder, she asked, 'What did you just say?'

Shaking her head, Hope did not reply. Instead, she wrapped her head into Alex's body, cuddling her.

'I'm sorry, Alex.'

'What for?'

'I should have understood when you heard the car door slam, and got up as fast as you could and got ready. I didn't think. It won't happen again. Next time, I will be up like a shot and have my stuff on. It would take him a minute to get up the drive and into here, walk along the corridor and get in. By that time we would be fully clothed. I would pick up a magazine quickly and pretend to read that. He wouldn't think anything of it. I would never want you to get into shit with him because of me. I promise.'

Gazing at Hope, Alex held her close, stroking her hair.

'You are very sweet but so innocent. I shouldn't be doing this and certainly not in my sitting room; it's just not …'

Hope stepped in, 'We don't have to do it here. We can go upstairs where if he came in, I could hide. There are enough rooms to hide in.'

'Oh yeah, he comes home and finds me in bed naked. And where would you be, in the cupboard? No, it's not right,' Alex announced, shaking her head, sighing.

Moving away, Hope's face went white as she bit her nails. Alex stood looking towards the fireplace. Noticing this, Hope bit harder, forcing her finger to bleed.

'But I thought you liked me, and that I made you feel good, and how you can talk to me, and tell me stuff about your tennis days,' she blurted.

Silent, Alex stared at her. Walking towards her, she took her hand and wiped the blood away with a tissue. Closing her eyes, she pulled Hope towards her. She took Hope's hand and led her out of the lounge into the dining room. Happily, Hope followed. Behind the door, Alex showed Hope a family photo.

'That's my parents and my sister. I love this photo of my dad.'

Hope squeezed Alex's hand, smiling at her.

'You look like him.'

Nodding, Alex turned and scanned the photo.

'You really worshipped him, didn't you?'

'Yeah. He was my hero. I confided in him so much; he was my rock. He was a great man.' She spoke softly, as her eyes welled up.

'Well, I can imagine he was, as you seem so nice too.'

Smiling warmly, Alex gazed at Hope.

'You have such innocence about you, I love it,' Alex replied.

Hope gently held Alex's chin and kissed her. Leading her out of the dining room, upstairs, Alex took Hope into a bedroom and closed the door. Hope sat on the bed. Alex joined her, pulling off Hope's jeans and top, kissing her body from head toe.

Chapter 19

The snow lay crisp on the rooftops from the night before as Alex climbed out of bed, pulling back the curtains, while Matt lay sleeping on this sombre Christmas morning.

She made her way downstairs, still in her pajamas, and slouched by her gift bag full of presents. She glared at them for some time, thinking how she would exchange every gift that day to have her father with them, making them laugh with his silly jokes. She went into the kitchen and made some coffee, switching her phone on. Immediately her mobile bleeped; she had two messages.

As she sat reading her messages, Matt joined her, handing her his handkerchief, smiling warmly. Immediately he sat close to her, embracing her, wiping the fallen tears with his fingers. Silent, he held her as she gazed out of the window, looking at the path of lightly covering snow. Slowly she pulled away from him, blowing her nose, avoiding eye contact.

'I know today won't be easy but your dad will be with you all day, with all of you. I have done my best to try and make today as special for you as I can,' he said, kissing her cheek, passing her the gifts to open.

Alex smiled unconvincingly, putting her hand in the bag, opening them one at a time, trying hard to show gratitude. As she delved to the bottom of the bag, she smiled, relieved to have finally opened them all. Leaning towards him, she kissed him on the cheek. Turning to face her, he kissed her. Instantly, she stopped him, frowning.

'What's up?' he asked with a shocked tone.

'Nothing,' she replied, with a catch in her voice, reaching for her phone.

Looking down, playing with his fingers, Matt sighed loudly. Alex ignored him, reading the screen on her phone, texting back. Glaring, Matt gritted his teeth, digging his fingernails into his fingers. Oblivious, she kept texting, raising a slight smile. Seconds later, she put the phone in her pajama pocket, and turned to face Matt, handing him his presents from under the tree. She kissed the top of his head, and sat down next to him. Smiling faintly, he began opening his small bag of gifts. As he did so, she took out her phone, smiling, as she read her text. Scowling, he finished ripping off the paper from his final gift.

'Thanks, angel. They are lovely,' he said, attempting to cuddle her.

Nodding, she finished sending her message.

'Who is it you keep texting?' he asked meekly.

Ignoring him, she slotted the phone back into her pocket, and kissed his cheek.

'Do I not get a kiss these days?'

Glaring, she shook her head.

'What was that look for?' he asked with a quake in his voice.

Placing her teeth onto her bottom lip, her face became red, as she stood staring at him, shaking her head.

'What is up with you, Alex?'

Bending down, she picked up the torn wrapping paper off the floor, refusing to look at him. Joining her, he helped pick it up, attempting to get close to her. Flinching, she crumpled the paper in her hands. Wiping his brow, Matt spoke softly.

'Angel, don't be like this. I know today is going to be tough but your dad wouldn't want you to be sad.'

Tossing the torn paper into the waste paper bin, she gave out a huge sigh. Advancing towards her, Matt grabbed her hand.

'Get off me, Matt. You are getting on my nerves,' she gasped.

'I'm getting on your nerves? Why? For buying you thoughtful things and being concerned about you?' he retaliated.

Raising her hands, Alex yelled, 'Just leave it.'

Watery-eyed Matt sulked, incapable of understanding Alex lately.

Lowering her tone, she took his hand, and looked at him.

Sensing his sadness, feeling guilty, she went next to him and said, 'Things just aren't the same and you know it.'

'What things? What are you talking about?'

Pausing, she stroked his face, deeply looking into his eyes.

'Well, I have looked at things differently since he died. Life is so precious and short.'

Touching her face, he agreed.

'You know, his death has made me see so much about myself, and us, and how things can never be the same anymore,' she admitted, sniffling, rubbing her nose with her sleeve.

Eyes wide, Matt scowled at her. Standing in the middle of the lounge, they faced each other. Barely able to speak, he mumbled, 'Alex, what are you talking about? Yes, you are devastated over your dad's death, but we are happy, aren't we?'

Closing her eyes, taking a deep breath, she paused for a moment. Opening her eyes, she saw Matt become tearful, as she opened her mouth, as though she was about to speak. Walking towards him, she rubbed the top of his shoulders.

'Come on, let's get ready,' she muttered.

'We are fine, aren't we?'

Forcing half a smile, she replied, 'Well …' she paused, looking at his anxiety, taking a huge breath.

With a tender glance, he moved next to her, calmly saying into her ear, 'I love you!'

Alex and Matt visited his parents, followed by a trip to her mother Eve's house, where Emily and her new boyfriend, Pete, were waiting to greet them. Alex embraced her mother as they both fought back the tears, trying to be brave for everyone, not wanting to spoil the day.

Eve and Emily had visited the grave earlier; Alex had not wanted to go, as she preferred to go with Matt to his parents' house.

After they had finished opening their presents, they sat reminiscing about Ken, and what he would be doing and saying now; talking fondly of him, helping to lift all their spirits, allowing them to look forward to a pleasant lunch as they made their way to the restaurant.

After lunch everyone visited Eve's sister Brenda's house, where other family members were waiting to give their presents to each other. As evening drew on, the day's events became too much for Eve and her daughters, forcing Eve to get upset in front of her family, much to her dismay, as she hated showing her emotion in public. Emily consoled her mother while Alex left the room, taking some fresh air as she stood at the back door. Some moments later Matt joined her, expressing his concern, much to her annoyance; she demanded to be alone, and gather her thoughts.

Hearing her mobile bleep, she reached into her coat pocket, seeing a message from Hope. Choosing to ignore it, she placed the phone back in her coat, fixing her gaze on the gate, sending herself into a trance-like state. Some moments later she took the phone back out, ringing Hope.

Playing party games with her family, Hope jumped up off the floor as she saw Alex's name flash up on the incoming call, almost as if her bottom had suddenly caught fire, running up to her room, taking the call in private.

'Hey. This is a nice surprise,' Hope admitted with an upbeat tone.

'Hi. Merry Christmas,' Alex replied quietly.

'What's up? You sound sad. And you shouldn't, you know,' she said.

'Why?'

'Because, silly, you are talking to me,' Hope joked.

Smiling uncontrollably, she replied, 'You see, this is why I like you.'

'Why?'

'You say such simple things with so much meaning.'

'Have you had a good day, then? Well, you know …'

'Yes, it was OK until now. Now I feel sad. My mum has just got upset so I have come outside out of the way to be alone. I hate feeling sad so I thought, I know, I'll ring Hope, she'll cheer me up!'

Hope chuckled as she joked, 'Oh, so you just want me to entertain you, then?'

Alex smiled more broadly than she had all day.

'Yes, you make me happy, I guess. You take me away from my problems. No one can do that but you,' Alex explained.

Hope became overwhelmed at Alex's comments, forcing her to cough to take away the lump forming in her throat.

'That's the nicest thing anyone has ever said to me,' she replied feeling choked, clearing her throat.

94

Feeling humbled, Alex understood how happy she could make Hope, with what seemed to her like simple comments.

'I can't wait to see you. I really can't. I'm more excited about that than I was about my presents today,' she said in a high-pitched voice.

'Really? Well, you can't have got many things, then,' Alex joked.

Hope's face flushed, and she laughed.

'Alex, come on, your mum wants to go home now. Who are you talking to?' Matt shouted from inside the door.

Alex did not answer but nodded her head in agreement.

'I'm going to have to go, sorry. I'll text you tomorrow?'

'Why, who was that shouting?'

She paused for a moment.

'Matt.'

'Oh right, I better let you go then.'

'OK, sweetie. See you tomorrow then.'

'Wait, before you go I want to tell you something,' Hope said softly.

'What? Quick, tell me, I have to go now,' Alex replied, shuffling.

'It doesn't matter. It was nothing,' Hope replied, disheartened.

'Bye.'

'Bye bye,' Hope replied as the call ended.

Hope sat on the end of her bed, unable to shake re-occurring thoughts about Alex and Matt together, feeling restless as she could not settle in one place. She rejoined her family, transfixed on the silver photo frame on top of the TV. Belle noticed her staring.

'Don't worry, I will get a family photo of us all to put in such a lovely frame. It has to be the best gift you have ever bought me; I really do appreciate that you have stayed in to save for it for me.'

Grinding her teeth, Hope looked away.

'What's the matter with you, boyfriend trouble?' David mocked.

Ignoring him, Hope sighed.

'She's weird lately, I don't know what's up with her,' Belle continued.

Chapter 20

Alex could not avoid telling Matt that she had planned a meeting with Hope at 1 p.m. He had presumed they would be spending the day together, and was disappointed. As a consolation she agreed to be home by teatime, offering to cook him dinner, allowing him to spend the afternoon watching sport.

Alex had arranged to meet Hope at their usual meeting point at the bus station. As she was preparing to leave, Matt saw her carrying a pink box under her arm.

'What's that you've got?' he quizzed.

Alex hesitated before answering, 'Just a little something for Hope; after all, it is Christmas.'

'Why would you buy her a present? You barely know her,' he said with caution.

'God, listen to you, Mr Scrooge. It's just some perfume.'

'Buy her what you want, it's nothing to do with me.'

'Exactly right, Matt. I will, regardless of what you say,' she said, offhand.

Matt lowered his head, wanting to avoid an argument as Alex turned, walking to the front door. He followed her, holding the door, grabbing her hand, forcing her to turn towards him.

'You isn't in a mood wif lil me, is ya?' he mumbled in the silly voice they used to one another.

'No, silly. I'll see you in a few hours,' she replied.

'Sure you isn't annoyed?'

'No, honest.'

'Lurve ya,' Matt said quietly.

Alex smiled, getting into her car, speeding off.

Hope had arrived early, unsure of the bank holiday bus timetable, standing on the corner, rubbing her hands together with her coat buttoned right up to the top to stay as warm as possible, while waiting excitedly for Alex.

Alex arrived ten minutes later than scheduled; Hope got into the car, immediately hugging her before placing her hands on top of Alex's hands.

'Do you know how cold it is out there? I was ten minutes early as well so I've been there twenty minutes,' she announced.

Alex grinned without speaking, staring intently at her, thinking how attractive Hope looked.

'To be honest, I'd have waited for you all day, in snow if I had to, just to be able to see you for one hour. Well, provided you warmed my hands for me,' Hope said with a jolly tone.

Alex smiled at this comment, placing her hand on Hope's face, running it up and down her rosy cheek, making Hope wriggle in her seat and fix her eyes on Alex, obliging her to stop.

'Sorry, that gave me a shiver.'

'What did?'

'When you touched my face.'

'You are crazy,' Alex joked, shaking her head.

'Yeah, you are right, crazy about you!'

Alex's face beamed.

Alex drove around the corner, parking the car, enabling them to exchange gifts. Hope bowed her head, looking into the red gift bag. Alex stepped out of the car and went to the boot, taking out a pink box, placing it on Hope's lap, lighting up Hope's face.

'Wow, pink. I love it. It's my fav colour!'

'I had noticed,' Alex replied, glancing at her pink coat.

Hope opened the presents one by one.

'Woo,' she said.

Tearing open her final present, taking it out of the box, with wide mouth and eyes, she said jubilantly, 'Oh my God, it's beautiful. I love it. It must have cost a fortune. Thank you so much.'

'I'm glad you like them. Here, put the bracelet on,' Alex recommended, placing it around her wrist, where it fitted perfectly.

'Like them? They are the coolest presents I've ever had,' Hope said euphoric, gazing at her wrist.

Alex held her hand tightly as they gazed into each other's eyes for a few moments. Looking down at her red gift bag, Hope sighed, as she reluctantly handed it to Alex.

'I'm sorry but I didn't wrap them; I put them in tissue paper instead. I hope you like them. I did have something else for you but ... well, but I have these instead. I feel crap because I had something very special that you could have used to put ... oh, it doesn't matter,' she expressed, shaking her head, rubbing her eyes.

'Hey, it doesn't matter what you have bought me; it's the effort that you have made, and the fact that you have made the effort to come and see me, that counts. I got lots of gifts yesterday, and do you know what...?' she paused, 'oh, I am just babbling,' she said, taking the presents out of the bag one by one.

As she reached in the bag, taking out the last one, she stopped, leaning over, kissing Hope softly, before ripping open the final gift.

'I'm sorry there isn't much but I am not a cheap skate, I did get you ...' Placing her hand over Hope's lips, Alex shook her head, grabbing Hope's hands, rubbing them.

'They are lovely, thanks.'

'Mmmm'.

'What does that silly noise mean?'

'Well, you have got me such nice stuff, and I bet Matt got you great things and look ... look at mine, but you know my stupid mum ...'

Alex took her in her arms, as they embraced, passionately kissing in the deserted side street. Transfixed on each other, they smiled tenderly for a few minutes.

'So what shall we do today, then? I need to go to the sales to take something back, but it will be very busy. Is that alright? Then maybe a drink somewhere after if you fancy? I'd say let's have lunch but I'm sick of eating. I'll get fat if I carry on like this.'

Hope nodded, seemingly uninterested.

'What's up with you?'

'Nothing. I just hate having to share you, that's all.'

Glaring, Alex held Hope's hand.

'You like me a lot, don't you? Maybe too much.'

'No, I don't,' Hope shrieked. 'You like me too, don't you?'

'Yes, but I have Matt and, well, he's my fiancé. And well, I'm not, I'm not gay.'

'And I'm not either. I could have a boyfriend if I wanted to,' she snarled.

'So, where are all these boys then?'

Going scarlet, Hope lowered her head, unable to make eye contact. Hope's heart began to beat fast, as though it was being pumped, causing her to take deep breaths. Alex's stomach began to knot, as she fiddled with her presents. Silent they sat, fidgeting.

'I'm sorry.'

'Me too,' Hope replied.

'I just don't know how to deal with all this; it's too much for me.'

'I don't really understand,' Hope commented, with a childish tone.

Raising a smile, Alex felt Hope's heart beat rapidly.

'Why are you smiling at me?' Hope asked, with a puzzled expression.

'Because you see everything so innocently. I have lost my dad, got engaged to be married and then met you. I am not sure if, and how to deal with it. If he had been ill, and died at night, in bed, at home, where we were expecting it, then it might have been easier to deal with. And maybe I would think fondly of my engagement party, but it was all so cruel. I can't bear any of it. Matt, my family and friends, all remind me of it all. I enjoy being with you, and I don't want you to leave my life,' she admitted, unable to hold back her tears.

Hope wiped Alex's fallen tears with her coat sleeve, gently running her fingers through Alex's hair.

'I will not leave your life. I really think that I …'

Alex cut in, preventing her words from coming out. 'Shhh. Don't speak, just hold me,' she whispered.

Clenching Alex, they cuddled for hours, making the car windows steam up.

Chapter 21

As Emily spoke, Alex's mobile beeped. She reached for her phone; as she read the message a huge grin took over her face.

'I bet that's her,' Emily guessed.

'Who?'

'That girl.'

'How did you know that?'

'Because you have a glow whenever she texts you, unlike when anyone else does.'

Alex grinned, replying with glee.

'You know, Emily, I think that I am starting to really like her a lot more than I should. I also think that I am going to suggest to Matt that we put the wedding on hold until I get myself sorted out.'

'What do you mean, sorted out?'

'I mean with money. We will not be able to afford the wedding we planned.'

'I thought that you were doing well in your business.'

'We are, but now that I'm part-time, I can't have a full wage.'

Frowning, Emily replied, 'When did you make this decision? You know, Alex, we all miss dad, but we are back to work, and were soon after his death.'

Screwing her face up, fidgeting on the couch, Alex did not reply. Leaning over, Emily slapped Alex's leg.

'For God's sake, Alex, you have got to snap out of it, and stop wallowing in self pity.'

Lifting her hands, Alex sat forward.

'How dare you say that to me? Do you have any sensitivity at all?' she bellowed.

Raising her arms, going beetroot red, Emily stood up, standing over her younger sister.

'Yes, Alex, we all know what happened, and where, and yes, that is tragic, not just for you, but for my mum and me too, but how come you are the only one who has to stay off for months, and are so sharp with Matt? You have always been the same ever since you hurt your arm; you wallow in self pity and expect us all to walk on egg shells around you, and pity poor you.'

Alex cut in,

'Yes, you are just jealous because I got more attention than you, especially from my dad. I could have been someone had it not been for that terrible fall. What did you do? You have made it based on your looks. Have you ever had any shit? I have always had to battle. You forget how much being off affected my school work and how much I fell behind. But who is the one with the degree?' she cried, standing up, walking towards the window, clenching her fists.

'You need to calm yourself down, Alex. Yes, what's done is done, and you have had it tough, but there are lots of people worse off than you; it hasn't been life threatening. You have had to face disappointments in your life.'

Alex interrupted, waving her hands in the air, 'And what disappointments have you had then?'

Shaking her head, red in the face, Emily picked up her tea, taking a sip.

'Come on then, answer!'

Slamming her cup down, Emily turned, facing her sister.

'You are spoilt, Alex, and you have been ever since you had your fall and couldn't play tennis competitively anymore. And now you have something else to be pitied for. Get a fucking grip and get on with your life. If you can't afford your wedding, have a cheaper one. I wake up every morning wishing he was still here. Do you not think I see his face, and his body crash to the floor? Do you not think I cry? And do you know what? I don't have someone like Matt to fall back on.'

Alex's mouth stood wide open, speechless for a few seconds. Emily paced the floor, wiping her brow.

Calmly, Alex asked, 'What do you mean? You have …'

Emily butted in, 'Yes, I do have him but Matt idolises you. I have had lots of boyfriends but I have never been proposed to.'

Feeling flushed, Alex took off her jumper, sitting down on the couch. Tearful, Emily joined her, searching for a tissue in her bag. Alex rubbed her sister's shoulder as Emily faced her, glaring.

'What are we like? We shouldn't be fighting. We only have each other.'

Alex agreed, trying to fight back her tears, sniffling.

'I just don't think getting married is right for me at the minute,' Alex explained, with a catch in her voice.

Looking puzzled, Emily, shook her head.

'Why is that so difficult to understand? After what happened, I think it's marred now.'

Disagreeing, Emily looked in her bag, hearing a phone bleep, looking at her phone screen. Alex checked her phone also, seeing a message.

Pointing, Emily scowled at her.

'This doesn't have anything to do with her, does it?'

'Who?'

'You said her name was Hope, didn't you?'

'No, I just think it's for the best at the minute. I need to sort myself out, you are right, and so a wedding isn't the best thing I need.'

Unconvinced, Emily sipped her tea.

Later that evening Emily sat by the fire, searching through family photo albums, gulping her red wine. Pete sat watching TV, glancing over at her, seeing her eyes fill up. She sat for hours, scanning over photos of herself and her family; finding an enlarged photo of a young slim girl holding a trophy, brimming from ear to ear, making Emily smile. Wading through the mountain of photos both black and white and colour, she put them in several piles, picking them up over and over again. Blowing her nose, she continued to search through until the early hours of the morning.

The following morning Pete got up first and went downstairs. He made his coffee, entering the sitting room, seeing the pile of photos on the floor, next to an empty wine glass. He leaned down, picking them up, finding many photos of an overweight teenager next to a slim pretty girl, and underneath, two slim girls in their early twenties. Next to them, he found several piles of a young, dark eyed girl with an older man with

102

broad shoulders and dark hair, playing football, tennis, riding motor bikes, and eating ice cream together, smiling. He put them back into their albums and left the room, heading into the kitchen.

Chapter 22

14 February

Matt opened the bedroom door, a heart-shaped balloon attached to the tray of food that he placed next to Alex. She sat up as he left the room, returning with a bouquet of a dozen red roses as well as a bottle of perfume and a large red velvet box of hand-made chocolates. He gave her a lingering kiss on her cheek, smiling profusely. Enthralled with her gifts, she opened her card, handing him his presents.

'Happy Valentine's Day, Angel. I hope you like your presents. I am going to make you a special meal tonight, so I will be in early,' Matt said, bouncing on his tiptoes, grinning.

'Thanks. I will look forward to that.'

'You never know, perhaps I'll get my reward later, do you think?' Matt teased as he kissed Alex, forcing her mouth open.

'We'll see', she replied, with a flat tone, as she began eating her croissant.

Matt smiled as he happily ate his breakfast, lying by her side.

'What are you doing today, then?' he asked.

'I don't know. Millie may come over,' she responded, reaching for her phone as it bleeped.

Alex smiled, placing the phone back on the table, getting out of bed, in search of the gift that she had bought for Hope, hiding it under her pillow, eagerly awaiting Hope's arrival, as butterflies crammed her stomach.

As the door knob turned, Alex beamed. Hope charged up the stairs like a herd of elephants running through the jungle, bursting through the bedroom door, hurling herself on the bed, flinging her arms around Alex, who lay there intrigued.

'Happy Valentine's Day, sexy lady,' Hope shouted.

'Happy Valentine's Day to you, too. I've missed you, little Miss Horny,' she replied, opening her eyes wide, licking her top lip.

Grinning, Hope took off her shoes and coat, and perched herself on the end of the bed, secretively hiding her gifts out of sight. Lying with her gift under the pillow, Alex fixed her eyes on Hope, opening them even wider. Hope attempted to pull back the covers, stopped by Alex as she yanked it close to her, right up to her chin. Surprised, Hope ran her tongue around her top lip over and over again, glaring at Alex. Alex lay motionless, draped in her bedcovers, staring into Hope's eyes. Hope stretched forward, gently holding Alex's chin, resting her lips on top of Alex's lips. Slowly, she licked Alex's top lip. Alex glared, turning her face away. Moving back, Hope stretched forward and reached in her bag of gifts, tearing open one of them. Hearing paper tear, Alex lay with her heart pounding out of her chest, unable to see Hope. Hope climbed back onto the bed, trying to pull down the bedcovers. Alex rived at them, preventing Hope from getting her way. Hope smiled, sliding down the bed, lifting it slightly, gently touching Alex's feet. Alex flinched away, leaving go of her tight grip, allowing Hope to quickly pull back the covers, viewing a naked Alex.

Their eyes met as Alex lifted her head towards Hope. Hope moved away teasing her, brushing her lips with her fingers. Grabbing Alex's hands, she handcuffed them to the bedpost. Alex's eyes lit up and her mouth gaped open. Pulling off her jumper and bra, Hope pressed herself against Alex, feeling their erect nipples entwined. Alex stared at her as Hope licked her body from head to toe, sucking on her toes, one by one. Alex moaned loudly.

Suddenly, Hope jumped off the bed and left the room. Lying naked with her stomach doing somersaults, Alex shouted for Hope. Silence fell, as her naked flesh begged to be touched. Quietly, Hope crept into the bedroom and mounted Alex, grinning. She placed a white scarf around Alex's head, blindfolding her. Alex groaned louder as Hope explored her body with her tongue, teasing her, as she kissed her inner thighs over and over again. Sucking on the top of her thigh, making Alex scream out loud, she moved her mouth towards Alex's soaking vagina, teasing her. Moving away, she got off the bed. Alex could hear rustling inside a bag, demanding Hope to satisfy her, lying trapped on the bed. Ignoring her request, Hope opened the jar, scooping in it, placing it all over her tongue. Lying helpless, Alex felt a cold, sticky substance touch her body, as Hope licked her nipples and stomach, advancing to her thighs. Leaning over, scooping into the jar, she rubbed Alex's lips and chin, licking it off. Moving down her body, she rived off her skirt and soaking knickers, buffing herself up and down Alex's sticky body, sucking on her neck, biting it, making Alex scream. Slowly she nibbled at her naked flesh, opening her legs wide, licking her soaking thighs, tasting her love juices.

After taking a hot steamy shower, the girls lay naked on the bed, arm in arm, gazing at one another. Alex reached under her pillow, passing Hope her gift, as her eyes lit up. Taking the gift, she smiled, transfixed on Alex. Putting the unwrapped gift next to her, she clenched Alex tightly. Placing her mouth over her ear, Hope spoke faintly, 'I love you!'

Alex pulled up at Millie's house. Brimming, knocking on the door. With flushed cheeks, she sat watching Millie iron.

'You look all hot and bothered, what have you been up to?' Millie quizzed.

Smiling, she ignored her, going into the kitchen, making herself a drink. Millie stared at Alex as she came back into the lounge.

'What have you been up to? Have you seen Benny?'

'No, not today. I saw him late last night. He took me out for a meal but I am getting sick of it all!'

'What do you mean? You adore him.'

Shaking her head, her eyes becoming smaller, she replied, 'Well it's killing me, him there with her and me here. I'm the part-time girlfriend, and it's no good. Affairs are a killer. Hope will feel the same as me; I sympathise with her.'

Frowning, Alex snapped, 'What do you mean? I'm not having an affair with her; we are just …'

Millie stepped in, banging the iron down, 'You mean, just friends? Alex, you might not want to hear this, but you are having an affair with her.'

Slamming her cup down, Alex lifted her hand.

'Don't be daft, we are just fooling around, that's all. She's a girl, for God's sake, and we are just having some fun. You told me to, didn't you?'

'Hey, Alex, why are you shouting? Have I hit a raw nerve?'

Alex shook her head, looking out of the window.

'You are seeing her. I mean, you are never off your phone. I hardly ever see you. When you are not at work, you are either with her, or on the phone for hours to her. It's just as well Matt works late.'

'Oh, Millie, don't be daft. She makes me feel good about myself and stops me thinking stuff.'

'Maybe she does, and I'm not having a go at you, but you are seeing her all the time. I told you not to let it get out of hand. I think you are falling for her.'

'Don't be fucking stupid!'

Pointing, Millie went on, 'What's up, Al, truth hurt?'

Lowering her head, Alex did not reply, taking a sip from her drink.

Seeing her best friend's unhappiness, Millie changed the tone of her voice, moving next to her.

'Look, Al, I'm just telling you how it is. Maybe it's time to admit this to yourself. Matt must see a change in you. You have cancelled your wedding, and when was the last time you slept with him? I'm only saying this because I care about you and don't want this to end in tears.'

Rubbing her face, Alex nodded.

'I know, Millie. It is getting out of hand. I have tried to stop seeing her but I can't. But I'm not sure this is what I want either. She's a girl for God's sake.'

'And?'

'But I'm not gay. I have never looked at girls like this before. I don't want to be gay,' she told Millie, bowing her head in shame.

'Alex, you have got to sort it out. You need time away, to think what you want, and who. If she was a boy, would you hesitate to leave Matt?'

Putting her head in her hands, she rubbed her eyes, moving her head from side to side.

107

Stunned, Millie cried out, 'Oh God, Alex, have you seen your neck?'

Panicking, Alex jumped off the chair, looking into the mirror.

'Oh fuck. What am I going to do?'

'You will have to put make-up on it.'

'And if that doesn't work, what will I do? Matt is going to be wanting an early night tonight. I can't have make-up on in bed,' she replied, with a shaky voice.

'Now answer me this, is it worth going through all this trauma and panic for a girl you only met a few months ago?'

Pausing, Alex sat staring at the floor. A few moments later, her phone bleeped, raising her spirits, replying. Walking into the kitchen, Millie mumbled something under her breath.

'What did you say?' Alex asked, putting the phone down by her side.

Returning, Millie looked at her best friend.

'I think that you have answered your own question by smiling your head off with that text, knowing you are going to have to come up with a good story for Matt.'

Accepting her words, Alex gave a massive breath. She picked up her phone, staring at the screen. Eventually she composed a text.

'I LOVE YOU xxxxx'

Chapter 23

Four months later

Emily lay sunbathing in the garden, checking her watch every so often, sighing loudly.

As the afternoon approached, she went into the house to cool off, wiping the mixture of tanning oil and sweat from her slim body. She made herself a salad and took a cold drink from the fridge as she checked her phone. She scanned her inbox, shaking her head, as she banged it hard on the kitchen work-top. Pacing the kitchen, she picked up her phone, placing it back down, over and over again, glaring at the screen. She left it in the kitchen, walking into the lounge, glaring at a family photo of Alex's engagement, making her cry. Sobbing, she sat on the edge of the couch, holding the photo frame in her hand, running her fingers over it. Wiping her eyes, she sat clenching the photo for ages with her uneaten lunch perched on the table next to her. Hearing a noise, she ran into the kitchen and picked up her mobile, clashing it back onto the bench.

Emily lay in the garden with her big shades on hiding her red, tearful eyes, checking her watch over and over. Every so often she went back into the house, glaring at her mobile phone.

As evening approached, she took her sun lounger back into the house, taking a shower, unable to hear her phone ringing. Stepping out of the shower, dripping wet, she heard her phone ring again. She dashed into the bedroom, answering.

'Hi.'

'Hi. How are you? What have you been up to today?'

'Well, I've been sunbathing all day. Why haven't you been in touch? What time will you be home?'

'Erm … I don't know. I am really busy at work and so it might be later, sorry'.

'OK, Pete. I will see you when you get in then? Shall I wait up for you?'

Pausing, he said, 'No, you get yourself out with your friends or go and see your Alex. She needs your support right now.'

Moaning, she replied abruptly, 'My sister is all over at the minute, and as you know, won't listen to me and take my advice. She goes mad if I say anything and so she's best left to sort it herself. I will just wait for you to come in. I haven't seen much of you …'

Pete stepped in, 'I have been working Em, you know that,' he responded with an unpleasant tone.

Changing her tone, Emily said softly, 'I know, baby, but I miss you and I …'

Pete interrupted, 'I have to go, Emily. I will see you when I get back. Don't wait up.'

Emily hung up the phone, sitting on the bed, drenched.

As the hours went by, she sat staring at the TV, unable to concentrate, with her half-eaten sandwich next to her on the couch. Deciding to reply to Alex's message earlier that evening, she composed a text.

'Hi sis. I kno it's really hard but you can't keep living like this. Matt really loves you & so u have 2 decide wot to do. U r changin & v. snappy with all of us. Plse sort it out. It isn't easy finding sum1 2 adore u. Hope does 2 I ges but Matt is yr rok. Do sumit bout it as it isn't fair the way u have been goin on for a while now. We r all involved as have 2 lie 4 u & I am not doin it 2 Matt anymore. He's a lovely guy.'

Chapter 24

'Hope, please tell us what's wrong. You have been in your room for two days now. You cry all the time, you won't eat, and you won't go to work. Please open your door and let me or your dad in,' Belle pleaded.

'I've told you, I don't want to talk about it. Just leave me alone,' Hope replied.

'No, I want to know. Is it boy trouble? We are all worried about you. It's your birthday in five days. Don't you want to plan things for it?'

Refusing to answer, Hope lay on her bed, sobbing uncontrollably.

'Hi, Al, I just thought I'd give you a ring to tell you that Hope has just tried ringing me again; that's ten missed calls in the past two days. I think that you should go and see her; the girl is distraught,' Millie explained in a concerned manner.

'Oh, Millie, I am trying so hard not to contact her but it's difficult. I feel awful; I think that I am doing the best thing, especially as I have seen how crazy she is about me, but it's breaking my heart when she sobs. I will give in if I talk to her. Please just don't answer, she may go away,' Alex replied in a desperate tone.

'Al, I don't agree. If she's making you that sad then you should still be with her. You have got so close to her these past months, you should really have visited her.'

'Please don't say that, Millie, I feel crap enough. Maybe I should ring her, then?'

'Yes, I would.'

'OK, I'd better do it now or I will have lost the momentum later. I'll ring you back when I've spoken to her,' Alex said, hanging up, searching in her call list for Hope's number.

Hope lay sobbing, holding onto her mobile, willing it to ring. Suddenly her mobile flashed an incoming call from Alex. Leaping off the bed, she pressed the answer button as fast as possible.

'Hello,' Hope said, high-spirited.

'Hi, Baby Bear. How are you?'

'Oh, I miss you so much. Please see me. Why have you had your phone off?'

'Because I'm trying hard not to contact you. It has to be over.'

'But why? I thought that you loved me?'

'Oh, Hope, please don't make this any harder than it is. I have explained my reasons to you. If you were older, I'm sure you would …'

Hope butted in angrily, wiping her fallen tears, 'Don't keep fucking saying that to me Alex. I'm not a baby. I do understand but I am so in love with you, I don't want to lose you.'

Horrified at Hope's tone, she blurted, 'Right, that's it. I'm not having you speak to me like that. Who the fuck do you think you are? I am in turmoil over all this. I don't want to hurt anyone but I'll tell you who is hurting the most, me!'

Sobbing, Hope sniffled, too distraught to reply. Silence fell. Alex rubbed her eyes, swallowing over and over again, feeling her heart pound out of her chest. Hope lay on the bed, trying to speak, as words failed her.

'I'm going to have to go, Hope. I can't bear this.'

'No, no, please don't. I'm sorry for shouting at you, I just can't take any of this, and want you so much,' Hope begged.

Shaking her head, Alex said faintly, 'I'm sorry, I can't, Hope. I am going to have to go, bye,' clicking off the phone.

Collapsing on her bed, Hope curled into a ball, pulling the covers over her, blowing her nose, rubbing her eyes, catching her tears.

Alex sat on the chair, holding her head in her hands, in despair.

Chapter 25

Three days later

'So what's going on?' David demanded.

'What do you mean?' Hope replied, trying hard to avoid further discussion, edging her way out of the front door.

'Well, you haven't come out of your room for almost three days, you have been crying a lot, you can't go to work, and now you are as chirpy as ever, off out, all dolled-up.'

'No, I'm not all dolled-up. I've got my old jeans on and a hooded top with my hair dragged back. And I'm not all happy either!'

'Yes, and a face full of make-up,' Belle added.

'Shut up,' Hope snapped.

'Hey, don't you speak to me like that. We have a right to know what is going on,' Belle said sternly.

'No, you don't, it's my business. I am not a kid.'

'Well, behave like a kid and we will treat you like a kid.'

Disregarding her father's comment, Hope walked out of the front door, slamming it hard.

'She's up to something she shouldn't be. I am sure of it,' David said.

'Yes, but she is right, she isn't a kid any more. What can we do? It will be boy trouble. It's bound to happen some time,' Belle replied.

'Yes, but she is our little girl, and we want to protect her. If she is seeing some loser, I will knock his head off, and she will be stopped,' he said firmly, knocking his hand off the coffee table.

Belle nodded in agreement with her husband.

Hope stood at the bus stop with butterflies running around her stomach, feeling sick to the pit of it. Pacing the path, she walked up and down in deep thought. The bus arrived and she sat near the back. She took out her mirror over and over, checking her make-up. She played with her fingernails for the entire journey. As she exited the bus she ran to the toilet, almost vomiting. She wiped her sweating brow, took a deep breath, and made her way along the path, walking briskly.

Twenty minutes later she arrived outside of an IT consultancy firm. Glaring inside, she stood for a few seconds, reaching into her bag, taking a sip of water, trying to quench her dry mouth. She stood with her heart beating so fast she thought she was having some sort of panic attack, before moving forward, taking a deep breath, pulling back the door. She entered the reception area and was greeted by a blonde girl.

'Hi, can I help you?' she asked.

Shaking, Hope replied,' Yes, is Alex in please?'

'Erm … can I ask who you are, please?'

Lowering her head, trying to stop her knees from trembling, she mumbled her name.

'Sorry, who did you say you were?' Jodie asked with a curious tone, looking her up and down from head to toe.

'Hope,' she replied with a tremble in her voice.

'Take a seat over there and I will ring her,' Jolie remarked abruptly, pointing to the leather sofa.

Shaking her head, Hope stood frozen on the spot, wiping her sweaty brow. Her cheeks were on fire, glaring at the ground. Jodie pressed the buttons on the phone keypad, glancing at Hope at the same time.

'Hello, Alex, I'm sorry to disturb you but I have a young girl called Hope in reception to see you.'

Shocked, Alex hung up the phone, running down the stairs. She pushed open the door, viewing a terrified looking girl with flushed red cheeks staring at the ground. As Hope heard the door bang, she looked up at Alex, filling up. Alex stood, unsure of what to do for a few seconds, conscious of Jodie watching them. Hope smiled at Alex. Her mouth opened as though she was about to speak, as Alex took her by the arm, ushering her out of the reception area up the stairs to her office.

Closing the door, Alex shook her head at Hope, as Hope burst into tears, clinging to Alex. Alex's heart began to beat faster as her mouth became dry. Hope clung to Alex's waist.

114

'God, Hope, what are you doing here? You can't come to my work. Matt is out with the other consultants but they will be back soon. You can't just turn up. This is my work. He will go mad if he thinks you have been here. He has suspected that there was something going on between us, and now Jodie will probably break her neck to tell him you were here. Why didn't you tell me?' she asked nervously, trying hard not to embrace her.

Unable to respond, Hope sobbed. Alex loosened Hope's grip to search for a tissue, wiping away her tears as quickly as they fell. She stroked Hope's face, feeling her cheeks burning, gazing into her tired eyes. She got Hope a drink, insisting she drank it, trying to calm her down, playing with her hair, as Hope sat composing herself.

'I can't bear to be without you, Mummy Bear. It is killing me. You won't answer my calls or texts. I had to come here; I didn't know what else to do,' she mumbled, tearful.

Touching her hand, Alex rubbed her fingertips over Hope's long fingers, as they stared at each other. Alex stroked Hope's face with the back of her hand softly, feeling every part of her face. Hope sat mesmerised, feeling calmed.

'It will be OK, Hope. Time is a great healer. It has only been a week. This time next month you will have moved on with a new guy and I will be just a memory.'

Shaking her head, Hope's tears began to fall again, as she stood up and walked towards the window. Alex moved next to her. Hope's arms lay by her side as Alex stared at her idle hands. Sniffling, Hope glared out of the window with her heart palpitating faster than ever. Suddenly there was a knock at the door. Darting to the door, Alex opened it.

'Hi, it's just me. Is everything alright up here?' Jodie quizzed.

'Yes, everything is fine. Hope is the daughter of a friend of mine and is upset about something; I will sort it out, don't worry, Jodie,' Alex replied, attempting to close the door.

Keeping it open, searching for Hope, Jodie commented, with a sarcastic tone, 'I have just rung Geoff to see how long they are going to be, and he says they will be back within half an hour.'

'Fine, whatever!'

Walking back towards the window where Hope stood motionless, Alex stood by her side, glancing down. She gulped and then took a tight grip of Hope's hand. Hope smiled as she turned facing Alex. Unable to make eye contact, Alex looked away.

'Why can't you look at me, Alex? Do you hate me that much?'

Disagreeing, Alex gripped her hand tighter.

'Well, what's the matter then? Don't you miss me?'

Pulling away, Alex moved, sitting back at her desk, placing her head on it. Staring at her for a few seconds, Hope sighed and then, advancing towards her, she leaned over her, holding her head, kissing her forehead tenderly. Alex did not move. Hope embraced her tightly. Alex stood up, opening the door.

'Come on, Hope, you have to go. I can't have you here. Matt will be back any minute. You can't keep hugging me; this has to end. You should never have come here. Please leave,' she demanded, with a catch in her voice.

Refusing, Hope sat on the chair, taking a sip of water.

'For God's sake, girl, what's the matter with you? I don't want you. I want and love Matt, so the quicker you accept that the better. Just go, will you!'

Devastated, Hope remained in the chair while Alex stood by the door, glaring at one another.

'Go, please, Hope. I beg you. Don't make this any harder. I am at work and I think I have done the right thing. You are young; you can't know what you want out of life yet. You are so pretty, I'm sure Mr. Right is just waiting for you.'

Beginning to cry, Hope stood up, banging the cup hard on the table. Alex turned away, refusing to look at her. Hope wiped her nose with her sleeve, approaching the doorway.

'I guess you are not the person I thought you were, Alex.'

'What do you mean?'

Composing herself, sniffling, she said, 'Well, I thought that you had lots of confidence and a high opinion of yourself.'

Frowning, Alex asked, 'What are you talking about?'

'You, Alex. You are meant to have such confidence but yet you don't have belief that I won't be with you, and will go off with a boy.'

'Don't be stupid, I don't think like that. I just think that you should decide what you want before you ruin people's lives!'

Pulling her face, Hope took Alex's hand.

'What do you mean? This isn't a game, Alex. I love you,' she said, heartfelt.

'Yeah, well, maybe you do but Matt loves me more and is older than you, and knows what he wants out of life. I am not sure you do, and I'm not prepared to ruin everything for a younger girl who may not really like girls.'

'But, Alex, you have never been with a girl before either. How do I know that you won't want to go back to Matt and have your flash lifestyle? I only work in a coffee shop. Yes, I am going to university soon, but am I good enough for you?' she said boldly.

Surprised, Alex moved next to Hope, looking at her.

Laughing, she spoke, 'You are too wise for your own good. You have an answer for everything. What happened to that shy girl I first met in that coffee shop?'

Smiling, Hope held Alex's chin.

'I guess she has had a good teacher, as well as growing up a lot. It makes such a difference when you know what you want out of life. I have to have the guts to go for it.'

Continuing to smile, raising her eyebrows, Alex asked quietly, 'And what do you want then?'

Hope moved her face next to Alex's, touching noses, caressing Alex's lips with her finger. Alex stood shaking with her heart beginning to beat faster and faster. Hope leant over to Alex's ear and quietly spoke. 'I want you, Alex. Not just for now to take you away from Matt but because I am helplessly in love with you. I want to be with you no matter what it takes.'

Breathing faster and faster, Alex did not respond. Hope moved her mouth towards Alex's lips, pressing them against hers. Closing their eyes, their mouths opened, making them kiss passionately. Hope closed the door with her foot, pushing Alex across the floor to lean against the desk, as they kissed. Hope licked Alex's ears and neck, while Alex fondled her breasts, pulling up her t-shirt to her neck, loosening her bra. Hope put her hand up Alex's skirt, touching her inner thighs, while they kissed harder and faster. Alex sucked on Hope's breasts, biting them, forcing Hope to yelp. Alex put her hand over Hope's mouth, forcing her silence. Hope pushed Alex onto the desk, riving off her skirt, forcing their pelvises together while Alex licked Hope's pert breasts, biting on them. Silent, they continued to explore each other's bodies with their mouths and hands, moving up and down on each other. Stopping, Hope stood up and gazed at her older lover for a moment. Slowly, she put her head in between Alex's legs, forcing Alex to groan. Suddenly Alex heard footsteps, making her panic. Stopping Hope, pulling away from the desk, she heard Matt's voice coming along the corridor. Terrified, she grabbed her skirt, quickly stepping into it as fast as possible, pulling down her top, glaring at Hope. Whispering to Hope, she indicated she hide in the vacant computer room next door. Shaking, Hope nodded and ran into the room next door, peering out from the square window, as Matt opened the office door. As he opened the door, Alex fixed her hair, taking a sip of water. Hope stood behind the door, peering out of the window in the door, taking deep breaths as quietly as possible. As Matt breezed towards his desk, kissing Alex on the cheek, Hope noticed a second door at the side, making her panic. Alex glared at the computer door, feeling her chest, realising she did not have her bra on. She paced up and down the room, rubbing her face.

'Are you OK, angel? You look a bit stressed.'

'Yes, I'm fine. I've just got a bit of a bad head, that's all.'

'Oh, OK,' he replied, unconvinced.

'Have the lads come back with you too?'

'No. They are en route though. I have just sent Jodie out to get me some paper for the printer in the computer room.'

'Why do you want to go in there? You have paper on your printer there?' she snapped, pointing to the paper.

'Alex, what is the matter with you? And why do you keep looking in there?'

'In where, Matt?'

As he pointed to the computer room, Hope noticed Alex's bra lying on the floor, making her chest palpitate, as she felt the sweat running down her back. Alex saw Hope looking through the glass as Matt went to the water dispenser in the opposite corner of the room. Hope pointed to the bra on the floor. Alex nodded, seeing it, kicking it under the desk, as she clenched her fists, feeling her palms sweat. Turning round, Matt looked at Alex.

'Are you sure you are alright, baby? You look all hot and bothered. Is the work too stressful for you as you have been coming in more lately?' he joked.

'Yeah,' she said, moving towards the computer door, trying to block it, her heart beating rapidly.

Matt emailed a colleague, allowing Alex to go into the computer room. As she went in, she heard Jodie coming up the stairs. Alex and Hope glared at each other, praying that Jodie did not come into the computer room with the paper. They both closed their eyes, hearing the door handle turn, sweat pouring down their backs. Hearing voices, Alex opened her eyes, moving towards the door, looking through towards Jodie, perched on the end of the desk with her short skirt, attempting to converse with Matt. Nodding, he fixed his eyes on the computer screen, doing his work. Quickly, Alex ushered Hope out of the other door, running along the corridor, and down the stairs as fast as they could. As Hope reached the door, with a tender glance, she whispered, 'I love you. Please don't leave me.'

Blowing onto her forehead, Alex let out a massive breath, trying to stop her tummy from churning. She glared at Hope's red-hot checks, besotted, before going back up to her office.

As Alex came into the room, Matt immediately looked up, smiling at her. Jodie got off the desk, standing up.

'Has your friend gone now then?' she asked.

'Erm … yes, she was only here a few minutes. She was upset, bless her; boyfriend trouble. Anyway, Jodie, Matt and I have work to do, so if you will excuse us,' she requested, escorting her out of the door.

'What friend?' Matt asked with a puzzled facial expression.

'Oh, just our Emily's friend's daughter who was a bit upset. Anyway, tell me how the meeting went.'

Chapter 26

Six weeks later

As Jodie drove Matt to the airport he sat pensively, unable to contemplate three days without his beloved Alex. He had tried in vain to shorten the trip, as well as arranging the visit for during the week, without success. Jodie had offered to drive Matt to the airport as it was on her way home; Alex had dropped him off at work, allowing him to pick up some paperwork on the way. As Jodie drove, he mused about three lonely nights without Alex.

Alex sat in a reverie at the bus station, waiting for Hope to exit, planning the wonderful things that they were going to do that weekend.

Hope had carefully arranged with Katie and Marco that she would use them as an alibi, claiming to have been invited on a weekend away to try new drinks samples with them, all expenses paid, allowing her to spend three days and nights with Alex.

Alex sat patiently as she saw the bus pull into the bus station. Hope leapt off, carrying a large holdall on her right shoulder, far too heavy for her slim shoulders. She wore a white knee-length, cotton dress with coloured patterns. Her hair rested on her shoulders in perfect shiny condition as she opened the car door, placing her bag on the back seat. Alex beamed as she saw this beautiful girl beside her, and she leant over, stretching across the passenger seat, to embrace her. Hope's face sparkled, emphasising her porcelain skin, as they kissed.

'I am so excited to be with you this weekend, you have no idea,' she said, with a high-pitched tone.

Alex smiled, taking Hope's hand as she pulled away.

'Did Matt get away OK? He won't be back, will he? I'm scared in case he is. I couldn't go through that again.'

'Yes, I dropped him off at work and Jodie took him to the airport. He has just texted me to say that the flight is on time and he is about to board. Don't worry, angel, it will be OK. Me neither, I was on edge about that so much, I was too traumatised to see you but I just had to. I couldn't wait any longer.'

Relieved, Hope leaned her head on the headrest, gazing at Alex, as electricity coursed through her body. Trance-like, she continued gazing, grinning from ear to ear, while Alex drove to her house in silence.

Alex pulled up onto the drive. She took the keys out of the ignition and turned to face Hope. Silent, they sat staring at each other. Hope gently took Alex's hands as they sat on her lap, locking them in between her fingers.

'I've missed you so, so much. I can't begin to tell you how much,' Hope said, filling up.

Nodding, Alex did not reply, grabbing Hope's hands tighter, transfixed on her.

'I have been so excited, unable to sleep, since you told me that he was going away, and that you wanted to see me, and that we could spend the weekend together. I have dreamed since that day at the hospital of sharing the night with you, waking up in your arms. It's a dream come true for me.'

'I know; me too. I'm really sorry that I have put you through so much upset; it wasn't my intention but it is so hard for me,' Alex confessed, tearful.

Unlocking her hands, Hope caught Alex's tears, wiping them onto her top.

'Please don't get upset; it's all behind us now. Let's just have a great time this weekend,' she said with an upbeat voice, grinning.

Alex smiled, touching Hope's face softly. Hope reciprocated with a kiss on the cheek and then leapt out of the car. Alex followed, taking Hope's holdall out of the back.

'So what is the plan for this weekend, then?' Hope asked, excitedly going through the front door.

'Well, what do you want to do?' Alex replied, raising her eyebrows.

'I just want to be with you and lock the door for three days without leaving.'

Alex chuckled.

'Well, we have to eat, don't we?'

'Eat what, though?' Hope teased.

'You are so naughty. I love it!'

Hope purred, going into the kitchen, following Alex. No sooner had Alex placed her keys on the bench than Hope grabbed her from behind, forcing her to face her. She grabbed Alex's chin, fixing her lips on top of hers, kissing her slowly. Without stopping, they kissed, wrapping their arms around each other, falling to the floor, embracing. Playing with each other's tongues, their jaws locked together with their eyes firmly shut. Holding each other tighter, they kissed passionately. Unlocking their arms, they grabbed each other's hands, huddled together, showering one another with kisses on the wooden floor. Their tongues explored one another's mouths, as they stretched out onto the floor. Continuing to embrace, Alex lifted her head up, leaning over Hope, taking the lead, kissing her softly. Alex stopped, gazing at her, and said, 'I love you.'

Beaming, Hope lay silent, as her eyes widened.

Alex took Hope's hand and led her into the lounge, taking Hope's shoes off, followed by her own, gently leading her onto the couch. Alex closed the curtains, lit the open logged fire, lighting candles, placing them on top of the fireplace and on top of the side tables. She lay next to her. Cuddling, they lay arm in arm. Content, Hope closed her eyes, clenching Alex close to her. Alex took off her top and bra, loosening Hope's bra. Hope pulled off her top and bra, allowing their naked flesh to touch each other. Feeling their soft, warm skin, they lay with their bodies entwined. Lying side by side, Hope pressed her breasts against Alex's, making their erect nipples touch. Hope gently rubbed her finger tips through Alex's hair, smiling faintly, before encasing her head into Alex's chest. With her eyes closed, Hope said quietly, 'I have missed you so much. I never want to be apart from you for this long ever again.'

Silence fell for a few moments until Alex muttered, 'Me neither. I can't bear to lose you.'

'Do you really mean that?' Hope asked, lifting her head up over Alex, staring into her eyes.

'Yes, baby, I mean it with all of my heart. I won't ever do it again.'

'Promise?'

'Yeah. It won't be you I will be leaving, Baby Bear,' Alex admitted.

Kissing Alex's forehead, Hope raised a smile.

Alex carried the pizza into the lounge, making Hope sit up. They sat by the fire with their bare shoulders, eating pizza, gazing at one another.

'What are you looking at me like that for?'

'Because I am so happy to be here with you, eating pizza by your fireplace.'

Goose pimples circulated around Alex's body from head to toe as she gently ran her fingers through Hope's shining hair, transfixed on her.

'You say the sweetest things.'

'Well, it's true, because most people take this sort of thing for granted but for us it's an extra special thing. I love it. But I love you more.'

'How much more?' Alex teased, leaning over, kissing her on the cheek, with a mouth full of pizza.

Putting her slice of pizza back down on the plate, she grabbed Alex's hand, staring at her.

'More than you could ever know, Alex. I love you with all of my heart.'

Alex's heart began to race, as the hair stood up on her arms. Reaching out, she touched the side of Hope's face with the back of her hand. Silently, they sat transfixed on each other, watching the candles flicker out of the corners of their eyes. Stopping their stares, they heard a mobile ring. Both of them ignored the phone, picking up their half-eaten pizza. Again the phone rang, making Alex, search for her phone. Sighing, she stared at the screen, feeling Hope's stare.

'I bet I can guess who that was then?' Hope remarked, nastily.

Nodding, Alex sent a text, returning back to eat her pizza.

'What did you say to him?'

Ignoring her, Alex took a sip out of her wine glass. Shaking her head, Hope sipped her wine. Alex moved closer to her, nibbling her neck, as Hope pulled away.

'Hey, what's up with you? I didn't answer him; I want to enjoy spending time with you, just you and me, but he is going to ring me when he is away. If I ignore him, it will make him panic. You don't want him to suspect anything, do you?'

Mumbling something as she drank her wine, Hope scowled at Alex.

'What did you just say there?'

Shaking her head, Hope continued to finish her food. Sighing, Alex stroked Hope's arm.

'You know this won't be for ever, Hope. I just need you to be patient with me for a bit longer.'

Snapping, Hope replied, 'Well, how much longer? I have waited for ages now. I may only be young but I am not letting you take the piss out of me. I will wait for as long as it takes but I need to know that you mean what you say and will be leaving him soon.'

Agreeing, Alex sipped her wine. Tossing her pizza onto the plate, Hope sat, glaring at the roaring fire flames.

'Hey, Hope, don't start and ruin this weekend. I can't help the situation I am in. I can't just leave. I mean, it would be a whole lot easier if you were older and understood, or had a place where I could come and stay. Where do you want me to go?'

Clenching her fists, Hope wriggled around on the floor.

'What's up with you?'

Biting her lip, Hope frowned at Alex.

Goading her, Alex went on, forcing Hope to stand up and sit on the couch.

'God, Hope, what the fuck is the matter with you? You see, this is why it's so hard when you are so young.'

Grinding her teeth together, Hope paused for a second.

'Alex, don't blame this on my age. You make excuses for it all the time. If you want to be with me, you will find a way. My family, your family, Matt, your house and business, are all major factors, but if you want me, they can be overcome. I hate it when you use my age, and how I don't understand, as a reason for living this way. I do understand that you live with a guy but are in love with a girl. And you need to see that I am torn apart by this triangle I am in. I find it so hard. He can give you everything, and I can give you nothing, but I have a full-time job now at the pub to be able to earn more money while I'm waiting to go to university. I did that for us. I can never compete with him, or give you what he can. Don't you see how much that kills me each day?' She spoke calmly, as she welled up.

Alex's stomach did somersaults, as she reached for her wine glass, speechless. Hope took a deep breath, putting her head in her hands.

'Do you know what surprises me about you?' Alex expressed, moving towards Hope.

'What?'

'Just how amazing you are for twenty. You are so expressive and you will never be beaten. You work so hard in that pub to get extra money for us and do double shifts so that I can see you during the day. I love that about you.'

Complimented, feeling very special, Hope closed her eyes, encased in pride at Alex's words, which lingered in her head.

'Well, do you know what I love about you?'

'What?'

'Absolutely everything: how sexy you are, how intelligent, strong, kind and how you make me feel. It hurts me lots sometimes the way you can be because of this situation that we are in, but as soon as you do or say something nice, all the pain goes away.'

'You are so advanced for your age with the things that you say. People my own age can't be as expressive as you,' Alex admitted, stroking Hope's face.

'I'm sorry for getting a bit annoyed at you; I know this isn't your fault, and it is harder as you need to find a home but I find it harder than ever. Please don't leave me because I tell you how I feel. I want you to respect me, no matter how young I am,' Hope replied, kissing Alex's head.

Mesmerised, Alex did not speak.

'I need to take a shower now and put my things upstairs. I won't be long.'

Nodding, Alex took the plates into the kitchen. She took her mobile out of her bag and listened to her voice mail. As she listened, tears rolled down her cheeks. Mumbling to herself, she said, 'Oh Dad, I wish you were here to help me. I miss you so much. You would advise me what to do.'

Glaring out of the kitchen window, she heard her phone ring again, answering, 'Hi.'

'Hi, angel. Where have you been for the last hour? I have been trying to ring you!'

'Oh, I was driving and I have just got in.'

'Where have you been?'

'To see Millie.'

'Oh, right. Well, I am here safe and sound; the hotel is great. I am going to meet Jan soon and they are taking me out for dinner. What are you going to do?'

'I am not sure yet. I may just stay in,' Alex responded, racked with guilt.

'I miss you lots.'

'How can you, you have only been gone a few hours, silly.'

'So that means that you are not missing me, then?'

'Well, not yet I'm not. Wait until you get back and then ask me.'

'OK, I will.'

'I am going to have to go in a sec as I have the bath on.'

'Oh, can't you talk to me for a bit longer? You isn't bothered 'bout me, is ya?' Matt asked in his silly voice.

Alex sighed, unwilling to answer.

'Oh, don't start this, boy. You know I'm bothered.'

'You isn't.'

Alex smiled as Matt continued in his silly voice.

'I am Matt. Now stop being stupid,' she demanded.

Silence fell.

'I love you.'

'Lurve ya too.'

'Lurve ya more,' Matt said.

Alex smiled.

'I am going to have to go now or the bath will be overflowing.'

'Shall I ring you later?'

'Well, just text as I may be out and then I may not hear it ring.'

'OK, well, I will text you later. Bye, angel. Enjoy your bath.'

'Bye, baby, I will, and enjoy your evening,' Alex said, hanging up the phone, rubbing her red cheeks.

She took a sip of her wine, swallowing over and over, trying to stop the lump in her throat. She sat on the stool, rubbing her eyes, making them sore. She stared at the floor, shaking her head. She heard Hope going across the landing. She stood up, swigged the remaining dregs of her wine, and went into the lounge. She lit more candles, put an extra log on the fire, and got a blanket from the cupboard, laying it next to the fireplace. She went back into the kitchen and took out some champagne from the fridge, and hand-made chocolates from a box, putting the champagne in a bucket, filling it with ice, and put the chocolates on a plate. She got two champagne flutes, and carried them into the lounge, placing them on the blanket. She took her trousers and pants off, and wrapped herself into the blanket. As she heard Hope coming down the stairs, she popped the cork, pouring it into the tall flutes.

Hope opened the door and sat next to her beloved, as she was handed the glass, and offered a chocolate, transfixed on Alex. She smiled profusely, surprised at Alex's efforts. Gazing at Hope in her dressing gown, Alex sipped her champagne, removing the robe with her eyes. Hope stretched out her legs, loosening her dressing gown, showing off her cleavage. Alex slowly took a bite from a chocolate, leaving the other half for Hope, gently slipping it into her mouth. Alex pulled down the blanket, showing off her naked shoulders, amazing Hope as she opened her mouth wide, licking her lips. Teasing Alex, Hope picked up her glass and licked the rim of it, staring at Alex. Slowly, she leaned forward and trickled the champagne on Alex's chest, making her flinch for a second before rubbing it around her nipples. Hope grinned, pouring more, licking it straight off. Alex lay passive, forcing Hope to take control. Hope rived the blanket off her, diving on top of her, nibbling her neck and ears. Alex turned her face away, tantalising her. Hope grabbed Alex's face, kissing it passionately. Alex attempted to throw Hope off her; Hope refused, grinning, grabbing Alex's arms, pinning them behind her head, holding them down, smothering her in kisses. Teasing, Alex stopped kissing, turning her face to the side, moving it backwards and forwards, touching

Hope's lips, attempting to kiss her, then moving away, until Hope forced her mouth onto Alex's, allowing them to kiss sensually. Again, Alex stopped, pushing Hope off her. Grinning, she stood up. Hope remained kneeling, grabbing onto Alex's feet, trying to pull her back down. Refusing, Alex moved away and opened the door of the lounge. Hope chased after her, running up the stairs behind her. Halfway up, she grabbed Alex's feet, tumbling her to the floor, lying on top of her back.

Screaming, Alex lay still. Hope pulled off her dressing gown and licked Alex's naked back. Slowly, she put her fingers on Alex's soaking wet vagina, playing with her clitoris. Crying out, Alex begged for Hope to put her fingers inside of her. Grabbing the back of her head, Hope satisfied Alex, making her orgasm within seconds. Collapsing on top of her, Hope gently kissed Alex's neck, making her turn round, allowing them to kiss, feeling their love juices running down their thighs. Sliding herself up and down Alex's pelvis, Hope ached to be touched. Playful, Alex would not give in to her, arousing her upper thighs with her fingertips. Suddenly, she stopped, sliding herself under Hope, licking around her vagina, feeling Hope's love juices on her face. Hope begged to be touched, pushing Alex's head onto her clitoris. Alex would not give in, gently moving Hope off her, standing up, taking Hope by the hand. She led her back down the stairs and into the lounge, blowing out all of the candles, leaving only the light from the fire. She ushered Hope onto the floor next to the fire, onto the blanket, gently kissing her. She stopped, taking a swig from the champagne bottle, hovering it over Hope's thighs, smiling mischievously. Taking another swig, she kissed Hope, passing the champagne into her mouth. Putting the bottle back down, she moved her head in between Hope's legs, nibbling the top of her thighs. Hope sat up, forcing Alex's tongue inside of her. Teasing, Alex stopped, leaning over the drinks. She took an ice cube out of the champagne bucket, smiling at her lover. She pushed Hope to the floor, teasing her with the ice cube, making her yelp out loud. Playing, she rubbed it onto her clitoris up and down and side to side, watching the water drip down her leg. She licked it off, touching Hope's clitoris with her tongue, making Hope gasp. Again, Alex teased her with the ice cube until it had melted. Then, she finally stimulated Hope's clitoris, getting faster and faster, forcing Hope's body to jolt, finally reaching her orgasm.

They lay huddled together inside the blanket, content, looking into each other's eyes for the rest of the evening.

The next morning Alex awoke early, reaching for her phone. She sighed, reading Matt's heart-felt messages, making her toss the phone onto the bedside table. She turned, staring at Hope sleeping peacefully, gently touching her forehead. For hours she lay next to her beauty until eventually Hope opened her eyes. Immediately, she gave a huge smile, cuddling into Alex's chest, kissing her cheek softly.

'I can't believe how great this feels, Mummy Bear. I feel so privileged to be here with you. I don't want this feeling to end,' Hope announced, feeling a warm glow all over her body.

'I know; me neither. I can't believe how nice it feels, here with you, waking up with you next to me rather than you just being my first thought. I could get used to this.'

Startled, Hope looked at Alex.

'Really? Do you really mean that?' Hope asked.

Quietly, Alex replied, 'I do mean it, yes.'

As she spoke her phone bleeped. Hope moaned loudly, while Alex leaned over to get it.

'I bet I know who this will be. Really, this is too hard for me. I would never give you ultimatums but I can't live this way. I love being here with you, and I know that this isn't your bedroom, but I don't feel too comfortable here.'

Alex's face became scarlet red as she replied to Matt's message. Pulling the covers back, Hope sat up. Alex continued to finish her message. Suddenly Hope grabbed the phone out of Alex's hand, snatched straight back by Alex. Gritting her teeth, Hope stormed out of bed. Riving back the covers, Alex went after her into the en-suite.

'Who do you think you are, pulling my phone off me? You are getting a bit too big for your boots. Don't dare do that again,' Alex said tersely.

'Why wouldn't you let me see what you were writing to that stupid fucking twat?'

Astounded, Alex retaliated, 'Yes, I know it's hard for you but still, there is no need for that.'

Pushing Alex out of the way, Hope went into the bedroom, searching for her holdall. Following her, Alex went on, 'What the hell do you think you are doing? Are you having a kid's tantrum because you can't get your way, and read my private messages?'

Ignoring her, Hope threw her clothes into her bag, biting the inside of her lips.

'Go on, Hope, that's it, be a child and ignore me. You see, this is why I can't leave him to be with you, as you are too fucking childish!'

Hope began to cry, feeling her heart pounding out of her chest. Alex saw this, sitting on the bed next to her.

'Why do you say such cruel things to me? I am bound to be jealous over him. I love you so much, and the closer you get to me, the worse I am with him. Maybe I shouldn't have called him that, but I'm upset and so …'

Alex cut in, dragging Hope to sit down. 'I know and I'm sorry. You are right but I do still care a great deal for him. It is an awful mess. You don't see and hear the things he says to me. He is pulling at my heart strings, and you are in the other direction. I'm so torn. I don't mean to be nasty to you, but I'm so frustrated. Please try to understand,' she begged.

Nodding, Hope stroked Alex's face.

'I'm trying to understand but you blame my age for everything. You know, Alex, my mum's friend has been having an affair, and is the other woman; you should see how she behaves. I think it's hard for anyone.'

Shaking her head, Alex gazed into her eyes.

'God, you are right, it's so hard on all of us, and you are so mature about it. Please don't let it spoil our day. Let's go for a nice walk after breakfast.'

'OK, Mummy Bear. And then can we come home and work up some calories before tea? I'm going to cook for us tonight.'

'What, pizza from the takeaway?' she joked.

Laughing, Hope replied, 'No, Chinese actually.'

Cuddling Hope, Alex whispered, 'Oh, baby, I love you so much. You are so, so strong-willed, and so funny too.'

Delighted, Hope squeezed her tightly.

The girls went for a walk in the nearby woods, arm in arm, enjoying every minute together; stopping when they were in a secluded spot to kiss, unable to keep their hands off each other. They walked for hours, taking a rest every so often. As they walked back to the house, Hope stopped, sitting on a large log. Looking anxious, she asked Alex, 'What happened the night your dad died?'

Lowering her head, Alex did not answer. Hope comforted her, playing with her hair. Silence fell.

'I'm sorry, Alex, I didn't mean to pry. You talk about your dad, and how much you miss him, but every time your engagement is mentioned, you go so sad, or your eyes fill up. You don't have to answer. I just want to know more, well everything about you really.'

Rubbing her eyes, Alex glared at the ground.

'Yes, my engagement was devastating. I guess you can figure that it was ruined. I don't want to go into it; not because I don't want to tell you, just that it upsets me too much. Can we just leave it please? Ask me something else instead,' she mumbled.

Holding her close, Hope nodded.

'OK, I have something else that I'd like to know. How did Matt propose? Was it very romantic? I bet it was.'

Shaking her head, Alex refused to answer, standing up, walking away, pulled back by Hope.

'Please tell me. I promise I won't say anything. I'm just curious, that's all.'

'Why do you want to know? To call him for being soppy, and very romantic?'

'No. Not at all, but I just don't want to duplicate something that he may have done, that's all,' she replied with a teasing tone.

Scowling, Alex snapped, 'What are you on about? I'm never going to marry a girl. That's mad.'

Dropping her head, Hope felt her eyes sting, wiping them. Her stomach did somersaults, as she felt sick. Realising Hope's sadness, Alex held her hand.

131

'OK, if you want to know, yes, it was very sweet, and romantic, but very subtle. It wasn't flash, and it wasn't in some posh place. It was at home and cost very little but I guess he had put a lot of thought into it. If I ever got proposed to again, it would be different, as the person would be different, and if I loved them with all of my heart, then it would be just perfect, no matter what they did.'

Hope gazed at Alex, squeezing her hand tighter than ever.

'I love you like that you know; with every tiny part of me. I adore you.'

'Well, will you wait for me then?'

'Yeah.'

Alex drove Hope home in silence, clenching her hand all the way. Hope stared out of the window, unable to make eye contact with Alex. She gulped over and over again, attempting to get rid of the lump in her throat. Alex, too, could feel herself getting upset, driving slower than usual. She arrived around the corner to Hope's house. They embraced tenderly for several minutes. Unable to hold back her tears, Hope began to cry, making Alex become tearful also. Finding it too difficult to say goodbye, Hope jumped out of the car and ran down the street, after spending three amazing days together. Alex sat watching her. As Hope got to the end of the street, she turned and waved, braving a smile. Alex drove off, wiping her eyes with her sleeve.

At the airport Alex stood pale-faced, composing a message to Hope. As the message was being sent, Matt came through the arrival gate.

A large grin came over his face, and he rushed over to her, hugging her tightly.

'Oh, I've missed you so much,' he said with relief.

Heartsick, she hugged him, closing her eyes with sadness, realising how out of control her feelings for a girl had become.

As they walked out of the airport to the car park Alex's mobile bleeped.

Alex read the message and excitement coursed through her body, as though she had just had a rush of blood to her head. She smiled with delight.

'Who is that texting, making you so happy?'

'Just Millie.'

He got into the car and leaned over to kiss her. Flinching, she moved her lips away, allowing him to kiss her on the cheek, unable to bear his lips on hers.

'Hey, what's up with you?'

'Nothing, I just don't like snogging in public. You know that,' she said harshly, staring out of the window whilst starting up the car.

Alex drove in silence as Matt talked about the success of the trip, and what revenue it would bring to the company.

'I have a surprise for you,' he said, high-spirited, as she pulled onto the drive, stopping the car.

'What?'

'I have booked for us to go away in January to the Bahamas in an exclusive five-star adult-only hotel. It's meant to be so romantic.'

Alex's heart sank, but she pretended to show enthusiasm.

Chapter 27

Christmas Day, 7.20 a.m.

Hope woke up early, excited about the day ahead, stretching over to her bedside table, reaching for her phone.

'Merry xmas MB im sooooo xcited 2cu 2day. I kno it wont b 4 long but id 4sake all of my xmas stuff just 2 cu on this spec day.'

9.20 a.m.

'Hello,' Matt said, stirring from his sleep, answering the telephone.

'Hi, son. Merry Christmas,' said Bill.

'Same to you, Dad.'

'We are going to come over to yours today instead of you coming to us,' Bill explained.

'Why? You never normally come over.'

'Well, your mum isn't feeling too good, and she thinks sitting in the house is making her worse, so she wants to get out for a change.'

'OK, Dad, that's fine for us. What time will you be here?'

'What time are you going to Eve's?'

'About twelve-ish.'

'OK, well, we will be there at about eleven. Oh yes, your brother has also invited you to his for tea.'

'Yes, I have just switched my phone on and read his text. OK, Dad, I will see you soon,' Matt responded, hanging up.

'That was my dad, they are coming here instead, so you will be able to see them now,' Matt explained to Alex as she lay pretending to be asleep.

Immediately she faced Matt.

'What do you mean, they are coming here?'

'Well, they said that they wanted to come and see us for a change, and now you can drop off Millie's presents on the way to your mum's, and still see my folks.'

'And what was that about your Steve?'

'Oh yes, we have been invited there for tea.'

'You are joking, we never get invited, ever. Well, I'm not going, and when your mum and dad are here, I will be at Millie's as arranged,' Alex remarked in a nasty tone.

Matt sighed, sitting up in bed.

'How is that going to look? They come over and you have gone to your mate's house? I mean, you don't need to be there all day. And then I go to my brother's alone because you don't like them. It's meant to be a day for families being together. You make me look stupid,' he complained.

Alex pulled the covers back, leaping out of bed, retrieving her mobile from the chest of drawers, sighing, looking worried, with sadness in her eyes.

'Cheer up, it might never happen,' Matt remarked as he studied her miserable face.

'It already has,' Alex replied, glaring at Matt with contempt.

'What do you mean?'

'I'm not having your lot thinking they can just dictate to us,' she said abruptly.

'Fine, Alex, I will tell Steve we are not going, and my mum and dad can't come over, and when they ask why, you can explain to them. How come you are so bothered about going to see Millie anyway? You never normally go over on Christmas Day.'

Without commenting, she read the messages on her phone.

'God, what do they say?' Matt quizzed.

'What?' Alex snapped, glaring at the screen.

'Well, you look like you are going to cry about what you are reading,' he commented unhappily.

'Shut up, you stupid idiot,' she said angrily.

Matt's eyes seemed to dim, almost as if the light shining inside them had gone out. He lay back down, turning on his side. Alex sighed more loudly, staring at the wall, wondering what she could do. Looking at the sadness and disappointment on his face, burdened with guilt, she got back into bed, cuddling him.

'You don't ever want to be with me, do you?'

'Don't be silly. I just hate my plans being disrupted, you know that,' she replied convincingly.

'But you can go to Millie's if you want. I know how hard stuff is for her this year with Benny, and you want to make her day special, but we can drop off there on the way to your mum's; I will sit and wait in the car for a bit if you want half an hour or so with her,' he said softly.

With inflated guilt, she tightened her grip on his strong, muscled body, barely able to look him in the eye, feeling his disillusionment on this special day.

'No, you are right, I won't go. Today is about being with your family and it means a lot to me to be there with you and to go to your Steve's too. I am sorry,' she said, holding him.

'Fanx, fanx very much,' he replied in his silly voice, his spirits rising.

Alex smiled, hiding her pain.

'Come on, let's open our presents,' he went on, feeling happy.

10.50 a.m.

Alex sat, holding her phone out in front of her, tapping her feet, as Matt took a shower, feeling heartsick, plucking up the courage to text.

'Merry xmas bb. Sory aint txt b4 now been opening gifts etc. did u get nice stuff?'

Send.

As Hope's phone bleeped she beamed, her anxiety lifting.

'thank god u hav replied. Was getting v. worried. Yes got nice stuff, did u? but can't wait 2cu the most. Wots the plan?'

Send.

Disgusted at the upset she was about to cause, Alex composed her message, feeling nauseous.

'Im so sory angel but can't make 2day. Matt stupid family makin it 2 Dificult 2 get away. It's 1hr round trip n then time 2gether cant get away. Im realy gutted honest + no how much u wantd me 2 cu2.'

Send.

As Hope read her message she felt an ache in her heart like never before and leapt off the chair, storming up to her bedroom. She sat on her bed with her head in her hands, trying to come to terms with the dejection she felt.

'Is ther no way at all? I hav2 cu cant bear it!!!'

Send.

'No I cant. can ring u tho. I will get awy 4 bit 2 do that. Promise.'

Send.

'Wen will that b? just tell me n I'll get out of the way of my family so that u can.'

Send.

'Oh Bb I am guttd u kno. Realy am. Sumtime afta dina. Smile 4me u kno Y?'

Send.

'Y?'

Send.

'Becoz I love you with all my heart.'

Send.

Viewing Alex's response, Hope grinned.

'I kno u do but you hav promised me so many times that u will leave. I need 2 know that nxt yr it will b me + u 2gether.'

Send.

As Alex was reading her message, Matt came out of the en-suite, dripping wet, frowning at her. Alex lowered her head, unable to make eye contact. She closed her eyes, taking in a deep breath. Matt's heart began to beat faster, sensing Alex's odd behaviour. He moved next to her, putting his hand on her shoulder. Without opening her eyes, she placed her hand on top of his, pushing down hard. As Matt kissed her forehead, she started to feel a trickle down her cheek. Biting the inside of his lip, Matt clenched Alex's hand tightly. Stuttering, he said, 'What's up, angel? You have been weird for months now. I barely dare ask you these days, as you always bite my head off.'

Refusing to answer, she stood silent, with her eyes firmly shut. Feeling sick to the pit of his stomach, Matt probed further.

'Come on, Alex, tell me what's wrong? Is it your dad? And if it is, then I suggest you get some help. I have done my best to be supportive, but now I think I am getting a bit sick of your mood swings and distance with me. Why take his death out on me?' he said, trying to stay calm, with his heart pounding out of his chest.

Opening her eyes, she shook her head, and her lips moved, as though she was about to speak. Changing her mind, she put her head into Matt's chest, beginning to cry. Comforting her, he felt her beating heart.

'I'm sorry, Matt. I know that I haven't been too good for a while, and no, it isn't all about my dad. Today isn't the right time and …' she paused, hearing her phone bleep. Immediately, she looked at her message, infuriating Matt. Feeling his palms sweat. Matt inhaled several times, watching Alex read her message, seeing a horrified look on her face. Walking away, she began composing a reply, going out of the bedroom along the landing. Clenching his fists together, biting his lip harder, he followed her, viewing the look of despair on her pale face.

Grabbing her shoulder, he scowled at her.

'Who is that? I bet I can guess? And it's because of your friendship with her that you are like this. Why did you stop talking to me the minute you got a text? You are always on that phone, and I'm fucking sick of it!'

Shocked, Alex put the phone in her pajama pocket, turning away from him, guilt-ridden. Red-faced, Matt wiped his sweaty brow, feeling nauseous.

'Show me your phone, I want to know what she says that makes you look terrified one minute, and ignore me, and ecstatic the next.'

Feeling as though her insides were about to boil over, Alex fell to the floor in a heap with her head in her hands, mumbling. Matt crouched to the floor, taking her in his arms.

'Tell me what's up, you look so sad. What is it with you and her?'

Silence fell, as they held each other.

'Alex, tell me.'

She did not respond, gripping him harder. Suddenly her mobile rang, startling her. Unlocking herself from his clutch, she reached in her pocket. Raising his arms, Matt grabbed the phone.

'Stop ringing her. I wish you would just leave her alone. If she doesn't want to reply to you then get lost,' he yelled, hanging up.

Astounded, Alex sat with her mouth gaped wide. Sitting back down on the floor, Matt's body began to shake. Looking at the anger on Alex's scarlet face, he wiped his eyes, reaching out for her hands. Refusing, Alex shook her head, disgusted.

'You couldn't leave it, Matt, could you? How dare you speak to someone like that? You didn't even know who it was. I am so surprised at you; it isn't you at all,' she confessed, quietly.

'It was just a very good guess, Alex.'

Composing a text, she ignored him. Tapping his fingers on the stair banister, he took large breaths. Tapping louder and quicker, seeing Alex text, Matt scowled at her. Alex finished her message and walked past him, going downstairs. Watching her take each stair, he sighed loudly, feeling sicker than ever. Reaching the bottom, she looked up to him.

'Are you coming down to open stuff, or are you going to ruin the day, and end up fighting with me?'

Shaking his head, he came downstairs and went into the lounge. Pacing the floor, he stared at her.

'God, Matt, what the fuck is your problem? I can't believe that I'm keeping my temper with you. Don't you ever take my phone, and be so nasty to my friends,' she shouted.

Feeling the hair stand up on the back of his neck and arms, he scrunched up the handkerchief in his pocket, walking up and down the room. Feeling the butterflies consume her stomach, she looked at her phone. As soon as Matt saw her take it out, he ran at her, pulling it out of her hands. Tussling over it, she rove at him, winning it back.

'That fucking phone is going in the bin. You can see how much it's pissing me off, and you are still doing it. You defend her, and I'm so, so sick of it. What is it with you and her? She's some dumb kid ...'

Alex butted in, pointing in his face. 'Don't you ever take my phone off me again. I am sick of this aggressive manner. And don't you dare call her names. You don't even know her.'

Infuriated, he turned his back, taking in large breaths. He sat on the couch, feeling his chest palpitate, touching the roof of his mouth with his dry tongue. Alex came and sat next to him, looking at him.

'I'm sorry, Matt, but I love her.'

Chapter 28

Emily hung up the phone, sitting back down next to Pete. She sat tutting, wiping her tired eyes. Pete sat transfixed on the football, picking at nuts from the bowl at the side of him. Leaning over, she kissed his cheek. Unmoved, he continued to watch the TV.

'Is there nothing else on?'

Shaking his head, he nibbled on the nuts. Putting her feet across him, Emily sat unhappily watching the TV. After a few moments Pete pushed her legs off him. Glaring at him, she put them back on, making him frown at her.

'Em, your legs are too heavy. Please get off me.'

Reluctantly, she moved them.

'Do you mind if I go out later? I need to go and see Matt. He's gutted.'

'Why do you need to go and see Matt? Surely you should be going to see your sister?'

'I have seen her but he doesn't have anyone to talk to. He's such a nice guy. You should take him out for a pint.'

'I would but I'm going out later to get pissed. I don't want him crying in his beer with the lads.'

Getting off the couch, she scowled at him.

'God, Pete, you are so unfeeling. Wouldn't you be gutted if I told you that I loved someone else, especially on Christmas day? Our Alex is so dramatic.'

Nodding, he continued to watch TV, eating his nuts. Walking out of the sitting room, Emily texted Matt, arranging to go and see him.

Hope lay in bed contemplating a new life with her beloved Alex, flattered at Alex's confession to Matt, smiling from ear to ear.

Alex drove to Millie's house, tearful. The minute she opened the door, Alex sobbed, unable to catch her breath.

Emily knocked on the door several times, trying the garage door, eventually getting into the house. Matt lay on the couch, staring at the wall in darkness. Shocked, Emily opened the curtains, sighting an unshaved Matt with red eyes. Comforting him, she shook her head.

'God, my sister is such a fool. What has she done to you?'

Moving his head from side to side, Matt did not answer.

Alex sat, unable to stop crying, comforted by her best friend.

Hope got out of bed and took a shower, arranging to meet her girlfriends in town.

Matt sat silently, allowing Emily to talk at him.

'God, Al, this is a mess, now isn't it? What the hell are you going to do?'

'I don't know. Since Christmas Day, he has hardly said a word. He hasn't slept in the same bed as me. He keeps crying all the time, asking me what she has that he hasn't. I can't take any of it. Hope thinks I'm going to leave him and get a flat, and my head is all over. I don't know if I'm coming or going,' she muttered, blowing her nose.

'I know, Al, it must be so hard but how can you go back now that you have told him about her? Do you not just think that it's gone too far now? As you said, he was suspecting something, with the way he behaved, so it had to come to boiling point. Do your mum and Emily know?'

'Yes, Emily does, and she has been really nasty to me about it, telling me how great Matt is; that isn't helping me. What shall I do? I mean, where do I go and live?'

'I don't know, Al, but you can rent somewhere if you want to until you can sell the house or whatever.'

'I don't know what I want. I just know that I really love her and it's tearing me apart. It isn't fair to any of us really, is it? But I don't want to tell people that I'm with a girl.'

Frowning at her friend, Millie shook her head.

'For God's sake, Al, don't be so pathetic; it's normal now, and if you are gay and love her, which you do, then you can't go on this way. It will destroy you all, and Hope will not wait for you for ever. She may be young, but she's strong-willed. You are not poor so you can get a place of your own.'

'But, what about work? We work together.'

Banging her glass on the table, lifting her hands above her head, Millie said, 'You are making excuses; if you really want to leave, you will find a way. You are a fighter, Al, and have achieved what you have because of your determination. And now you are too gutless to make yourself happy.'

Not responding, Alex took a sip from her drink.

Hope sat in the bistro with her friends, pretending to listen to their Christmas Day stories, planning their New Year parties, unable to stop thinking of Alex, and how different her life was going to be.

Emily made Matt lunch, despite his refusal of her making it. She sat perched next to him, handing him his handkerchief to wipe his eyes.

'So, what has actually been said then? I know she says she loves her but you know our Alex, she can be so dramatic at times. She may just be infatuated with her. I'm sure that you will be OK.'

Tossing the half-eaten sandwich on the plate, he shook his head. Placing her hand on top of his, she nodded her head.

'No, you are wrong; I know she loves you very much.'

'Maybe she did, or still does, but she is in love with her. I see the way she looks at her, and the way that she can make her smile. I know that she has been having an affair for some time now. I just know it,' he admitted, as tears rolled down his pale face.

Guilt-ridden, Emily, turned away, picking up her sandwich from her plate.

'I love her so much. I couldn't bear for her to leave me.'

Chapter 29

'Good afternoon, can I help you?' said the blonde receptionist.

'Yes, I have an interview with Mrs. Turner and Mrs. Briggs for the Education Sales Coordinator position,' Alex replied.

'OK. Take a seat over there,' the receptionist replied, pointing to the designated seating area.

Alex acknowledged her, and decided to go to the toilet to check her hair and make-up. She was wearing a green skirt suit with a white shirt and green scarf, black tights and high-heeled black shoes with a green bow on the side. She returned to her seat.

'Hi, Miss Thomas, would you like to come this way?' a lady said, approaching Alex, her hand held out.

Alex stood up, shaking her hand firmly, and was led into the interview room and asked to sit down.

'Hi, Miss Thomas, I am Mrs. Briggs. I am the training manager. You have already met Mrs. Turner, she is the sales manager,' she said, as Mrs Turner stood up to greet Alex.

Alex shook her hand.

'So, Miss Thomas, tell us a little bit about yourself. I can see from your CV that you have your own business?' Mrs. Briggs said.

Alex looked confidently at both ladies, speaking with clarity.

'Well, yes, I left university and then I did some sales work as well as some private tuition. Then I met my boyfriend, and he was very good at IT, so we decided to start up our own consultancy business.'

'So why, if you don't mind me asking, do you want another job, if you have a successful business?' quizzed Mrs. Briggs.

'I don't mind at all. Our business is doing well but I seek a new challenge now; we have built up a very good clientele and so, to be frank, the company name virtually sells itself, and, well, to be honest, I want to use my degree in English more, otherwise it was just a waste.'

Both ladies nodded, making notes.

'But selling books is a different thing altogether, as is leading and motivating a team to do so. Why do you think you could fulfill this role?' Mrs. Turner asked.

'Well, I think that sales are the same whatever you are selling. If you know your product well, and have the ability to get someone to believe that they need what you have, then you have sold it. It doesn't matter whether that is beer, books, computer maintenance or software.'

'Yes, I agree, but we are not the cheapest book company and people are often put off by that,' Mrs. Briggs commented.

Alex smiled graciously as she went on. 'I agree that selling an expensive product can be hard, but if you market it correctly then you have a chance. How hard do you think it is to tell someone that your fees are one hundred pounds per hour?'

'Yes, but no one else may be able to fix things like your company can so they will pay,' Mrs. Turner responded.

Alex replied immediately.

'I agree, but your books are the best option if you want to pass your GCSEs as they include every aspect of the curriculum, which your competitors cannot, explaining it in a way that is pupil friendly,' Alex said boldly.

As Alex made this comment the two ladies glanced at one another out of the corners of their eyes.

'It's nice to know that you think that of our books,' Mrs. Turner said, pleased.

'Yes, I do, I have looked at them, and at some of your rivals', and as I have a degree in English, I can see good explanations that will work, and bad ones. Any teacher you approach, highlighting this factor, will want to buy your books, irrespective of the price, and that is what I would tell my team, if I were offered the position.'

As Alex talked further, Mrs. Turner glanced at her with a sparkle in her eye. After several minutes of questions from both ladies, all of which Alex answered with ease, she was thanked for coming, and was informed that they were looking for someone to start within the next month, which suited Alex owing to her imminent week's holiday in the Bahamas in eight days' time, and that they would notify her if she was successful later in the day.

'Wow, she was very good, she had an answer for everything,' Betsy said.

'Yes, she knows fine well how to run a business and so this will be a walk in the park for her. Do you think she will gel with the other members of your team?' Ailsa asked.

'Yes. I liked her; she has something different about her.'

'Yes, me too. I just don't get why she would want to leave a thriving business where she is on Easy Street,' Ailsa remarked.

'Maybe it is like she said and she needs a challenge, or she may want to get out of her partner's hair. They could be going through a bad patch. His loss is our gain. She could sell sand to the Arabs,' Betsy replied.

'Yes, you are right,' Ailsa responded.

Alex drove out of the car park en route to work. Matt had gone away for the day on business, making things a lot easier.

Late into the afternoon, her phone rang. Searching in her bag, she answered, 'Hello?'

'Hello, is that Miss Thomas?'

'Yes.'

'Hi, this is Betsy Turner from Lessons R Us. I would just like to say that if you would like it, the position is yours.'

'Really? That's great, thanks', Alex replied, upbeat.

'Great, well, welcome aboard. I will send you a letter to confirm but we would like you to start training as soon as you can. Did you say you were going away soon?'

Alex paused.

'Yeah, I guess I will have to go, in just over a week, so I could start training in three weeks' time if you want?'

'Oh, I would be more enthusiastic to be going away if it was me,' she joked.

Silence fell.

'OK then. I will write to confirm this. Enjoy your holiday and I will be in touch.'

'Thank you. Bye.'

'Bye.'

Alex immediately telephoned Hope to inform her of the good news.

She did not answer, prompting her to phone Millie instead.

'Hi, Millie.'

'Hi, flower. How did you get on with the job?'

'I got it; they have just rung to tell me. I am over the moon.'

'Excellent. I bet Hope will be pleased.'

'Yes, she will. I have just tried ringing her but she must be at work as she didn't answer.'

'Well, once you get your foot in the door you can do whatever you want.'

'Matt doesn't know that I've applied, but at least now I can get some relief from him.'

'Yes, and now there is no excuse for staying with him any longer. It must be fate for you and Hope.'

'Mmmm,' Alex replied with a deflated tone.

'Yes, well, if it turns nasty…'

Alex cut in, 'It would never be like that with Matt, we are so close.'

Chapter 30

Hope stared out of her bedroom window as the rain thrashed against the pane. Her heart felt numb, almost as though it had stopped beating. She stared into the back garden, fighting hard not to visualise Alex lying naked in Matt's arms, sipping cocktails in paradise without a thought for her. Since Alex's departure three days ago, her sleeping pattern had been erratic. She was desperate to erode the recurring images of Alex and Matt in her head, and was barely able to eat without feeling nauseous. As she deliberated over the agonising days left, she visualised herself in place of Matt, raising a smile, helping to ease the pain of her deep longing to be with Alex.

Alex had texted every day, and had even managed to telephone her for a few moments, much to Hope's surprise, but delight, both aching to hear the other's voice.

Matt lay on his sun lounger in paradise as the sun basked his perfectly toned body. Alex had just creamed his back as he rested peacefully in the mid-afternoon sun. Alex lay alongside him, saturated in tanning oil, in deep thought, gazing around the idyllic gardens surrounding the swimming-pool area, with small bridges around the outside of the pool and tiny alcoves where she could see lovers smooching together. Her gaze fixed on the large palm trees, swaying slightly in the breeze from the sea, making her fantasise about a new life. The more she pontificated, the more unhappy she became, forcing stomach cramps. Agitated, she sat up, looking at Matt through her dark shades, feeling a tear trickle down her bronzed cheek. Turning her face away, she stared at the lovers in the distance for some time. Matt lay on his stomach with his eyes shut, unable to see his fiancée's anxiety. She tiptoed across the ground next to the beach bag with all of their belongings in, it perched next to Matt's sun lounger. She slithered her hand inside the bag, trying to be as quiet as possible, feeling her stomach cramps worsen. Quietly, she retrieved her mobile phone, scanning the screen.

Feeling her stomach knot tighter and tighter, she placed it back in the bag, tiptoeing back to her sun lounger. She sat trying to read her magazine, reading the same article over and over without understanding its context. She glanced at her watch, sighing. Sitting forward, pulling her legs up to her stomach, attempting to ease her pain, she sat transfixed on Matt. Again, she glanced at her watch, deciding to take a swim, creeping about. Matt lay still as Alex entered the pool. She swam up to one of the bridges and sat under it, unable to maintain composure. She began to cry.

On the penultimate evening, she attempted to ring Hope, pretending to Matt that she had to go to the in-hotel shopping mall for last minute gifts. Demented when the call could not be connected, she rang Millie.

'Hi, Millie.'

'Hi, flower. How are you? Having fun? I got your text to say how fab the hotel was.'

'Yeah, it's amazing; it's so posh, but ...'

Millie interrupted.

'Hope has been fretting like a new puppy as you never text her back and she sends you lots.'

'I know, that is why I'm ringing you. My fucking phone won't connect with her and it's driving me nuts. I could burst out crying.'

'Oh God, you are joking?'

'No, Mil, I'm not, and I will have to be quick as this costs so much, and when I try to ring her I get her voicemail, so it costs me every time.'

'She has texted me a couple of times to ask if I have heard from you.'

'Oh, really?'

'Yes. Are you having fun, then?'

'It's so nice here, it's like paradise, but I can't stand it, if you want the truth. I can't wait to be back. It's so romantic here and I am just with the wrong person. Matt is oblivious, it's horrendous.'

'I knew you would be like this, and she will be the same.'

'I know. Will you text her and tell her why I cannot contact her, and how much I miss her? The holiday has made me see that I can't live this life anymore. I have been saying it for a few weeks now but now I know when I get back, I have to leave him.'

'Good for you, Al. It will break his heart though, so be prepared for a battle.'

Silence fell. Alex felt an overwhelming sickness.

'I'm going to have to go. I will be back in two days; I can't wait. Well, in one way I can't, but in the other I am dreading all the trauma.'

'God, Al, I know.'

'Will you text her for me?'

'Sure, Al. Bye, and enjoy the sun. Use the time as your thinking time.'

'OK, bye.'

Alex hung up the phone, gathering her thoughts for a moment, going back to her room.

Hope poured the wine into the glass, spilling it on the counter as she tried hard to concentrate.

'Are you OK, Hope? You look very sad,' Katie said, standing behind the bar next to her.

'Yeah, I'm fine,' Hope replied unconvincingly.

'You don't look fine. It isn't very busy tonight so you can go soon if you want.'

'No, I'd prefer to work, it keeps me busy.'

'You look like you have got the worries of the world on your shoulders. What's up? You can tell me.'

'Nothing,' she snarled, handing over the drinks.

'Hey, don't snap at me like that, I was just being nice. You snotty cow,' Katie said, annoyed.

Hope stared at Katie, walking away as she searched for her mobile in her bag. Katie went over to Marco, where he was conversing with customers.

Ecstatic, she read the message waiting for her.

'Hi hope, it's Millie. Alex has rung n wants me 2 tell u that her phone aint wrking properly 2 yr netwrk n she is pissed off

wif it n wants u 2 kno that she's missin u sooo much n can't wait
2 b bak. Take care x'

'I think that you should have a word with that little shit,'
Katie explained to Marco.

'What? What are you on about, woman?' he said harshly.

'Well, she was rude to me and I'm not having it.'

'You are always like this with her. Are you jealous of her or
what?'

'No, why would I be jealous of her?'

Marco looked his fiancé up and down from head to toe with
a sarcastic glint in his eye.

'Well, maybe because she is a babe and you are not.'

'You shit. I can't believe that you would say that to me. Is
that why you want to promote her to head bar person?'

'No, I want to do that as she is very good with the
customers and works hard for us; she does double shifts so that
we can go out, and she looks after Grace in the bar too. She is
nice and, yes, I do like her, and maybe if you made more of an
effort, then the customers would drool over you as they do her,
and the other sexy bar staff that we have. Do you think I'd
employ ugly girls?'

'Who do you think you are talking to?'

'Let's not argue again. Leave her alone. You are picking on
her and she looks sad,' Marco announced, ogling Hope across
the other side of the bar.

Katie saw this look.

'Well, get over there and serve with her because I'm sick of
you and I'm going upstairs to watch the TV,' Katie replied,
storming off.

Marco walked over to Hope.

'Are you alright?' he asked, placing his hand on her
shoulder.

'Yes, I'm just a bit tired, that's all. I haven't been sleeping
too well,' Hope replied quietly.

'You should stay back with me and have a drink to wind
down after work.'

Hope looked at him sternly.

'No, I have to go home. I want an early night. I'm shattered.'

'Are you sure?' he said, winking at her.

'Yes, positive, thanks,' she responded, walking away.

'I think he likes you. You want to watch him,' a customer added.

Hope looked at the man with distaste.

'Don't be daft, he has someone and, well, I'm not interested,' she replied, unable to escape the pangs of jealousy over Alex, and the engulfing misery she felt, missing her with every inch of her body, wondering if she would ever leave, and be with her.

As their last evening arrived, Matt sat dejected at the prospect of going home the following day, unlike Alex, who seemed in better spirits than she had for days, the sadness slowly lifting from her eyes, allowing them to sparkle once more in the moonlight. As Matt sat sipping his coffee, Alex decided to try once more to telephone Hope, getting up from her seat in the beautiful restaurant that had been recommended to them, pretending to go to the toilet, aching to speak with her.

Praying that it would work, she nervously pressed the button.

'Hi, angel, it's me,' she said in a high-pitched, excited voice.

'Oh my God, I can't believe it's you. Oh, Mummy Bear, I have missed you beyond words,' Hope replied, overcome with emotion.

'Hey, what's up? You aren't crying, are you?'

'Yeah, because I'm so happy that you have rung me. Are you having a good time?'

'Well, the place is like paradise, and it's very posh, but I wish you were here with me.'

'Really?' Hope replied, surprised.

'Yes, really. I miss you so much. And I have something that I must tell you when I get back. We must sit down and talk.'

Hope felt her heart sink, feeling her mouth go dry.

'Oh right,' she murmured faintly.

'Don't worry, baby, it's good. I can't live this way, I'm going to leave ...'

The phone cut off.

'Hello, hello, Mummy Bear, where have you gone? What did you just say? What did you mean, leave what?'

Silence.

Realising Alex had been cut off, Hope began to whimper, with her heart pounding out of her chest. She sat on the stool, taking deep breaths, aching for Alex to come home.

Alex returned to the table, looking pale.

'You don't look very well, angel, are you alright?'

Unable to make eye contact, Alex replied, 'Yeah.'

'You look radiant tonight, if I may just say. I'm so proud to be here with you,' he said, taking her hand across the table, staring into her eyes.

Nodding, she glared at the menu, fighting back her tears, hiding behind it. Matt stared at her for a few seconds, shaking his head, welling up. He gripped her hand tighter, closing his eyes, squeezing it tighter than ever.

As Alex and Matt sat on the aircraft she glanced at him whilst he slept, resting on her shoulder. She looked at his perfect skin, mouth and hair, wondering why she did not lust after him, and never had, if she was being honest with herself, as she did for Hope. She placed her hand across his lips, confused about why those lips did not make her face tingle, and her lips feel numb when they kissed her. She reminisced about when they had first met, and how handsome she had found him, how his kindness and thoughtfulness led her to believe that he was her soul mate. She reflected upon the day he proposed to her, how romantic it was, causing sadness to well up inside her, knowing what she had to do when she got back.

The more she thought, the more agitated she became, listening to his snores, as she shuffled restless in her seat, forcing her to turn the radio on.

'You look into my eyes, I go out of my mind, I am madly in love, but I feel so unkind, coz I live a lie, and I just wanna cry...

'I'm in far too deep, I'm unable to sleep, coz you're all that I see and you're all that I breathe, and I know that it's real, with the way that I feel...'

As the words resounded in her head, goose bumps formed all over her body, causing her to shiver, closing her eyes. Mesmerised, she lingered over every single word, realising how apt this song was for her.

Chapter 31

Alex woke up early after a virtually sleepless night, provoked by the prospect of seeing Hope at lunchtime that day, as Matt lay sleeping peacefully. She carefully stepped out of bed, eager not to wake him, and took a shower. As she showered she fantasised about Hope, bracing herself for an unforgettable day with her, one she had longed for throughout her trip to the Bahamas: the longest eight days of her entire life.

Hope had not slept at all apart from the odd catnap, tossing and turning in sheer delight at the thought of seeing Alex the following day, as she watched the clock, willing the time to pass more quickly.

The moment her parents left the house, she sprang out of bed, taking a shower, envisioning Alex's naked body, creating a spine-tingling feeling all over her body.

Alex quietly got ready in one of the spare bedrooms, shaking with nerves of excitement.

Hope could not decide which outfit to wear, trying on virtually all her wardrobe, frantically pulling clothes out at a rapid rate. She perfumed her body from head to toe in Alex's favourite perfume, tantalising herself as she wondered what attire Alex would be wearing, and if she would be able to resist her superbly tanned body.

Alex kissed Matt's forehead as he remained sleeping, leaving a note by his bedside.

She opened the front door, and realising she had a flat tyre, she screamed out loud. Checking her watch, she began tapping the side of her head, pondering. After letting out a huge sigh, she went back into the house, slammed her keys on the bench, scribbled a note to Matt and left, closing the door without making a sound.

She drove with speed in anticipation of her rendezvous with Hope.

Hope left the house in a hurry, late for the bus, running down the street as fast as her slender legs would carry her, desperate not to miss it. As she sat on the bus, her heart pounded in her chest, causing breathlessness. Her palms sweated and a permanent smile glazed over her face, as she sat restless on her seat.

Alex arrived at the bus stop, in her usual spot, ten minutes earlier than planned as the spine-tingling prospect of seeing Hope became overwhelming. Her heart raced in anticipation of the bus arriving at the terminal. At first she could not see her, then finally she saw the top of her head, reinforcing the heart-warming feeling she was experiencing.

Hope could hardly exit the bus quickly enough, shoving passengers out of the way, enabling her to leave faster. Her body tingled as she ran to her beloved Alex. To her surprise, Alex had got out of her car, for the first time ever, and was waiting by the passenger door, breaking into a smile the moment she saw Hope running towards her.

As Hope approached the car both girls held out their arms, embracing one another with devotion, clenching each other tightly.

'Oh my God, I have missed you so much. Please never go and leave me again,' Hope begged.

Alex pulled her head back, staring at Hope, holding her in her arms.

'I almost forgot how gorgeous you are. You look radiant. Your face is glowing, and as for that smile of yours, I could just stare at you all day.'

Hope beamed from ear to ear, kissing Alex softly on the lips, expressing her attraction. Glaring at the people at the crowded bus stop, Alex moved away, releasing her grip on Hope as they continued to transfix on each other.

Alex wore faded blue jeans with a red three-quarter length coat that she had buttoned up to her chest and a red V-necked jumper. The red in her coat and jumper brought out the copper tones in her dark brown hair, emphasising her bronzed face and chest.

'I can't believe how brown you are. I look like chalk next to you,' Hope joked as she grabbed Alex's hands.

'Well, that was the point of going and getting a tan.'

'You were already brown before you went, so now you look even browner.'

'Come on, let's get in the car, it's freezing,' Alex requested.

As soon as both girls had shut their doors, they kissed passionately. Alex grabbed Hope's face, holding her chin as she spoke.

'I have missed you so much, angel. I cannot explain it in words.'

Hope purred as electricity coursed through her whole body. Her eyes widened, sparkling, as they gazed into Alex's dark, hazel eyes.

'You are looking at me with that deep penetrating look. Stop it!' Alex teased.

'Because I am thinking about how much I have missed you, how much I adore you, and how I yearn to show you,' Hope said in a seductive tone.

'Really?'

'Yeah. I knew that today would be very hard for me.'

'What do you mean?'

'I want you right now. You look amazing and I have missed you like someone would miss their crutch if they couldn't walk, and even that doesn't come close. As I sat on the bus I imagined you naked with your pert little brown boobs lying next to me and your fab brown legs wrapped round mine, and I could feel my face getting hot and my lips tingling.'

'Your lips were tingling?' Alex quizzed.

'Yes, but not on my mouth,' Hope teased, moving closer to Alex.

'You are such a dirty girl,' Alex said, in a low-pitched voice.

Hope stared at her.

'I have met no one like you ever. There is so much I love about you,' Alex admitted.

'Like what? Like how headstrong you are and how expressive and how sexy and horny you are and ...'

Hope surged forward, grabbing Alex's face, devouring her lips.

'No. Not here, Hope,' Alex insisted, driving to a secluded area. As she stopped the car, barely able to restrain herself, Hope grabbed Alex's face, kissing her passionately, their lips entwining.

As the kiss lingered, Hope wrapped her arms around Alex's neck, and they nibbled each other's necks.

'Oh God, I love you so much. I wish that we could go somewhere and just lie in each other's arms naked and then fall asleep together.'

'Will Matt be going away soon?'

'Don't talk right now about that stuff, we will talk later, just show me how much you've missed me,' Alex demanded, lunging towards Hope.

They kissed hard and fast, tearing each other's clothes off, unaware of the other car nearby.

'Oh God, I want to feel your juicy fanny on my hands. I want to sit on your face while you suck hard on me,' Hope confessed, panting.

Alex moaned, aching for her pounding clitoris to be touched. Hope tore off Alex's shirt, biting on her nipples, forcing her legs apart. Unable to open them wide enough, due to lack of room, Hope climbed into the back of the car, pulling Alex with her. Excitedly, they laughed, kissing each other's necks and boobs. The car windows steamed up, preventing them from seeing the car with two passengers, watching them.

'God, Hope, you are driving me crazy; I want to make love to you so much, I can't resist you. I need to taste that sweet taste of yours now,' Alex said, forcing Hope's skirt up, yanking down her tights as best as she could, banging her arms on the window.

'Try and sit on my face,' Alex insisted, attempting to push Hope on top of her, making Hope bang her head on the roof.

Laughing, they smothered each other's necks in kisses, licking the other's ears. Alex managed to get Hope's tights down enough to stick her tongue inside of her, forcing Hope to groan loudly as her juices soaked the top of her thighs.

'Oh, that feels so good; you have no idea what you do to me. Oh God, suck harder. Oh God, that feels amazing. I am going to come so fast today,' Hope expressed, sitting on Alex's face, with her naked back against the cold leather passenger seat, feeling her whole body tingle, making the hair stand up on the back of her arms and neck. Alex licked harder and faster, satisfying Hope. Suddenly, they heard a car screech up next to them. Alex immediately stopped, hearing a car door close.

'Quick, stop, Hope. I can hear someone,' Alex demanded, with an unsettled tone.

Hope moved to the side, pulling up her tights, searching for her top and bra. Alex fastened her shirt as there was a tap on the car windscreen. Jumping forward, Alex panicked. The girls looked at each other, fearful. Again, there was another knock; this time it was harder. Alex rubbed the steamed window, feeling her heart race. Startled, she saw a tall, stocky man in a black uniform. Frozen on the spot, she sat, stuck to her car seat, as he glared at them.

'Could you step out of the car, please?' the man asked, in a forceful manner.

Terrified, Hope looked at Alex, unsure of what to do, forcing her shoes on her feet, fastening her bra at the same time. Alex nodded, slowly getting out of the car. As she stepped out she saw a car opposite her with two elderly people shaking their heads in disgust.

'Can I ask what is going on here?' the policeman requested.

Hope crawled out of the car, standing by Alex's side, trying not to shake as her knees knocked together. Fretting, Alex replied, 'Erm … we were just having a bit of fun. I was tickling her, and we got a bit carried away.'

'Really? Well that isn't what we got reported to us. What relationship is this girl to you? Well …' he went on.

Hope stepped in, 'She's my…'

Alex knocked Hope's elbow, stepping in, 'I'm her friend, and like I said, we were in the back mucking about.'

Sternly, the policeman leaned forward.

'Can I ask what your names are, please? You do know that it's an offence don't you?' he said, with a nasty tone, taking down the registration number.

'What is?' Alex asked, barely able to get her words out, as she watched him jot down each letter and number, panic-stricken.

'Indecent exposure. It's sick as well when you are both …'

'Both what? Are you being discriminative against us, sir?' Hope asked meekly, feeling her heart pound out of her bony chest.

Shaking his head, the policeman tore off the sheet of paper, logging it with the rest of his paperwork in the back of his log book.

The girls stood, shaking.

'If I ever see you two again up to no good, I will arrest you both, and I'm sure your husband…'

Hope burst in. 'She's not married,' she insisted, abruptly.

'Well, your fiancée then. I'm certain he won't be amused to come to the station for you, and see your charge. I have your details now, and I will have you if I see that car again around these parts. In fact, I will look out for it. It's not normal, I tell you.'

Feeling sick, with her teeth chattering together, Alex asked, 'Why have you taken down my registration? What will you do with it now?'

'Why do you look so guilty? Should I run a check on it? Is it your car?'

Alex gulped, breathing slowly.

'Yes, it is mine.'

The policeman smiled and took out his phone from his top pocket, about to call in to the police station with the registration number, terrifying Alex as she stood frozen on the spot, when he received an emergency call.

He answered the call, rushing to his car. As he opened the door he stopped and turned to the two girls standing still, almost stuck together.

'You should both be ashamed of yourselves. I just know there is more to this than meets the eye. You are lucky I have to go,' he shouted, getting in the car, starting up the engine.

Alex did not comment, accepting his words without retaliation. She got in the car without looking at Hope, driving off.

'Are you hungry? What do you want to do now then?' Alex asked, deflated.

Red-faced, Hope clenched Alex's hand.

'He was such a dickhead, and a homophobe. Please don't let him get to you. I love you so much. It isn't about what sex you are, it's about how you feel about each other.'

Alex shrugged her shoulders, replying, 'If only it was that simple.'

'Do you know what?'

'What?' Alex said.

'I fucking love you, sexy lady, and it is as simple as we want it to be,' Hope confessed, staring at her.

Unconvinced, Alex shrugged her shoulders. Hope stared at her, placing her hand on top of Alex's hand.

After a moment of silence Alex opened her mouth as though she was about to say something.

'What?' Hope quizzed.

Alex turned to face her, taking a deep breath, and asked, 'Do you really wish that you could be with me all the time and live with me as a proper couple?'

Startled, Hope replied, 'What a crazy question. You don't have a clue what that would mean to me. My heart rejoices with just a mention of it.'

'But don't you think that you are too young to have a house and so on?'

'No. I am twenty-one soon. I couldn't think of anything better than going shopping with you, and ironing for you, and doing the housework.'

'You say that now, but once the novelty has worn off then it may not appeal to you as much.'

'That isn't true. You can't say what will be, and how I will be, until we do it. I just want you.'

'But what about your job and your parents? They will go mad.'

'Yes, but it's my life. I am so miserable right now. I don't want anyone but you. They will have to accept me or lose me.'

'But do you want people to know that you are gay? I hate the idea of that if I'm honest.'

161

'I don't really care that much. It's more normal these days. I won't like being judged but I am not sure that will happen. I would be proud to be seen out with you. It's the person I love, and if that is a girl, then so what? People will have to get over it. It's their problem, not mine'

Alex stared at Hope as an unusual look came over her face. She reached out for her hand.

'You are amazing for someone so young. You are brave and go with what you think. I admire you and I can learn from your thinking pattern. I have oodles of confidence but when it comes to saying I love a girl, and daring to be seen as a couple in public, I shy away from it. Does that make me a coward?'

'No, not at all. It may be because I have not lived the heterosexual life but I could live it if I wanted to. I just adore you too much to ever want anyone else. It isn't about a man or woman, it's about you, and us.'

As Hope spoke, tears came into Alex's eyes as Hope's powerful words overcame her; an unprecedented feeling.

'Are you crying?'

'Well, I feel a bit choked, yes. Your words are comforting me a lot. I have never heard you talk like this before.'

Hope's face shone with elation – she loved impressing Alex.

'I am really tired now, baby. Do you mind if I take you home? It has been quite a day.'

'No, of course I don't. Even if I only saw you for one hour it would be OK for me – as long as I can feel your hand in mine. And yes, I agree, it has been quite a day; we will have to be more careful next time,' she chuckled.

'I love you so much, Hope,' Alex said with more meaning than ever before, holding her hand firmly, looking deeply into her eyes.

Chapter 32

'You are so brave, I am so proud of you,' Emily said, clenching Alex's hand with a look of admiration in her eyes.

'Do you think so? What is our mum going to say?'

'It's not about her, it's your life, and you can't go on like this anymore. Did you go and look at that flat?'

'Yes, I really liked it; it was very modern, and will suit me fine, until we sell the house or Matt buys me out.'

'But you are not going to move Hope in straight away, are you?'

'No. I want a little time on my own to just date her without the anguish of lying to him, and to be able to just stay in on a Saturday night, have a glass of wine and watch a DVD, which will be a real novelty to us. Also, I don't think it would be fair to Matt to see me living with her. I couldn't do that to him. After almost eight years it is going to be so hard, and I will miss him, and the life that we have lived, but I know that I can't go on like this any longer – it's killing all of us.'

'You seem to have really thought it through. When can you move into the flat?'

'Next week, but I am going home to tell Matt now, he should be in from work,' Alex explained with a catch in her voice, as her eyes filled up.

'Oh, Alex, I don't envy you, he will be totally devastated. He will not give up without a fight. I feel so sorry for him, he has been like a brother to me, but you are my sister and so I stand by you. I can still be there for him too though,' Emily replied, in low spirits.

Alex gasped, cheerless, covering her eyes with her hands.

'Hey, don't worry, I will stand by you. Not many people have the guts to follow their heart, and give up their lifestyle, and a man who dotes on them, to go and live a gay life with someone ten years their junior.'

'Is it brave or stupidity?'

'I think that it's the right thing. She loves you, that is obvious. Yes, she is quite young, but she knows her own mind and how you make her feel. When I went out with you both I saw how she gazed at you with such affection and how she was very comfortable to demonstrate that affection in public. You had the problem with it, not her.'

'I know, and I think I will struggle with that at first, but she doesn't care, and so she can help me, I think, to be brave enough to admit it and be happy to be with a girl,' Alex confessed unconvincingly.

Emily nodded, holding her hand tighter, in a show of support.

The girls sat conversing in the coffee shop drinking their coffee and tea for some time before Alex plucked up the courage to go home.

'Are you sure you are going to be OK?'

'I don't know; it all depends on how he reacts, I guess,' Alex said, feeling her stomach ties itself in knots.

'Well, ring me whenever you want. You can come and stay at mine if you like. And tell Matt that I am here for him anytime too, day or night.'

Alex stared at her sister, frowning.

'OK, well … I don't really know what to say, to be honest,' Emily responded, kissing her sister fondly on the cheek.

Alex did not speak as she went towards her car, dragging her feet behind her.

'By the way, I almost forgot, have you told Hope about leaving him? What did she say?'

'Yes, I told her yesterday when she came over. We sat and chatted and I told her that I was going to tell him today. She is a bit unsure I will do it as she has no confidence in my love for her. I blow hot and cold, but I just hate the triangle. Plus, she thinks that I will go back to him anyway and leave her. It's awful,' Alex answered, pale-faced as she drove off, slowly making her way home.

As she drove home, she deliberated on exactly what she would say to Matt in her head, initiating an ache like never before. Her heart began to beat faster and faster and she struggled to breathe normally, emphasising her dismay as she drove in silence. She arrived home and saw Matt's car on the drive, making her heart palpitate more and more, feeling as though she was about to vomit.

She sat for a moment, bracing herself for the unenviable task ahead. She got out of her car and entered the house, breathing heavily.

Matt had begun preparing dinner when she walked into the kitchen with a ghastly pale look.

'Hi, angel. Oh, you look awful. Are you ill?' he said, rubbing her shoulder.

'No, I'm not ill – well, I do feel quite sick actually. Stop doing that and come and sit with me. I must talk to you. The longer I leave it, the harder it will be,' she replied, pensive.

Sensing a problem, his heart started to beat at a rapid rate.

'What's up? Has something happened to your mum or Emily?' he asked, feeling his body beginning to shake.

'No, it's nothing like that. Please come and sit down next to me,' she said, perching her bottom on the edge of the couch, leaning forward, gripping his hand, gazing at him.

'Alex, you are scaring me!'

'Matthew, you have to listen to me; this was not an easy decision ...'

He interrupted.

'You never call me that unless there is something wrong or I have done something wrong,' he said nervously.

'Let me finish, please, or I will never say it. This is the hardest thing that I have ever had to do in my whole life, something that I never thought that I would do.'

Matt's hands began to shake as Alex gripped tighter.

'I can't be with you anymore.'

'No, please, no, don't say that,' he yelped, pulling her towards him, embracing her in his arms.

Alex pulled away as she went on. 'Listen to me. I am not proud of what I have done but I am in love with someone else,' she said in a shaky voice.

Matt put his head in his hands. Alex stood next to him, trembling.

'Is it her?' he said faintly.

Alex hung her head in shame.

'Who is it?' he demanded, raising his voice.

' If you mean Hope, then yes.'

'I can't get my head around this. I'd thought that you may have got over this infatuation that you had developed with her?' he screamed, pacing the floor.

'Don't be stupid, Matt. Do you think that I would joke about something like this?'

'Do you love her more than me?' he asked, beginning to sob.

Overcome by the devastation she was inflicting on her fiancé, her body began to quiver. Desperate not to magnify his grief, as he wiped his eyes, sobbing uncontrollably, she grabbed him, squeezing him tightly. As this inconsolable feeling intensified, Matt became breathless, collapsing on the couch in a state of shock, as snot poured out of his nose.

'Do you love her?' he muttered almost incomprehensibly.

'What? I can't understand you.'

'Do you love her?'

Alex hesitated for a moment, reluctant to accentuate his pain, staring at him.

'Please, tell me.'

'Yes, I do love her very much, but I still love you.'

'So are you leaving me for her?'

'Not really. I want to be on my own for a bit, but Matt, I can't live this life any longer.'

'What do you mean?'

Alex moved closer to him, wiping the moisture from his nose, attempting to calm him down.

'Calm down, sweetie. You will make yourself ill. Come on, take deep breaths,' she begged, stroking his forehead.

'I don't care if I make myself ill. There is no point to anything anymore, not without you.'

'Matt, it will be hard at first but it will get better.'

'What does she have that I don't? And I never knew that you were gay.'

Hearing the word 'gay', she winced in disgust, reluctant to accept her sexuality.

'I'm not gay,' she growled.

166

'Well, you must be something to fall in love with a girl.'

Without replying, she wiped away the fallen tears from his soaking face, distressed.

'So have you had sex?'

'Matt, don't ask me this stuff, it will just make it really painful for you.'

'I want to know. You owe me that, surely?'

'OK, yes, I have had sex with her.'

'Where?'

Realising the shamefulness of her actions, she closed her eyes.

'Please don't say you did it here – I couldn't cope with that. Please, no!'

'No. I may have kissed her here and stuff, but we never went to bed,' she lied with shame.

Desperate not to hear what Alex uttered, he put his hands over his ears, muffling out the sound, as his heart wrenched, crumbling on the couch, his breathing worsening. Alex moved next to him, unable to rally her sinking heart; she began to cry, burying her head in his chest, as the reality of a life apart sank in.

'I'm begging you not to leave me,' he said.

'Matt, don't do this. I love her, and it is not fair to do this.'

'Well, I don't care if you love her. You can still see her and have me too. I just can't be without you,' he begged.

'Don't be silly; you don't know what you are saying. That's not right. I can't do that.'

'Well, leave her then. Surely all these years count for something. Think of all our memories, and all of the things we have shared together, and this great life we have built up over the years, and how I nursed your dad in my arms as he …'

Alex cut in, red faced with her frustration.

'Matt, you are making this so hard for us. And what do you mean, the great life we have together?'

'Well, you want for nothing. All of your friends will envy you.'

'Why? Because I have got a nice house and car? Don't you see that there is more to life than that? Hope has taught me so much.'

Matt sobbed, unable to hear her words, putting his fingers in his ears. Alex ceased talking, feeling her heart caving in. She stroked his back as he lay curled up on the couch like a new puppy in his basket.

'I want you and I will do anything to stop you from going to her. I will do anything!'

'But you are missing the point. I really love her. Surely you don't want me to be with you, and be miserable, when I want someone else?'

'But we have never been apart, so why don't you move out and get a flat, and then I will just see you on the weekends, and see how it goes?'

'I am going to do that. I have seen a flat and I can move in next week, but because I am leaving you and need to move out until the house is sold.'

'Oh God, you can't go straight away,' he yelped as his distress increased once more.

Alex sat silent, wiping her wet face, listening to heart-rending stories about their past, as he tried to persuade her to change her mind about splitting up, guilt-ridden about her actions for so long. He clung to her body, smothering his head into her chest, refusing to let go, as he whimpered, re-telling events gone by of everything from their first date to his proposal. Alex held him, feeling so much pain about, seeing his distressed state, and how hard it would be for him to see her go. She sat for hours, holding his head, and wiping his eyes, and nose, before she finally stood up.

'Matt, I can't take any more; it's breaking my heart. I have to do this or I may lose her.'

'Oh no, so you do love her more than me? You don't care that I am heartbroken, you just care about her?'

'That isn't true but I cause her endless pain; I spare yours for mine, and hers.'

'What do you mean?'

'Well, I do try to stop the way I feel about her by pushing her away and being unfair to her at times, and ...' She stopped for a second. I have forced myself to love you more like ...'

Matt burst in, 'Like her you mean?'

Alex refused to answer.

'Can't you try harder then?' he begged.

'But I have tried and it's getting harder and harder. Don't you care about me?'

'You know I do, angel,' he said, grabbing hold of her.

'So why don't you want me to be happy, then?'

'I do, but we can be happy. I will try harder.'

Frustrated, she put her hands onto her face, rubbing her mouth.

'But it's not about that, don't you see?'

She paused, looking at him, before going on, 'I have met Hope, and …'

Matt stepped in, 'But I love you with all my heart. And I know that it is more than her, so why can't you just be with me for that?' he pledged, gripping onto her.

'Come here,' she replied, kissing his forehead, seeing his desperation.

Matt sobbed in her arms as he contemplated a single life.

'Please stop crying, it's killing me seeing you like this.'

'Then stay with me.'

'But that's blackmail.'

'It's not. It's love!'

Alex sighed as she stood up.

'Where are you going? Don't go, I beg you,' he cried, grabbing her arm firmly.

Alex flinched away, freeing her arm, running upstairs to pack her belongings.

'No, come back!' he said, chasing after her, pulling the holdall away, attempting to stop her departure.

'Matt, stop it, please. This is unbearable, I cannot take it.'

'I can't help it. I need you.'

'OK, well, just leave me alone for a few days to have some thinking time', she said, feeling pressurised.

He paused for a moment.

'No, because you won't come back once you go.'

'I will as all of my stuff is here. I just need space, I will be in touch,' she explained, packing her bag quickly, as tears rolled down her bronzed face, desperate to get away from him.

'Where will you go? Your mum will go off on one at you leaving me. She will never accept Hope, and therefore she will be a nightmare with you.'

Alex glared at Matt as the realisation of the anguish that lay ahead, after she had left him for a girl, took hold, instilling doubts in her mind, as she made her way to the front door. He swiftly followed her, tumbling to the floor, sobbing at her feet, grabbing her legs, dragging her away from the door as she tried to shake him off and his grip tightened.

'No, please don't go. I don't want to live without you. I am devastated. Please, I will do anything!'

'Matt, please don't do this. I know it's hard but this isn't fair to me,' she begged, detaching herself.

'No. No!' he pursued, lying in a heap on the floor with his head against the door.

Unable to cope with his distraught state, she ran out of the house, starting up her car, trying to make a quick exit, as Matt lay motionless at the front door. She sped off the drive, fighting the urge to return and check on him.

As she drove, she heard her mobile ring. Choosing to ignore it, she drove on. For several minutes it rang relentlessly, forcing her to check it. Emily, Hope and Matt had all telephoned, leaving voicemails. Matt's voicemail had been impossible to understand owing to his sobbing.

She deleted it immediately and pulled over to the side of the road to compose a text message.

'Hi bb sory haven't answered u. I have tld him n he is so upset I am v. worried bout him. Have lft wif my stuff n gonna stay at Emily's 2nite or may go 2 hotel. Will contact u lata but need bit of space. Was the worst fing had 2 do. Gunna b so awful 4 him. My heart feels so sad but I want u so got2 stick2 it.'

As Alex sent her message, another one came through.

'Angel plse cum bak im in bits just been sick n can hardly catch my breath just wanna hld u. please don't go2 her. I love you so, so much ill do anything at all. Plse just hold me 2nite. I can't take it xxxxx'

As Alex read the message, nausea came over her, making her retch. She quickly opened the car door and vomited. She sat stupefied, holding her phone out in front of her, deciding to turn it off, as she drove to her father's graveside, gathering her thoughts.

She stood staring at his gravestone, sobbing profusely. Her fingers were freezing from the chilling fog, as she stood, talking to his gravestone. Eventually, she made her way back to the car.

Emily sat with her mobile in front of her, staring at the screen. Deciding to call, she put the phone to her ear and listened to the ringing tone. Shaking her head, she sat staring at the TV, unable to concentrate.

Matt sat on the kitchen floor, sobbing, looking up at the cupboards.

Alex made her way to a hotel, breaking her heart as she drove.

Hope sat eating her dinner with her family, barely able to swallow her food, feeling it stick in her throat. Her mobile sat in her pocket, as she willed it to bleep, pretending to listen to her sister.

Emily began pacing her sitting room floor, gripping her mobile. Again, she made a call, reaching a voice mail. She sighed, hung up and pressed another button. It rang out, making her scrunch her lips tightly together, pondering what to do.

Matt could barely see for tears, pulling himself up from the kitchen bench. He opened the cupboard door and pulled out tablets from the medicine cupboard. He lined up a concoction of tablets on the kitchen bench, filling a glass with tap water. He wiped his eyes, sniffling, taking a sip of water. He took a deep breath and rang Alex – her phone was turned off.

Emily stood in the kitchen tapping the bench. She made another call from her mobile; again it just rang out. Demented, she grabbed her car keys off the bench and left the house.

Alex registered into the hotel, and went into her room, sitting on the bed, staring out of the window.

Hope left the table, leaving almost a full plate of food and went to her room. She rang Alex and was connected to her voice mail, making her fret, as she sat on her bed.

Alex sat for some time, staring into the darkness of night. She thought about her father, and how she yearned to be able

171

turn to him for advice. She worried about Matt, and how he would cope without her, but mostly, she thought about Hope, bringing a smile to her withdrawn face. Then she switched on her phone, telephoning Hope.

Hope's phone rang, making her jump with shock. She saw Alex's name on the screen, accentuating both excitement and nerves.

'Hi,' Hope said, upbeat.

'Hi, baby. Are you OK?'

'Yes, Mummy Bear, I'm fine. Are you OK? Where are you? I've been really worried about you,' she blurted.

'Calm down, Hope, I'm fine. I'm at ...'

Hope's stomach did somersaults, as she interrupted, 'You aren't with Matt, are you? You are not going back to him when he begs you, are you? I will leave tonight if you want, and tell my mum and dad. They will go mad but I want to be with you so much ...'

'God, slow down. Don't worry. No, I am not going back. I have done the hard part now. We could never go back.'

'Promise?' she asked sheepishly.

'Yes, I promise, silly. Matt was in a state when I left him, but he will get over it.'

'I am so happy that you have done it; I never thought you would. I love you so much. I will make you so happy. Honest!'

As Hope comforted her with her words, Alex began to cry, knowing she had made the right decision.

Matt leaned over the bench, playing with the row of tablets. He took a handful of them, inhaled and rang Alex. It was engaged, making his anxiety worsen. Realising he had lost her, and with her words about her love for Hope resounding in his head, he closed his eyes and picked up the tablets, shoving them in his mouth.

Emily drove fast, anxious about having to stop at every traffic light. She arrived at the house and exited the car, slamming the door. She ran up to the house, banging on the door with her fist. She stood for a few seconds, deciding to try the back door. As she opened the back gate and walked along the side of the house to the patio doors, she saw someone lying on the floor. Her heart started pounding.

Alex hung up the phone to Hope, smiling. She put it down next to the window and went into the bathroom. It bleeped, indicating a message. She walked back into the room, and pressed the voice mail button. She played it again, unable to make sense of it. Panicking, she rang Matt.

Emily had got into the house, edging open the patio door. Matt lay semi-conscious. She sat him up, asking him what he had taken. Immediately she dragged him to the sink and poured him some salty water, forcing it in his mouth. She dialled for an ambulance, talking to Matt at the same time, trying to keep him awake. He vomited all over her shoes, making her yelp out.

'Oh, Matt, they are my favourite shoes,' she joked, trying not to allow herself to panic.

Alex rang Matt over and over without any answer, making her anxious. She sat biting her nails, making them bleed. Her mouth became dry, forcing her to swallow. Feeling guilty and uncomfortable at the state she had left him in, she decided to return home to check on him.

The ambulance arrived and the paramedics lifted a semi-conscious Matt into it.

'Will he be alright?' Emily asked, with a scared tone.

'Yes I think so. It looks like he has taken a mixture of things but none look too harmful. He doesn't seem to have taken paracetamol, so that's good. Are you his wife?' the paramedic asked.

Emily shook her head, lowering it, as she followed a dazed Matt into the ambulance, en-route to the hospital. She stroked his brow and held his hand.

Alex pulled up on the drive and went into the house. The house was in darkness as she searched for Matt, shouting his name. The more she searched, the more frightened she became. She went into the kitchen and saw the mess of tablet bottles all over the bench, making her heart feel heavy. She heard a knock on the door.

'Hi, Alex. I have just seen Matt been taken away by an ambulance on a stretcher. I think a girl was with him. It might have been your sister. The car is outside. Did you see it?' Betty, the next door neaighbour, said.

Alex gulped, putting her hands over her face.

'Oh my God. No!'

She rang her sister but there was no reply. She slammed the front door and made her way to the nearest hospital. As she drove, Emily called her informing her about Matt.

She arrived at the hospital and parked her car in a loading bay, running into reception. As she gave her name she felt a tap on her shoulder. She turned.

'Oh God, Em, it's you. What happened? How did you come to be at the house? Did he ring you?'

Emily cuddled her sister, and led her to the waiting area, finding them a seat in the crowed room. She placed her hands on Alex's lap. She shook her head and glared at her sister, tutting.

'What are you looking at me like that for?'

'Why do you think? Your fiancé has just tried to take an overdose. What did you say to him? You don't deserve him,' Emily replied abruptly, rolling her eyes.

Standing up, Alex became red-faced, moving away, to the coffee machine. Emily sat staring at her. She returned and banged her coffee on the table next to her.

'Why were you there anyway? Did he call you?'

'I tell you what, Alex, it's just as well I did go over, as I found him. Who knows what might have happened had I not got there in time. You and your big mouth, I dread to think what you told him. You can be so fucking cruel.'

Alex burst into tears as her name was called. They both stood up. Alex put her hand out, stopping her sister from advancing forward.

'I will go in and see him, thanks. You can see him later!'

Emily sat back down, enraged.

Alex was escorted into the cubicle where Matt lay with tubes around him, resting. As she walked in, the doctor followed her.

'Hi, I am Doctor Jones. Matt is going to be fine. We have done some tests, and pumped his stomach out. He had taken sleeping tablets, vitamin tablets and some antibiotics. Most of it has been flushed out but we don't think he took too many. He is quite tired at the minute so we are letting him sleep. I don't think he wanted to end his life. He has spoken to another doctor who deals with this stuff and he said that he just wanted the pain to go away, and wanted to go to sleep for a while.'

Alex began to sob, holding Matt's hand tightly.

Chapter 33

Three days had passed since Matt had been admitted to hospital. He had refrained from admitting the truth to his family, backed up by Alex, who had been advised by the doctor that he needed stability and could attempt something at any time, caused by his distressed state.

As she stood in the kitchen making his dinner, she stared out of the window. She felt a trickle down her left cheek. Quickly she brushed it off, glaring at the empty, large garden, causing her to go into a trance. She had not noticed Matt coming into the kitchen, wrapping his arms around her. Immediately, she winced away, looking at him with distaste.

'Hope, what are you being so dreamy about, staring at the glass? It will not pour itself,' Marco teased.

Hope smiled, ignoring him.

Alex could not bear to make conversation at the dinner table as she pushed her food around her plate. Matt looked pale and washed out as he scraped the plate, playing with his food, unable to eat it.

Hope served the customers with a permanent smile.

Matt put down his knife and fork, reaching across for Alex's hands. Alex closed her eyes, lowering her head, as she felt his hands in hers. She took a deep breath before opening her eyes, trying hard to avoid eye contact. Matt clenched tighter. Alex sat for some moments until eventually she pulled her hands away. His eyes welled. Again Alex bowed her head.

Hope conversed happily with the customers, laughing and joking in high spirits.

Feeling sick to the pit of her stomach, barely able to make eye contact with Matt, Alex stood up, clearing away the plates. Matt followed her, wrapping his arms around her waist as she stood next to the sink, doing the dishes. Standing behind her, he embraced her tightly, placing his head on her shoulder. Alex sighed quietly, closing her eyes, scrunching them together, gritting her teeth, standing motionless.

Hope cleared the glasses, dropping two of them, seemingly miles away in deep thought. Quickly she picked up the broken glass, helped by Marco, beaming from ear to ear, as he tried to touch her hand.

Alex finished the dishes and moved away from Matt. She went upstairs and ran a bath. Her hands began to shake as she wretched to be sick. Feeling unsettled, she sat on the edge of the bath, watching the water pour out. Suddenly she felt her face, realising she had tears flowing down her withdrawn cheeks. She sat for a moment, then she stood up and glared at herself in the mirror. Shaking her head, she rubbed her red eyes. Matt entered the bathroom. Immediately, he touched her face with the back of his hand, desperately attempting to smile. Glaring back, she walked out of the bathroom. Matt switched off the tap, following her into the bedroom. Feeling unsettled, as she went to take her suitcase out of the wardrobe, Alex rubbed her eyes, preventing the tears from falling out. Panic-stricken, Matt began to wobble, making him unsteady on his feet, leaning on the bed. He tried to settle his nerves, breathing in and out. Alex stood, willing herself to have the strength to ignore his distressed state, refusing to look at him. She stood still on the spot, hearing Matt's breathing worsening as he became distressed. Tears began to flow down his cheeks as he stared at the lady he loved, praying she did not pack her suitcase that stood upright on the floor next to the wardrobe. Within seconds, she went over to him and took his head, placing it into her chest, hugging him tightly. Together, tears trickled down their faces.

Hope left work with a kick in her step, sauntering home, unable to stop grinning. She reached in her bag and took out her phone. She rang Alex but as she did not answer; undeterred, she composed a text.

'Hey, Mummy Bear, I can't stop smilin and I am sooo happy that u hav finally left him 2 b wif me. Its v. xcitin. I kno u need a bit of space, and that's y I haven't been in touch much but I kno we can b gud 2gether. U r all I hav ever wantd. I will make u so happy. I am so in love wif u. gudnite. Sweet dreams xxxxx'

Chapter 34

Alex sat in her car, waiting for Hope at their usual place, with intensified agony. Some moments later Hope arrived, running to the car with excitement at seeing her beloved Alex.

'Hi, how are you? How's things? Have you seen Matt? Is he OK with things? I am so excited,' she blurted.

Alex gazed at Hope, grabbing her hand.

'Let's go somewhere quiet,' she said in a pained tone, her eyes dimming.

'Why, aren't we going to yours?'

'No,' Alex said, driving off.

Hope stared at Alex. Aware of her unhappiness, a nervous, nauseous feeling settled in the pit of her stomach.

'What's up? You look tired but you still look gorgeous,' Hope commented, transfixed on Alex.

Alex sat silently as her sick feeling increased, glancing at Hope out of the corner of her eye.

She pulled into a disused factory, turning to face Hope, locking their hands together.

'You are scaring me. What is wrong? You have gone back, I can just tell. Please tell me that you haven't?' Hope agonised.

Shutting her eyes, Alex swallowed before speaking.

'Oh, Baby Bear. I'm sorry,' she said with a catch in her voice.

'Oh no, I can't bear it,' Hope cried.

'Listen to me.'

'Go on, then.'

'Yes, I have gone back but …'

Hope stepped in.

'But why? I knew you would. I just knew it. I can't take this, my heart is broken in two,' she screamed, pulling her hands away, beginning to cry.

'Oh, Hope, don't do this. I can't stand any more pain. I feel like I am bleeding, it hurts that much. I know that you will probably hate me, but if you were older you might understand.'

'Understand what? That you just piss me about all the time? One minute you want me, the next you don't. What about me and my feelings?' she said with anguish, as the tears flowed down her perfect cheeks, dripping onto her chin.

Alex took a tissue out of her bag, slowly beginning to wipe away Hope's tears, struggling not to cry, swallowing hard to combat her emotion.

'That isn't how it is. You have got to believe what I'm trying to tell you. If you were in my shoes, you might have understood, but as you aren't, you don't get it.'

'Get what?'

Alex sighed, wiping a tear from her left eye.

'It's not easy when you are with someone who idolises you, who you have built up a life with, and who tries so hard to please me, and I feel ill that I don't feel the same way about him. He loves me so much; he can't cope without me.

'It has destroyed me to see him in such a state. I am doing what I think is the best thing.'

'The best for whom? What about me, and my pain?' Hope bellowed, becoming angry, tears pouring down her face.

Alex tried to comfort Hope, but Hope pushed her away, looking at her with disgust.

'Baby, if you were older you might ...'

Enraged, Hope cut in, 'I am fucking sick to death about you going on and on about my age. Yes, I am younger than you but I can be in love and be younger. I know that you don't love him like you do me, and if he cries when you want to leave him, then it isn't right as we are all so miserable. I can't take anymore of this love triangle. I can't ...' she paused, trying to compose herself. 'I can't,' she said, looking away from Alex, lowering her head. 'I just can't, Mummy Bear, I'm sorry.'

Hope flung open the car door and jumped out of the car, banging it shut as she ran along the road, sobbing. Alex sat watching her succumbing to her anguish, crying profusely.

The next day

179

'Hi, Mummy Bear it's me. I can't bear 2 b without u. I haven't stop crying since I left u. I want u 2 b wif me. I hate u wif him. Do u fink that u will ever leave him for me coz I can't wait much longer.'

Alex read Hope's text feeling relieved, helping to ease the nervous, anxious feeling she had endured from the moment Hope left. Immediately she replied.

'Oh baby I'm so happy that u hav got in touch. I was so devastated yesterday wen u left like that. I didn't get the chance 2 explain things but it doesn't matter now. There isn't an excuse 2 make u feel better. Yes I will leave him. I just need more time.'

Send.

'Do u really love me? Y didn't u run after me yesterday? I wantd u 2 so much.'

Send.

'Oh I wantd 2 but thort that I wud make things far worse. Yes I do realy love u and wen the time is rite I will show u. u hav 2 trust my love 4 u is v. strong and real. I won't let u dwn.'

Send.

'We'll c then won't we!!'

Send.

Chapter 35

Hope had tried over and over again to refrain from contacting Alex, relenting the moment Alex got in touch.

For weeks they had been in contact as much, if not more than ever, meeting up in secret as often as possible but never at Alex's house, and never for long periods of time, much to Hope's sadness. Acknowledging this misery for them both, Alex decided to plan a full day trip away to the beach.

The sun bathed the deep blue sea as the waves gently rippled the shore. Hope lay in her bikini reading her book as Alex lay beside her drenched in suntan oil. Peeking over the top of her book, Hope gazed out to the sea, viewing people taking a dip. Feeling over heated, she put down her book and sat forward. She started stroking Alex's soaking arms very gently, causing Alex to startle. Immediately she smiled at her beloved Hope, looking her up and down. Hope continued to stroke her arm, moving up to her chest and neck, relaxing Alex who lay watching her, grinning. Gently Hope eased herself forward on the lounger, allowing her to reach across Alex's body, touching her stomach and upper thighs. Alex's face brimmed as she allowed Hope to continue. Discreetly, Hope softly kissed Alex, arousing them both. Carefully, so they could not be seen, Alex sat up and covered herself over with a towel, pretending to dry herself from the mingle of sweat and suntan oil, while Hope pretended to dry her back, sitting very closely. Slowly, Hope put her hand inside the towel, rubbing Alex's inner thigh and crotch area. Amused, Alex giggled, viewing a man coming up towards them. The more Alex giggled, the more Hope teased her, making her groan very faintly. As the man approached them, Hope took away her hands and began to massage Alex's shoulders, gently brushing her lips on the back of her neck, turning Alex on even more. The man stared at them as he passed them, turning back to look at them.

'You are so naughty,' Alex whispered.

'Mmmm, I know I am,' she replied, licking Alex's outer ear very softly.

Alex moved forward, scanning the nearby area.

'I think that we should go for a walk, don't you?'

Hope's face beamed, nodding. She stood up and put her flip-flops on. Alex took away her towel after drying herself off. Together, they walked off along the beach, brushing each other's arms, trying hard not to gaze at each other. Their feet pressed into the hot sand as they took small strides, enjoying the hot sun on their backs. They walked along the pier, smiling happily at each other, not noticing the packed beach. They walked for some time before finding a deserted spot.

Alex found a deserted area surrounded by rocks. Slowly, she placed her hand in Hope's hand, leaning forward, kissing her. Gently, they moved back onto the rocks, lying on them, as Alex lay on top of Hope, kissing her harder then slowly, teasing her with her tongue. Gazing into each other's eyes, Alex caressed Hope's thighs and crotch area, making Hope beg to be touched. Slowly, she ran her fingers up and down her body, looking into Hope's eyes. She stroked her face, rubbing her fingers over Hope's perfectly shaped lips. She moved down her whole body, kissing and licking every inch of it, tantalising Hope, making her groans intensify. Gently she pulled back her bikini bottoms and began to lick her swollen clitoris, making it wetter and wetter, as the sun shone on them, making Hope's hair shine even more beautifully. She opened Hope's legs further, caressing her thighs whilst gently touching her vagina with her saturated tongue, making her slowly move her pelvis up and down Hope's leg. Groaning with pleasure, Hope lay over the rock, allowing Alex to make love to her. She changed from licking her clitoris to sticking her tongue very gently in and out of her. As she felt Hope about to climax, she took away her tongue, slowly placing two fingers inside of her, penetrating them deep inside of her, forcing Hope to cry out. Gently, she rubbed her fingers inside of Hope, sliding them in and out very slowly. Feeling Hope's body judder, she moved close to her, lying by her side, staring at her, continuing to slide her fingers deep inside, making them go slightly faster, allowing Hope to climax. Easing Hope off the rock and onto the sand, she held her

182

tightly, feeling Hope's body relax, almost spasm-like, embracing her softly. Without speaking, she got on top of her and positioned her leg on top of Hope's, taking off her bikini bottoms, enabling her to feel Hope's warm, wet vagina next to hers. Softly their bodies mingled, feeling the warm sand encasing them, as they buffed themselves up against one another, transfixed on each other, kissing passionately. Slowly, they climaxed in synch with each other's bodies.

'I am so in love with you,' Alex whispered as she reached her climax.

Hope smiled, increasing her confidence.

'Do you mean that?'

'Of course I do, why would you doubt me?' Alex asked, stroking Hope's arm, melted by her beauty.

'Well, things haven't been the same since your decision to stay. I will just never understand and I'm not sure that my heart can take it.'

Panic-stricken, Alex sat up, clenching Hope's hand. Transfixed on her she said, 'You have to trust me, I'm working on things. I just need more time but I have to admit, it is unbearable at home with him. I am too soft, I should never have been emotionally blackmailed, and I'm not sure that I'm ready yet.'

Shaking her head, Hope replied, 'Emotionally blackmailed, what do you mean? And ready, ready for what? I don't get what you are saying to me. I just think you make one excuse after the other; it kills me every day as I ache to be with you. What life do I have with this double life that I lead?'

Chapter 36

Nine weeks later

'Come on, Hope, we are leaving this bar now. You are very drunk and you need to get home,' Linzi said.

Hope ignored her friend, continuing to dance from one side of the dance floor to the other, eyeing up two men. Linzi stood at the side of the dance floor with her hands on her hips, shaking her head, staring at Hope. Hope turned her back on her friend, making advances towards both men, dancing closely in between both of them. Amber joined Linzi at the edge of the dance floor, sipping her drink.

'We need to get her home. I don't know what's wrong with her tonight. She has been like this all night, flirting with every man that she sees that seems to show her attention. I wouldn't care but none of them have been good looking,' Amber stated.

Linzi agreed.

Hope danced for a while until one of the men lunged forward, grabbing her waist, dragging her towards him. He attempted to kiss her, pushed away by Hope, making her leave the dance floor and stand with her friends. Barely able to stand up, Hope attempted to string a sentence together. The girls took Hope by each hand and steered her out of the club. As they walked along the road either side of Hope, keeping her upright, Hope's phone rang. She ignored it. Again it rang.

'Aren't you going to see who that is ringing you at this time of night?' Amber asked.

Hope shook her head. Some moments later they arrived at their apartment. They escorted Hope into the bedroom, allowing her to collapse onto the bed.

The next morning Hope woke up feeling unwell. Her eyes stuck together and her head hurt. She lay motionless for a few seconds before rubbing her eyes. Her unwashed-off mascara stuck to her eyelashes, making it difficult to open her eyes. She lay listening to the birds chirping, feeling the hot sun beaming into her window. She dragged herself out of bed and made her way into the kitchen, taking a bottle from the fridge, gulping the contents down. She retrieved her phone from the bottom of her bag, tipping out its contents onto the bed. She glared at the missed calls and text messages, making her heart beat faster and knots form in the pit of her stomach. As she read her messages over and over again, and listened to her voice mails repeatedly, her heart started to pound out of her chest, making her feel sick, rushing to the bathroom, vomiting.

Emily sat watching Pete as he mowed the lawn. Unhappy about their cancelled holiday, she sat drinking wine on the patio. Her mobile phone rang.

'Hi, little sis. How are you doing?'

'Hey, I'm demented if you want me to be honest.'

'Why, because of Hope?'

'Yes, how did you guess!'

'Well, she is entitled to have a laugh you know. It's normal for her to want to go away on holiday with her friends. You can't go with her, or should I say, won't, and …'

Alex butted in, 'I can't go, Em. You know that, so why are you being sarcastic about it? If Matt didn't still, and hadn't, put so much pressure on me, I would be free now, and I could be away with her and I would be a part of her big fuck-off birthday party too.'

Emily paused, viewing Pete empty the grass into the dustbin, taking a sip from her glass. He turned, giving off half a smile. Emily waved him over, seeking affection, rejected by Pete, preferring to get on with the gardening. Shaking her head, she took another sip of wine.

'Did you just hear what I said, Em?' Alex requested.

'Yes, I heard you, and you moan on about Matt. And all he is guilty of is loving you. You take his love for granted. Is it really such a hardship to be adored the way you are by him? He would do anything for you and always wants to be by your side. You are so lucky and you don't see it,' she remarked with a harsh sounding tone.

Alex sighed loudly, feeling unwell.

'Maybe you are right. Hope hasn't even replied to my messages. I never normally am the one to message the most, but being away is really getting to me and I'm finding it hard being around Matt without her, but as you say, she's young, and away having such a good time, she can't seem to contact me. I will just have to see what great things I have, eh?'

'Yes, Alex, you will. Matt is wonderful; you are the envy of so many. Trust me, good men like him are hard to find,' she replied quietly.

Alex nodded her head.

'Anyway, tell me, why aren't you going away? I thought that you had it all booked, going away for some quality time together?'

Fixing her eyes on Pete, shaking her head, Emily took a deep breath.

'We were, but Pete told me that we had to cancel it as he can't take the time off work. He is off for the next few days, and is going to do some DIY, but he needs to go in at the back end of the week so our holiday, that we would be on right now, had to be cancelled.'

The girls lay around the pool by day and partied by night, getting very drunk, especially Hope.

Alex deliberated over Hope's every move – what she was doing, places she was going and who she may be with, feeling very jealous and anxious, especially as Hope refused to reply to any of Alex's messages.

Hope sat at the bar, glaring at her phone. She sat for some time reading her messages again and again, making her smile. Amber and Linzi were at the bar chatting to boys happily. Hope preferred to sit people watching, grinning at her numerous messages.

'I hope that whoever that is, they are worth it,' a voice said.

Startled, Hope looked up, seeing a girl with bobbed blonde hair and blue eyes staring at her. Her bronzed body emphasised her blonde hair as it glowed immaculately in the sunlight.

'Sorry?' Hope replied.

Smiling from ear to ear, the girl replied, 'I was just wondering why you were not over there with your friends, getting those cute boys to buy you drinks. Obviously, you have someone back home that you are loyal and faithful to, and can't stop reading his messages, eh?' she replied with a sarcastic tone.

Raising a smile, Hope shook her head.

'Yeah, something like that, although, I don't know why I bother as I feel that I'm just wasting my time and beating my head off a brick wall. I have come away to get away from it all but it doesn't leave my thoughts or my heart,' Hope said, screwing up her mouth, sighing.

Sitting down, the girl edged herself next to Hope.

'Well, we can't be having a lovely girl like you sitting all sad when you are on holiday, so let me go and get us some cocktails. Oh, and by the way, my name is Poppy,' she said, standing up and walking off, oozing confidence.

Hope smiled, enjoying Poppy's forward nature. Poppy returned with a pitcher of cocktail and two glasses filled with crushed ice. She sat close to Hope, enough to allow their naked fleshed legs to brush against each other, as they both wore short skirts. Poppy wore a low-cut top, emphasising her large, pert breasts. Her teeth were perfect as she smiled at Hope, pouring the drinks with her long thin hands. Hope caught sight of her large cleavage as she poured the drinks.

'So, tell me all about you then,' Poppy requested.

Hope smiled as she took a sip from her cocktail glass.

'Mmm, this is good. Thank you, you are so kind. Do you normally come up to strange girls and start up a conversation?' Hope joked.

Both girls began to laugh. Gazing at Hope, Poppy replied, 'No, not that often, but it has been known. I guess I am a sucker for pretty girls. And besides, I thought you needed a distraction from your mobile phone.'

Hope giggled, sipping her drink.

'So, come on then, the suspense is killing me, tell me all about you. I can see you are a girl of mystery.'

'Well, what do you want to know?'

'Everything,' Poppy replied with a seductive tone, making eye contact, illustrating her perfectly applied eye make-up.

'Erm … well, I'm called Hope and I'm twenty-one in five days' time.'

'And are they your friends, that you are here with?' she asked, looking over at the girls, drooling over the boys at the bar.

'Yep.'

'Why aren't you here with your boyfriend, or is he taking you somewhere else later?'

Hope blushed, lowering her head.

'Oh, sorry, have I said something to embarrass you, Hope?'

Hope paused, staring at her for a few seconds.

'No, of course not. And to answer your question, no, I don't have a boyfriend,' she declared, standing up, squeezing past Poppy, as she made her way to the toilet.

Poppy followed her with her eyes, all the way to the toilet, checking out her small bottom, tightly fitting around her short, linen skirt and long slender legs. Hope returned, sitting close by Poppy. Poppy eased herself closer as they drank their cocktails conversing with one another. Hope's phone rang, and immediately she searched in her bag, taking it out. She stared at the incoming call as her eyes widened and her heart thumped out of her chest. Poppy stared at her new friend, intrigued. Hope ignored the call as she held the phone in her hand, staring at it, waiting for the anticipated voice mail. Continuing to stare at it for several seconds, Poppy commented, 'Whoever Alex is, he or she must be special, as you are willing that phone to work some magic right now; maybe you are trying to beam him or her to you.'

Seemingly unable to hear Poppy, she sat transfixed on her phone. Poppy stood up and went to the bar. On her return, Hope had placed it back in her bag, feeling deflated. Her eyes had gone smaller as her tummy did somersaults. Poppy sensed Hope's sadness, placing her hand on top of hers, looking into Hope's big green eyes.

'You know, whoever that person is, they are not worth it, if they are making you sad like this, and stopping you from answering the phone. It's not right when it's like that.'

Hope glared at her.

'You don't know me or the situation, so I don't want you to make a comment if that's OK. In fact, I don't want to talk about it,' she snapped, taking her phone back out of her bag, placing it on silent, tossing it back in.

'Alright. Well let's forget back home and just have a good time. You are on holiday, for fuck's sake!'

Hope took a large breath, followed by drinking a full glass of mojito in one go.

Smiling she commented, 'Yes, you are right, life's too short, let's party.'

Grinning, Poppy brushed her leg closer to Hope as they chatted.

'Would you like to go somewhere a bit different to here?' Poppy suggested.

Hope nodded and stood up, noticing that her friends had left the bar.

They left the bar, en route down the street. Poppy gazed at Hope from the corner of her eye.

'It's just down this back alley here,' Poppy said, directing Hope down the side street. As they got to the corner of the road, Poppy turned left and opened the door to the bar on the corner. As she opened the door she viewed men and women intimately huddled together, holding hands and kissing, both in secluded booths and around the bar area and dance floor. Hope stood with her mouth wide open, scanning the room, searching every inch of it. Poppy grinned, watching her. They made their way to the bar and Poppy ordered a round of drinks, while Hope stood fascinated with her surroundings. Poppy escorted her to a quiet spot with low couches and placed her hand on Hope's bottom, ushering her to the couch, sitting right next to her. Hope stared at a female couple close by, kissing. Unable to take her eyes off them she felt herself becoming aroused, making her eyebrows rise and the palms of her hands sweat.

'Are you OK? I haven't offended you, bringing you here, have I?'

'God, no, not at all. It's really cool. I like it.'

Grinning from ear to ear, Poppy leaned across and whispered, 'Alex, she's a girl, isn't she? Is she your girl?'

Smiling, Hope looked at her and said, 'Yes, and well … kind of …'

Moving closer, Poppy brushed the back of her hand onto Hope's face, staring into her eyes. She moved her hand onto her hair, playing with it. Hope took a deep breath, unsure of how to react, leaning forward, reaching for her drink. Poppy took the glass out of her hand, banging it down onto the table, grabbing Hope's chin, forcing her back onto the seat, kissing her.

Alex could not settle at home, pacing the floor, checking her phone every minute, feeling nauseous.

Poppy led Hope to the dance floor, smooching with her, kissing her.

Alex decided to visit her father's grave, feeling tearful.

Hope danced the evening away with Poppy without checking her phone at all.

Alex drove in a trance for hours, avoiding contact with Matt, as he rang and texted her several times.

Poppy and Hope left the bar and headed for the beach.

Alex pulled over and rang Hope, unable to help herself from her overwhelming longing to hear her voice.

Hope and Poppy walked hand in hand to the beach. As they got to a remote area, Poppy dragged Hope to the floor and put her hand up her skirt. Hope's heart began to palpitate at a rapid rate, almost as though it was going to come out of her chest. Suddenly, she pushed Poppy off.

'I'm sorry, I can't do this. I like you, you are very pretty, but I can't do this to Alex. I love her and all I can see when you kiss me, and I close my eyes, is her.'

Annoyed, Poppy stood up.

'Well, if you are that much in love, why aren't you here with her, and why don't you answer your fucking phone to her? And, if you love her that much, then you shouldn't have let me kiss you, and enjoyed it so much.'

Shaking her head, Hope said, 'No, you don't understand our relationship, and when I was kissing you, after a few seconds, I was wishing it was her, and imagining it was. I guess I thought in my mind it would be a way to get back at her, but I can't do what she does. I just can't.'

Tears began to trickle down her face. Poppy shook her head, walking off, shouting with her back to Hope. 'I think you need to sort yourself and her out. You are very pretty and so don't waste time with people who won't be with you.'

Hope took out her phone, seeing two missed calls from Alex and a voice mail, making the tears fall heavier down her cheeks. She listened to her voice mail as she walked back to the main street. She began to sob uncontrollably, making her ring Alex back.

Alex lay awake, staring into the darkness of night while Matt lay sleeping peacefully. Immediately she heard her phone vibrate, turning to see who it was. Viewing an incoming call from Hope she darted out of the bed and raced down the stairs. Her hands were trembling as she pressed the answer button.

'Hello,' Alex said, ecstatic

'Hi,' Hope replied with a very sombre tone.

'Oh God, Hope, why haven't you answered me all this time? I have been demented.'

Hope continued to cry, without being able to get any words out.

'Hey, don't cry, you will make me even sadder. Are you having fun?'

Silence fell as Hope sobbed, trying to catch her breath.

'Hey, angel, don't cry. It's all going to work out. I have realised so much since you have been away. I just can't do it anymore, as I have told you all week in your voice mails. I am not being fair to you, me or Matt. We are all miserable and need to be together.'

Trying to compose herself, Hope began to murmur something.

'What did you say? I didn't hear what you said.'

Mumbling, Hope said, 'I have been to a gay bar tonight, and it was really good and …'

Alex cut in, feeling her hands trembling and her knees knock together. 'You haven't been with anyone in there, have you? What were you doing in a gay bar?'

Feeling her teeth chatter together, Hope's need to unburden her soul, due to her inability to keep anything from Alex, made her say very timidly, 'Well, this girl came over to me in a bar and we went to this gay bar together, and she kissed me, and then tried to put her hand up my skirt, but it made me feel sick, and all I could think about was you, so I stopped her, and pushed her away. I only did it to feel wanted, and to see if I could do what you do with Matt but, Mummy Bear, I couldn't do it. I just want you. You are all I want. I'm so sorry, I just …'

Hope could no longer speak, due to her overwhelmed state.

Beginning to cry, wiping the tears from her face, Alex's lips quivered, as she attempted to calm down Hope.

'Oh, Baby Bear, I'm sorry. I do understand why, and thanks for telling me. We can't go on like this. I know why you do things, and I can't blame you. We are going to have to sort this and I need to show you what you mean to me. Please have faith in me. I won't let you down. Enough is enough.'

Chapter 37

Hope sat in the hairdresser's staring into the mirror as the stylist curled her hair while another girl manicured her nails.

'Are you excited for your big party tonight?'

Hope nodded.

Alex sat staring out of the bedroom window. Matt came behind and wrapped his arms around her. Alex stood motionless, proceeding to look out of the window. Matt caressed her neck, gripping her waist tighter. Pulling away, Alex moved.

'God, Alex, what is the matter with you? Can't I even hold my fiancée? I can't remember the last time we had even a snog, never mind sex.'

Alex frowned at him, squinting her eyes.

Feeling nerves encase his stomach, Matt did not probe further, choosing to walk out of the room, rubbing his tired eyes. Alex went into the en-suite and washed her face in cold water, staring into the mirror. Quietly, she said to herself, 'I can't do this any longer. I can't go on another day.'

Belle came to pick Hope up from the hairdresser's, beeping the horn outside. Hope paid and left, getting into the car with her hair, make-up and nails done to perfection.

'Oh, Hope, you look nice.'

'Thanks,' she replied quietly.

Belle shook her head, tutting. Hope scowled at her mother.

'You are just never satisfied. There is just no pleasing some people,' Belle commented with an angry tone.

Hope ignored her mother, sighing loudly, taking out her phone, seeing a message, prompting a smile.

Belle moaned.

'I'm pleased something has cheered you up. For someone who has just had a full pamper in the hairdresser's, to look all glam for your twenty-first party tonight, you are not exactly in the best of moods. I just don't know what is the matter with you. But I know one thing, you are never ever off that phone. One minute your face lights up, and the next minute, it is sad and miserable. I will never work you out.'

Alex rang her mother and invited her out for lunch, leaving Matt to do as he wished, much to his displeasure. She beeped the horn and sat waiting. Her armpits were sweating and her mouth felt dry. Her mother got into the car and they drove off.

As soon as they arrived at the restaurant, Alex ordered a bottle of red wine, taking a large gulp the second the waiter poured it.

'What's up with you, you seem nervous?' Eve asked.

Alex ignored her, taking another large drink from her wine glass. Eve peered at her daughter over the top of the menu, sensing Alex's sadness. The waiter came over and took the order. Alex continued to drink more wine, pouring more into her glass.

'You have the car, don't forget. You are driving so I would go easy on the wine,' she commented with a stern tone.

Alex glared at her mother, before lowering her back to reach for her phone that she had just heard bleep.

'Hey sexy wot ru up 2? I've just had my hair curled + I hav had my makeup done. I luk v. sexy lol. I'm so guttd u cant be wif me 2nite + share this big nite wif me. Wen will we ever b 2getha? Its just not rite. I cant stand it much longer xxx'

Alex's eyes welled up, making her go to the toilet and wipe her eyes. She stared into the full-length mirror, composing herself, willing herself to pluck up the courage. She took in a deep breath, going back to her seat. She sat down and took another large sip of wine, placing it back on the table. Eve frowned.

'Can you please not drink so much? You have the car!'

Alex snapped at her mother, raising her eyebrows and screwing her face up, making her nose wrinkle as she blurted, 'For God's sake, can you stop going on and on? You are like a broken record. I haven't even drunk the full glass yet. I am stressed out.'

Eve pulled a strange looking face, commenting, 'Stressed? What have you got to be stressed about?'

Alex lowered her head.

Eve took a drink from her glass, transfixed on her daughter.

'Come on, spit it out and tell me what's the matter.'

Alex took another drink. Her eyes filled up, forcing a tear to trickle down her face. Sensing her daughter's distress, Eve reached across, taking her left hand, stroking the top of it. Neither of them spoke for a few seconds until Alex said very quietly, 'I can't live like this anymore. I am so unhappy, Mum, I don't love Matt the way I should, I love ...' She paused, seeing her mother's astonishment, shaking her head.

'I just don't want to be with him. I have tried so hard; you have no idea just how hard, but I am staying to make everyone else happy to my own detriment.'

Eve closed her eyes, rubbing them, shaking her head.

'What would your father think? He thought the world of Matt. You are making a very big mistake. He is your soul mate. He is very good for you and you will never meet anyone to feel for you the way he does, and for how well matched you are.'

'I don't want to hear this. I am sick of hearing it. Emily says it all the time. Yes ...'

Eve butted in, 'Well maybe Alex, because it's true. Emily would give her right arm to have what you do and you are going to throw it all away? For what? Don't tell me there is someone else?' she asked, with an unpleasant tone.

Alex poured some more wine into her glass. Her mother glared at her. She took a large drink, whilst frowning at her mum, becoming agitated.

'Don't start about me drinking. I can see you looking at me about to say something. Well don't.'

Shaking her head, Eve sighed. Alex began to tap her fingers on the table and bite her lip.

'So why are you so unhappy? I thought you loved him.'

Alex started to rub her face, tapping her feet on the wood flooring.

'You just don't get it, do you?' she said sharply.

'No, I don't but I tell you this much. I don't care what you say, you are making a big mistake. No one else, whoever they are, is right for you. You believe what I'm telling you. You just won't listen.'

Alex slammed her glass onto the table, and began to raise her voice as she spoke, 'No, there isn't anyone else, I just don't want to be with him. Yes, he is lovely and I do love him, but I am not in love with him; do you want me to be with someone and not be happy?'

'Shhh, stop shouting. The whole place can hear you.'

'I don't care. You are annoying me.'

'Well, I care, so stop shouting. You need some sense knocking into you. And I mean, where will you live? You won't be able to maintain your lavish lifestyle if you leave. You will be straight back.'

Alex gritted her teeth together, retaliating, 'It isn't always about fucking money though. I can earn my own money.'

Eve scrunched her face up in disgust, leaning across the table.

'Do you have to use the foul language? There is no need for it; and stop losing your temper. He is a good man and I feel heartily sorry for him. He adores you; you will break the poor lad's heart. How could you, Alex?'

Alex began to cry, putting her head in her hands.

Hope took out her silver dress, silver and white heeled shoes and her silver necklace and began to get ready. Every second she checked her phone.

'Come in flower, you look upset. Are you OK?'

'No, not really.'

'You look smart. Have you been out?' Millie asked, fixing Alex a cold drink.

Alex nodded.

'Al, what's up? You look so sad. I can hear it in your voice every time I talk to you.'

Alex put her head in her hands and began crying. Millie went over to comfort her best friend.

'Al, you can't go on like this. You have to do something or it is going to change you as a person.'

'I am changed as a person. I am a lost soul with no purpose in life. I am destroying Matt and Hope. It can't go on. I am demented that it's her big bash tonight. I should be there with her. It's not right.'

'Al, you have one life and you have to go with it, and follow your heart. Fuck those who will not accept you.'

'I know, but I can't bear being judged by people. What will they say?'

'Who, Alex?'

'Hope's family, Matt's family, and my own, as well as my friends and neighbours.'

'Oh, Al, I think that you seem to have issues about what everyone else thinks of you, rather than your own happiness. Hope doesn't seem to mind people's opinion of you both; she adores you and just wants to be with you. She doesn't care and neither should you.'

Alex nodded, wiping away her tears.

Hope left the house en route to the hotel function room booked for her party. Her family had already left and had sent a taxi to collect Hope. She looked at her phone over and over, feeling anxious. She arrived at the hotel, greeted by her father.

'You look very nice; a proper grown-up woman,' David commented.

Hope smiled, searching in her bag for her lipstick, putting some on as she walked to the room, checking her phone at the same time. As she opened the door, her eyes widened and her face beamed, sighting all her family and friends. As she closed the door they all began to sing Happy Birthday to her. She greeted her family, followed by her friends, accepting her many gifts as she stood there, the belle of the ball. The room was filled with silver and pink balloons, matching Hope's outfit. Her cake was in the shape of a shoe – silver and pink. Her father brought her a large glass of chilled white wine, placing it in her hand as she rived open her many presents.

Alex returned home and paced the floor, ignoring Matt, who seemed distressed. She took a bath, lying in it for ages until the water went cold. Suddenly she got out of the bath and went into her dressing room, searching in her wardrobe for clothes.

Hope sat conversing with Amber and Linzi about her holiday as Marco joined them, bringing a bottle of champagne. He poured the girls a glass, handing Hope hers, staring into her eyes.

'You look so sexy tonight. I just can't believe how gorgeous you are,' he declared.

'Thanks,' Hope replied, feeling flattered.

'Maybe we can have a dance later if you want?'

'What will Katie think?'

'I don't care what she thinks.'

Hope lowered her head, seemingly uninterested as she looked at her phone again.

Alex put on her outfit, searching in her wardrobe for appropriate shoes to wear.

Hope danced happily with her friends as her mother and sister joined them. Hope scowled at her mum, moving away from her.

Alex put on her shoes and went into the bathroom to put on some make-up.

Hope went to the buffet, taking some food, as she walked back to her seat. Her mother came over, introducing her to Paul, a friend of her work-mate, trying to match-make. Hope dismissed Paul, wandering off, watched by Marco, unable to take his eyes off her.

Alex went back into the bedroom and took out her holdall, filling it with clothes.

'Come and dance with me, Hope,' Marco requested, pulling him towards her.

Hope pulled away, making excuses, going to the toilet.

Alex took a huge breath as she walked down the stairs. She stood at the bottom of the stairs, her mouth was dry and her whole body could not keep still. She turned the door handle with her shaking hands. Matt sat slouched in the chair, looking sad. He stared at her ready to go out, feeling his heart beat at a rapid rate. He sat forward, trying to breathe calmly, blowing in and out. Alex's heart started to pound out of her chest as her stomach tied itself in knots. She advanced towards him, perching herself on the end of couch. His hands began to tremble as he struggled to keep them still, making Alex even more nervous. He saw her holdall, forcing him to lunge forward and grab her.

'Please, angel, don't go. Please don't leave me. I couldn't take it a second time. My heart can't take anymore of this. Where are you going all dressed? Are you going to be with her?' he asked, with a quaking voice.

Alex bowed her head, trying to get the words out of her mouth. Without looking at him she said faintly, 'I can't do this anymore, Matt, it's not fair on any of us, least of all you. I should have gone the first time but you put pressure on me with what you did. It's not about me, and my happiness and ...'

Matt stepped in, trying hard to breathe, feeling breathless, 'And her, it's about her. You want her more than me. I should come before her.'

Standing up, feeling worked up, she said with a harsh but nervous tone, 'Yes, Matt, you have come before her; I put you before her the last time. I love her and I suppose that makes me into girls. I can't stand being apart from her. You know this and yet you keep me here with you and try to put emotional pressure on me. Well no more, I've had enough. And I'm sorry, but I'm not sitting here again and listening to you pour out your heart to me, it's too hard. I have to go, sorry.'

Looking astounded at her seemingly harsh comments, Matt began to sob, standing up, trying to pull the bag out of her hands. Alex pulled it back, advancing to the front door, determined to leave.

'Please don't leave, angel, I won't be able to cope. I am nothing without you,' he announced, falling to the floor.

Alex looked at his pitiful state, remembering the last time, giving her the courage to open the door and walk to her car. Her heart felt heavy and her teeth began to chatter as she threw the bag on the back seat. Matt stood by the car sobbing. Tears began to trickle down her face but the unhappiness she felt drove her forward, as she got in her car and sped off the drive without being able to look at Matt. She sped round the corner and pulled over, composing herself. She sat for several minutes pulling herself together, taking deep breaths, wiping the tears from her wet eyes. She took out her phone and could barely press the buttons caused by her trembling fingers. After several minutes of pressing the wrong keys she finally hovered her finger over the send button, reading it back.

'Hi baby. I'm comin 2 to that party now 2 get u once & 4 all. I want the world 2 kno that we r in love & on the biggest milestone of yr life so far, I shuld be ther. I will be 20 mins.'

Send.

Chapter 38

Alex drove at a rapid speed, eager to maintain the momentum she had gained.

Hope sat with nerves of excitement, wondering what to do. Standing up, she went over to her mum and dad, asking to speak with them in private. Belle and David looked at each other with suspicion, surmising something was up, judging from the unprecedented facial expression of their daughter. As she ushered them into the corridor, suddenly her whole body froze, making her stand statue-like as her parents stood next to her, forming a circle. Hope attempted to speak, opening her mouth, but nothing came out.

'Come on then, spit it out. What's up?' Belle asked with a nervous toned voice.

Hope's legs started to vibrate against the wall, struggling to keep them still.

'My word, Hope, what are you shaking for? You look terrified. Tell us what's up. Is it some boy upsetting you?'

Hope shook her head, afraid of their reaction but at the same time elated at Alex's declaration of love for her, and their unity at long last.

'For heaven's sake, what's the matter?' David shrieked.

Looking at her watch, realising Alex would not be long to arrive, she closed her eyes, inhaled and then let out a huge breath, blurting, 'Alex will be here soon. She is coming to be with me, and we are together. We love each other.'

Belle's face became scarlet red as David raised his hands in the air, disgusted. Hope opened her eyes, glued to the wall, incapable of moving a single muscle.

'You better be fucking joking. What have we told you about her? Is there something wrong with you?' David screamed.

'You are not being with her, and she is not coming here making some big scene, telling everyone. No way!'

Hope closed her eyes again, gulping, attempting to drown out the onslaught by her parents. David and Belle stood becoming more irate. Hope ignored them, standing with her back firm against the wall, preventing her from falling to the ground. Both of them moved closer to her, standing with both of their faces pressed against hers. David pulled her hair back, whispering with an intimidating tone.

'Make sure that she does not come in here or I will not be responsible for my actions. She is a dirty, filthy lesbian, and I do not want to look at her. She turns my stomach.'

Hope turned her head to the side, determined not to listen as her eyes remained firmly shut. Belle grabbed her arm and said, 'Your dad is right. You will never be with her; over my dead body. She is never going to be with you. I am not having any daughter of mine being a lesbian. It's sick and not right, so forget about it. Go back in there and tell her not to come…'

David interrupted, 'And we have told you before, but I'm telling you again for the last time, you are not seeing her anymore. If you do, I will kill her.'

Hope opened her eyes and pulled away from her mum and dad. Red-faced, she gritted her teeth.

'Don't you ever threaten her. I love her and she loves me. We are in love and no matter what you say, we are going to be together. I want her and I am going to be with –'

Belle cut in and slapped Hope hard across the face, making Hope run down the corridor.

Belle and David looked at one another, shaking their heads, unsure of what to do.

Hope ran into the room and took out her phone, frantically pressing buttons as fast as possible. She attempted to ring Alex but got put through to her answerphone, terrifying her. David and Belle stood in the corridor, plotting what to do. Hope rang Alex repeatedly, leaving voice mails, telling her what had happened. And not to come into the hotel, advising her to go to a nearby hotel and wait for her.

As soon as she left the message, Macy came over, insisting to know what had happened. Trying to keep things as normal as possible, Hope dismissed her question and led her to the dance floor, pretending not to show her fear, as she attempted to move her body in time with the music, panic-stricken.

Alex arrived at the hotel some moments later, not checking her phone. She sat for a few seconds, composing herself, before getting out of the car. Immediately as she closed the door, she felt a pull on her hair. Startled she turned to see a man and a woman in her face, enraged. The woman grabbed her throat and clenched her teeth together. Alex stood aghast, attempting to shake off this angry lady, but as she tried, the man pinned her back, forcing on her shoulders.

'Stay away from our fucking daughter or I swear I will kill you. You are not being with her. I will not allow it. Leave her alone, you filthy dyke. You are sick and disturbed and you are not brain washing our Hope to your ways.'

Shocked and mortified by his comments, Alex turned her head for a split second before replying, freeing herself from their grip.

'Don't you dare talk to me like that, nor call me that terrible word. I am not like that and I am not sick. I love Hope and I want to be with her and she loves me and…'

Belle moved in closer, placing her hand over Alex's mouth.

'Your fucking words disgust us. Our Hope does not love a woman like you with your flash car and job. You are influencing her and I will not have it,' Belle said, screaming in Alex's face. Alex moved away once more, as they began a tussle, joined in by David. He grabbed her arm, allowing Belle to punch her in the face, making her nose bleed. Alex wriggled her body, striving to set herself free of them both, but David grabbed both of her arms behind her back, squeezing them tight, paining her, fearing he had broken her weaker arm, forcing her to stop, allowing Belle to strike her again. She seized her throat, forcing Alex to cough, finding it hard to breathe.

'Tell me you won't see her again or I will knock you black and blue,' Belle demanded.

Alex shook her head, refusing to give in. David then pulled her arms tighter, hearing her scarred arm crack, making her cry out in pain. Sensing her pain he grabbed her neck.

'I'm fucking telling you, stay away from her or I will kill you. Do you hear me? Go back to your boyfriend or we will come to your house and tell him what a dirty lesbian you are.'

Letting go of her neck, sensing her shortage of breath, Alex began to cough. David let go of her arms, pushing Alex to the floor. Walking off, David shouted, 'I'm telling you, if you know what's good for you, you will keep away, and don't dare tell her either. She's having a good time so just leave it!'

Alex crawled to her car, wiping the blood from her nose with her sleeve. She sat with her back to it, bewildered.

Hope checked her phone over and over with her heart in her mouth as she walked on and off the dance floor. Viewing her parents walk towards the bar, she glared at them with contempt.

Chapter 39

Alex checked in to the nearest hotel that she could find and dragged herself up the staircase into her small room. She sat staring at the hotel walls, feeling her battered face and neck. In a trance, she did not hear any call or texts from either Matt or Hope.

Hope worried frantically all night as her evening drew to a close, glaring constantly at her phone, demented about Alex's whereabouts, fearing she had not left Matt.

Feeling numb, Alex could not bear to speak to Hope as her phone bleeped over and over. She lay in darkness all night, bewildered, fully clothed.

Hope tossed and turned, her stomach churning, as she ached to hear from Alex.

As the sun rose, shining through the window, Alex lay motionless, feeling empty and unable to keep a thought in her head. Drained and sore, she took her phone from the side of the bedside table. She listened to her numerous messages from Hope and then from Matt, bursting into tears. Unable to shake the cruel words of Hope's parents, they resounded over and over in her head, making her run to the bathroom and vomit. She returned and lay back on the bed, wiping her tired eyes.

She lay all day and night, refusing to take any of Hope's or Matt's calls, feeling numb and frightened. She deliberated over her life, loathing herself and who she was, desperate to change the way she felt.

The next day she took Matt's call, needing to hear the security of his voice. Afterwards she spoke to Hope, accentuating her self-loathing, listening to Hope's declaration of love for her, and how she yearned to be made love to, cutting the call short, as the ruthless words of Hope's parents spun around in her head like a record on repeat, churning her stomach. She hung up the phone and sat on the edge of the bed, staring out of the window into the darkness of night, eventually lying on the bed and falling asleep.

The next morning she awoke early and lay thinking for hours. Eventually she got up and got dressed, packing her bag. She went to reception and checked out of the hotel and got in her car. She looked in the mirror at her bruised face and lowered her head in shame, driving off.

Chapter 40

As the days passed by, Alex concentrated more and more on Matt, spending as much time with him as possible, often ignoring Hope's texts and phone calls, incapable of hearing her voice without aching to be with her.

Hope could not believe the turmoil she suffered without the woman she loved by her side. She agonised over the lack of response from Alex, making her fear the worst, sensing that she had not left Matt. She could not stop visualising them together: what they were doing, where they were going, were they having sex, causing her sleepless nights, during which she was consumed with jealousy. She had texted Alex, explaining how devastated she was by her parents' reaction, surmising this was the reason for Alex's return to Matt, angering her.

Alex dismissed Hope's desolation for her return home, refusing to allow Hope to see her bruised face, focusing her attention on Matt, feeling secure and loved.

Hope could hardly stomach to be in the same room as her parents and could not speak to them without feeling distaste. Her parents watched her every move, demanding to know her whereabouts, frustrating and upsetting Hope, resenting them more and more each day. Desperate to be away from home, Hope dreamed of a life with her beloved Alex more than ever.

Out of blue she decided to go to the hairdresser's and get her hair cut short.

Chapter 41

'God, Hope, you gave me a fright,' Alex said in an uneasy tone, staring at Hope's new short haircut.

'Sorry. Do you like it? Please say that you do,' Hope replied with agitation.

Alex rolled her eyes with displeasure, staring harder at this short haired girl before her, undecided whether she liked it shorter.

'What are you looking at? You hate it, don't you? Oh God, I'll die if you say you hate it.'

Glaring at Hope, Alex commented, 'Yes, it's awful, you look like a fucking boy. What possessed you to get it done?'

Feeling her heart sink and her pain engulf her Hope felt as though she had been punched and kicked; her head and stomach ached, creating a sickness that was unlike any feeling she had ever had before.

Alex sensed the hurt she was causing with her words, unrelenting.

Bowing her head, Hope began to cry. Feeling like she was being stabbed, not able to make eye contact, knowing how painful her words were, Alex stopped, staring out of the window. Hope wiped her face and took a small gift bag out of her large handbag. She placed her hand on Alex's leg. Alex took a deep breath, refusing to look at Hope. Hope grabbed Alex's hand, gripping it tightly, closing her eyes.

'In fact, you are knocking me physically sick, it's that bad. I hate it. I am sick to death of you, do you know that?' Alex said, facing her.

Quietly Hope said, 'I have some things I bought and did for you. I know that my mum and dad put a spanner in the works for us, and how angry you are at me, and I guess this is why you are being standoffish with me, but as I have missed you so much, I got you these.'

She put the gift bag on Alex's knee. Alex screwed her eyes tightly together, shaking her head. Barely able to make eye contact, she looked into the bag.

Struggling to hide her emotions, willing herself not to cry, Alex took out her gifts: her favourite sweets, a heart pin badge, a teddy key ring saying 'miss you' on its tummy and a CD with a piece of paper attached.

'Wow, these things are so thoughtful. What's this CD?' Alex quizzed.

'Look and see. I made it myself. I hope you like it,' Hope said with joy.

Alex opened the piece of paper, reading each part carefully, her eyes and mouth opening wide in amazement at receiving such a special gift.

'I cannot believe this, angel. Where do you get these ideas from?' Alex asked in awe.

'From you, Mummy Bear,' Hope replied, grabbing Alex's hand, gripping it tightly.

'I can't get over this. You have put all the songs that are special to us, or which express how you feel, and you have written why next to each one. Our song is there of course, "Unbreakable", and I like this one the best, the one about puppy love,' Alex said with glee as her eyes softened.

'Do you like them?' Hope asked, upbeat.

Incapable of hiding her feelings, she smiled from ear to ear, clenching Hope in her arms.

'Of course I do. You are so sweet, baby, but...'

Hope stepped in, kissing the side of Alex's neck. Alex closed her eyes, allowing Hope to carry on. Suddenly the reality of what had happened with her parents made her feel uncomfortable, pushing Hope away.

Feeling dejected, unsure why, Hope resumed her position, attempting to kiss her lips. Alex moved away, shouting, 'For God's sake, Hope, get off, not in public. How many times have I told you this?'

Lowering her head, feeling sad, Hope looked out of the window. Alex started up the car and said, 'Come on, I will drop you off at the bus stop. I wouldn't dare attempt to take you home or your fucking mental family may come at me with an axe.'

Hope did not comment, fixing her eyes on the path. Alex drove her to the bus stop, leaving the engine running. Hope took off her seat belt and leaned across to Alex.

'Why are you so nasty? I don't get you at all. I don't know what is wrong with you. I should be the one being mardy with you.'

'How do you figure that out?' Alex snapped.

Feeling nervous but determined to say, Hope stammered, 'Well, you left Matt to be with me but again, you go back. I know my mum and dad aren't happy, and I told you not to come to the party but I did say that I would come later, despite them knocking my head off, but you didn't contact me and left me worried to death about you. I don't think that you will ever leave him; you just make excuses up all of the time and I am really…'

Alex burst in, 'You are really what, Hope? Sick, fed up? Well good, leave me then.'

Shaking her head, Hope got out of the car and slammed the door. She walked quickly to the bus stop, furious. She stood waiting, getting angrier, mulling things over.

Alex sped off, feeling tears trickling down her face, confused.

Hope took out her phone and composed a text.

'Yeah Alex mayb I will leave u. I'm sick 2 death of yr xcuses. I'm not waitin 4eva 4u. If u lovd me that much it wudnt matta wot my mum + dad sed 2 me, I'd go thro hell 4 u. U musnt lov me enuf or u wudnt care!!'

Send.

Chapter 42

Hope lay on her bed shaking as the fear of their love affair ending became a harsh reality. Thoughts of being unloved circled around her head, again and again, as she cried into her pillow, wondering how she could make Alex love her more.

Determined to lift her depression, she rang Macy, asking her to go out, desperate to take her mind off things for a while.

She took a shower and got ready, before heading off to meet Macy in town.

She fought hard to shake off her sadness, a feeling she had learnt not to show in public, as she laughed and joked with her friend, flirting with boys as they tried to attract her attention.

'Hello, girls, can I buy you a drink?' Marco said, winking at Hope.

'Hi there. Yes, that would be great, thanks. We'll have two Southern Comforts and lemonade, please,' Hope replied.

'OK,' he responded, walking off to the bar.

'He fancies you, Hope. He isn't that bad looking and he has quite a good job, owning a bar,' Macy pointed out.

Hope turned up her nose at Macy's comment, watching the man at the bar, as her heart remained sad.

'There you go, ladies. By the way, you both look very nice,' he said, returning with their drinks.

Macy and Hope smiled in acknowledgement of his charming comments.

'I love your hair, it's very sexy. You look fucking gorgeous; you are the best looking girl in here tonight,' he commented, giving Hope the once-over.

Hope smiled, flattered by his comments, taking a sip from her drink.

'I'm just going over there to talk to Paul. After all, three is a crowd,' Macy teased, moving away.

Hope grabbed her arm and said, 'No, don't leave me alone with him. Stay with me.'

Macy shook her head, ignoring her request.

'So, Hope, do you want to go somewhere more quiet later?' Marco asked, pushing out his chest.

'Why, where is Katie tonight? You shouldn't flirt with me, you are my boss.'

'Yes, I know that, but I can't help it if I find you beautiful, can I?'

Hope smiled with increased confidence.

'I guess not. Do you really like my hair?'

'Yes, why do you ask? It makes you look prettier – well, no, that's not possible,' he said in a seductive tone, running his fingers through her hair.

'Oh, nothing, it's just that some people have said that they don't like it.'

'Well then, they need glasses. It's turning me on just looking at you.'

Hope blushed.

'Stop being silly, Marco, you are just teasing me, I reckon.'

Marco gazed at Hope, moving closer to her, placing his hand on her bottom, much to her dissatisfaction. She flinched away.

'You have never guessed, have you?'

'Guessed what?'

'I have always fancied you, from the day that you first came into the bar.'

'No you haven't, you flirt with loads of girls.'

'Yes, true, but I have always liked you the most, but I knew that a sexy siren like you would never go out with an old guy like me.'

'You are not old.'

'Well, I'm a lot older than you. I bet you go for younger sexy men with great six-packs and sports cars.'

'No, I don't. I like them older,' Hope said, her thoughts wandering.

'Really? Well, we have even more in common than I thought,' Marco replied, placing his hand on her bottom again, reaffirming his interest.

Hope stared at him, enjoying the attention, allowing him to keep his hand where it rested.

212

'I hope we can get closer. I like you so much,' Marco divulged.

Hope nodded, trying to reciprocate her feelings towards him.

'You must have a boyfriend, and I bet if you do he adores you, and you give him the runaround. I know if I was your boyfriend I'd be putty in your hands,' he teased, moving his hand up her back.

Hope paused for a moment, wondering how to answer.

'No, I don't have a boyfriend.'

'I can't believe that at all.'

'Well, it's true.'

'So are you a virgin, then?'

Hope began to snigger, fantasising about her lovemaking and erotic behaviour with Alex.

'Why are you laughing? It's a simple question.'

'Nothing, it's a private joke. Well, yes, I guess I am,' she teased.

'You guess? You either are or you're not,' he responded.

'I am, then.'

Marco's face lit up as he took a packet of cigarettes out of his pocket.

Looking unhappy as he puffed on his cigarette, she said, 'I'm just going to talk to Macy. I'll come back.'

'OK, well, I'll be here waiting for you.'

En route to the toilet, she checked her phone, agonising over the fact that she had not received any messages from Alex, causing resentment to circle her head again. As anger overcame her, she stared at herself in the mirror, willing herself to no longer be Alex's plaything, going back to Marco.

Marco and Hope chatted for some time while she regularly checked her phone. He bought her drink after drink and they both got more and more drunk. Hope enjoyed the attention Marco gave her. He made her feel wanted, but still she could not escape thoughts of her beloved Alex.

As the evening drew to a close Marco asked Hope to go for a walk.

At first she declined, until recurring resentment about Alex and Matt being together made her reconsider. They walked up the deserted streets and he grabbed her hand before stopping next to a wall and kissing her.

As he kissed her with his smoky breath, Hope felt nothing, unlike the goose bumps and tingling-toe reaction that a kiss from Alex ignited. After a short kiss Hope pulled away, loathing the feeling of his lips pressed on hers.

'What's up? Why did you stop?' Marco asked.

'I'm just tired. And you have a girlfriend who is my boss too.'

'I know, but it's just a kiss and I can't resist you. I don't fancy her anymore.'

'Yes, well, I've heard all this before. I'm not getting into this.'

'What do you mean?'

'Nothing, it doesn't matter. She may not be my favourite person in the world but I'm not being the bit on the side,' Hope announced forcefully.

'I never asked you to be. You sound bitter over something.'

'No I'm not,' Hope snapped.

'Alright, I was just joking. I am not happy, Hope, and everyone at work knows that. If it wasn't for Grace, I'd have left Katie ages ago. I'm just looking for the right girl to make me happy and who I can share my life with.'

As Hope listened, she yearned for Alex to speak those same words to her, but the harsh reality of Alex and Matt stared her in the face.

'Can I take you out tomorrow?' Marco requested.

'I have plans, sorry.'

'OK, well what about you staying behind one night after work and we can chat? I'd love to treat you the way you deserve to be treated. I want to take you away on weekends, out for meals and out for the day.'

'What about Katie?'

'What about her? If you say you'll come out with me, I'll say anything to get away from her.'

'Really?' Hope asked, surprised at how much he seemed to like her.

'Sure. Here, there's some money for a taxi, I want you home all safe and sound,' he replied, walking her to the taxi rank.

Hope stared at Marco, willing herself to find him attractive, looking at his short dark hair and dark eyes.

'Here's a taxi. Thanks for the money. Bye,' Hope said, jumping into the taxi as fast as she could.

'Can't I have a kiss?' he asked, leaning into the taxi, grabbing her chin.

Hope quickly kissed Marco, quickly pulling away, as the taxi drove off.

She arrived home, got undressed and went to bed, lying riddled with guilt at kissing Marco, feeling as if she had cheated on Alex. As she lay there, thoughts of Marco quickly left her head and she fantasised about her beloved Alex, and how much she desired her, despite Alex's aloof manner towards her.

The longer she lay there thinking about herself and Alex, and all their wonderful memories, the happier she became, making her put her fingers inside her pajamas. She felt her wet, pulsating vagina, aching to climax. She disrobed Alex in her head, imagining her naked bronzed body, intensifying her arousal. She rubbed her soaking finger up and down her palpitating clitoris, faster and faster, barely able to keep still, enjoying the sexual gratification, aching for her lover to make love to her again.

Chapter 43

Hope stood waiting outside a pub on the outskirts of town; her hair shone in the moonlight, complementing the sparkle in her eyes and the glow from her perfect cheeks. She wore more make-up than usual. She had bought a new (shorter than usual) skirt and wore her knee-length high-heeled black boots.

Marco arrived slightly later than planned owing to family commitments. He wore black jeans with a V-necked red jumper, a black leather jacket and black cowboy boots. His hair was slicked back with gel.

'You look very sexy tonight. I love short skirts and boots like that,' Marco explained, transfixed on her.

'Thanks,' she replied, entering the bar.

Marco went to the bar, ordering a bottle of red wine as Hope took a seat in the far corner, out of view.

'You are so pretty. I can't wait for you to be back at work tomorrow. I've missed you so much, it isn't the same without you,' he said, sitting next to her, lighting up a cigarette.

Hope grinned, feeling flattered, taking a sip of her wine, broken-hearted at the prospect of losing Alex.

'You are very slim, aren't you?'

'Yes, but so are you. Your suits are always two sizes too big for you at work. It's funny,' she said, laughing.

Marco pouted.

'I'm not that thin. Don't you think I'm sexy, though?' he joked.

Hope looked at his dark eyes and jet-black, thick hair, scanning his slim lips and small dark eyes.

'Yeah, you must have been a model in Italy. Were you?' she teased.

'Yes, I was very good looking when I was your age.'

'How old are you now?'

'How old do you think?'

Hope paused for a moment, noticing the slight wrinkles around his eyes and forehead.

'I don't know, thirty?'

'Almost. I'm thirty-one.'

Hope smiled, taking out her phone, scanning her inbox, as sadness enveloped her.

'You are always looking at that phone and now you look very unhappy.'

'I'm fine. So, tell me more about you. Where did you meet Katie and how did you propose?' she asked, sipping her drink.

'I don't want to talk about that or her. I'm with her for the sake of Grace and the pub, I guess, but that's it. I want to leave her.'

Hope listened, believing him as he spoke.

'So why don't you leave her, then?'

'Well, I'm just waiting for the right girl to come along for me and then I will.'

'Yes, that's what they all say.'

'I mean it,' he said, waving his hands in the air.

Hope lowered her head, reading the menu.

'Are you hungry?'

'No, not really. I've felt sick all day.'

'Why is that? Are you nervous to be out with your boss?'

Hope grinned.

'No, not quite.'

Marco moved closer to her, placing his hand on her left leg. She flinched away, feeling uncomfortable.

'What's up? Don't you fancy me?' Marco enquired, putting his arm around her.

Hope stared at him, trying hard to be attracted to him, studying his features.

'I don't know. I haven't really thought about you in that way before, to be honest.'

'Oh well, you will have to try, because I would like us to get to know each other a lot better.'

Hope smiled, making an excuse to go to the toilet. In her absence, Marco had moved closer to where she had been sitting, forcing her to sit even closer to him.

As the evening drew to a close, Hope agonised over kissing Marco, staring at his dark Italian features as they walked to the taxi queue.

Around the corner he pulled her to one side, kissing her, pressing his erect penis against her leg as she struggled to feel aroused.

'You are amazing. Can I see you tomorrow after work? Stay late and we can continue where we left off,' he said, transfixed on her, in awe of her beauty.

Unsure of what to say, she agreed, heading quickly for the taxi queue, eagerly waiting for her taxi to arrive. As she looked at Marco's slim body thoughts of Alex remained with her, and she visualised her dark (like his) hair and eyes, and bronzed skin, causing a tingling feeling to start off inside her. She imagined Alex's pert breasts and her shiny shoulder-length dark hair, bringing a glow to her face.

'What are you grinning at?' he asked, trying to smooch with her.

Dismissing his advances, she reached into her bag, searching for her phone, engulfing her with sadness, as she forced herself to come to terms with the realisation of Alex's lack of love for her.

'Oh, nothing,' she replied, grabbing him, allowing him to kiss her.

Chapter 44

Three weeks later

Millie exited the car in tears, slamming the door so hard she almost shattered the glass. She stood wiping her eyes, watching Benny speed out of her street, refusing to make eye contact with her. She stood frozen on the spot for a few seconds, feeling nauseous. Her phone began to ring, making her reach in her bag.

'Hi,' she whimpered.

'Hey, what's up, Millie? Are you OK? You sound upset,' Alex asked with a concerned tone.

'No, not really.'

'Oh, you sound so sad. We are a right pair. I am gutted too. I just can't seem to function.'

'Yeah, I can imagine. Are things no better?'

'No. In fact they are worse. I hate my life so much and hate myself for being so weak. I should take control of things and not let anyone interfere in my happiness.'

Looking puzzled, Millie scratched her eyes, walking towards her front door.

'You need to sort this out. Have you not heard anything then?'

'Not a thing!'

Shaking her head, Millie closed the door behind her.

'You are so stubborn, Al. I would sort that out if I was you. I have told you that she won't wait for you for ever and would get sick. There is always a straw that finally breaks, you know.'

Massaging her eyes hard, Alex gave out a huge breath.

Millie continued, 'You need to fight for her and make the first move. She is sick of the whole thing, bless her, and I would be going down there and sorting it out.'

'But what if she doesn't answer when I ring her? It will kill me.'

'Well, you should try.'

Agreeing, Alex changed the subject, listening to her friend's heartache.

Hope sat staring at her phone, deciding what to do. Nervously, she pressed the keys on her phone pad, composing a text. Immediately she received a reply, creating nerves in her tummy. She stared at the phone before finally replying, throwing it on the bed, as she took a shower.

Alex hung up the phone and stood thinking. Minutes later she took a deep breath and pressed the call button on her phone.

Hope got out of the shower and opened her wardrobe, quickly finding something to wear. She put on her clothes and went into the bathroom, doing her make-up.

Alex hung up, deciding to ring back, determined to leave a voice mail. As the phone rang out, butterflies encased her stomach, making her breathe faster. As it clicked to voice mail, suddenly her mouth dried up, and she could not speak, hanging up.

Hope finished getting ready and packed her bag. She strolled downstairs, glaring at herself in the full-length mirror on the stairs, moving her head from side to side.

Alex took her keys off her desk and left the office, seemingly in a hurry.

Hope stood on the street corner waiting, looking anxious, glancing at her watch.

Alex drove to Hope's work and went into the bar area.

Hope looked at her watch over and over again as she stood there.

Alex left the bar en route to the town centre.

As she drove down a side street, she slowed down. Suddenly her hands began to freeze against the wheel and her heart plummeted; she slowed down to be certain of what she was seeing. Immediately, she saw Hope standing on the street corner, carrying something in her hand. Hope wore a short skirt, high-heeled shoes and a short jumper with a shirt underneath.

Despite her efforts, Alex could not make out every feature, but she was able to see the amount of make-up she wore, more than usual, thinking how lovely she looked, although not in her

220

usual classy style. Alex's tongue stuck to the roof of her mouth as she watched her smile at him and get in the car, which quickly sped away. Alex drove to the end of the street, stopped the car, leant out of the door and vomited on the pavement.

Alex's heart was shattered; she struggled to keep calm as a heart-wrenching feeling overwhelmed her, something that she had never felt before, and she wondered what to do.

She sat in a trance, staring at the road in front of her, consumed with jealousy, visualising them together, tortured over what she could do.

After some time she started up the engine and slowly drove off, her hands trembling on the wheel.

She arrived at Millie's house, craving her advice and support. As soon as Millie opened the door, Alex fell to the floor, broken, sobbing.

'My God, what's happened, flower? Are you all right? You look awful,' Millie commented with fear in her voice, helping her friend to get up from the floor.

Alex lay in a heap next to the stairs like a helpless rag doll, attempting to speak.

'You won't believe it, Millie. I saw it with my own eyes and it is killing me. I can't get the vision out of my head, I want to keep being sick,' she replied, sobbing.

'Who? I don't understand. Calm down. Come on in here and sit down,' Millie responded, helping Alex into the living room.

'Hope. I saw her with that Marco. The reason why she doesn't contact me anymore is because she's seeing him. How could she?'

Millie looked sad, embracing her friend.

'You are joking, though?'

'I'm not. I went to the bar to see if she was at work and her friend said that she was in town, so I thought that I would drive by to see if I could see her, and I saw her waiting on the street corner, and then he came and got her. She had an overnight bag too,' she wept.

Millie cuddled Alex's limp shoulders.

'I guess she wants attention from him, and you haven't been too nice to her lately, but it's a rotten trick to not tell you. She should have rung and told you if she's seeing someone else.'

'But I can't believe how this is making me feel. I'm in bits. I want to just curl up and die. It feels as bad as when my dad died. I can't take it, and how do I go home in this state? If only I had got a back bone and stood up to them.'

'I don't know what you are talking about. You will have to see her and tell her how you feel,' Millie replied, looking mystified.

Alex wiped her face, not answering.

'Can I ask you a very direct question as your best mate? But you must be honest with me.'

Alex stared at her friend, fearing the question, nodding nonetheless.

'Are you forever pushing her away and using her parents and Matt as an excuse for your fear of being gay, and how you may get judged?'

Alex wiped her eyes, pausing for a few seconds.

'I try hard for Matt as it would crush him, as I've seen, and I hate hurting him, but yes, I am scared of how much I love her and how she may hurt me too.'

'But you still haven't answered what I asked.'

'She isn't bothered, Mille, and that's all there is to it. I am a fool for all I have gone through and agonised over for her.'

'But you love her, Al, and that's why.'

Pausing, Alex sat glaring at the carpet.

'I have had enough, she is making a fool of me and doesn't deserve me. Matt loves me and so...'

Millie butted in, 'You need to stop doing this.'

'Doing what?' Alex replied, raising her hands.

'Clinging to him when you are upset over her and she is hurting you. Get stronger, Alex.'

Frowning at her best friend, Alex stood up, made her excuses and left. Furious, she took out her phone and rang Hope.

Hope saw the call from Alex as she sipped wine with Marco in the wine bar, making her panic. She quickly went outside and took the call, feeling her hands shake.

'Hello,' she said sheepishly.

'Well, hello, stranger. Long time no speak? Are you finally answering your phone?' Alex scoffed.

Silence fell.

'What's wrong? Cat got your tongue?' Alex snapped.

Feeling on edge, Hope felt her mouth dry up, incapable of responding.

Becoming scarlet red, Alex did not relent, going on, 'So why haven't you been in touch then? And don't try and be clever by not fucking answering when I rang you earlier. Don't you think I deserve an explanation?'

Hope's stomach was tied in knots as she struggled to speak.

'Yeah,' she murmured.

'I'm not sure I want to hear it as all you do is lie. You are a liar and I'm sick of it, and you,' Alex said in a nasty tone.

Hope's heart began to beat faster. Aware of how annoyed and disappointed Alex was with her, barely able to tolerate the idea of Alex attacking her yet again with her cruelty, she blurted, 'I couldn't wait for you for ever.'

Alex fell silent for a moment.

'What did you just say?' she growled.

Hope stuttered, 'It's not working and I don't think there's any point in going on. Do you?'

Alex's chest began to tighten, digesting Hope's words, which sank into her heart, making it ache worse than ever before.

Silence fell as Hope stood trembling. Her teeth started chattering as she attempted to compose herself.

As silence continued, Alex's pain grew, fuelling her tears. Determined to maintain her dignity, she went on, 'Well, you have just saved me a job to be honest.'

'What do you mean?' Hope asked nervously.

'I've been sick of you for ages and you were too thick to see it,' Alex said with aggression.

Hope fell silent again as her chest began to tighten, taking deep breaths.

Alex continued as her mouth became dry, fighting back her tears.

'Yes, well, I'm pleased that you have met someone because I love Matt and I don't, and if I'm being truthful, never did, really love you; it was all about the sex and I am tired of you. I have been trying to find the words for weeks. It has been wonderful not having to see you or contact you,' she said with exaggerated cruelty.

Hope could not listen anymore to the vile things that Alex was saying to her, proving what she had suspected all along, cutting her with every nasty word spoken, almost as though she was there in front of her, slashing her arm with a knife.

'I'm going to have to go. I'm sorry, I can't take any more of what you say,' Hope said softly, hanging up the phone, devastated. Alex made her way to her father's grave, sitting on the gravestone, sobbing like a child, feeling physical pain, unburdening her soul, feeling guilty at her lies to Hope.

Hope went back to the bar and got drunk, spending the night with Marco.

Chapter 45

Alex had agonised about Hope's declaration about Marco to her for the past six days. She could not eat, sleep or apply herself at work. She put all her efforts into Matt's birthday, forcing her pain and misery to the back of her mind, determined to give him a good day, which he deserved.

As Emily wandered around the shops, she received a call from Pete informing her he would not be able to attend Matt's birthday dinner, insisting on having to work late. She clashed down the phone and went to the toilet, re-applying her make-up. She left the toilet and headed for the restaurant. She took out a large gift bag and walked to the restaurant. She arrived and greeted everyone, giving Matt a lingering hug and kiss on the cheek. Alex sat drinking wine, conversing with everyone. Emily sat close by Matt, handing him the gift bag, watching him as he tore open every present, while Alex fixed her attentions on their guests.

As the night went on, Alex drank more and more, keeping as far away from Matt as possible, allowing her sister to distract him.

As the evening drew to a close, Matt came and sat close by Alex, making her flinch away. All night he had watched her glare at her mobile over and over, sensing the sadness consuming her. As they sat finishing their drinks, Emily moved towards them and began chatting to Matt, who seemed distracted. Alex pretended to show interest in their conversation until she received a text, making her seem uneasy, unnerving Matt. Alex became transfixed in a text frenzy, dismissing everything and everyone around her. She became restless and seemed angry as she received the bombardment of texts. Matt questioned her, making her angry, lashing out at him in front of their guests. Matt's face became beetroot red, insisting that he wanted to go home, infuriating Alex as they left the restaurant suddenly.

As they waited for the taxi to arrive, Matt paced up and down. Alex stood, desperate to check her phone, but did not attempt to do so. The taxi arrived and they got in. Alex's phone vibrated in her bag, forcing Matt to tutt loudly, urging the taxi driver to turn his head. Matt tapped his fingers on the door panel, biting his lip. Alex tapped her feet, feeling irritated. As soon as the taxi stopped, Alex jumped out, walking briskly to the front door, secretly reading her message, while Matt paid the driver.

He clashed the front door, searching for Alex, who had switched off her phone. She stood pouring a glass of wine as Matt came in, scowling at her. Taking a sip from her glass she turned her back on him. Standing viewing her back, he ran his tongue over the top of his teeth, playing with his chin. Alex took a deep breath and turned to face him, smiling. Matt's face became more scarlet, unable to hide his anger.

'You weren't exactly being very nice to me tonight, were you?'

Alex dismissed his comments, glaring at him before brushing past him, going into the living room. Matt stood, enraged, following her.

'You showed me up in front of our family tonight and I'm getting sick of it, and your moods!'

Shaking her head, she ignored him, showing little respect, making him worse. He moved up and down the floor, taking deep breaths.

'You don't have any respect for me, do you? You show me no affection and I can't take it anymore. I am sick of it. I won't be treated this way,' he said abruptly, feeling his stomach cramping.

Alex began to get annoyed, banging her glass on the table.

'Oh, stop being dramatic, Matt. I went to lots of efforts for your birthday and arranged all that and so…'

He stepped in, getting closer to her, 'No, your Emily did most of the arranging and talked to me all night, as you didn't seem to want to, until of course that phone started, and then you were engrossed. I wonder who that was, eh …' he said with his arms above his head.

Standing up, she responded, 'Don't you dare start, Matt. I won't have you talking to me like that.'

226

Shouting, he said, 'And don't you take the piss out of me, Alex. I am sick of you with that fucking phone. In fact, where is it, I am going to smash the fucking thing off the wall so that you can't use it. It drives me mad how you are glued to it. But to do it when we are out, that's just rude,' he insisted, searching in her bag, finding her phone.

Becoming irate, Alex snatched the phone out of his hand, screaming at him, 'Don't you fucking swear at me.'

Horrified, Matt knocked the phone out of her hand, making it fall onto the floor. Livid, Alex picked it up, running upstairs, fearful Matt would damage her phone. He went after her, determined to seek the truth.

'So who have you been texting? And why have you been so fucking miserable? In fact, tell me the last time you kissed me, or told me that you love me. I would do anything for you but you treat me like shit. I am the biggest mug ever.'

Alex looked at him, unsure of how to answer. Matt went up to her face, demanding her to answer.

'Get away from me, Matt. You are scaring me and I don't like it. You have no idea about me so I am not going to explain anything to you.'

'Why not? I thought you were hard and tough.'

She walked away from him, attempting to diffuse the situation. Matt would not let it rest, feeling his wet brow as the sweat poured out of him.

'Just tell me it was her that you were texting; tell me!' he demanded.

She refused to answer, clenching her teeth.

Destroyed, Matt's eyes sunk into his head, walking out of the room. He went downstairs and took his phone, slamming the front door. He made a call as he walked down the street.

'Hi.'

'Hi,' Matt replied.

'Are you alright?'

'No, not really. I am sorry to say this but I have taken all that I can and I am at the end of my tether. I am crushed but I know that she doesn't have any respect for me. I am sorry to ring you as it puts you in a difficult position, but I have no one else to talk to and I need someone to …'

She cut in, 'It's fine, Matt. I'm pleased that you have rung. I am here for you.'

Chapter 46

Five days later

Hope sat on the bus, a bundle of nerves, as excitement overtook her emotions.

Alex concentrated hard on thinking negatively about Hope, and how she had betrayed her, sitting at the bus stop outside her house, refusing to collect Hope from their usual spot at the bus station ten miles away, wanting to emphasise her lack of feelings for her.

Sitting in the car, Hope embraced Alex tightly, gazing into her eyes, her deep love shining through, as much as ever before. Alex noticed this immediately, allowing her anger to dissolve in Hope's arms.

'I've missed you so much,' Hope said, choked.

Alex stared at her, feeling the same, but somehow she could not find the words to convey this as she drove the short distance to her house. Hope gripped her hand, feeling a rush of electricity surge through her whole body, as much, if not more, than ever before. Alex too felt an amazing glow in the pit of her stomach, making the hairs on the back of her neck and arms stand up.

As she pulled onto the drive, both girls leapt out of the car, aching to be in each other's arms again. Alex slammed the front door, locking it behind her, enchanted by Hope in her faded blue jeans and long white and blue stripy jumper. Her hair was pulled back in a very short, messy ponytail. She wore limited make-up and looked very tired, but still Alex wanted her.

Without hesitation, Hope tore off Alex's coat, throwing it to the floor as they made their way up the stairs, one by one, pulling off each other's clothes, kissing passionately. Alex pushed Hope onto the bed, ripping off her white lacy thong with her teeth, licking her vagina, placing her fingers in her mouth, teasing Hope, swallowing her love juices.

'Oh God, your pussy is soaking wet,' she announced, breathless, moving towards Hope's breasts with her saturated lips and dripping chin, rubbing her juices all over them.

Hope lay gasping, putting her fingers inside herself, unable to sustain the pleasure-pain any more, rubbing her clitoris harder and harder. Alex moved on top of Hope, grabbing her arms, preventing her from touching herself. She pinned her arms back, getting on top of Hope, kissing her neck then biting it. Hope cried out, trying to move her hands to touch Alex. Again Alex grabbed her wrists, pushing them above Hope's head as she lay groaning. Alex put her fingers deep inside Hope, taking them out, rubbing her fingers all over her mouth, making Hope drool, trying to lunge forward to lick it all off. Alex grinned. After a few seconds of licking her lips, she gently slid forward, touching her face onto Hope's, allowing Hope to slowly lick her bottom lip, making them both moan loudly. Slowly, Alex buffed herself up and down Hope, their vaginas touching, gazing into each others eyes. Hope wrapped her arms around Alex tightly, feeling her naked flesh against hers. Their bodies moved gently in synch with each other, feeling their warm moisture on one another as they tenderly stared into each other's eyes. Just as they were both about to climax, Hope stopped, pushing Alex off, leading her by the hand into the bathroom. She turned on the shower and led Alex into the shower, allowing the water to wash over them. They stood caressing each other with the hot water bouncing off their skin. Hope took the shower head off the wall and placed it on Alex's vagina, watching the hot water jet inside of her, much to both their satisfaction. She clenched Alex close to her, kissing her, rubbing their wet breasts together. Alex gently ushered Hope against the wall and took the shower head out of Hope's hand, gently letting the water stimulate Hope's enlarged clitoris, making her cry out. In unison, they fell to the ground, rolling around the floor.

Matt left work and headed for town, heading for the restaurant.

Hope sat in the car, gazing out of the window, looking unhappy. Alex drove in silence, willing herself to open her heart to Hope. She drove feeling nervousness consume her whole body, preventing her from concentrating on the road, almost crashing into the car in front. Hope did not flinch in her trance state, glaring out of the window. Driving as slowly as possible, Alex finally reached the bus stop, forcing stomach cramps, feeling unwell. As she stopped the car, Hope did not turn to look at her and opened the car door. Alex's heartbeat was faster than ever, making her feel as though she was having a palpitation. Hope put her left leg out of the car, tilting her body. Alex's hand moved as though she was going to grab her but moved it back, unable to make any contact as her arm suddenly froze. Hope said goodbye faintly, closing the door, walking down the street, dragging her feet. Alex sat watching her, unable to move from the spot, feeling magnified pain. She watched Hope turn the corner, turning glaring at Alex as she went out of sight. Alex sat for some time before driving off.

She drove for hours in silence, mesmerised. Eventually she returned home to an empty house. Her mobile bleeped.

'Hi, it's me. I guess there's no point in meeting again. U clearly will never leave him. Goodbye Alex!'

As Alex read her message, forcing tears, Matt came in, unable to make eye contact with her. He walked past her and went upstairs. Alex followed him some time later and got into bed and lay on her side as far away from him as possible.

'Where have you been tonight? You have been out every night this week,' she queried.

'Just out in town with my friends,' he replied with a sheepish tone.

Chapter 47

Seven months later

Matt sat sipping his wine, enjoying his female company. He happily ate his starter and main course without looking at his watch.

'You are looking better in yourself; your cheeks are rosy, but then again you are drinking wine and that may be helping,' his companion teased.

Matt smiled. The waiter came over and handed them both the dessert menu. Matt's face beamed as he salivated over which to choose from.

'I think you should get that,' she said, pointing.

Matt peered over the top of his menu, grinning. The waiter took their order as Matt went to the bathroom. He returned and took out his mobile.

'Hasn't she sent you a message asking where you are?'

'No,' he replied, lowering his head. His eyes suddenly lost their glow as he picked up his wine and took a large gulp.

'You are not meant to drink wine like that,' she joked.

'I know, but …'

His companion butted in, leaning across, taking his hand.

'It's OK that she doesn't text or ring. She will probably be busy or something.'

Matt nodded, unconvinced, as the desserts arrived. He played with the chocolate sauce and ice cream around his plate for ages before eating it.

'She won't care where I am; I'm sure she likes me out. In fact, I think she's out with her new friend from work. If I wasn't with you, I would never go out for meals or the cinema. And if she is there then she's either doing something or is miles away from me and hardly has anything to say. Her eyes look so sad all the time. I wish sometimes that she would do us both a favour and leave me.'

Glaring at him, leaning into him, stroking his arm, she replied, 'Well, if it's that unhappy, why don't you leave her? Is it ever going to get any better? Maybe it's for the best as you are both so miserable, and that's the saddest thing.'

Feeling choked he bowed his head, refusing to answer. She took a sip from her wine, gazing at him. Matt continued to drink his wine, pouring more into their glasses, finishing the bottle off.

'At least she's not at work right now, surely that must be better?'

He paused for a few seconds and then he answered, 'Well, it is a bit strange; I miss her business brain but I think that to seek another job, when she is needed with me to help it expand, says it all. She was looking for independence, and now she has it. And I suppose I don't have to look at her miserable face all day as well as at home.'

Alex decided to stay out after work and go for a drink with her new boss, partying long into the night.

Chapter 48

Alex and Betsy had found a mutual bond, a bond that she had not thought possible when they first met. Betsy was everything Hope was not: successful, ambitious, her own person (without any parental influence), with her own car and house, and she was her own age.

Betsy had a very athletic body; a body she had groomed herself, with daily trips to the gym. She was very fit and loved all sports. She had shoulder-length dark hair, dark eyes and very tanned skin. Alex saw Betsy as a female version of Matt, with her dark, toned, athletic body and dark eyes.

As the weeks went by the chemistry between them was augmented as Alex's forced Hope out of her thoughts.

Betsy had invited her to her friend's party. She wore a very short denim skirt, showing off her amazing toned, bronzed legs. As the evening moved into the early hours of the morning, the two work colleagues became closer, kissing with passion for several minutes as their physical attraction for each other became apparent, aided by the copious amounts of alcohol they had consumed.

Alex happily snogged her friend, enjoying this intimacy between them. For some reason, neither lady wanted to take their intimacy a step further, preferring just to kiss, their arms locked around each other's waists.

Alex staggered home at 4 a.m. (usual for her during the past few weeks). Matt lay restless in bed, pontificating over her whereabouts for the past eight hours.

The following day she awoke feeling uncomfortable about what she had just done. She stared at Matt, knowing that her unyielding love for Hope, despite her efforts to distract herself, had not diminished. She ached to hear her voice and kiss her lips; Betsy could no longer distract her thoughts.

Chapter 49

Three weeks later

Every morning Alex woke up with the same sick feeling in the pit of her stomach, thinking of Hope the second her eyes popped open.

She had continued spending time with Betsy, enjoying discovering her new friend, without combating her desire for Hope or quelling the months that had passed by since Alex had hung up on Hope, without any correspondence whatsoever. Alex had remained true to her word, refraining from giving into temptation and finding a way to contact her. To her surprise, Hope had not made any contact with her, much to her devastation.

Alex decided to wander into town at lunch time, trying to motivate herself. As she sauntered by the shop windows, she glanced at the spring fashions. She walked around searching for a new outfit to cheer her up. Whilst perusing the display windows, she stumbled across a skirt and jumper, making her go into the shop. She looked round at some other items that she liked, picking some up and taking them to the changing room. She went in and tried them all on, taking her time, glaring at herself, making sure she looked right in them. She decided to buy them all, handing the sales assistant the tag, holding the items across her arms. As she walked towards the counter, she heard voices behind her. Then she felt her shoulder being touched. Startled, she looked up. Scowling at her were Hope's parents. Immediately, feeling intimidated, she flinched away, dropping her clothes. Quickly, she bent down, retrieving them as her hands began to shake and her mouth dried up. Belle bent down, pretending to help her, allowing her to whisper in her ear.

'I'm so pleased we have seen you here today because we have news for you.'

Alex stood up, moving away, feeling herself getting worked up. She stared at Belle without speaking, trying to remain calm. David tutted at Alex, shaking his head. Alex attempted to move away but Belle grabbed her arm and continued with a condescending-toned voice. 'As I was saying, I have great news, Hope is living with Marco and they are very happy. I knew she wasn't a filthy dyke like you, and that it was you all along trying to brainwash her. You disgust me.'

As the words fell out of Belle's mouth, Alex felt augmented pain, feeling her face starting to numb. Maintaining her dignity, she shook her head, frowning at Belle, freeing her arm. Quietly, she said, 'Get your arm off me, and I am not having you call me names.'

David stepped in, 'Whatever, we don't care what you say. You just stay away from our daughter as she is very happy. And you know what will happen if you dare get in touch with her. You had your warning the last time. Next time you won't be so lucky.'

Becoming both angry and emotional, Alex picked up her clothes and briskly walked out of the shop.

She ran to the nearest toilet, feeling the tears streaming down her cheeks. She locked herself in the cubicle and sat composing herself. Feeling worthless, the tears continued to flow. Suddenly she heard her mobile bleep. She reached in her pocket, taking it out.

'Hi it's me. How r fings? I'm ok. Got sum news. I live wif Marco now but I still miss u. Mayb we cud meet up sum time?'

Livid, Alex stopped crying, feeling anger consuming her. She read the message over and over with the words of Hope's parents resounding in her head, making her even worse. She took a deep breath and began pressing the phone keypad so fast she had to start again as she kept pressing the wrong keys. Her fingers trembled as her face went a deep shade of red.

'I TOLD U BEFORE & IM TELLIN U AGAIN STOP TEXTIN ME AS U HAV SOMEONE ELSE. IM PLSED U R LIVIN WITH THAT WOMANISER, U MAKE A GUD COUPLE. I DON'T LOVE U ANYMORE SO GET THE MESSAGE & PLEASE LEAVE ME ALONE!!'

Hope read her message and started to cry, unable to believe Alex's cruelty.

Chapter 50

Jodie sat staring at Matt across the open-plan office: staring at his smouldering good looks. Matt noticed Jodie looking at him, blushing as their eyes met. He stared at her long blonde hair and young looks before concentrating on his work covering his desk. After a few moments Jodie plucked up the courage to email her boss. Matt read the message, feeling flattered as he quickly replied.

'Hey Matt, you look very cute today!'
Send.

'Thanks, so do you but then again, you always do!'
Send

'Wow. I'm flattered, especially by someone like you.'
Send

'What do you mean?'
Send.

'Well, someone who is as successful as you and so cute with it ☺'

'God, I never think of myself like that. You are very kind. I don't think Alex deserves you.'
Send.

Matt read her message, puffing out his chest. Jodie sent another message.

'Do you want me to stay late tonight and help with any work you may want doing? In return we could go for a drink after if you want?'
Send.

'I'll bear that in mind, thanks. I will have to go early tonight as Alex is cooking for me and as we are rarely in the house at the same time these days, I will have to take advantage of it.'
Send.

'She is so lucky to have you. Maybe we could go for a drink after work tomorrow night or something? You can tell me how amazing you are!!'

Send.

As Matt continued to exchange emails with Jodie, who was sitting merely a few feet away, his mobile bleeped.

'Hi sweetie. Can we take a rain check on 2nite? I'm havin 2 wrk late. I won't b in til late as im goin out 4 a drink with Betsy after. Cu when get in xx'

Matt read his text message, shaking his head, tutting.

He sat for some time before emailing Jodie.

'Hey, change of plan. If you fancy helping me out tonight with this extra work then I would be grateful and then maybe we could go for a bite to eat? My treat as a thank you for your overtime?'

Send.

'Yes that's great. I'd love to ☺ '

Send.

Matt continued with his work for the duration of the afternoon, until the staff left, leaving him alone with Jodie. She perched herself on the end of his desk, flicking her long blonde hair from side to side, gazing into his eyes.

'You are so attractive, Matt. I have to admit something to you.'

'What?' he asked, intrigued.

'I have liked you for ages but as you are my boss, and live with my other boss, I haven't dared tell anyone, as I guess I haven't dared admit it to myself,' she said firmly.

'Well, why now?'

'Because I just can't keep it to myself any longer.'

'But I'm your boss.'

'Yes, I know but you like me too, I think?'

'Well, to be honest, I haven't really thought about it,' he said, looking to the floor, fiddling with his tie.

'Well, think about it now,' she replied in a seductive voice, lunging herself towards him, showing off her cleavage. Matt, feeling extremely flattered but guilty, stood up, pretending to look out of the window in an attempt to distract himself. Jodie boldly stood up too, moving next to him and taking his hand in hers.

'Do you want me?' she whispered.

Matt flinched away, thinking deeply.

Jodie grabbed his hand once more, softly kissing him on the cheek before moving away.

'Come on, we have work to do.'

Jodie nodded.

Matt returned home at 9.50 p.m. to a dark and empty house. Alex had gone out to dinner with Betsy and their other work colleague, Sebastian, finally returning home at 11.35 p.m., much to his disapproval − he had ended the evening with Jodie early, feeling guilty, wanting to see Alex. He lay silent as Alex undressed, climbing into the warm bed beside him.

'Where have you been till this time?'

'Out with my workmates, I told you so. Are you going to moan about it?' she said sharply.

'I'm not going to moan. I just thought that I would come home early and see you. I was looking forward to having a nice romantic meal with you,' he said, kissing her cheek.

Feeling guilty, she turned to face him, kissing him. Matt responded, attempting to take things further, pushed off by Alex.

'You don't want me anymore, do you?' he asked bluntly.

'Oh, Matt, not this again; go to sleep.'

Matt sighed, feeling foolish.

'You still love her, don't you?'

Alex ignored him as her desperation to be with Hope overwhelmed her, concentrating her thoughts on her, mishearing his words as he spoke.'

'Are you listening?' he asked in annoyance.

'Hey, don't talk to me in that tone,' she replied.

'Well answer my fucking question then.'

'What fucking question?'

'About her and don't swear at me. I'm not the shit off your shoe. I demand you to respect me, even if you don't love nor want me.'

Alex touched his face, seeing his anger, realising the impact of her behaviour finally breaking him.

'I'm sorry for being so snappy all the time, and yes you do deserve respect. I just need to sort my head out that's all. Just bear with me.'

'For how long? I can't live this life for a moment longer.'

Hearing his words run through her body, overwhelming her, she began to fill up. She turned away from Matt and lay for hours wondering what to do, feeling so unhappy. Matt also tossed and turned long into the night.

As the light started to shine into their bedroom, Alex turned and cuddled into him.

'What are you doing tonight?' he asked

'I don't have any plans. I have quite a bit of work to do so I will probably do that. What about you?'

He paused for a few seconds, replying, 'Yes, I'm going out tonight with a friend for dinner.'

Matt sat waiting for his dining companion as his mobile bleeped.

'Hey Matt. How ru? U lukd so cute 2day. I cudn't take my eyes off u. Do u want 2 do dinner tomorrow nite? We can stay late & finish the P+D contract & then go 4 food, my treat'

As Matt read his message, about to reply, his companion arrived, gazing at him, smiling from ear to ear.

Chapter 51

Three weeks later

'So are you going to tell her, then?' she asked.

'Yes. I will go home and tell her now, it's over between us. It has been coming for a long time and I can't live with her any longer.'

'What will she say?'

'She won't care.'

'Surely she will be gutted. I dread to think what she will say. I bet she will go crazy when she knows it's me. I bet that's the end of me and her.'

'No. I will be giving her what she wants. She can finally go after her dreams.'

Not answering, she took his hand, staring into his eyes, desiring him.

'I will go home now and tell her. I don't know where I'm going to live as she will surely kick me out.'

'Will you tell her about us?'

'No. I don't think that's wise, do you?'

'No, but she will have to know eventually.'

'I know.'

She kissed him, making him feel special, giving him the confidence to end his troubled relationship once and for all.

Matt walked through the door, surprised to see Alex at home, happily preparing dinner, making his announcement awkward.

'Hey, sweetie, I thought that I would finish early and cook us something nice, make a change from you doing it all the time. Are you OK? You look tired.'

'I am tired. I haven't been sleeping very well these past few weeks so after tea I think I'll have an early night.'

'Surely not that early? I had hoped that we could have our dessert in our room,' she said, attempting to show enthusiasm, sensing his unhappiness.

'I'm tired,' he announced, going upstairs to get changed.

Dismissing his 'odd' behaviour, she continued making dinner.

They sat across the table eating, Matt looking uncomfortable, playing with his food with his fork.

'What's up with you?'

'I don't think we are working out. We are not the same anymore, are we? I was looking at our engagement photos the other day and we are not like we used to be, and we are drifting more and more. We live separate lives,' he blurted out.

Alex's stomach began to tie itself in knots as nerves engulfed her.

'What do you mean? Do you want to break up?' she asked softly.

'I don't want this anymore. I've had enough.' He spoke looking deep into her eyes.

'But I don't get it,' she said, dismayed.

'You don't want me and I have finally come to terms with that. I still love you but you have chipped away at me and now I can't take it for another day.'

'You haven't just decided this. There's someone else, isn't there?' she said, feeling her cheeks flush.

'No. I've told you. It's about us and no one else,' he responded, looking away from her.

Alex stood up, staring at him, becoming angered by the finality in his tone.

'So that's it, because you say so? What about when you begged me to stay, and I really loved someone else with my whole heart, and you went on at me to stay.'

'Yes, I know, and I'm sorry for that, but if you had really wanted her you would have gone regardless.'

'You liar, you begged me on your hands and knees, you went on at my mum and sister to change my mind and the more I fell in love with Hope, and didn't want you, the nicer you were to me, offering to tend to my every whim. You are pathetic,' she shrieked.

241

'Well, maybe I have been, but not anymore. I don't want this and so that's how it is,' he said coldly.

'You selfish bastard; I lost the one person that I truly loved to stay with you, and went through torture, because that's what it was like, especially on the holidays we had. I went to please you because I felt very guilty and didn't want to hurt you, but now you want to go, and tough shit for me whatever I say to you. If I beg are you going to stay then?' she asked sarcastically.

'No, I'm not. I have a new chance and I'm not blowing it. We are dead wood and so …'

Alex interrupted.

'We have been like this for ages but you would never have it. How many times did I try and tell you, but no, you just wouldn't hear of it, so what's changed? Who is she? I know you too well,' she screamed, leaning over the table towards him.

'It's nothing, just a few drinks and dinner after work. It's not about her, it's about us, you and me!'

'Who the fuck is she?'

Matt stared at Alex, nervous, deliberating his next move. Alex stood over him, goading him to admit what she sensed, with blazing eyes.

'Come on, Matt, don't be a wet fucker all your life,' she tormented him.

'Her name isn't important,' he murmured, dropping his head, closing his eyes.

'Just tell me!' she demanded.

Matt walked away, desperate not to disclose her name. Alex followed him, unrelenting.

'Tell me her name. Do I know her?'

Feeling increased nausea, he could not look her in the eye.

'Oh my God, it's not who I think it is, Matt, tell me it isn't,' she begged, feeling her knees starting to buckle.

Matt's tongue started to stick to the roof of his mouth, preventing him from speaking as he went to the kitchen and took some water from the fridge. Alex went after him, shaking.

'Who is it? I know her, don't I?'

Sensing her anger and frustration, scared, he said in a timid voice, barely legible, 'Yes, you know her. I'm sorry, Alex, it just happened. I don't want to hurt you.'

Swallowing, she closed her eyes, fighting back her tears. He approached her, touching her arm. She pulled away, continuing, 'Tell me who it is, I have a right to know. Tell me, for fuck's sake!'

He took a sip from the bottle, trying to hold himself together, desperate not to fall apart. He opened his mouth but no words came out, making his whole body freeze. Clenching her teeth together, she went next to him and knocked the bottle out of his hand, hurling it to the floor. He quickly picked it up, wiping away the water. He stood up and she glared at him. Feeling uneasy, he bowed his head in shame.

'Tell me who it is, Matt, please,' she pleaded

He nodded his head, walking away from her, mumbling a name under his breath.

Alex's hands trembled, terrified of who it might be.

Matt's heart raced at a rapid rate, becoming unwell. Alex went next to him, forcing him to look at her.

'Please tell me. I beg you.'

He closed his eyes, trying to prevent his body from shaking. Without looking at her, he said quietly, 'Jodie.'

'From work?' she asked, shocked.

'Yes'.

Unsure of how to feel nor react, she replied, 'How has that happened?'

He opened his eyes.

'Well, she really likes me. She is nice and …'

Jealous, Alex stepped in, snapping, 'And I'm nice too. I have stayed with you and tried so hard; you have no idea what it's like for me.'

'How hard it's been for you? Are you joking? You had an affair behind my back, and I know you still see her, and love her a lot. I am happy for you and her. Go after her and see if you can get her back. I'm setting you free, finally; be happy rather than sad,' he said harshly.

'I can't believe how unfeeling you are being because that stupid little girl has flicked her hair at you and flashed her knickers. How long has it been going on? This is where you have been when you have been coming in late, isn't it?'

'Well, not always,' he said with a mysterious tone.

'How long?' she shouted, picking up the plate of food, launching it at him in temper.

Matt ducked under the missile of food, which hit the wall behind him, as he attempted to restrain her.

'Get off me now,' she responded, freeing herself from his grip, watching food drip onto the floor from the wall.

'Don't be like this. I'm sorry but I know you don't want me. And she does. And you can pick that food off the wall. I have had enough of your temper, Alex. No more!'

He walked out of the kitchen and mounted the stairs, taking out a holdall from the cupboard. He went into the wardrobe and began tossing in items of clothing.

Alex stood in the kitchen, glaring at the food dripping from the wall, destroyed. Matt came into the kitchen with his holdall and said, 'OK, I'm going now. I will be back in a few days when you have calmed down to get some more things. Bye, Alex.' He turned, determined not to turn back and see her upset, willing himself out of the house. He got in the car and sped off the drive, wiping his eyes.

Alex collapsed on the floor, sobbing.

Soon after her mobile rang.

'Hi, Alex. Are you OK?' Emily asked.

Whimpering, she replied, 'He's left me. He's gone.'

'Gone? Gone where?' she asked, surprised.

'I don't know, but he's gone and I can't believe how cold and unfeeling he was with me.'

'I know, Alex, but you treated him so badly, and didn't deserve him.'

'Thanks, Emily. Kick a girl when she's down. How uncaring are you? In case you have forgotten, you are my sister, not his.'

'Yes, I know I am, and I love you, but you have been all over the place for so long now, and haven't been good to be around. He's a wonderful man and has not deserved what you have done to him. You would have left him ages ago if Hope hadn't got with this guy.'

'That's not true!'

'Well, where has Matt gone, and did he say why he's finally going? I can't believe it.'

'God, Emily, you sound like you are happy for him to have left me.'

Stuttering, feeling guilty for her harsh words, Emily responded with a more sympathetic tone. 'No, I'm not. Of course I care about you. But now he has ended it, saving you from the agony, then maybe you can get on with your life and be the real you.'

'What do you mean, the real me?' Alex demanded.

'Well, you know.'

'No, I don't know what you are talking about.'

'Well, that you can come out and admit who you are.'

Feeling embarrassed and uncomfortable, Alex lashed out, 'I'm not gay. I just don't think that Matt was the right one for me, that's all. I mean, he isn't the man I thought him to be, especially leaving me for another woman.'

Immediately the hairs stood up on Emily's neck and arms, feeling goose bumps all over her body.

Anxiously, she quizzed, 'What, you mean he's left you because he loves someone else, and wants to be with her?'

'Yes, Em, and I'm knocked sick.'

'Why? You didn't want him,' she retaliated.

'Well, it still hurts to leave me for someone else. I do care about him and never wanted to hurt him. This is why I stayed for so long; you know how he pulled at my heart strings. Now there is someone else, he's off. I'm gutted.'

Understanding her sister's devastation, Emily began to cry.

'Oh, I'm sorry, Alex. It is hard, but you didn't want him and if he is loved by another, then you have to let him go. You know deep down it is the decent thing to do.'

Realising her sister's harsh but true words, Alex wiped her face and stood up.

'I know, but I can't believe he's actually leaving me.'

'I know, but trust me, he will be really happy with this girl. I bet she really loves him.'

Puzzled, Alex agreed.

'Shall I come over later and we can talk about things?'

'No. I just want a bit of me time. And I don't want you ringing Matt either. Just leave him alone to be with her. He will have gone straight there, I'm certain.'

245

Startled, feeling her stomach tie itself in knots, Emily replied, 'What do you mean, gone to her, do you know who she is?'

'Yeah. That tart from work. He has been seeing her for a few weeks now.'

Shocked, Emily's mouth dried up, hanging up the phone, flabbergasted.

Alex took a deep breath and began to clean the food from the wall.

Chapter 52

One week later

'OK, Paul, we have one more job to go before the end of our shift,' he said, driving into the housing estate.

'Yes, Peter, I know, we could get a flyer if we get this done sharpish,' Paul replied, viewing the large houses with envy.

Paul and Peter got out of the van, scanning the front garden, wondering where the most suitable spot was.

'This looks nice and posh. I wonder where they are going to go from here,' Paul said.

Peter shrugged his shoulders, going to the back of the van, retrieving his spade. Paul followed, taking out the sales board.

Alex had taken some holidays, trying to evaluate her new life. She had used the week to go for walks along the beach and spend time at home, coming to terms with her two broken relationships.

Standing in the kitchen, tidying up, she started to hear a banging noise. At first she dismissed it, continuing with her chores. As the noise increased, she moved into the lounge, peering out of the window. To her astonishment she saw two men banging a sales board into her front lawn, making her feel sick. In a state of panic she ran outside.

'Excuse me. I think that you must have the wrong house?' Alex said anxiously.

Both men turned to face her, stopping their work.

'No, we have got the right address,' Paul said.

Alex walked towards the men.

'Can I see your paperwork then, please?'

Paul nodded, walking to the van, retrieving the documentation, handing it to Alex.

She scanned it very quickly, hoping that a mistake had been made, but to her horror the paperwork was correct.

She immediately ran into the house, slamming the front door, and rang the estate agents. The estate agent informed her that Mr. Harris had requested that the house be put on the market, and that the property had already been valued and photographs taken. Alex became very angry, realising Matt's deceit; he had told the estate agents she was out of the country on business to avoid having to get her signature on the sales agreement. She watched the sales board being erected, shaking in anger at Matt's deception and his clandestine activities, never having dreamt that he could behave in such an outrageous manner.

She fell back onto the couch, beginning to cry, bemused. After a while, she composed herself and reached for her phone, dialling the numbers with quaking fingers.

As she dialled his number, her hands began to tremble, and her teeth to chatter, unprecedented, as she had always maintained complete control with him.

'Hello,' he said.

'Hi. It's me.'

'Oh, hi. Are you OK?'

'No, I'm not. I never would have believed it had I not witnessed it with my own eyes and heard what the estate agents said. How could you, after all these years together?'

Matt began to stutter, startled by her discovery.

'Well, erm, I just thought ...'

Alex blurted, 'Are you stupid? How did you think that I wasn't going to find out when I would see the board, and then when people wanted to come for viewings? How dare you go behind my back and lie like that. I am so hurt by what you have done. I just can't get my head around it,' she shrieked.

'Well, I just thought that it would be quicker and easier if I sorted it as we have to move forward now and get the ball rolling.'

'But you could have told me. I had to see them come and put it up, and I didn't know anything about it. You need my say-so before decisions are made on our house. It is wrong what you have done. I could get it taken down and refuse to sell.'

'Well, no, you couldn't, because I will go and see a solicitor, and you will be made to sell. I am paying all the bills and will maintain the payments until it sells. It may take ages and so I thought the sooner the better.'

'But you have only been gone for one week. How cold is that, Matt? And where are you living?'

'Well, erm …'

Alex interrupted, 'With her?'

'Well, sort of,' he replied, stammering.

'What do you mean, sort of?'

'Well, yes, I am.'

'After one week? Are you mental? You hardly know her,' she shouted.

'Well, that's up to me, isn't it. You didn't want me, and treated me badly so I have gone, and am starting to rebuild my life. I have wasted so much time on us, and all that dead wood, and now I won't let the grass grow under my feet for a moment longer. I won't let you make me unhappy for another day,' he yelled.

Alex's took deep breaths, attempting to quash the lump in her throat, trying to retaliate. Silence fell.

'Alex, I don't want to hurt you but you have to understand why I have left you. Do you get it? I loved you so much, and I suppose …'

In a very timid voice, slouching into the couch, Alex asked, 'Do you still love me?'

Matt paused and then replied, 'I think I do, but you hurt me so much, I am not in love with you and I wouldn't come back.'

Alex nodded as a tear trickled down her face. Taking a deep breath, her mind wandered to Hope, realising she had to fight Matt back.

'Erm, so what are we going to do financially then?'

'Well, what do you mean? I guess we half the house profit and the little savings we have.'

'And what about the business? It's half mine,' she said sternly.

Matt sighed.

'Don't sigh, Matt. I helped build that business up, and you know it.'

'I know but we can't sell it, and I am not sure if I have the revenue to buy you out. It is doing very well though, so it would be a shame to sell what we have achieved.'

'I agree, but if you want half of the house, I want half of that. I am entitled, and now, as you seem to be doing, I have to think of me now, and put myself first.'

Silence fell as Matt pondered.

'Why don't I get the house profit and sign the business over to you? That sounds fair.'

Shaking his head, he replied, 'The business isn't worth as much as the house if I sold it.'

'No, but with your on-going client build-up, it soon will be and more. If not, I am still entitled to a cut in the profits and a wage as I am the other director. Up to you, Matt.'

'OK. Yes, we can do that. I will go to the solicitors and have the paperwork drawn up. I will have to go now. I will be in touch,' he said with an aloof manner, putting down the phone.

Alex threw herself onto the couch, bouncing as if she was a rubber ball, completely devastated by the prospect of this different life suddenly thrust upon her, causing her body to shiver, her teeth to chatter and her hands to tremble, as the idea of life, a life she had shared for almost nine years, without Matt began to sink in, accentuated by his callous attitude and seeming lack of love for her.

For hours she sat curled up on her couch thinking about him, and the precious memories of their life together, realising the pain she had caused him with Hope, wondering if this new life forced on her would be worth it. She felt numb as to how she would manage without him after all the years together. The more she thought, the more anxious and scared she became, her thoughts turning more and more to her father, and how much she wanted him to comfort her.

As darkness set in, Alex continued deliberating about her life, slumped on the couch. She analyzed Matt and Jodie's relationship, assuming that she had set out 'to get her boss', wondering whether it was him or his position that she was enraptured by. The more these thoughts swept over her, the more she philosophised about Hope and Marco, making her green with envy, barely able to hold a thought in her head about their intimacy. The more she attempted to dismiss these flashes in her mind, the more prominent they became, struggling to subdue the image of them together. Quickly, she forced her mind onto Matt and Jodie, lessening the pain she had suffered in stewing over Hope and Marco.

Chapter 53

Millie wandered around the shops searching for Benny's birthday present. She walked round and round the shops, checking her phone over and over again, making her sad. As she rummaged round, she heard shouting, looking up. To her astonishment she viewed a young, slim, attractive woman with a dark haired man, screaming at each other, creating an audience in the middle of the shop. He squalled at her, riving the items out of her hand, making her go bright red. He hurled obscenities at her, belittling her. Millie stood in the corner out of sight, watching everything, fascinated. The young woman looked at him with resentment, leaving him, marching out of the shop. He stood for a moment, expecting her to return, before leaving, going in the opposite direction. Millie followed the girl a few moments later, walking briskly to catch up with her. She walked behind her, seeing the girl go into a shop and try clothes on. She waited for her to come out of the shop, pretending to walk into her by accident.

'Hi there, I thought it was you. How are you?' Millie quizzed.

'Hi. Yes, I'm fine, thanks,' Hope replied.

'Are you having a spending spree?'

'Yes, I guess so. It cheers me up,' Hope said, trying to force a smile.

'Cheers you up? I thought that you were really happy? I hear you have got a boyfriend, and that you live with him.'

Hope's eyes began to dim as though the light switch had just been turned down, not replying.

Millie probed further.

'So what's he like, this Marco?'

Sensing Millie's probing, Hope snapped, 'He's lovely, and we have just moved into a new posh apartment. It's fab.'

Millie nodded.

'Oh, that sounds good. Have you heard about Alex?'

Hope's eyes widened, replying with an upbeat-toned voice, 'No, what about her?'

Smiling, Millie said, 'Well, her and Matt have finally split; the house is up for sale. He is with someone else.'

Hope's mouth gaped, unable to shut it. She stood dumfounded.

'Maybe you should give her a ring. She misses you, and still loves you very much.'

'No, she doesn't love me. If she did, she would not have been so nasty and told me never to contact her. I got sick of that. Marco left Katie weeks after meeting me. That's love. Alex never really loved me. I know she didn't.'

She lowered her head, fighting not to cry. Millie could see Hope's sadness, placing her hand on her shoulder.

'You are wrong, Hope. I think you still love her too and maybe it's time you met up and talked. She thinks of you, and talks about you all the time.'

'Look, it's over between us. We have both moved on. It's too late for us even if they are split up. I mean, if she loved me that much, why hasn't she told me, and been in touch? She isn't bothered enough. I have Marco now and I care a lot for him. He treats me well.'

'Yeah, right,' Millie mumbled under her breath.

Hope did not hear her. 'So is Alex OK on her own?'

'Why are you concerned?'

'I'm not really, well, I am, but I have someone else now and …'

Millie stepped in, 'You still love her don't you?'

Refusing to answer, Hope bowed her head, biting the inside of her lip.

'I'm going to have to go now. Tell Alex I was asking after her,' she said, walking off.

Dismissing Benny's present, Millie found a bench and rang Alex, excited about her news. Alex listened, desperate to text Hope, and hear her voice, but deciding to leave her alone, unsure of what to do. As she hung up the phone she decided to accept Mike's invite for a date.

Chapter 54

Christmas Day

As the sunlight shone into Alex's bedroom she lay motionless, dreading the day ahead. With sheer determination and willpower, she had battled with the hustle and bustle of the shops, buying her usual thoughtful gifts for her family and friends. Unenthusiastically, she had agreed to 'party nights' at her house over this festive period, before moving out in February the following year.

She had lost her spirit and sense of humour. Her face had become pale and gaunt as she had battled with the months of torture.

She reached over to her bedside table, switching on her mobile, hopeful of texts, staring at it for several seconds, willing it to beep with messages. She had four messages, from Betsy, Sebastian, Jessie and Emily, all wishing her a Merry Christmas, raising a slight smile as she lay back, feeling alone and empty. She reminisced about past Christmases with Matt, and the Christmases without her father, especially the first, deciding that nothing made her feel as depressed as she now felt.

As she lay there, the prospect of spending the day at her mother's with the rest of the family, a time she had always enjoyed, filled her with dread. She would prefer to remain at home, lying in bed feeling sorry for herself. She stared at the ceiling, coming to terms with this overwhelming sadness that exhausted her, her eyes filling with tears.

Some moments later she decided to get up, got dressed, had a coffee, and left the house, heading for her father's grave.

As she drove away from his graveside, she put on the radio, where Christmas songs played merrily. Unable to bear listening to them, she put on her love CD from Hope, which made her sob profusely, playing the same song over and over again. She drove along dreaming that one day they would be reunited, and that nothing would prevent their love, as she felt the powerful words from the songs absorbing into her veins. Suddenly she started to gain confidence in who she was, and what she wanted from her life, especially after her short dalliance with Mike.

She adjusted the volume, belting out the songs, lifting her dejection about the day ahead. The more she listened to it the more courage and self-belief she gained.

She arrived at her mother's and sat for a moment, gathering her thoughts.

She got out of her car, taking out her gifts, creating a faint smile. As she walked with her gifts, she knew that only she could seek happiness by choosing a new life, augmenting her determination.

Later that evening Alex returned home to an empty house and emptied her bags of presents. Again she glared at her phone, creating a sickness, despondent at the lack of response. After sorting out her gifts, she sat, aching to text Hope, but decided to telephone Millie, seeking, as always, her advice.

'Hi, Millie. Merry Christmas. How are you? Have you heard from Benny?'

'Hi, flower, same to you. Yes, he texted this morning and I was over the moon, but now I'm gutted, all alone, knowing that he's with her. It's a killer, eh?'

'Yes, but he will be thinking about you, I bet.'

'Mmmm, maybe. It still hurts, though. What about you – heard from her?'

'No.'

'You're joking? Matt hasn't texted even?'

'No, but I didn't really want him to. We have both moved on. I went to my dad's grave and admitted to being gay, and told him how much I love Hope. I seem to have been uplifted since.'

'Ah, Al, I'm pleased. Once you've accepted it then that's half the battle; now the hard part is getting her. She'll be back, I'm certain of it. Believe me, she is still so into you. He's just rebound. You watch her change once she gets bored with him, if she hasn't already. I've heard it all from Benny. Trust me. That girl's feelings were too strong, and the way she looked when I mentioned your name … it's till there, I'm certain.'

As Millie continued to speak, Alex's phone beeped. Eager to see who the message was from, she immediately went to the coffee table, retrieving it.

'Merry xmas Mb. 2+3 xxx'

As she read her message, tears of elation filled her eyes. In shock, she yelped, 'Oh my God, Mil, guess who has just texted me, and what she's said. I can't believe it. It has made my Christmas. I can't remember the last time she said it to me in our special way. It means even more. Oh God, I'm a jittering wreck, what will I say back?' she asked nervously, hands trembling.

'What the hell has she said?'

'That she loves me. You know, 2+3, and called me Mummy Bear too. God, Millie, what shall I do?'

'2+3. I can't remember why?'

'Oh, just our code for I love you in Italian so that no one would guess what it meant if they ever got hold of our phones.'

'Oh yes, I do recall you telling me that before. Anyway, text her back saying the same thing; I'm telling you, she's letting you know how she feels. You can get her back, I'm certain. I'm so pleased that she has texted, but to say that is very special, especially as she has not been in touch. But true love never dies. I told you she was trying to push you away and give herself time, forcing herself into him. Now you must go for her, and don't stop till you get her.'

'OK, Millie, I will. I need to go and compose what I'm going to write. I'll ring you later. Bye.'

Hanging up the phone, she stood composing her text, dancing around the room. Wanting to say so much but refraining, she decided that something short but meaningful would be the most suitable message.

'Merry xmas 2u bb. U hav made my day the best 1 ever. 2+3 2u more than u will eva kno!!!'

Send.

Within seconds a reply came back.

' ☺ mine 2. I mean it. I kno that I've been awful 2u but I'm gonna stop all that. We need 2 tlk I kno. I will ring u soon. Plse giv me time but I will n I wanna cu n hold u in my arms. Cu v. soon xxxx btw, I realy miss u more than u cud kno.'

Send.

As Alex read her message she ceased dancing and began to cry, quickly replying,

'Oh I fink I do kno as I'm missin u just as much. Can't wait 2cu. I will giv u time angel xxxxxx'

Send.

Alex sat down feeling her chest tighten. Suddenly, she fell to the floor on her knees, clasping her hands together, closing her eyes, whispering,

'Thank you, Dad, I knew that you would help me. Merry Christmas.'

Chapter 55

Two weeks later

'Hi, is that Millie?' a timid voice asked.

'Yes. Who's this?'

'It's me, Hope.'

'Oh, hello there. How are you? Did you have a nice Christmas?'

Hope paused.

'It was OK. What about you?'

'Oh, not very good, to be honest.'

'I need your help, please.'

'What the hell's up?'

'I don't know what to do. I wouldn't dare tell Alex or she'd go mad,' Hope confessed, her voice beginning to crack.

'What? You can tell me, and I will help, if I can.'

'Can I come and see you? But don't tell Alex, I beg you, or I won't tell you.'

'Yes, of course. When?' Millie said, concerned.

'Today, if you can make it? I will get my mum's car.'

'Have you passed your test?'

'Yes, I passed it three days ago, and I have been saving for a car, and I have put in for a few jobs …'

Millie interrupted, unconvinced that she was telling the truth.

'How come you haven't told Alex? I would have thought that would have been the first thing you would have done. You have been trying to pass it for years, and it would help you two so much.'

'I know, but I wanted it to be a surprise, and I'm amazed I did pass, because my head is battered right now. I can hardly think straight.'

'Well, Alex will be over the moon, and I mean elated.'

Hope went quiet for a moment, before continuing, 'So can I come and meet you in an hour's time? What about going to the coffee shop I used to work in?'

'Yes. I'll see you there, and don't worry, I will sort it out. Bye.'

'Bye.'

Millie sat deciding whether to inform Alex about their meeting, deliberating for some time, concluding that she would go alone and see what the problem was. She took her coat, heading off to meet Hope. She arrived at the coffee shop and saw Hope sitting alone in the far corner, drinking tea. She walked over to her, apprehensively. Hope wore a long mustard coat with a matching hat. She looked pale, but as attractive as ever, and her large eyes shone brightly.

'Hi. How are you? You look a bit worn out and tired, but you do look well.'

'Thanks. I haven't been sleeping too well. My eyes feel as heavy as lead,' Hope replied, lowering her head in shame.

'So what's up?' Millie asked, sitting opposite her.

'Oh God, Millie, what a mess.'

'What?'

Hope became anxious, unable to speak for a moment, closing her eyes in shame at her actions, confessing to the best friend of the woman she was still in love with.

Millie reached out and placed her hands on top of Hope's, feeling them trembling, gripping tighter.

'What is it? You can tell me.'

'I'm pregnant, Millie,' Hope said quietly.

'Oh my God,' Mille responded in disbelief.

'I know. What a mess. I don't know where to turn. I need help.'

'Have you told anyone?'

'Just my best mate, Macy, but I swore her to secrecy.'

'Well, firstly, I have to ask, why you are in such a state about it? If you are happy, and have been together a while now, then it should not freak you out so much,' Millie pointed out calmly.

'You know why.'

259

'Why?'

'Because of Alex and stuff.'

'OK, Hope, this is serious, and as you have asked for my help, I will have to say what I think, and ask you some very direct questions, and I want a true answer or you could end up ruining your whole life. I don't mean to be nasty but it has to be said,' she explained, raising her left hand.

Hope stared at her, agreeing.

'Right, first thing, are you still in love with Alex?'

'I don't know.'

'OK, do you miss her, and feel a pain inside because you ache to be with her?'

'Yes.'

'When you are with him do you wish it was her?'

'Yes, most of the time. No, in fact, all of the time.'

'Why won't you see her?'

'Because I'm scared.'

'Of what?'

'Not being able to let her go once I see her. It's too hard to look at her, and not kiss and hold her.'

'So you still fancy her, then?'

'Well, I guess so, but I haven't seen her for so long.'

'Trust me, if anything, you will want her more. She looks better than before so why wouldn't you?'

Hope shrugged her shoulders, taking a sip of her tea.

'You have pushed her away all this time, haven't you?'

'Yes, I guess so, but she won't want me. I know she will go back to him.'

'Listen to what I tell you. She loves you so much. You have no idea what she's gone through over you. Yes, she cares for him, and is very sad that they are over, as a break-up is very hard, especially after all the years they were together, but she is in so much pain over you, and loves you more than ever.'

'Really?'

'Yes, flower, trust what I say. She would be devastated if she knew that you were telling me that you're pregnant.'

'So why did she never leave him for me? And why was she so nasty to me, and told me that she didn't love me?'

'Well, let me ask you this. Why have you been awful to her now that you have a boyfriend? You have said you don't love her, and never did, and you love him more. You have torn strips off her. Is it to get her back?'

'No,' Hope snapped.

'So why?'

'I don't know.'

'Because you are pushing her away, and trying to be faithful to him.'

Hope dropped her head, nodding.

'I'm right, eh?'

'Yes,' Hope admitted faintly.

'And so why did she do it? She had him, and tried, just like you have. But you still love her, and didn't mean it, so it was the same for her. No, it isn't acceptable, and I used to tell her not to behave that way with you, but you two have always been under pressure. What you both need is time away to see if there is anything worth saving.'

'But what about Marco? He left Katie and Grace for me. I'd feel crap. We have a flat and a life.'

'But you are not happy. You have tried to bury your head in the sand and it has taken this to shake you up. You don't want his baby, do you?'

'No, I don't. He cares a lot for me but he can be awful to me and shout at me. He is quite controlling and I don't lust after him as I did Alex.'

'I'm sure you do, and Alex loved Matt, but she was never in love, and neither are you, or why would you be gutted to be having his child? Because then that would be you trapped for life, and you know that you love a woman. You never thought they would ever split, and so you went on the rebound, but you can't get her out of your head, can you? Despite how much you have tried.'

'No, I can't.'

'Be honest now, how much do you think about her?'

'All the time.'

'So, you haven't seen her for nine months, you live with another man, but you think of her, and want her all the time, yes? Do you think those are the feelings of someone who's over her?'

'No, I know that, and so that's why I texted her on Christmas Day, and why I really have been trying my best, and saving a bit too, for a car. But this happening has thrown me. I'm scared to have an abortion.'

'Don't have one. Keep it, and maybe you and Alex could bring it up.'

'No way. I would only want our child together. I don't want anyone else being a part of our lives. I want to have Alex's child,' she spoke, tapping her hand on the table.

'Well then, you have answered your own questions, Hope. I could bang both your heads together as you are both so sad, and yet you are both too stubborn. I don't know about kids, but in time, when you are happy as a proper couple, then maybe she will.'

'But what if she leaves me if I leave him for her? I couldn't cope with that at all. I'd be crushed for ever.'

'Why?'

This question prompted a flood of thoughts to fill Hope's head.

'I love her too much, and she hurts me so easily.'

'Doesn't your boyfriend do that to you too?'

'No, not really. We argue quite a bit at times but it doesn't get to me much. Not like she did.'

'That's called being in love.'

Realising Millie had spoken the truth, Hope felt a sense of relief overcome her, making her beam.

'Yeah. I guess so. I really love her, and I'm on edge a lot, wondering what she's up to, and who with. But what about Matt? And if I leave Marco, and he comes back for her?'

'Hope, she loves you, and would never take him back, but you have to leave Marco as you are not happy, not stay with him to hedge your bets, in case you and Alex don't work out. You and she have the love, so that's a big help. You are not in love with him.'

'No, not at all,' she said, screwing up her face, wincing.

'Yes, but you are missing the point. He doesn't make you feel like she does, does he?'

'No,' Hope replied, shaking her head, accepting her love for Alex.

'So I guess you are right to have an abortion.'

'Yes, I think so. A baby should be made out of love, and if we can't do it like that, the conventional way, then it should certainly be brought up with love, and I wouldn't have that with Marco around. I just want to do everything with Alex.'

Millie smiled, clutching Hope's hand in reassurance.

'You seem very sure of what you want?'

'I am. I have had lots of time to think, and think, and think some more. I am sure what I feel now and want.'

'And what about your parents and friends? Do you care what they will say when you are with a girl?'

'Not really. If I have her to be with I could go through whatever my family and friends say.'

'Good for you.'

'So what do I do now?'

'You need to set up the termination.'

'Yes, I know, but I'm scared,' she said, clenching onto the tabletop with her fingertips.'

'What of? You get put to sleep.'

'Do you?'

'Yes.'

'Will you come with me?'

'Of course. What about Alex, what will you tell her?'

'I don't know, but I want to have the abortion as soon as I can, and then talk with Alex about her and me, and then I will explain to him. The lease is up for renewal in two weeks so this is a great opportunity. We have been arguing a lot lately. But, oh God ...' Hope stopped talking, suddenly fearful, nibbling her fingernails.

'What?'

'I'm in a bit of debt. Marco wanted things for the flat, and I have to pay the rent, and he wanted nice things for Grace for Christmas, and he pays loads for her and for his car, so I have got a loan and stuff on my credit card. Alex will go mad.'

'Oh, right. How much?'

'Five grand loan and nine hundred on my card,' Hope confessed, shaking her head.

'Alex won't go mad. She loves you and will help you.'

'Really?' sounding surprised.

'Yes. Don't worry. Get an appointment with your doctor, and if that's what you want, then go for it, and I'll help you.'

'Thanks. I don't want to tell Alex just yet. Promise me you won't?'

'Oh, Hope, that's putting me in an awkward position as she would really want to know.'

'Yes, but I just need to sort it out in my head. It's a lot to deal with: leave him, get rid of the baby, and tell Alex I've lied, and do still want her. She'll go mad. My mum and dad will flip and I'll be disowned. I don't need Alex to get angry with me too as I have allowed myself to get pregnant to him. Please understand,' Hope begged.

Millie, realising Hope's situation and anxiety, agreed to her wishes, standing up and embracing her.

'Alright, I'm doing it for you both. I'm here for you, but please ring Alex and tell her you are missing her.'

'No, if I hear her voice I'll want to be with her, and will confess what is going on, and I need a clear head. I'll text her.'

'OK. Well, I'll give you a ring tomorrow to see how things are going. How far gone are you?'

'About eight weeks. I've been to the doc's and he's making an appointment at the hospital for me. Macy said that she'll come with me.'

'Oh, so you had already made your mind up, then?'

'I guess so.'

'What did Macy say?'

'Nothing; she thinks I'm too young, and jumped in too quick with him anyway, so she thinks I'm being sensible.'

'You are. You have really grown up. Alex will be so impressed.'

Hope beamed and her eyes lit up.

'You reckon?'

'Definitely!'

'I can't wait to see her. I'm so excited.'

'And she will be too. I'm going to have to go now. Where have you parked your car?'

'Just round the corner. I'm dying to tell Alex. When all this is over, I'll drive to her work. She'll be chuffed, I hope.'

'She will be,' Millie replied as they left the coffee shop, walking side by side until Hope reached her car.

'This is me,' she announced with joy, opening the car door.

Millie stood watching her start up the engine, seeing with her own eyes that she had passed her test, knowing how happy her friend would be.

'Good for you for passing. You take care. Alex will be so proud of you. Give me a call tomorrow, and text Alex,' Millie suggested nervously.

'I will,' Hope responded, driving away with confidence.

Millie waved, making her way back to her own car, relieved that Hope had finally admitted how she felt for Alex, knowing that she had been right all along, creating a smile.

Chapter 56

Ten days later

'Come on, we're going to be late,' Macy announced, standing at the bottom of the stairs.

'I'm coming. I'm just packing my bag,' Hope replied, packing her dressing gown into her holdall.

'OK.'

Hope came down the stairs, entering the lounge with her blue-and white holdall on her shoulder, looking withdrawn and very slender, as her black fitted trousers hung loosely around her legs and bottom.

'I'm ready.'

Macy turned to her friend and smiled.

'You all set, then?'

'Well, yes, I guess so,' Hope replied with uncertainty, in deep thought.

'Are you sure this is what you want? I mean, Marco thinks that you have just come back to stay at your mum's for a few days due to an argument. He doesn't know how serious it is.'

'What do you mean? I thought that you told me I was doing the right thing?' Hope snarled.

'Yes, I do, but I think that he could help you through it. He gets off scot-free, and it's not fair, all this secrecy. You should tell your mum too; she'd agree for you to get rid of it, I'm sure, as you argue all the time.'

'Mmm, well, I'm not so sure about that. She would rather have me with him than the alternative; she doesn't care that deep down she knows that I have been living a lie.'

Macy looked puzzled as they made their way to the car.

'What do you mean, live a lie? You are going back to Marco, aren't you?'

Hope shook her head.

'No, I don't think that I can. I must tell you something, but not today. I will, though.'

Intrigued, Macy glanced at her friend as she drove to the hospital.

'You are as deep as the ocean, you. Poor Marco – he thinks it's a lover's tiff, and you are aborting his child and never going back to him.'

'Don't say that. Anyway, let's change the subject,' Hope insisted, fidgeting.

Alex drove to work thinking about her beloved Hope, as she did every day, and about the message she had sent to her on Christmas Day, making her beam. Hope had been in touch via texting, but put off the idea of meeting up, making Alex suspect something was up. As she drove she felt edgy, mulling over the various texts sent over the past week, making her reach for her phone and ring Hope. As she listened to the ring tone, eventually reaching her voicemail, she became anxious, knowing that Hope never turned off her mobile.

She arrived at work extremely unsettled, incapable of concentrating on the day ahead.

She made various efforts to contact Hope, only to reach her voicemail over and over again. She explained her worries and fears on the matter to her work colleague, who agreed that it seemed rather 'odd' and suspicious, advising her to go and see her at the bar or at her flat, to ease her mind. Alex deliberated for a while before leaving the office, taking her mobile with her.

'Hi, Millie. Listen, will you do me a massive favour, please?'

'What's up?' Millie asked nervously.

'I've been trying to ring Hope for an hour and her voicemail is all I get, and she never has her phone off, so I am more suspicious now. I'm going to go to her work. Will you come with me?' Alex begged.

Millie sighed, hating lying, stuttering, 'Erm, I can't, not really, I have to go out and I've got no petrol at all. Just leave it and it will sort itself out. Honest. Trust me.'

Alex paused for a few seconds, sensing the uncomfortable tone in her best friend's voice.

'Millie, what the hell's going on?' she demanded.

'Oh God, Alex, I'll have to tell you as she will be like a worried rabbit there all alone.'

'What do you mean?'

'Look, she rang me about ten days ago, and said that she had something to tell me, and could I meet her, begging me not to tell you. I went and, well, wait till you hear this, she declared her love for you, and said how much she had tried to stop loving you but couldn't, and how she forced herself to want Marco, but didn't feel the way she had for you. Just as I told you ...'

Alex butted in, 'You are joking? Did you have to force it out of her or did she just tell you?' Her face became numb and her hands started shaking.

'A bit of both, but she wanted to tell me that she's pregnant and that ...'

Alex interrupted. 'Oh my God, no. Please God, no,' she cried.

'Calm down and listen. She realised that she didn't want to keep it, and asked for my advice. She wanted thinking time, and I just didn't want you to go on at her, and you would have, and so she asked me not to say anything. That's why her phone will be off as she's there now at the hospital.'

'What, having the abortion?'

'Yes.'

'Oh my God, bless her. Is she alone? Does he know?' she asked, fretting.

'Her mate was dropping her off, but she will have to go through the procedure alone, and then I said that I'd pick her up later, and she's going to stay with me tonight, just so that her mum doesn't ask any questions.'

'What do you mean, her mum? Don't you mean Marco?'

'No, she said that she had walked out on him the other day. She has left him and is back at her mum's.'

Stunned at this information, Alex felt her heart begin to race, causing a shortness of breath.

'Alex, what are you doing? I can hear you breathing very strangely. Are you OK?'

'No, I can't breathe too well. My heart is racing and missing beats. My chest is palpitating. I'm going to have to go into the office and phone Betsy to tell her that I'm going home. I can't take it. What time is her operation?'

'I'm not sure, she just said in the morning sometime.'

'I'm coming to yours now. Is that alright? I can't believe all of this. My head is going to burst. She loves me still, are you sure?' she asked, flapping.

'Yes. There's lots to tell you. She's tried so hard for you, and to show you how serious she is about you. I'll tell you when you get here. She's yours. I told you she would come back and want you.'

Incapable of fully comprehending what Millie had just declared, Alex could not think straight. She ended the call and headed back into the office to call Betsy and inform her that she had to go home.

'God, mate, you look ill. Your cheeks are all flushed. Are you OK?' Jessie asked.

'No. No, I'm not. It's Hope, she's pregnant and is having an abortion today, and wants me, and has left him,' she blurted, attempting to dial Betsy's phone number with shaking fingers.

'Calm down. Here, let me dial for you. You are in no fit state,' Jessie said, placing her hand over Alex's, helping to settle her shakes.

Alex nodded, collapsing on the chair as her heart and head raced.

Macy arrived at university guilt-ridden that she had left her friend all alone to abort her baby. She thought that Marco should be there with Hope, helping her through this very difficult time, instead of serving pints, flirting with the local girls, absolved of any responsibility for his girlfriend. These thoughts circled in her mind over and over, and she was able to absorb nothing whatsoever, staring at the blank paper in front of her in the lecture theatre.

Alex drove to Millie's house like a Formula One driver trying to win a Grand Prix, yearning to find out everything that had been going on with Hope over the past few days. Banging her car door hard, she ran to Millie's front door in anticipation.

'God, Millie, I'm a total wreck. For God's sake, tell me everything. I don't know how to feel but my chest feels like it's getting tighter and my head like it's going to explode. I'm so worried about Hope at that hospital. I'm like a blob of jelly,' she blabbed, entering Millie's house.

'I told you this would happen. I never expected the pregnancy, though, but I think that she knew all along how she felt, and so when she found that out, it made her realise for certain; perhaps it's a good thing.'

'I want to go and see her now. She will be so scared there all alone.'

'You can't, flower, they won't let anyone in the ward. She'll be fine, honest. She's a tough cookie, her, mind.'

Alex's eyes widened and she smiled with pride.

'I know, and that's why I love her with all of my heart. She makes me so proud.'

'Well, get this, she's passed her test ...'

Alex butted in, 'Wow, you are joking. When?' powerless to hide her excitement.

'Not long ago. She had it all planned that she would come and show you at work, but when all this happened it changed things. That's why she didn't want to talk to you until she had sorted it. She thought you would go mad and think less of her.'

'Don't be crazy. I love her. Wow, I'm so impressed that she's passed. I will buy her a car. Oh, Millie, I'm so happy that she still loves me, but I'm very concerned about the abortion. I hope that she's sure of what she is doing. I can't put any of this into words. I'm quite numb.'

Macy left her lecture without learning anything, worried about her friend, unsettled at the thought of her being all alone in hospital, feeling more and more annoyed that Hope had spared Marco the trauma of going through this with her. She glanced at her watch; it was 11.35 a.m. She knew that Hope would either have had the operation or would be about to have it. Without reason, she decided to telephone Marco.

'Hello?'

'Hi, is that Marco?'

'Yes.'

'Hi, it's Macy. I have something to tell you. Hope is pregnant and is at the hospital right now having an abortion,' she blabbed.

'What?' he replied, stunned.

'You heard. So what are you going to do, then?' she demanded.

'Why hasn't she told me? I want to know which hospital she's at and I'm going. Is it mine?'

'You selfish bastard, what do you take her for? She has been nothing but loyal to you and helped look after your kid. She has paid for the holidays, and the flat; she's in a load of debt, so how dare you say that?'

'Listen, don't ring me saying all this. I left my girlfriend for her and my little girl …'

Macy interrupted, 'Yes, but you weren't happy with her so it wasn't exactly that hard to do.'

'Well, this is not relevant right now. I want Hope back with me and so I'm going down to that hospital right now. Which one is it?'

'You'd better be nice to her. I've seen you having a go at her. Why do you think she left?'

'It was just an argument. Every couple has them. Please tell me the hospital.'

Macy gave him the information he required. He thanked her and left the bar immediately, heading for the hospital, enraged.

'So what time do you think she'll be ringing you?' Alex asked.

'I would say within an hour or two,' Millie replied, glancing at her watch.

'When she rings, then, don't tell her I'm here, and agree to go for her, but I will go instead, and then she can come back home with me.'

'Yes, I think that is the best thing to do.'

'Hello?' Belle said.

'It's me, Marco. Why haven't you tried to stop her? I thought you liked me and didn't approve of her leaving me?' Marco asked with an irate tone.

Confused, Belle replied, 'I don't know what you are talking about.'

'She didn't tell you, did she? The sly little bitch.'

'Sorry? What are you talking about?'

'Hope is pregnant; her friend just rang me and she is having an abortion today. I am on the way to stop her.'

Thinking quickly, Belle responded, 'Pregnant? Well, that's good. I can't believe she doesn't want kids. You have to stop her, Marco. Maybe we should come too. That way she might listen?'

'Yes, good idea. I am on the way now as she has to be stopped.'

'Yes, I agree. If she keeps it then ...' She paused, her mind wandering.

'Yes, sir, can I help?' the nurse asked.

'Yes, I want to see my girlfriend now. How dare she abort our baby without my knowledge,' Marco screamed.

'I'm sorry, sir, but you can't go through there,' she replied, refusing access to the ward doors.

'I want to see her now. I want to talk to her. It's my baby too.'

'Sir, I'm sorry, but if you don't calm down, I will have to ring security to come and have you removed. You will have to wait until she is discharged.'

'What do you mean? She will have got rid of it by then, though, won't she?'

'Take a seat. Can I get you a tea or a coffee? Give me her name and I may be able to give you more information.'

'No, thanks, I don't want a drink. She's called Hope Reagan.'

'Right, I will see what I can find out,' the nurse replied.

Marco nodded, sitting with clenched fists.

After a while the nurse came up to him and said, 'I'm sorry, but we cannot give any information except to say that Miss Reagan has not been discharged yet. When she is, she will come out of this area, and only then can you see her.'

'So when will that be, and does that mean she's got rid of it?'

'I don't know, sir. I cannot give out any information. It is up to the patient to inform you. You are welcome to sit here if you wish.'

'I will,' he retorted in an abrupt manner.

The nurse walked off. Marco stood up and began pacing the waiting room, looking at his watch every few minutes.

'God, Millie, there's your phone, quick, get it, is it Hope?' Alex asked, frantically searching for Millie's phone.

'OK, calm down. Yes, it's her. Hello?' Millie answered.

'Hi, it's me. I'm ready now if you can come, please?' Hope asked in a very weak tone.

'Yes, sure. How are you?'

'I'm so tired. I just want to get home.'

'No bother. I'll not be long.'

Millie hung up the phone.

'Right, she's ready. Good luck. Do you want me to come with you?'

'No. I'll be fine. Thanks, Millie,' Alex said, embracing her friend.

'Be gentle with her,' Millie urged as she stood waving at her front door.

Alex nodded, speeding off, heading for the hospital.

She drove as fast as she could with very mixed emotions: excitement, nerves and anxiety.

She arrived at the hospital and parked the car near the entrance.

Belle and David got out of the car and headed for the hospital in the opposite direction.

Alex walked in and gave Hope's name as well as hers to the nurse. Marco overheard Hope's name being mentioned and approached Alex; she recognised him immediately.

'Who are you? How do you know my girlfriend?' he demanded.

Alex's mouth became dry as her stomach churned.

'Erm...' she stuttered.

Marco glared at her before catching sight of Hope out of the corner of his eye, coming through the double doors. She moved slowly towards them, feeling very weak and tired, seeing both Marco and Alex standing before her, causing her to panic.

'Hope, my darling, what have you done? Why didn't you tell me? I would have stood by you. Come home and we can talk,' he said, reaching out for her hand.

Hope looked over his shoulder at Alex, realising that Millie had informed her. Uncertain what to do, she took Marco's hand, lowering her head, avoiding eye contact with Alex, standing frozen on the spot as her legs began to turn to jelly.

As they moved forward near the doors, the door burst open and in walked Hope's parents, looking angry. Immediately, Hope's stomach turned inside out; unable to move, she stood motionless, terrified. Her whole body shook, feeling Alex staring into her back, desperately wanting to go near her. Belle grabbed her hand, not seeing Alex behind her, shaking her head.

'Tell me you didn't do it, please, no!' Belle shrieked, worried.

Hope bowed her head, desperate to leave the hospital. She pulled her hand out of Marco's, standing still circled by her parents and Marco.

Marco faced her, frowning, unsure of her actions. Destroyed, Hope started to cry, feeling exhausted. Alex stood behind her, petrified of what to do, feeling her legs turn to jelly.

'Come on, let's get you home and we'll talk there. Who is she?' he asked, turning to face Alex, standing a few feet away, grabbing Hope's hand. Neither Hope nor Alex spoke as they stood transfixed on each other, scared how to react. Angry, Belle pushed past Hope, attacking Alex.

'I have fucking told you to stay away from her. Get out of here now or I will kill you!'

Shocked and bewildered, Hope's heart pounded so fast she thought she was having a heart attack, unable to move. The nurse stepped in, putting her hands in between them both, informing security. Knowing they were being watched, David pulled Belle away from Alex, calming her down. Marco stood dumfounded, clueless about what had just taken place. Alex did not fight back, moving away. She stood clenching her teeth together, motivating herself. She looked at a frail and scared Hope before her, knowing she had to take action. The nurse escorted everyone out of the building, aided by the security officer. Marco tugged at Hope's arm, desperate to get her into the car as quickly as possible. Belle and David followed, looking back, glaring at Alex, who stood still, unsure of what to do. She clenched her fists as she watched Hope being manipulated away from her, looking weak and too tired to fight back. Her mother walked close by, ushering her forward, eager for her to leave with Marco. Hope looked back at Alex, smiling.

'Don't look at that filthy bitch. She is no good for you. You have a life with Marco and he loves you,' Belle insisted as David nodded.

Marco stopped still, glaring at Hope.

'Who is this woman? What do you mean, forget about her?'

'It doesn't matter who she is; she is not important!' David shrieked.

Hope shook her head, devastated at her parents' behaviour, resenting them.

Alex closed her eyes in fear of what was to come, marching after them. She placed her hand on the back of Hope's shoulder, heart-sick.

'Don't go with him; come with me,' Alex begged with a trembling voice.

Hope looked relieved, staring at her, willing her to take her in her arms, as she pulled away from Marco.

'Who are you? Get away from my girl.'

'I'm not your girl,' Hope insisted.

Alex smiled, feeling bold and confident, refusing to be intimated by anyone any longer.

Belle was just about to lash out at Alex again as Alex caught her arm, grabbing it, startling and frightening Belle.

Pointing, and gritting her teeth together, she said calmly but forcefully, 'Don't you dare hit me. I have had it with you. I won't be bullied anymore; we love each other and if that makes us gay, then so be it. We are who we are. And if you would rather have her with him and saddled to a kid, than be with a woman, you are evil.'

Hope smiled, feeling loved that Alex had stood up to them, helping her gain confidence, sticking her chest out.

Belle stood speechless, turning to her husband for support, who shook his head in disgust. Marco looked bemused, grabbing

Hope, hurting her arm. Both David and Alex stepped in, dragging him off her.

'Who are you?' Marco demanded, pointing at Alex.

Pausing, she took a deep breath, determined to admit her feelings without feeling guilty or embarrassed.

'I am the person who loves Hope the most. I let her go once, and that was stupidity' – glaring at Hope's parents – 'but I will not let her go and be with you as she loves me, and I love her,' she admitted, fixing her stare on each of them in turn.

As Alex spoke, pride engulfed Hope, overwhelming her. Marco looked at Hope and her parents, who lowered their heads, looking disgusted. Hope moved close to Alex, taking her hand.

'Are you a fucking lesbian, then?' he demanded, ogling Hope.

Hope paused, looking at Alex, boldly squeezing her hand tighter.

'Answer, then!' he shouted.

'Yes, if that's what you want to call me. I love this woman, and have for years,' she replied steadfastly.

'And I love her too. I would give my life to be with her,' Alex added in support, tightening her grip.

'You little bitch. How could you? I won't allow this to happen. You love me. You live with me,' he screamed.

'I don't love you, and I moved out, in case you have forgotten. I don't want to fight in the car park. And I don't want your kids either. I don't want to hurt you but I want to be truly happy. I have tried, Marco, but I can't. I know it's difficult to get your head around right now, but I have been living a lie and it has to stop now,' Hope said, her eyes dimming.

'I cannot believe it. You bitch,' he said, pushing Hope's shoulder.

'Right, that's enough. I know that you are upset, and shocked too, but now is not the right time for you to hurl insults at her. And don't dare touch her. Come on, angel, let's get you home,' Alex said calmly, moving away.

'You shut your mouth, you vile, dirty dyke,' Marco bellowed.

Feeling cut to the quick, but determined to carry through her actions, Alex responded, clutching Hope's hand tighter, marching to the car. 'Think what you like, you narrow-minded, ignorant man. Get in the twenty-first century; being gay isn't a disease or a crime. You are as bad as those two, who don't want their daughter to be happy. They will do, and have done, anything to get her away from me. Well no more. I love her and won't allow this to go on.'

She threw Hope's bag in the back of the car, gripping her hand as Hope sat bewildered with what had just happened. Marco shouted obscenities that neither the girls could hear as the car muffled out the sound. Belle turned to David and said, 'Come on, let's go; I will never accept them two and she will never be welcome in our house, but what can we do?'

David agreed, walking to their car.

Alex held Hope's hand throughout the car journey to her house without any dialogue between them. They arrived on her drive. Alex stopped the car, took off her seat belt and turned to face Hope.

'Are you OK, Baby Bear?' she asked, gently running her fingers on Hope's withdrawn face.

'I feel a bit numb, to be honest. My head is spinning. I don't feel like talking too much. Will you just hold me?' she asked quietly.

Alex nodded, playing with Hope's hair.

'Come on, let's get you in here where it's all warm,' she suggested, getting out of the car, retrieving Hope's bag.

As the girls entered the house, Hope collapsed on the couch. Alex took off her shoes and coat for her, wrapping her dressing gown around her slender body, getting her a glass of water.

'Thank you. Will you turn off my phone, please? I can't bear to talk to anyone today. I will face it all tomorrow.'

'Sure, angel.'

Hope smiled at Alex, tired but relieved, as the sparkle in her eyes shone through. Alex returned her smile, placing the glass on the floor next to her.

'Lie next to me. I just want you to hold me, and not let go ever,' Hope begged.

Alex did as she asked, cuddling into her back as they lay locked together, spooning.

'I'm sorry for all this pain I've caused you. I have behaved so immaturely,' Hope said faintly.

'Don't be sorry for anything. It has all happened for a reason. We have both had to go through the pain to prove our love, and if you want the truth, love has to be tested. You are the person I admire the most, as well as my dad, that is. To do all this alone shows how strong you are. I'm so proud of you, and honoured that you love me this much. I am a different person to when we were last together. It will all be different now, I promise.'

Hope faced her, gazing into her eyes with devotion.

'Promise me something?' she asked.

'What?'

'Never leave me,' Hope whispered.

Alex's face beamed.

'I promise,' she replied, kissing Hope on the cheek.

Hope smiled back, placing her head on Alex's chest, closing her eyes.

'I love you more than words can describe,' she admitted.

'Me too; I will never let you down again,' Alex said heartfelt.

Chapter 57

The following morning both girls woke up simultaneously, gazing at one another, joyful, lying side by side, their bodies locked together. They lay silent, hugging tightly, for some time, savouring the moment of finally being together after so long.

'How are you feeling today?' Alex whispered.

'One hundred times better for being here with you,' Hope said softly.

'Oh, that's so sweet.'

Hope purred, embracing her more tightly as she spoke.

'It all starts from now, then, eh?'

'Yes, I guess so. We will have to face the crew,' Alex answered nervously.

'I'm scared. I feel so crap about Marco. Will he be OK?'

'I don't know, but if you are not certain …'

Hope interrupted.

'No, I am. I want you. I just mean that it's going to be tough. He wanted another child, that's all, and I suppose …'

Alex stepped in, 'I know what you are going to say. I know one day you will probably want children.'

Hope nodded, unsure what to say, still numb about the abortion.

'Don't worry, it will all work out for us, you know.'

Hope bowed her head, unconvinced. Realising Hope's uncertainty, Alex turned to face her, gripping her hand.

'Don't worry, everything will be fine; trust me!'

'I hope so. I feel terrible that I have aborted my own child but …'

Alex stepped in, 'I know you do, angel,' she said, kissing Hope's soft cheek.

'I just want to have kids with you and not for him to be in my life. Do you think I did the right thing? Am I a bad person?' she asked, getting tearful.

Alex sat up, leaning over Hope, stroking her left cheek.

'No, Baby, you are a wonderful person. I adore you, and if you made the decision to abort the baby then it was right and I support you.'

Hope smiled, feeling reassured, kissing Alex softly. Suddenly she pulled away, pondering.

'Oh, I've just thought, where am I going to live?'

'Well, with me silly.'

'I know, but I can't move in here, can I? You are moving out in a few weeks.'

'Yes, but I have got a flat sorted that I'm going to rent while I look for somewhere. I'm putting in for a new job with more money, so if I get that, then I can buy somewhere. I will get a lot from this house but I want to save some too. What about your job?'

'Well, I have been looking, and I have put in for two jobs, both with more money, so fingers crossed. And now that I've passed my test, it should be better.'

'Yes. You can stay here with me until I get the flat sorted and then you can move in with me. Your mum and dad are going to go wild. I'm dreading that. And what about your friends?'

'I know. It's going to be awful but I've done the hardest part. I love my family very much, but I love a woman, and that has to be told. What about you and your mum?'

'Yes, I know, but if you can do it then so can I. I take a lot of inspiration and courage from you. You make me want to be a better person, and you give me so much strength from what you do.'

'Oh, wow. You are so nice. I am so lucky to have got you back,' Hope confessed, as her huge eyes sparkled.

'Yes, you are definitely lucky to have me, that's for sure,' Alex joked.

Hope giggled.

'You make me laugh. I have missed that humour more than I thought I would. I missed everything.'

'I have to know something,' Alex said.

'What?'

'Did you mean what you said about your sex life with him? Because Matt didn't come close to how you made me feel,' Alex said, shaking her head.

Hope unlocked her body, staring at Alex.

'If I'm being honest, and let's face it, I have lied all the time to convince myself, then no, it wasn't the same at all. The sex was OK at first; I put up with it, but he couldn't make me lust after him, nor give me that electricity when he touched even my hand as you gave me, even right from the start with him. Looking at you makes my whole body go numb, and when you touch me, well, I cannot describe it.'

Alex's heart began to flutter, listening to her beloved Hope, transfixed on her.

The girls lay locked in each other's arms, with their legs wrapped around each other, content. All of a sudden, Hope began to fidget, seemingly anxious.

'Why were you so nasty to me? It broke my heart. You said some cruel things and one thing that hurts the most is would you have ever left him, had he not left you?' Hope said quietly.

Alex paused before sitting up, staring at Hope, taking her hand tightly.

'Oh, Baby Bear, I'm sorry. I know I gave that impression but it was, like I've said, to push you away. You are all I want. I know that I was all over the place but if you really want the truth, I was afraid of who I am.'

Surprised, Hope frowned.

'I don't get what you mean.'

'I was ashamed of who I was. I couldn't bring myself to declare my love for a girl so I hid behind Matt. And yes, I would have left him. He put so much emotional pressure on me; that was so hard but I was getting braver and braver with who I knew I was, and when I was ready, I would have left him. Had he not gone, I would have. I was at the end of my tether. Once he left, I had breathing space to realise things. I hope you can forgive me,' she begged, squeezing Hope's hand tighter.

Hope's heart began to melt as her stomach did somersaults. Her face brimmed.

'Of course I can forgive you. I do forgive you. I wasn't perfect either. But you promise you won't ...' she paused, that you won't ...'

Alex leaned forward, kissing her softly, whispering, 'No, don't worry, I will never ever go back to him. I'm yours for ever. I lost you once, I won't again. And your family will not break us either!'

'I know. I will handle them. They seem to hate you but I won't let them be awful like my mum was at the hospital.'

'Yeah, and the rest of the times,' Alex mumbled under her breath.

'What did you say?'

'Oh nothing, angel, it's unimportant now.'

'Your mum, dad, and friends, and mine, may not accept us at first, or never in your parents narrow-minded thinking mode, but when they see that we are very much in love, and have come all this way, they may come around. I have enough money to keep us going while you look for a job, and I won't pressure you to do certain jobs. You be what you want to be. I couldn't love you any more no matter what you do. I mean this,' Alex said with a sparkle in her eyes.

'What about Matt, though? I'm scared!'

'What of?'

'Of you leaving me for him. He can give you so much more than …'

Alex cut in, 'No, don't finish off that sentence. It's not about money or even security anymore. I pissed about for three years, toying with the prospect of loving you, with more passion, and spark, than I did this good man, who doted on me and gave me everything, and that was very hard to accept. He is the normal, accepted life, and I tried and tried to do it, but I couldn't. I came to realise after you left me that we were ruined, and had been the minute I fell in love with you. I was falling deeper and deeper with you, without knowing. I guess all my friends, and Matt, could see it, but I couldn't.'

'So why were you so nasty to me, and why did you say such hurtful things? It killed me, and so I went to Marco to feel wanted.'

Alex dragged Hope's slender body next to her, placing her head on Hope's chest.

'Well, to be honest, it was the triangle we were in. I would resent you, as it felt weird to me, and then with the prejudice I had to endure, it made me lash out at you. I knew you would feel rejected, and try to either ease your pain or get at me, to hurt me, by lying, and this would drive me crazy, and help me push myself away from you, as I could never prove it, given the secrecy we had to maintain. Can't you get that?'

Hope lifted her head up, staring into Alex's eyes.

'Yes, I can now, but I couldn't at the time. For so long I thought that you didn't care, and so I would try hard to make you want me more, by lying, when in actual fact, if I'd just got my act together, and supported you more with Matt, you would have loved and respected me more, and then I would have given you the security and confidence to leave him. I'm sorry for being so infantile,' she explained, clenching Alex.

'I know, but it was meant to happen. I'm pleased in a way because I wasn't ready to accept who I am. That took a while'.

Hope agreed, kissing Alex on the side of her neck as she snuggled into Alex's naked body.

'What do you mean, though, by prejudices?'

Alex paused for a few seconds, squeezing Hope harder.

'Oh, nothing. I guess I mean you have to feel the shit to feel the benefit. If it had been too easy, we'd have never known how strong our love is, nor appreciated it when it came back. I have passed all the tests, and so I'm sure.'

As a shiver went down her spine, Hope stroked Alex's face.

'You mean that, I can tell!'

'Yes, I mean it!'

Hope nodded, accepting what Alex had said, kissing her softly on the lips.

'I really, really love you,' Alex said, reciprocating, lingering her lips onto Hope's lips.

Hope purred, grinning from ear to ear.

'Shall we get up and check your phone to see what has been said?' Alex asked.

Hope covered her face with the bedcover.

'Oh God, I daren't put it on, Mummy Bear,' she said, hiding away. Alex put her head under the covers, kissing Hope's cheeks over and over.

'Come on, Baby Bear, be brave. I'm here to protect you with all my might,' she joked, attempting to ease Hope's anxiety.

Hope looked deeply into her eyes.

'I fucking love you,' she whispered.

Alex purred.

'Come on, we have got to face it all some time. Before we can decide what to do, we have to know what to face first,' she said, getting out of bed, retrieving Hope's phone from her bag, pretending not to illustrate her fear.

She switched it on with trembling fingers while Hope lay fearful under the bedcovers. Within a few seconds it began bleeping over and over again as she passed the phone to Hope. Refusing to take it, Hope threw it on the bed.

'You have to just face it,' Alex said.

'You read them for me,' she replied timidly.

Alex sighed. She took the phone and began reading the messages. Marco had texted, telling her how disgusting he thought it was, her friend Macy and a work colleague told her that she wasn't normal, and her mother had texted to say that she was going to be killed the minute she set foot through the door. The more she read, the more sick she felt, from the pit of her stomach. Demented, she listened to three voicemails from Marco, Katie and her father, all being very unpleasant, deleting them as soon as she heard the harsh words spoken by people who were meant to 'love' Hope. She could not understand the unacceptable obscenities from Marco and Hope's father. Her chin dropped.

'So what are they saying? Anyway, I don't want to know, to be honest, who has contacted me.'

'Marco, Katie, Macy, your mum and dad, and some girl from work, who are all pathetic.'

'So he must have told everyone. Great!'

Alex got back in the bed, holding Hope very close.

'It will be fine. I will protect you. I know it will be tough for us but we'll get through it. I'm strong and will be your rock too, angel. Don't worry,' she said with a reassuring tone, kissing her forehead tenderly.

Hope looked at Alex, seeing her eyes sparkle, making her feel better, able to raise a slight smile. Suddenly her phone rang, causing Hope to jump in sheer panic.

'Oh my God, who is that?' she yelped, searching for her phone.

'It's your sister.'

Hope took the phone, gulping with fear, inhaling before answering.

'Hello?'

'Hi, Hope. It's me. Where are you? Are you with that lady?'

'That lady ... do you mean Alex?'

'Yes. I wasn't sure what you called her. My mum didn't say her name, sorry.'

'Oh, OK. Have you been told to ring me to get me to come home, because I'm not going to, and you can all hurl abuse at us, but it won't matter,' she shouted.

'No, I rang to see how you are and where you were. Marco has been round shouting his mouth off. I'm pleased you have left him.'

'What has he been saying?'

'Just that you are a horrible dyke, and how you took him for a mug, and how he is disgusted that he left Grace with you. He is very nasty and bitter towards you. He said that if you dare come near his daughter, he'll get the police. Dad kicked him out in the end and told him that you are better without him. He said that you have to come and get your stuff or he will put it in the street, and that you'd better leave your key.'

As Hope listened, her heart began to fill with sadness that the man she had cared for, and who she had lived with, could be so callous and heartless towards her. Viewing her sadness and pained eyes, Alex left the room, allowing her to deal with her feelings in private.

Hope's eyes welled with tears and she struggled to speak.

'Well, I will come over now as he will be at work. Will you ask Dad if he will come with me?'

'Right, hold on. I will go and ask him for you.'

Hope sat waiting for his response.

'Hi, Hope. He said that it was your mess, and that you have to clear it up, and you should think before you do stuff. I'm sorry, but you know what he's like. I think that if you are gay, and are happy, then it is fine. I am here for you, and if anyone says anything to me, then I will go mad. It's your life so live it your way. We are who we are.'

'Thanks, sis. So do Mum and Dad not want me back, either to get my stuff, or talk to them?'

'Just come over and they will talk to you.'

'OK, well, bye, then.'

'Bye.'

Hope sat staring at the phone, plucking up the courage to phone Marco, eventually making the call.

'Hello, what do you want?' he answered with aggression.

'Just for you to stop being nasty to me. I want to come and talk to you, and get my stuff, in a nice way.'

'Do you now?'

'Yes. I can understand that you're upset but …'

He butted in, 'Upset, you stupid, filthy dyke; you lied to me all along. How long have you been fucking her behind my back?'

Hope began to tremble.

'It's not like that. Why are you being so horrible? I can't help that I love a girl, and neither can she. I never cheated on you with her. I wouldn't. I do still care about you,' she replied in a quaking voice.

'Don't you ever say that you care for me. I left my family for a lesbian; how daft am I?'

'But I didn't ask you to leave. Did I? You wanted to.'

'Yes, because I wanted you.'

'But you didn't love me, you hardly knew me that well, so…'

He interrupted, 'So what? I want you out of my life for ever. I don't love you. You revolt me.'

Hope began to cry.

'Marco, why are you being so awful?' she whimpered.

'What the fuck do you expect? You aborted my baby, and then say you are gay, and love another woman, and always have. So what was I? A game to get her jealous?' he asked angrily.

'No. It wasn't like that.'

286

'Well, you must have been with her for a bit to feel that way. I could see it in both of your faces, and that you had known each other for a while, so when?'

Hope stammered, 'I was seeing her for a couple of years before I started seeing you. I met you and finished with her.'

'Why?'

'It's a long story.'

'So is she gay, then, too?'

'She had a boyfriend, they were getting married ...'

He stepped in, 'So you came along and broke them up too?'

'I didn't break you and Katie up. You didn't want her, and that had nothing to do with me. I do care for you, and have tried so hard, but I couldn't stop loving her.'

'So you have lived this secret and lied to me all this time? It makes it worse.'

'Not really. I have not lied about anything. You didn't ask me,' she murmured.

'Well, I want you out and there is no way you can work here. I will pay you for the month, and that's only as I have to, as it is the law. I will give you a reference but I don't want you to set foot in the bar again. Leave your key and I will get stuff for you to sign for the tenancy agreement and that's it,' he said harshly.

'What, just like that?'

'Yes, just like that.'

'What about our photos and stuff like that, and the things I bought for the flat?'

'What about them? I will need them here. I have put all the photos in the bin. They are lies.'

'They are not. We had some special times and I will always remember them.'

'Well, I won't. If you come later today or tomorrow I will have sorted stuff out, and have it ready for you to sign, and then you are out of my life. I will text you when it's done and then I never want you to text me again,' he retorted, hanging up.

Hope sat on the bed crying. Alex entered the room, bringing her a cup of tea.

'Here, have this. I know it is hard but I had all this with Matt and we had been together for so long. He's hurting, and is bitter at the moment, so try and take a lot of what he says with a pinch of salt – he won't mean it. He cares for you,' Alex explained, putting her arm around her shoulders.

'He wants nothing more to do with me and says that I cannot go back to the bar ever. How nasty is that?' she said, as tears fell down her cheeks.

'I know it's very hard when they turn nasty, but do you really want to go back to the bar? Sometimes it's better to just move on. I have had to do that with Matt, and we had such a closeness, but it's the right thing to do I think. It's too hard for them.'

Hope nodded, gazing at her beloved.

'I have an idea. I think that we need it,' Alex expressed, tapping her finger over her lips.

'What?'

'Well, I saw this promotion the other day on the net for a holiday to New York. I really want to take you. I think we should go and get away for a while, get to rediscover ourselves, and each other. What do you think?'

'Wow, a trip to New York! Oh, yes, I would love to be going away with you, especially there. How posh. It's my dream place.'

Suddenly her chin dropped, guilt evident in her eyes.

'What's up?'

'I have got something to tell you and I'm so ashamed. I ran up debts for the holidays and lifestyle we lived, and now he won't even let me have the things I bought. But anyway, I have no money – well, apart from a bit I saved for a car – to bring to us, and no job now either …'

Alex grabbed Hope's hand, squeezing it tightly, fondly looking into her eyes.

'I know you have some, Millie told me, and it's not that big of a deal, I will sort it, and I know about the job, but you are a very intelligent girl, and will get work. I will help you to be who you want to be. That's what love is all about. I know that now. You take the rough with the smooth. I hope that I'll get another job, and I'm getting quite a bit from the sale of this house in a few weeks, so I am going to save it all and then buy something smaller. I will be able to keep some savings to help you out too. It's OK, I have enough to make us comfortable,' she said reassuringly, rubbing Hope's arm with the back of her hand.

'But I'm worried that I can't give you the lifestyle he could.'

Alex shook her head, tutting.

'You are very silly, Hope. It isn't about money. Yes, we had it good but I was unhappy, and now all I want is for us to live comfortably. It will be good to share what I do have with you and that means more to me than anything. No money can make you love them. I learnt the hard way,' she said, rubbing Hope's cheek.

'You really do love me, don't you?'

'Yes, but I love the tough Hope who will fight hard to get what she wants, and so you have to go and see your mum and dad, and then get your stuff from Marco, and sign whatever you need to. We can go away after all that on our romantic trip to recharge the batteries, before my move, then come back and get on with our lives. It will be a new, fresh start for us.'

'I can't wait to be with you. I want to be with you for the rest of my life,' Hope said, leaning forward, kissing Alex passionately.

Chapter 58

Hope stood outside the door, trembling in fear, terrified to turn the handle and go inside. She could hear her mother's voice in the lounge, making her feel worse. She retched, her stomach cramping severely, as she stood there for what seemed like an eternity. Eventually, she placed her hand on the gold handle, slowly opening the door to the lounge, where her parents and sister sat watching TV.

Immediately they stared at her; her parents gave her a very disapproving look while her sister smiled in admiration of her bravery.

Hope stood almost frozen to the spot in the doorway, trying to speak, but words failing her.

With a look of disgust her mother spoke.

'So you finally show up, then?'

'Yes, I thought that I should,' Hope admitted in a trembling voice.

'I guess you will want your clothes, then?' David asked.

'Well, yes, if that's OK?' she asked timidly.

'Well, they are your clothes after all, so go and get them, and then you can be on your way,' Belle remarked without compassion.

'But I want to explain stuff to you both first and let you know where I'm living ...'

Belle interrupted, 'We know where you are living, with that disgusting bitch. If I ever get my hands on her, I'll kill her.'

'Why, Mum? That's awful. You made her, so if she's gay then it's your fault,' Amber said.

'Shut up,' Belle said sharply.

'I knew you would be like this so I will just get my stuff and go. If you are not willing to listen then I'm not going to stand here and be abused, nor Alex either. You don't even know her. She's a very good person and really loves me. Surely you want me to be happy?' she queried, perching on the arm of the chair next to her sister, quaking in her shoes.

'It's not right. And to abort a baby? How did we bring these up, Belle?' David said, looking at his wife.

Belle shook her head.

'I mean, the way you treated Marco is terrible; no wonder he hates you,' Belle commented.

Hope lowered her head in shame as Amber rubbed her shoulder.

'Don't listen to them. You weren't happy, but you did try to love him and make him happy. I admire you as you are following your heart and being brave. You knew what these two are like' – she pointed to her parents – 'and how un-accepting they would be, and what Marco would be like with you, and so it would have been so much easier to keep that life, but you are strong, and brave enough to do it. It's the norm now.'

'It's not the norm. The norm, Amber, is to get married and have kids, not cavort with a woman a lot older than you,' Belle snapped.

'Marco is older than me and you never went on like this,' Hope screamed.

'No, but we weren't over the moon about it. They are both far too old for you. You are going to ruin your life,' David said, tutting, pulling his face.

'But I think that if I had had Marco's child then that would have ruined my life, can't you see that?'

'Well, we will never accept her, and so you can do what you like. You are old enough now, but we won't be a part of your life,' David said.

Belle glared at him, as did the two girls, disapproving of his words.

Tears began to well in Hope's eyes. She sat in silence, feeling sick to her stomach.

'Well, your dad doesn't mean that. We do want you in our lives, it's just that she's not welcome here, and we will not come to your house either. Speaking of living arrangements, what's happening? I hear she has split with her fiancé, so where are you living?' Belle asked.

'We are living in her house, but it's sold and so we are going to rent this lovely flat while we look for a house.'

'So who is paying for you? You don't even have a job,' David quizzed.

'Alex is paying. I am looking for a job. I have an interview as a receptionist at a school Alex knows.'

'She must have money if she can pay for a posh flat, and keep you,' Belle said.

'Well, she has a good job and her and Matt had their own IT business, so she got the house and he got the business.'

'So you have a rich girlfriend?' Amber joked.

'Ugh, don't say that word in here. It's just turned my stomach,' Belle explained.

Hope's eyes became heavy, emphasising her pain, causing a tear to fall onto her pale cheeks.

'I'm not a freak, Mum. I love Alex. She's a very nice person who will look after me and me her. You would like her if you weren't so much of a homophobe. We can't help who we are but I'm not ashamed. She means everything to me. I know I have lied to you, as you threatened me before …'

David butted in, 'Yes, you were told and you betrayed us. How can we forgive you? And she's got some nerve as well.'

Belle glared at David, making Hope suspicious.

'What do you mean by that?'

Belle shook her head, fixing her eyes on David.

'Well, just that she …'

Belle stepped in, 'That she had the nerve to come to the hospital and show us all up.'

David bowed his head as Hope stared at her mother, suspicious.

'Yes, and that she dared to keep it a secret knowing she shouldn't.'

'Well I'm not a child and I wasn't then. I loved her, and due to your narrow-mindedness, you wouldn't approve, we had to do it in secret …'

Belle cut in, 'But it wasn't right, she had a fiancé. I bet she broke his heart too.'

'But she wasn't happy. No, she wasn't proud of what she did to him, but now he has someone else, and says that he's happy, and so why should we both be miserable, and me hurt Marco, just to please everyone else? When I found out that I was pregnant, I had to get rid of it. No, I'm not proud to have done that, but I would be living a lie, and what life would that have been for the baby? Would you have wanted that, then, just so I was "normal"? It's pathetic.' Hope spoke bravely, standing up. Belle and David shook their heads, refusing to accept her explanation.

'I came here today to explain to you what was happening and where I live. I will give you my address when we move, as I'm going to New York for a few days in two day's time, so that we can have a break and sort ourselves out, and if you want to visit me, you can, but at least you know where I am. Alex says that you are welcome any time. She has a good career and is very intelligent. If you weren't so stubborn, you'd like her. I won't let you take my sexuality out on her. She has enough problems ...'

David interrupted, 'Why, do her parents hate her being a dyke too?'

Hope's face became angry, and she started pacing up and down.

'Don't say that word, it's awful. If you must know, her dad is dead, and he idolised her, so I'm sure he'd just want her happy. And as for her mum, I don't know, she's gone to see her now. But it can't be any worse than with you two. Anyway, I'm going now. You know where I am if you want me. I'm your daughter; I haven't committed a crime, I am in love with a girl, that's all, and I have the balls to finally come out and admit it. As our Amber said, who has more sense than you two, I should be admired, not judged,' she retorted, stomping out of the sitting room, going upstairs to gather her things, followed by her sister.

Belle and David looked at one another.

'She is our daughter, David. I hate this as much as you, but he didn't really make her happy, and we knew deep down that she was still mucking about with her, when we told her not to, and threatened her. I don't want to lose her. We will have to keep in touch with her.'

Alex walked into her mother's lounge, where Eve and Emily sat waiting to hear her announcement. Legs wobbling, she sat down, looking pensive. Hands shaking, she glanced at Emily, who looked grave, in anticipation.

'So what's all this about, then?' Eve asked.

Emily and Alex made eye contact, knowing what was about to be said.

'This is not easy for me, as I know that you won't approve, but I'm just going to have to say it. I'm in love with a girl,' Alex blurted.

Eve winced. Emily sat in silence as Alex went on, 'This is why I wasn't able to marry Matt. About three and a half years ago I met this girl in a coffee shop, and at first we were friends. She helped me through my dad's death but then we got closer and …'

Eve cut in, 'What do you mean, three and a half years ago? You and Matt have only been split up for nine months or so. I don't understand.'

Alex put her hands over her face.

'You had an affair, didn't you?' Eve demanded.

'Yes, but I couldn't help it,' Alex explained.

Eve stood up, moved towards her daughter, cracking her cheek with the side of her hand. In shock, Alex jumped up, feeling her painful face. 'What was that for?' she screamed.

'Because you are a disgrace. I'm ashamed of you. He was a lovely lad and you did that to him,' Eve said, clenching her teeth together.

'Don't hit me. I can't help it if I love a girl.'

'Well, you should have had more respect for him than to do that. He gave you a great life. The problem with him was that he was far too soft with you. Who is she? I'm ashamed of you.'

'Mum, don't be so awful to her. She wasn't happy. She loves Hope and she's a nice girl,' Emily said, clashing her cup down on the table.

'Hope? What kind of a name is that? What does she do, and how old is she?'

Both girls looked at each other, knowing Eve's likely reaction the moment Alex admitted the truth about her.

'She's almost twenty-three, and she used to work in a pub near where she lived, but she isn't there now, as she was going out with the owner, and she can't work there now ...'

Eve intervened.

'Well, that's smart. You mental case, have you gone mad? Some younger girl with no prospects or job; you are not right in the head. You are not normal,' she commented harshly.

Alex began to get upset.

'Don't be so nasty to her. She loves her ...'

Eve stepped in. 'Love, love? She is deluding herself. You want to get to the doctor's to get something. You are round the flaming bend. I cannot believe it,' she screamed.

Alex felt ashamed. Her self-worth dented, she retaliated, 'I knew you would be like this. Matt took off with another girl ...'

Eve butted in, 'Well, do you blame him?'

'Let me finish. He took off and left me high and dry, without compunction. I know what I did but I tried so hard to love him, and to feel for him as I did for her, and you know, after all those years with him, I never felt the way she made me feel. Yes, she doesn't have lots of money or a great job, but he had all that, and I was so miserable. If I'm a mental case for wanting to be truly happy, and all those years I thought I was but wasn't, then so be it, I don't care. She really loves me and I do her. I make my own decisions and so does she. She is intelligent, and with my help she will get the career she wants. It's not all about having lots of money. I have faith in her. I am gutted that you are ashamed of me. You hurt me saying these things, but my dad ...'

Eve cut in, 'Your dad will be turning in his grave now. He will be so disappointed in you. I am.'

'No, he wouldn't. He wanted us both happy. Yes, he loved Matt but he wasn't for her. I'm proud that you finally dare fight her back and admit who you are. And yes, I agree, Matt surprised us all. He acted very cold,' Emily interjected.

'Oh, so you knew, then? And you let her carry on? You are just as mental,' Eve bellowed, with angry eyes.

'You are so nasty. Alex, don't listen to her. She is happy, and if you keep going, you will lose your daughter. Hope loves her, and they have both been so unhappy for so long, and I'm relieved that they are finally doing something about it. It has been slowly destroying them both. If you haven't been able to see it then you need to look harder. It's quite normal these days. And it doesn't matter what sex you are as long as you both love and want each other with all of your heart,' Emily divulged.

'No, it's not normal. I mean, I just want normal kids who get married and have children, and yet my two haven't got any. What did I bring up?'

'Right, that's enough, I'm not having this. I love her and I don't want Matt or any other man. Yes, she's ten years younger than me but she makes me feel alive. She, apart from my dad, is the strongest person I know, and I adore her for it. Matt was weak, and yes, I did love him, we had great times, but I have never felt for him as I do for her. She can make my day with just a smile, and break my day with a bad word. We have a spark and chemistry, and my dad would be proud that I have the nerve to face you, and change my whole life. And I will prosper without Matt. It was me that made him, and I will have a good life where I'm happy. You are my mum and I love you. The three of us are all that's left now in this family and so we should be looking out for each other, not being awful. If you are going to be so against me, what chance do I have with the rest of society? If I'm not normal in your eyes, then so be it, but I won't go back. Accept it, or I will keep out of your life,' Alex said in a resentful tone, storming out of the house, banging the front door with force.

Eve sat stunned, shaking her head in disbelief.

'Don't push her too far, Mum, or you'll lose her. She's your daughter. You were very harsh, and she expected it, but you will have to come round and accept Hope too or lose out on having Alex in your life. She's right, we are all we have now. She's hurting also. She didn't want any of this but can't help it. I'm proud of her, as she really has battled with herself for so long; it has slowly been destroying her.'

'Well, I will, then, won't I?' Eve replied, turning up her mouth in disapproval.

Alex drove home bewildered by her mother's extremely harsh words, arriving to see Hope's car on the drive, helping her to smile as she entered the house.

Hope sat depressed, pretending to watch TV.

'How did it go?' Alex asked, kissing her softly.

'Badly!'

'Yeah, I can imagine. So when will they be coming to kill me?'

Hope stared at her.

'Never. I'd lie down and die before letting anyone hurt you,' she said, grabbing Alex close to her. They embraced one another for a few tender moments. Then Hope asked,

'How did it go with your mum?'

Alex sighed before answering.

'The way I expected, although she cracked me across the face.'

'Really? Why?'

'I told her I had an affair with you and she was ashamed of me for Matt.'

'Oh, I bet she'll hate me, then?'

'Well, she will have to come round.'

'Yeah. I really learned today that I love you so much and I have done the right thing. It's going to be tough getting people to accept us but we have got over the worst part.'

'I know we have and I don't regret my decision either.'

'Me neither. My mum and dad were nasty to me, and may never accept us, but as long as I have you, I can manage. I can manage anything. I'm so happy to be here with you, going away in two days' time, and getting our apartment. It's all my dreams come true – well, except for one.'

'What's that?'

'Well, for you to be proud of me when I get a career of my own. I'd like to train to be a primary school, teacher part-time perhaps, like I was meant to before I got with Marco. I want to make something of my life.'

Alex stared into her eyes.

'I'm already proud of you, angel. I am so in love with you,' she confessed, heartfelt, eskimo kissing her.

Hope purred.

297

'We are going to have so much fun in New York. I hope our room has a jacuzzi.'

'Why? It is a five-star hotel, so I think it has one in the gym area if it doesn't in our room.'

'Well, I want to catch up on all I've been missing out on for all this time. We have so much ground to make up for and new things to try,' Hope replied, trailing her fingers over Alex's mouth.

Chapter 59

'Quick, Hope, get your bags, the taxi's here,' Alex shouted.

Hope stood up, taking her suitcase to the door, grinning from ear to ear, peering at her beloved. Alex wore a pair of fitted faded jeans with rips in the knee and buttock area, a short blue denim jacket and a pair of brown boots with three-inch heels and a buckle at the side.

As Alex went towards the front door, Hope stared at her backside, seeing her white silky pants and brown bottom through the rip, making her blood pressure soar.

At the airport Hope sat staring at Alex and her beauty, scarcely able to comprehend that as she sat in the departure lounge, her destination New York, she was finally with the woman she loved. She closed her eyes, silently thanking God for answering her prayers, before opening them, grinning, and reaching for Alex's hands. At first Alex felt uncomfortable, moving her hand away, looking around to see if anyone had caught a glimpse of the gesture. Undeterred, Hope subtly took her hand once more, smiling profusely at Alex, illustrating by the glow on her face how elated she was to be sitting alongside her, as her girlfriend. Alex glanced at her, seeing the euphoria on her face induced by the fact that she was holding her hand, and allowed it to remain locked in Hope's hand for a few seconds, until she moved it away.

Alex read her magazine, barely able to concentrate, aching to lean to her left and kiss this beautiful girl sitting next to her, but she did not dare. The girls sat silently, both fantasising about the amazing things they would see, and do, in this fantastic city together, making them both smile broadly, each pretending to focus on her magazine or book.

Finally, to their joy, the flight was called, and Alex stood up. Hope stared at her, puzzled as to why she had got up, gathering their belongings, when they had called for 'first class and business class' passengers only.

'Come on, get up, we are off, my cute little muffin pie,' Alex said, excited.

Hope smiled, remaining seated.

'Come on, or you will miss your champagne.'

'What are you on about? It's just for the first-class people, isn't it?'

Alex, feeling like a child in a sweet shop, ecstatic, announced to Hope to her surprise that she had upgraded them to business class.

Hope's eyes shone brightly, and she leapt off her seat, retrieving her items from the floor, hurrying forward. At the front desk Alex handed over the tickets. The airline employee took them, wishing them a good flight.

They made their way to the aircraft, to be greeted by an air steward, who directed them to their seats. Once the section was all seated, and ready for take-off, an air steward came round offering everyone a glass of champagne. Joyful, Hope beamed, sinking into her 'sofa-like' seat. Another flight attendant followed handing out a menu with choices for lunch and afternoon tea; she explained to the girls that she would attend to their every request throughout the flight, much to their pleasure. Absorbing the moment, Hope pinched her arm re-assuring herself that it was real, before gently leaning into Alex, stroking the back of her hand. Alex took Hope's hand, looking around nervously, making eye contact with other passengers.

'So, nice surprise, eh?'

Hope pondered for a second.

'Yes, I am taking it all in. These armchairs are brill, they go back like a bed, and there is still so much room. I feel like a superstar,' she replied, dancing in her seat.

'You are a superstar, my superstar,' Alex expressed, gazing into her eyes, slightly brushing her face as discreetly as possible.

Hope's eyes widened as she reached across, kissing Alex softly on the cheek, unable to resist her, whispering into her ear, 'I love you.'

Alex's face glowed.

'You think this is posh? You ain't seen anything yet. We are going to have the time of our lives. Make the most of everything here. I'm going to treat you like a princess to show you how much you mean to me. I've been saving up for a while and wanted to treat you specially as I know how hard it's been for you. I just want to do so much with you here and enjoy every second of our time.'

Hope took a large breath and exhaled slowly, mesmerised by her beloved girlfriend.

After a short wait in the airport they finally made their way to their hotel in Times Square. Hope could not believe the sheer opulence of the hotel front entrance and reception area, with its marble flooring and walls and dangling chandeliers. Their baggage was taken to their room while they checked in. They were given a brief introduction to the tourist attractions available, and the best restaurants to dine in, as well as a discounted voucher for certain department stores. Although it was still rather cold outside, the receptionist explained how lucky they were to have such mild weather, unlike previous years at this time.

They took the lift to the third floor to their room, a junior suite which Alex had reserved without Hope's knowledge. As the door opened, the sheer delight on Hope's face was a sight to behold.

She stood with her mouth wide open, trying to see as much as possible, gazing at the king-size brown leather bed with brown and cream sheets and suede cushions. As she went further into the room she viewed a cream vase holding a bouquet of flowers on top of a coffee table.

'Wow, look, they have put flowers in our room too. I cannot believe how posh this is,' Hope said, thrilled.

Alex laughed, walking towards the flowers, picking up the tag, showing it to Hope, who read:

'2+3 for ever xxxxx.'

'Oh, you are so thoughtful. I am the luckiest girl alive. I am going to wake up from this dream eventually,' Hope said, her eyes shining brightly. Alex took her hand, leading her into the bathroom. Hope gazed at the marbled floor and walls, and the dual white oval-shaped sinks with gold taps, matching the bath and separate shower cubicle, big enough to fit a family in. Alex stood behind her, holding her waist tightly.

'What do you think, then?'

'It's amazing. I have never been in somewhere so posh. The bath is massive and it has holes in the side,' Hope said, puzzled.

Alex grinned.

'It's a whirlpool bath; just the same as a jacuzzi really. That's why it's so big, silly girl,' she teased.

Hope purred, holding onto Alex's arms around her waist, both savouring the moment, until the bellboy with their luggage knocked on the door.

Alex gave him a tip while Hope dived onto the king-size bed, placing her watch on the glass bedside table with its cream marbled legs.

'Come and lie on this bed with me,' she said suggestively.

Alex smiled, shaking her head, unpacking her suitcase, putting her items in the larger of the two cream wardrobes.

'So you get the biggest wardrobe, then?' Hope joked, watching her unpack.

Alex nodded, continuing to unpack as Hope got off the bed, opening a cupboard door on the wall. Behind it was a large silver plasma TV attached to the wall. Alongside it was a cream mini-stereo system with a rack full of CDs and DVDs.

'Oh, wow, this TV is so big, and look at all the DVDs,' Hope said, grinning from ear to ear.

Alex glanced over, while continuing to unpack.

'It's fab here. What is that over there next to the seating area?' Hope asked, pointing.

'I think that's a fridge.'

Hope went to investigate, opening the cupboard door.

'Yes, it is. Oh, look, they have bottles of Coors. You love them, and mini bottles of pink champagne, water and Coke.'

'Great, I'll have a Coors now, please,' Alex responded.

Hope took out a bottle, unscrewing the top, giving it to Alex. She walked back to the fridge and took out the mini bottle of pink champagne, grinning. Transfixed on Alex in her ripped jeans, unpacking, she began to strip off her clothes, tossing them to the floor. She lay naked on the bed, taking the bottle in her hand. Alex turned, mesmerised by her amazing body, stopping what she was doing. She stood still, watching Hope sipping from her bottle, deliberately missing her mouth, allowing the champagne to drip down her chin and onto her breasts. Licking her lips, Alex tore off her top, standing watching Hope who poured the champagne onto her chest, allowing it to run down her body. Alex lunged forward and dove onto the bed, tearing off her jeans as quickly as possible. She licked off the champagne. The more she licked, the more Hope poured, opening her legs, pouring it onto her crotch area, saturating it. Getting excited, Alex grinned, taking the bottle from Hope. Hope lay groaning, screaming out as the cold liquid dripped onto her thighs as Alex poured it on bit by bit, catching it with her mouth. She pulled Hope's legs apart, kissing her inner thighs, forcing Hope to grab her head, attempting to put her tongue inside of her. Alex teased, refusing, playing with the champagne, lacing her legs and thighs with it, making her wetter and wetter. Alex stopped and jumped off the bed, finding the belt from the dressing gown in the bathroom. She returned, smiling mischievously at her lover, embracing her passionately. She placed the belt around Hope's eyes, covering them. Hope smiled, enjoying Alex taking control.

'Oh God, I want you so much inside of me. I want to feel your tongue, licking me. I can't wait to come all over your face with my juices dripping down your face,' Hope said, licking her lips. Alex began, dripping champagne all over her body, making Hope cry out as she didn't know what to expect next.

'God, I am going to make you scream and beg for me inside of you,' Alex insisted.

'God, I want to be made love to so much. Lick my pussy, really sensually and make me come so hard.'

Alex stopped and moved up to her ear, whispering, 'Yes, I am going to show you what you mean to me with my tongue.'

Feeling her whole body go numb and tingle with excitement, Hope turned and stuck her tongue deeply into Alex's mouth, kissing her for some time, making their bodies move together, enrapturing each other.

Alex moved all over her body, finally taking the bottle and swigging it. She then lowered her body, gently putting the champagne into Hope's vagina, pushing it inside of her, causing bubbles. Hope cried out, expressing her pleasure, making her clitoris throb. Alex teased Hope farther, licking the end of her

303

clitoris for ages, licking all around it and in the middle of it, forcing Hope's cries.

'Oh my God, you are so fucking amazing in bed. I am so turned on by you. I adore you more than you can ever imagine; you are so gentle with me,' Hope gasped, moving her pelvis up and down the bed.

Alex smiled, feeling more and more aroused as she pleasured her beloved. She licked very gently, putting cold champagne inside of her, making Hope scream out loud. As she licked gently, she put her fingers inside of her, deep onto her g-spot, pressing onto it, pulling back her fingers back, creating an amazing sensation. Hope yelped loudly, her body jolting.

'That is fucking fantastic, what are you doing?'

Alex ignored her, going deeper, staring at Hope so besotted, slowly moving her fingers inside of her, feeling her moisture drip out of her, arousing Alex even more. For a split second, she pulled her soaking finger out and licked off Hope's love juices, aching to taste her. She put her fingers back inside, maintaining the position of her fingers, staring at her sexy girlfriend until Hope could not take anymore, screaming at the top of her voice. Unable to keep her body still, her vagina tightened up, as though it was going into a spasm as she ejaculated onto Alex's hand, feeling the squirt and pressure onto her hand as Hope orgasmed over and over. Alex stopped and took off the belt. Hope's body could not keep still, overwhelmed her as tears flowed down her face. Alex cuddled her tightly, kissing her softly. Hope tried to speak but words failed her as she lay speechless, trying to calm down. Alex felt her heart beating faster than ever before, placing her hand over her heart.

'I love you so much, Hope, and that was amazing.'

'What was that? I don't know what happened there. I can't keep still, I can still feel you inside of me. I am overwhelmed, Alex.'

'You had a female ejaculation. I love you with all my heart,' she said, wiping Hope's wet cheeks, placing her head onto her chest, cuddling her.

They left the hotel, walking around Times Square, viewing the amazing billboards with their colourful adverts, and then down a side street, where they caught sight of a gay male couple holding hands, prompting Hope to pluck up the courage to take Alex's hand, which hung loosely by her side. Immediately Alex flinched away, much to Hope's disappointment.

A woman walking behind them stepped forward and whispered in Alex's ear, 'It's OK to hold her hand here in New York, you know. There are so many gay people here. No one gives a rat's ass. Even straight people hold hands with their girlfriends and no one gives a damn. I tell you what, I'd gladly hold her hand. She's awesome.'

Stunned, Alex glared at the tall black woman, who smiled as she continued down the street.

'God, these people are so forward here,' Alex said.

'Yes, but I like it. Now give me your hand before I get upset,' Hope joked, reaching out for her hand.

At first, for a few steps, Alex would not succumb. Slowly she put her hand alongside Hope's, gently rubbing her fingers across her hand, finally taking it boldly. Hope happily locked hands as they wandered up and down the streets, feeling at ease with each other, catching sight of other gay couples, arm in arm, and hand in hand, making Alex feel somewhat less anxious. She giggled as a passer-by commented, 'Nice ass.'

After a short wait in the queue on Broadway, Alex finally got her tickets for *Mamma Mia*, much to her delight.

They sauntered on, taking in the sheer wonder of this magnificent city. A man holding bus tickets approached them, selling tickets for the city bus tour. Happily, wanting to see as much of the city as possible, they bought their tickets, getting on board.

'This bus takes you all over. I would like to see Ground Zero and the guy said that it stops there, so can we get off and have a look?' Hope asked.

'Yes, sure.'

Hope leaned over, kissing Alex on the cheek as they took their seats on the upper deck. A couple sitting opposite smiled, catching a glimpse of the girls, so madly in love, trying to hide it from the world.

They sat content on the bus, listening to the tour guide giving information about the area, when Alex overheard someone mention the Empire State Building.

'Yes, I really want to go there. It will be so romantic to see the whole of New York at night when it's dark,' she whispered.

Hope nodded, looking at the shops as they went by.

'Here is our stop. Come on, let's get off,' she declared, standing up.

Alex followed, exiting the bus, heading towards the site of Ground Zero. Walking slowly, arm in arm, they arrived at the site where the Twin Towers used to be. Instead of a building, they saw a hole in the ground with a large pile of rubble, cordoned off with steel fencing. Many people had gathered round to read the signs, seeking information on what had happened. Hope wandered around, reading everything in detail, trying to imagine what the site must have looked like at the time and how the people must have felt, causing a tear to roll off her cheek onto her chin. Seeing her distress, Alex comforted her.

'Can you imagine how awful it must have been here?' Hope said quietly, wiping her eye.

Alex agreed.

'What's that over there on that wired fence?' Hope asked, looking straight ahead.

'I don't know. Come on, let's go and have a look.'

As they got closer they saw colourful plaques representing different flags from all over the world. Hope seemed intrigued by this, and bent to read the information plaque at the end of the wall.

'Alex, come here,' she shouted.

Alex walked towards her.

'What?'

'All these plaques have been sent by children all over the world, expressing their sympathy for the victims. Oh, it's so sad,' Hope said, bringing a tissue out of her coat pocket, wiping her damp eyes.

'I know. It is so great to see this lovely colourful wall. It shows how many people cared, especially young children,' Alex replied, putting her arm around Hope's shoulder.

Hope smiled, embracing Alex, as they contemplated the great loss suffered by thousands.

'I'm so sad for all these people and their families, but I tell you what, if anything like that happened to you, I'd end it there and then. I would want to be with you wherever you were. I couldn't stand it,' Hope said, squeezing Alex's waist tighter.

'You are such a softie, aren't you?'

'Yeah. Come on, let's get the bus back to our hotel. It takes you all over, and we have these passes for two days, so we can go all over on it, hearing all about the area. I love it here already,' Hope said, her eyes gaping.

Hope hopped off the bus, followed by Alex, and they made their way back to their hotel, hand in hand, taking the lift up to their room.

Within seconds Hope had switched on the whirlpool, taking all her clothes off, tantalising Alex as she stared at Hope's amazing figure, fancying her more and more. Hope went next to Alex, rubbing her hands all over Alex's naked body, smiling profusely. She clenched her close to her, making their breasts touch, placing both hands on her bottom. Alex closed her eyes, feeling Hope's silk-like back. Tenderly, they stood, feeling one another's naked, warm flesh, feeling their bodies surge with electricity, magnified together. In unison they both explored each other's body with pleasure, standing in the middle of room. Slowly, Hope ran her fingertips onto Alex's cheeks and chin, moving down to her neck with her eyes closed. Alex stood still, enjoying Hope's gentle touch. Hope took Alex by the hand, slowly leading her into the bathroom, stepping into the whirlpool, followed by Alex, feeling the bubbles tickle their feet. Lowering them into the water, Alex sat in front of Hope, permitting Hope to drape her long legs around Alex's body, feeling the warm bubbles encase both of them. Savouring the moment Hope held her closely, resting her head on Alex's wet shoulders. She began kissing Alex's neck and ears, pleasuring them both, forcing Alex to turn round, covering each other with kisses.

The next three days were hectic. They had visited Chinatown, which Alex loved, bartering with the locals, buying pirated bags and sunglasses to give away as presents. They had toured again on the bus and visited Central Park, taking a very romantic horse-and-carriage ride around the perimeter, during which Hope presented Alex with a red rose that she had bought from a flower stall on the roadside nearby. They had watched *Mamma Mia* on Broadway, which they had both enjoyed, and dined in nice restaurants recommended by the locals.

On their final evening, saving the best until last, Alex had arranged for them to spend their last moments going up the Empire State Building. She had asked the hotel receptionist to book this for them, to avoid them having to wait in the long queues.

As they left the restaurant and got into their cab, Alex announced to Hope what she had arranged. Joyful, Hope was barely able to sit still in the cab, in anticipation of seeing this great building. They arrived at the entrance to the building, walking past the queuing public, heading for the queue for the lift to the top, eagerly awaiting their turn to get in it. After a few short moments, they entered the large gold lift, packed with people from all over the world. Alex had brought gloves and scarves for them both to wear, knowing how cold it would be at the top. As they left the lift, heading outside, she handed hers to Hope.

'Oh, Mummy Bear, you are so thoughtful. I can't believe that you have arranged this. Wow, look over there,' she said, pointing at the Statue of Liberty. Alex nodded, in awe of the fabulous view, walking towards the edge, craning over fellow tourists, all seeking to view as much of the city as possible from this great height. After a few awkward moments the family in front of them moved, allowing the girls a clear view of this incredible city.

'God, I never envisaged that the view would be this beautiful. Look at all the dazzling lights of the bustling city down below and all the tall buildings. Look, there's the Chrysler Building too. It's so amazing,' Alex said, upbeat, her spine tingling.

Hope clutched her hand. Gazing at her, she said, 'It's so romantic and peaceful up here. I cannot explain in words how happy I am. I have been thinking all day of a word or a group of words to define my joy at being with you on this fantastic holiday. I have so many memories that will fill my memory bank for ever. You have made it so special.'

'Me too, it has been the best holiday ever for me, and I mean that.'

'Really?'

'Yes, and you know what?'

'What?'

'This is just the start. I'm going to make you so happy, and you are me. We are going to go back home stronger, and fight back if we get any hassle. You heard what that gay guy said to us in that bar the other day − it's not about sexuality, it's the person, and how they make you feel. If someone of the same sex makes you feel as one from the opposite can't, then so be it, and if you are comfortable with it, others will be too. He's right,' Alex explained, smiling at her beloved Hope.

'I know you are right, but I'm dreading going back as I'm scared.'

'What of?' Alex quizzed.

'Well, that I'm not going to be good enough for you. It's not real here, and we can pretend, but back home we can't. I have no job or money and I'm in debt. I hate sponging off you all the time. I want to make you proud of me.'

Alex took Hope's other hand.

'You will, angel. I have put a good word in for you for that job, and it's quite good money. You can always do courses to better yourself, and get to see what it would be like to work in a school, as you want. I will support you if you want to do a B.Ed degree. I am your partner now and we are a team. We will clear your debt, and then you can start afresh.'

A tear trickled from Hope's eye and goose bumps stood out on her body. Holding Alex's hand very tightly, entranced, she said, 'I feel like the luckiest girl alive. Not only am I so in love with you, but you really love me, and believe in me. You will give me your world, and stand by my side, helping me to be better at whatever I do. I always thought that I was going to have a shit life and meet idiots. Marco wasn't bad to me but no one could be anywhere near as good as you. And to imagine the thought of not getting you back, and losing you to another girl, knocks me physically sick.'

Alex's face shone with the reflection of the moonlight. Happily listening to Hope, she felt a warm glow all over her body. Feeling bold, she lunged forward, kissing Hope softly. Hope's eyes lit up. Sensing Alex's courage, she whispered something in her ear, grinning. Alex pondered for a moment, nodding. Hope locked her arm into Alex's arm as they walked towards the exit, smiling broadly.

They exited the taxi and walked the short journey along the street where both of their eyes widened, seeing all of the gay people, happy in their surroundings. As they entered the first bar that they came across, Alex clenched Hope's hand. Feeling her nerves, Hope stopped and kissed Alex passionately, watched by some onlookers. Feeling somewhat uneasy, Alex looked straight ahead as they made their way to the bar, clinging onto her beloved. Immediately, Alex downed her drink as fast as possible, ordering another. They walked around the bar, looking at everyone and everything, absorbing their surroundings. Alex caught her eye on two girls devouring each other on the dance floor, then viewed many men kissing, relaxing her. Feeling less anxious, she sat close to Hope on the couches, her heart filled with pride. She drank from her tall glass, finishing it off, darting off the seat, ordering more drinks from the bar, whilst Hope sat content looking round at the different looks and attitudes of the packed bar. The waitress chatted to her at the bar, being friendly, making Alex feel more and more comfortable in her unfamiliar surroundings. She sat back down and embraced Hope, feeling aroused. After several drinks, she led Hope to the dance floor, smooching with her, surrounded by beautiful men and women all enjoying themselves. Like children in a sweet shop both girls fixed their eyes all over for a few seconds, turning their attention to each other. Alex leaned into Hope and said, 'There are so many gorgeous women in here tonight but you are the best looking by far.'

Hope grinned, dancing even closer to Alex, rubbing herself against her. Aroused, Alex grabbed her chin, devouring her lips. She took her hand and dragged her off the dance floor, taking her outside. She turned the corner, finding a deserted alleyway, pulling Hope towards her. She pressed her against the wall and pulled up her skirt. Hope's heart began to beat faster and faster as she pulled up Alex's skirt, kissing and biting her neck. Together, they put their fingers inside of each other's pants, rubbing their throbbing clitoris, feeling it get wetter and wetter.

'God, I'm so horny and turned on; I'm going to come so quickly,' Alex said, breathless.

'Me too. You are so raunchy and dirty, I love it.'

They kissed harder and faster the more turned on they felt, making both of their hearts pound more. Hearing sounds, Alex's blood pressure soared, as they tried to keep as quiet as possible, touching one another, making their bodies jolt and their pelvises move faster and faster until they both stopped, finally reaching their climax at the same time. Transfixed on each other, they smiled, making Hope speak. 'This has been the best holiday ever. I worship you. Thank you so much.'

Chapter 60

Alex turned the corner into her street as Hope lay sleeping, exhausted from the journey home, to find Matt's car on the drive. She pulled up behind both Hope and Matt's cars. She stared at Hope, not wanting to disturb her, quietly closing the door, leaving the suitcases, nervously opening the front door, unsure how to interpret Matt's return.

The lounge door was closed; she opened it to find Matt sitting on the couch watching TV in his suit, looking pensive as he stared at the set. As she came through the door, he immediately smiled at her, jumping up, kissing her on the cheek. In astonishment she drew back, dismissing his advances.

'What are you doing here?' she asked nervously.

'Hi. I rang your Emily and she said you were away for a few days. I have been staying since Wednesday. I'm sorry but I had nowhere to go,' he replied, his eyes pained.

Unsettled at his presence, knowing how awkward it would be with both him and Hope staying, she spoke abruptly.

'Well, you can't stay here, Matt, no way. You can't just let yourself in. You no longer live here and, well … it's awkward now.'

'What do you mean? I just wanted to talk to you as things…'

Alex interrupted, 'Oh, so you and her have split up and you are coming crawling back to me, then?'

Matt scowled.

'Well, yes, we have split up, but it never felt right with her. You know how I felt about you, and so I thought that we could chat. I know we are over, as you treated me so badly, but I just hated how things became, and I wanted to come and see you and hopefully put it right.'

Alex paced up and down the lounge, anxious about Hope waking up, feeling her heart thumping in her chest. She responded, 'You've got a nerve, haven't you?'

'What do you mean?'

'Matt, I don't hear hide nor hair of you for months, you just leave without a kind word to me, put the house up for sale, ask for the business to be in your name, throw money at your new woman, and now it's over, you think you can just come back, and what? Be friends? I don't get what you want?'

Matt, feeling embarrassed, closed his eyes, sighing. He approached her, grabbing her hand.

'I just want to make it all right again and be nice.'

'No, Matt. If you hadn't split with her, you wouldn't be here. This is my house now, you have no right to be here. I want you to go.'

'Why are you being this way with me? You look on edge, and why are you keep looking outside, who is there?'

Taking a deep breath, pushing out her chest, she blurted, 'Hope is outside Matt, asleep. We have just come back from holiday. We are back together and we are both very happy. I just want to be left alone and get on with our lives. The past is the past.'

Sad, he bowed his head. He rubbed his face as Alex stood in the middle of the sitting room.

'Oh, right, I see, well, I will go then and let you get on with it. I was pathetic back then, and you are right, I have no right here. Here is your key and good luck,' he said, handing her the key.

She smiled, kissing his cheek.

'I hope you get happy one day.'

'Thanks,' he replied, heading towards the front door. He left and got in his car, speeding off. Alex stood for a few seconds and then went to the car and woke Hope, leading her into the house.

As Matt drove down the street, Emily drove past him, making them both pull over and engage in conversation, happy to be reunited.

Hope lay on the couch half asleep, smiling at her lover. Alex lay next to her, cuddling her warm body.

'I am so in love with you. I am so excited for Christmas and you know how much I hate Christmas these days.'

Hope nodded, closing her eyes, squeezing Alex more tightly.

Chapter 61

Christmas Eve

'Good morning, Mummy Bear,' Hope said, staring at Alex as she woke up.

Alex grunted, with one eye half open, cuddling into her until they were locked in each other's arms, warming themselves from their body heat against the cold morning frost that stuck to their bedroom window. Alex, still half asleep, closed her eyes, trying to go back to sleep, as Hope lay wide awake, gazing at this dark beauty that lay in her arms, excited about the festive period ahead. She lay there scarcely able to believe that they were finally sharing a Christmas together, speculating about the days ahead, making herself move closer to Alex, covering her in kisses.

'I can't believe this is happening and I'm not dreaming. I am so excited about these next few days; it's my prayers answered after all these years. It couldn't be any more perfect if we tried. We have our presents wrapped under the tree, all the lovely food to share and cook for one another, we have been invited to your mum's house for lunch, which I am so thrilled about, and to your sister's for Boxing Day for turkey and chips. We have this lovely house, I have a good job, and I am going to university next year to do my B.Ed, and you have new job too. It's perfect; after all the problems and struggles we have had for so long, we have finally made it. I can say with all my heart that I'm so happy,' Hope whispered.

Alex opened her eyes, staring at Hope, smiling broadly. She stroked her flawless complexion.

'Wow, you are so pretty; your eyes are the most beautiful I have ever seen. They shine like a diamond in the sunlight, and are so big and green, and your eyelashes are so long. Even first thing in the morning you look radiant. I feel so lucky to have such a beautiful girlfriend.'

Unable to combat her desires any longer, Hope gently kissed her.

'What was that for?' Alex asked happily.

'Because you are my girlfriend and I am allowed to do that. Besides, I can never resist you, you should know that by now, and if you don't get up soon, I will have you in here all day, making mad passionate love to you, and then we will never get anything sorted,' she teased, kissing Alex tenderly again.

Alex shook her head in amusement.

'What?' Hope asked.

'You.'

'What about me?'

'You are a one-off, I'll tell you that. You are a little minx. I don't know where you get your sex drive from at all.'

Hope purred, opening Alex's pajama top.

Alex rolled away playfully.

'Come back, I want you right now,' Hope said in an amused tone.

'No. It's not Christmas yet,' Alex teased, getting out of bed, tugging the bedcovers off Hope.

'Hey, I'm freezing. Put them back over me or come back to bed,' Hope squealed.

'No, naughty girl. It's time to get up. We have got lots to do today, me especially,' she explained in a mysterious voice.

Hope stared at her, pulling the bedcovers back over her goose-pimpled body.

'What do you mean?' she questioned.

'Well, I have one or two last-minute things to get so I'll have to get going.'

'Like what?'

'Now that would be telling, wouldn't it?' Alex said, kissing Hope's cheek, walking into the en suite, watched lasciviously by her beloved, who was smiling happily.

Noticing this sparkling smile, as she sat on the toilet peering at Hope lying in bed, Alex commented, 'What are you smiling your head off about?'

Hope did not answer.

'Tell me, then,' Alex pleaded.

'Well, I'm just so happy, that's all. Are you going to get me more presents? I hope you like mine. I have even bought you 'housey' things. I love this room − in fact all the rooms really. I think I would make a good designer,' she teased, scanning the red-and-cream décor.

Alex laughed as she stood brushing her teeth.

'What are you sniggering at?' Hope asked.

'You. I thought of most of the designs for the rooms. What are you like?'

'No, you never.'

Alex laughed. 'Yeah, yeah, whatever. I am the house guru, not you.'

'No, no. It has been a joint effort. We make a great team.'

'Yes, I guess we do. I love my idea of all white for the sitting room. I'm so surprised that you have managed to keep it so clean,' Alex joked, sliding back the wardrobe door, searching for an outfit to wear.

'Excuse me. I clean the house almost every day. You don't do that much in it,' Hope said drolly.

'I know, angel, but I work very hard, and long hours, to help us have nice things. Are you getting out of that bed? Don't forget, you are visiting your mum and dad today and so it's time to get up, lazy lump,' Alex said, full of beans, taking out a dress.

'What are you getting that dress out for?'

'I'm meeting my friends in town for a drink later, and then I thought that you could come and meet us. We can have a few drinks, come home, have some nice food, and chill, whilst waiting to see what Santa brings for you tomorrow.'

Exiting the bed, Hope grabbed Alex, embracing her tightly.

'What's that for?'

'I just love you so much. If only you could know how much. Just watching you taking out your clothes, meeting up tonight with your friends, having some drinks, and then coming back home to our house, is just awesome. I hope I make you as happy as you do me. My heart beats faster as soon as I hear your voice or see you, and when I think about something nice that we will be doing, like today and tomorrow, my whole body gets goose bumps. Here, feel my arms,' Hope urged, stretching it out.

Alex grinned with mischief.

'What are you grinning at?'

'The best things come to those who wait,' she replied, kissing her on the lips, moving into one of the spare bedrooms, getting dressed.

Hope's face beamed as she went into the en suite to take a shower.

Alex made a percolator of fresh coffee, the smell wafting around the kitchen area, as they sat at the breakfast bar sipping their hot coffee and eating Christmas cake. Alex's hair hung loosely around her face, falling onto her shoulders, as she sat running her fingers through it. Her tanned face emphasised her sparkling white teeth, matching her dazzling dark hazel eyes and long dark eyelashes, as they sat chatting to one another.

'So, what are your plans today, then?' Hope enquired, intrigued.

Alex smiled.

'Well, I have a few things to do now and then I want to visit Millie and exchange gifts; we said that we might have lunch together. I am at the hairdresser's at four and then I said that I would meet the girls in town at about six, hoping that you could meet me about seven thirtyish, have a drink with us, and then we can do whatever we like afterwards. What do you think?'

'Yes, that sounds great to me. I am going to see my mum and dad; I may go and see a movie with our Amber and then I want to visit Macy for a bit. We might go for a drink. And then I will come home and make myself look beautiful to meet you.'

Alex's eyes looked heavy and sad as she took a sip from her cup, shaking her head.

'What are you shaking your head for? You look sad all of a sudden. Are you thinking about previous Christmas times with Matt, wishing you were with him?'

Alex tutted.

'No, silly. If you must know I'm thinking about this time last year, and how I never imagined that twelve months later I would be in this lovely house, drinking coffee with the lovely aroma wafting through the kitchen, with you sitting opposite me, and how things seem to be working out for us after all these years. We have had three miserable Christmases and finally we get what we've always dreamt of. It's very special and I feel so lucky and grateful. You know what they say is true. The best things come to those who wait. And God, have we waited and gone through some shit,' she said with moist eyes.

Hope nodded her head, pondering on previous years apart, when she longed for this moment, urging her to lean forward and take Alex's hand.

'Yes, I know. This time last year I was with Marco, aching with the worst pain ever to be with you. I always imagined it to be good but never this fantastic. I can't believe that I have done so well at work with my promotion in such a short time to head receptionist, and to be able to go to university next year, and this lovely house. And do you know what makes me so happy?'

'What?'

'That your mum has invited us both for Christmas lunch. I know that you wouldn't have gone if she had said I couldn't come, but you love being with them, and so it would have been very sad for you if you hadn't gone.'

'I know. She is coming round to us, and will make you feel very welcome. I think when she went to see that fortune teller, who described my dad so well, and said the things he'd say, it helped her to come to accept it a bit better, by explaining his acceptance and joy at my happiness.'

'I wish my mum would go and see her, then,' Hope said with sad eyes. Alex nodded.

'I know, me too, but they will have to come round eventually. At least people at work are fine about it for both of us and Macy is OK now, she has accepted us. In fact she loves coming over, apparently. Your cousins are fine with us, as are your Amber, and Ben. We can take her out over the holidays somewhere if she wants. I am sad about your parents, but at least you go visiting them. It could be worse. I hope they will accept me in time.'

'Me too; they are just jealous because I'm so elated with my new life. They will have to get used to it as it will not change.'

'Are you sure?'

'Yes. I'm yours for ever, Mummy Bear.'

By the time the afternoon set in Alex had visited the shops she needed to visit, putting the final touches together.

With time to spare, she visited her father's grave.

She walked slowly to his gravestone, standing rubbing her gloves together, wrapping her scarf more tightly around her neck, buttoning her long red coat up to keep as warm as possible in the freezing, icy conditions. She placed a bunch of flowers on his gravestone then stood for a while, glancing around at the many people visiting their loved ones, before staring at his stone again. Her face shone, emphasising her rosy cheeks, as she marched back to the car, before heading for Millie's house.

Hope had gone to lunch with Macy. They exchanged gifts, happily conversing about their lives. Hope left Macy to visit her parents, delivering the gifts that had filled her car boot.

Alex arrived at Millie's house, knocking on the door with an armful of presents, grinning from ear to ear. Millie opened the door, greeting her best friend.

'Come in, flower, out of the cold,' she said, kissing her on the cheek, as Alex passed her the gifts. They went into the lounge and she sat down on the couch.

'You look very happy. Your face is glowing,' Millie commented.

Alex giggled. 'Yes, well, it is Christmas. The birds are chirping, the sun is shining, even though it is zero degrees outside, and we all have our health and strength, so why shouldn't I be happy?'

'I know, it's great to see. This time last year you were so pale-faced with the saddest eyes in the world. I'm so happy for you. When I think of all the times you were in such a state, and now look. I told you it would all come good in the end,' she said in an upbeat tone.

Alex agreed, taking off her coat.

'I know, I cannot even imagine how it used to be. When I think about it, my stomach goes into spasms, and I feel sick. What we all went through. Remember the day of the abortion and him calling us such cruel, nasty names? Hope never talks about the abortion but I know she would like kids with me someday.'

319

'Yes, I do, and when Matt left, and then when he was waiting at your house when you got back from New York. And all those many, many times that you would come here in despair, wondering what the hell you were going to do, and if you should leave him or not. How things change,' she reminisced, standing up and going into the kitchen.

Alex nodded. Millie returned with a bottle of champagne and two glasses. She popped the cork, pouring the champagne into the glasses, handing one to Alex, before putting the bottle back into the fridge, pouring orange juice in her glass.

'Cheers, Al, I think it's time to celebrate. Here's to our new, and well-deserved, future. And Merry Christmas, flower. We can have the Christmas, and New Year, that we have both wanted for so long,' she said, beaming.

Alex smiled, slurping her champagne.

'Yes, it has been an extremely painful journey. But if I have learnt anything from all this heartache, it's that you have to fight for what you want, and never stop trying. No one is going to come and make things easy for you, handing it out on a plate. I have worked so hard at the office to get my promotion, and Hope too. I'm so proud of you also for finally getting rid of Benny ...'

'I know, but you don't see it when you are in it. I knew that he wasn't good for me, and would never be mine, and if I'm being truthful, I didn't really want to be with him; he wasn't good enough for me. But now look at Tom and all the joy he's brought to me lately.'

Alex agreed, going into the kitchen to top up her glass. Millie followed her with a somewhat anxious expression.

'I've something to tell you, Al, and I want you to be the first to know.'

'What?' Alex asked, her stomach churning.

'I'm pregnant, about seven weeks, I think.'

Startled but happy, Alex cuddled her friend.

'Well, this calls for a second toast, then. I wondered why you had put orange juice in yours and were just sipping it. I'm so happy for you. Tom is such a nice man. I could tell when I met him how nice he was. He was so accepting of me and Hope. She thought he was charming and he is. He has a good job and wants to take good care of you. And I tell you what, if anyone deserves happiness after all this time, it's you,' Alex expressed, embracing her friend.

Millie smiled graciously.

'You too, though, Al. Hope is a very lucky girl; how she handles your wit and crazy personality, God only knows,' she teased.

Alex laughed, returning to the lounge, sitting on the couch. Suddenly a mysterious look came over her. Millie noticed this, prompting her to ask, 'What's that look for? I know that look, you are up to something.'

Alex smiled broadly, without speaking, gulping her champagne as she checked her mobile.

'Tell me, then.'

'What?'

'I don't know but you have that look.'

'What look?'

'Just like you are up to something.'

'Like what?'

'Well, I don't know. Do you have a surprise gift for Hope, like a new car?'

'She has a car,' Alex said, placing her hand over her mouth, suppressing her sniggers.

'Oh, Al, I've told you my secret. Tell me, please.'

'I will tomorrow. I will ring you, I promise,' she said, unrelenting.

Millie stared at her, wondering what she was going to do, knowing full well she had something up her sleeve.

After a nice evening, basking in the Christmas party ambiance in the town bars with her friends, Alex met up with Hope, enjoying the great atmosphere together. They stood gazing at one another, grinning like Cheshire cats to be sharing their first Christmas Eve together. They both looked stunning as they stood hand in hand in their party dresses.

Alex even plucked up the courage to kiss her gently in a crowded bar, feeling comfortable about having just declared to the whole bar that they were 'an item', stopping any unwanted male attention to either of them.

After an hour Hope asked to go home, so that they could snuggle up by the fire, watching the evening Christmas film. Alex led her by the hand out of the bar, flagging down a taxi. They sat side by side in the back, the driver peering at them in his rear-view mirror, driving in silence, as both girls seemed oblivious, devoted to each other.

'So have you had a good time, then? Is it busy?' he asked politely.

Hope acknowledged his question.

'So where are you off to now, then? Another party?' he enquired.

Their eyes fixed on one another as they smiled happily.

'No, we are off home to watch a nice Christmas film,' Alex replied boldly.

Raising his eyebrows, he stared, puzzled.

'So, are you sisters, then?'

'No,' Hope giggled.

Alex paused for a moment. Bravely, she answered, 'No, she is the complete love of my life and we live together as a couple.'

Hope grinned from ear to ear, her body oozing with goose bumps, looking at Alex with pride.

Without hesitation the taxi driver responded sincerely, 'Well, that's so nice to see, and what better time to see it than at this time of year. I wish you lots of happiness.'

Alex's face glowed as Hope clutched her hand, lingering a kiss onto it. All of a sudden snowflakes began to fall onto the window.

Looking out, they saw the white sky.

'It looks like you two may get a perfect Christmas if this snow keeps up and we have the fairy-tale white Christmas,' the driver said.

Both girls nodded, and a few moments later he pulled up outside their house. Hope reached into her bag, then leaned forward and paid the taxi driver, giving him a large tip.

'Merry Christmas,' Alex said, exiting the cab.

'The same to you both; enjoy your night,' he said, smiling, as he drove off.

Alex took out her key and opened the front door. Hope followed, taking off her high-heeled shoes in the hallway. Alex put the lights on in the lounge and lit the fire, as Hope went into the kitchen, taking a pizza, potato wedges and breaded cheeses out of the freezer, placing them in the oven. She opened a bottle of red wine, pouring measures into the large wine glasses that she had taken from the cupboard. Alex entered the kitchen, casting her eyes over Hope from head to toe.

'Wow, you look stunning this evening. I was the proudest person in that whole bar, you know,' she said, approaching her.

Hope purred, blushing at the same time.

'What are you going red for?'

'Because you make my heart glow with all the sweet things you say, and as it's you saying them, they mean even more. It is already the best Christmas of my entire life and tomorrow hasn't even arrived yet.'

'I know. I think that we should quickly go upstairs and put our pajamas on and then we can relax and watch our film,' Alex suggested, kissing Hope's cheek softly.

'Yes, but you know what, it's not the same wearing old pajamas on Christmas Eve,' Hope said in a deflated voice.

Alex shook her head, smiling profusely.

'What are you grinning at?'

Alex took Hope by the hand, leading her up the stairs into their bedroom. As she pushed the door back Hope saw a pink box with a huge pink ribbon on top of the pillow on the bed. She turned, looking at Alex, jumping up and down.

'Did you think I had forgotten, then?' Alex said, grinning.

'Forgot what?'

'Just go and open it. It's your first Christmas present,' Alex explained, leading Hope to the parcel, watching her as she untied the silk bow. Hope's eyes lit up as she pulled open the box, finding a brand-new red silk pajama top with matching shorts.

'Oh my God, how did you know about this tradition?' she asked with glee, hugging Alex.

'I remember the first Christmas I was seeing you, and you texted me telling me that you had just had a bath and been given your Christmas pajamas that all three of you got to wear every year. It was always my dream to be able to buy you a pair when you were finally with me. It makes me so happy to have fulfilled my wish on this special evening,' Alex admitted poignantly.

Ecstatic, Hope grabbed Alex, squeezing her tightly, kissing her. Alex stopped kissing her, itching to speak.

'Come on, I want to share a very special moment with you. Put your jim-jams on and I'll put mine on, a clean pair for Santa, and then let me share a great memory with you. Hurry up,' Alex requested, euphoric.

Intrigued, Hope quickly did as Alex requested, the two of them getting undressed simultaneously. Alex ran downstairs, making Hope wait impatiently on the bed, until she was ready for her. After a few long moments Alex came upstairs, taking Hope's hand, leading her to the lounge.

As she opened the door, the fire stood blazing in the centre of the dark room, the flames lighting it up, catching the reflection of the tree lights that glowed from the silver-and-white Christmas tree, making the matching white stockings, with their names barely visible in silver, shimmer in the light. Alex led Hope to the window, where they could see large snowflakes falling to the ground. She stood behind Hope, holding her waist tightly, watching the beautiful picture outside their window, the tree and firelight emphasising the darkness outside, contrasting with the covering of snow on the ground. Alex could feel Hope's quickening heartbeat pounding through her flesh as she placed her warm hands on her silk-skinned back. They stood there silently, enjoying the falling snowflakes. Some moments later, Hope turned round, hugging Alex tightly, resting her head on her shoulder, looking at their gifts to one another under the tree, wrapped in their favourite colours, pink and green. Alex held her proudly in her arms as both girls' eyes shut firmly as they savoured this special moment, butterflies fluttering in their stomachs.

'This is the most perfect Christmas I could have ever dreamt of. Thank you. You are my world,' Hope whispered.

As they remained locked tightly together, Alex smiled devotedly, pressing herself harder against Hope's body, her eyes fixed on the snow-covered pavement. Flooded with emotion, she said, 'This is the nicest feeling I have ever had, you know. I haven't had the easiest route to get here; you know – my life, and how sad I have been at times, especially when I was younger, but I'm finally here, and if I died tonight, I would end my journey feeling accomplished.'

After a few seconds Hope pulled away, softly kissing Alex, looking deeply into her eyes, gently running her finger over her cheek, smiling heartily. Sharing a special moment, they stood mesmerised by one another's presence, absorbing their passionate love for several lingering moments.

'It's ready,' she shouted from the kitchen, opening the oven door.

Hope put the food onto the plates, carrying them into the lounge, where Alex was nowhere to be seen. With a puzzled look on her face, hearing a noise from upstairs, as if furniture was being moved around, and a rustling of paper, Hope smiled as she visualised what Alex was doing, thinking she was organising her presents for the following day. She put the food on the table, informing Alex again that it was ready, and sat down, munching her pizza.

Some moments later Alex came into the sitting room with an unparalleled glow.

'What have you been up to?' Hope asked, bemused.

Alex, eager to divulge her surprise, glanced at her watch, smiling broadly as she took a slice of pizza from the plate, sitting alongside Hope.

'Tell me. You know how impatient I am with surprises,' Hope said, glaring at Alex, enjoying her pizza.

'You should know by now that the best things come to those who wait, and then when they come, they are awesome,' Alex joked.

Hope signified her contentment, eating her food.

Throughout the film Alex stared at her watch over and over again, trying in vain to will the time to pass more rapidly. After some time Hope noticed this, questioning it, ignored by Alex, who continued to stare at the TV screen. Hope happily lay alongside her until the film had ended, when she stood up, indicating that it was bedtime. With a look of panic, staring at her watch, Alex attempted to keep Hope awake, enticing her to watch another programme. Hope declined, making her way to bed. Once again Alex stared at her watch, whispering to herself,

'What will I do to keep her awake for the next forty minutes?' She sat for several seconds before coming up with an idea, quickly turning off the TV and the fire, running upstairs, going into the spare room, anxious that Hope should not uncover her plan.

Hope had got into bed and was resting peacefully as Alex frantically checked over the spare room. Her heart had started to beat faster than ever, her mouth becoming dry, as she nervously waited for the next thirty minutes to pass. She went into the bedroom and turned the light on, pretending to look for something.

'What are you doing, Alex? I can't get to sleep with the light on. Whatever you are looking for, can you look tomorrow? It is going to be such a busy day at your mum's house. I'm quite nervous, and I'll need all my strength for that, so I must rest now.'

Alex dismissed her comments, leaving the light on for a few minutes longer, before finally getting into bed, much to Hope's approval. They lay hand in hand as Hope spoke in a very tired tone.

'Thanks for the best Christmas Eve ever. Sometimes I'm not sure that my heart can take all this happiness. I am the happiest person in the whole world.'

Alex squeezed her hand tighter, engulfed by nerves, lying next to her silently. Hope closed her eyes, nodding off as Alex began to mumble in an attempt to combat Hope's sleep for a while longer, glancing at the clock (11.52 p.m.) As she talked about her father, Hope lay motionless, dozing off. Suddenly she awoke, startled.

'What's that noise?' she asked, befuddled.

'I'm not sure, it sounds like a song to me,' Alex responded apprehensively.

The noise became louder as Hope lay there, trying to make out where it was coming from and what it was.

'Yes, it's a song. It's coming from outside, I think.'

'Maybe you should go and see?' Alex suggested hopefully.

'No, you go and see. It's our song, though, listen …'

Alex lay smiling from ear to ear as the song got louder.

'It is our song, "Unstoppable"; where is it coming from?' Hope asked, sitting up.

Alex pulled back the bedcovers, bouncing off the bed.

'Come on, let's go and see where it's coming from.'

Hope got out of the bed, rubbing her eyes, following Alex out of their bedroom, along the landing, where the sound became louder.

'It sounds like it's coming from in there. Open the door and see,' Alex said.

Hope did as requested, thrusting the door open, standing silently.

Alex carefully took her hand as Hope stood stiffly on the spot, with her mouth wide open, gazing at as much as her eyes could take in, as the music played in the background.

'Merry Christmas, angel,' Alex announced in a joyful tone, glancing at her watch (12.04 a.m.).

Speechless, unsure of what was happening Hope nodded, meticulously scanning the room. Alex stood there, taking a large, deep breath before revealing the fruits of her detailed planning, leading Hope around the room from left to right. Immediately Hope noticed the bouquet of roses in the centre of the bedroom, with the biggest pink satin bow she had ever seen, attached around them.

'Don't look at them just yet, all in good time.'

Overwhelmed, Hope agreed, as her heart pounded, faster than ever before, making her cheeks flush. Alex led her to the wall on the left-hand side, pushing the silver-and-red 'I love you and Merry Christmas' helium balloons to one side, allowing Hope to see the cards and photographs stuck behind them. Shaking her head in sheer amazement, Hope studied them.

'This was the first card I ever sent you. Oh God, I can't believe that you still have it, and the first letter too. I have everything you have ever given me, even cinema tickets, but I never knew you kept everything too,' she announced, in a high-pitched voice, shaking her body, mesmerised by Alex, unsure at this stage of the significance of it all.

Guiding her along the wall, anti-clockwise, Alex pointed out a menu. Hope put her hand over her mouth, amazed by Alex's memory.

'Wow, Tacos. That was the very first place we went. Look, another card, from when you first told me that you loved me, and what picture is that? It's the only picture I ever had of you when you were with Matt. I kept that under my bed, you know,' Hope said, unable to contain her excitement.

Alex smiled, moving her around the wall, as Hope struggled to absorb all the sensations evoked, her heart glowing inside, unlike anything she had experienced before. She saw a photograph taken in New York, of them both standing on top of the Empire State Building, bringing the biggest smile to her face so far.

'Why have you done all this? I don't get it,' she said, kissing Alex tenderly.

Ignoring her, Alex came to the end of the wall, smiling at Hope with a sparkle in her eyes, reflecting the moonlight outside, leading her into the centre of the room, where the bouquet sat on top of the table.

'Oh my God, you are the most romantic and thoughtful person I know. Wow,' she said, bedazzled by the two plump pink and three plump red roses in amongst the beautiful hand-tied flowers, sprayed with silver.

'So you guess what that means then?'

'Of course I do,' Hope said, feeling her whole body tense up, reading the card for confirmation − '2+3 for the rest of my life xxxxxxxx.'

'Well, now for the final gift.' Alex spoke with fulfillment.

Hope stood there, numb, open-mouthed, overwhelmed by Alex's surprises, as Alex went to the cupboard, bringing out a huge balloon imprinted with 'This love is Unstoppable' in pink letters, and a small silver box with a green bow and pink wrapping paper saying 'Be mine' with red hearts all over it. She picked up the box, which was attached to the end of the balloon, holding it in her hands, nervously glancing at Hope, thinking how beautiful she looked. Hope put her hand over her mouth once more as Alex tore the wrapping away from the box, placing it in Hope's hand. Moving closer to her, her hands trembling, she said,

'Hope, Christmas is the time to share with the people you love, and so it is on this Christmas Day that I have chosen to declare my ultimate love for you. I lost you once but I will never allow that to happen again. Therefore' – she paused for a moment – 'I would like to ask you to make me the happiest woman alive, and marry me, so that we can spend the rest of our lives together.' She opened the box, taking out the ring with its large square solitaire diamond.

Hope began to cry, overcome by Alex's proposal. She looked at the beautiful platinum ring, glistening in Alex's hand, before gazing at this amazing woman standing before her, shaking her head in disbelief. Alex took the ring out of the box, waiting for Hope's response.

'Well ... will you?' she asked, quaking.

'Of course I will. This is all I've ever wanted. I cannot come to terms with it all. It's too much for me,' Hope blurted in bewilderment, allowing Alex to place the ring on her finger, which had to be held still by Alex.

It fitted perfectly. Alex stood staring at her wife to be with a huge smile, casting a glance out of the window, where the snow continued to fall slowly to the ground.

Euphoric, Hope grinned at the realisation that her dream had become a reality. She stared at the fabulous ring sitting on her finger, jumping up and down.

'I never imagined that you cared for me this much. I cannot believe you had all these ideas. I'm dumbstruck, to be truthful,' she said, looking round, adoring the crowded room, full of their most precious and poignant memories, brought to the fore by her beloved girlfriend.

'Well, I told you that if I ever got married it would be special and for ever, so in order to express this I had to do something very meaningful and special to us. I love you with every part of my body and soul. Merry Christmas, Baby Bear. Do you like the ring?'

'Like it? I adore it, but nowhere near as much as I adore you. I'd put a plastic band around my finger as a ring just to be engaged to you. You will never know how much I love you. My whole body aches for you twenty-four hours a day.' She spoke with widened eyes, grabbing Alex's hand, moving towards the window, holding her around the waist.

They contentedly watched the snow fall on this early Christmas morning, kissing each other's flushed cheeks with rapture.

Chapter 62

'Come on, Hope, it's after one and we were meant to be there at twelve thirty. Have you put all the presents in the boot of my car?'

'I'm coming,' Hope said, coming down the stairs.

'You will have to take your ring off until I have announced it officially to my family.'

Hope pouted but indicated her agreement, staring at her dazzling ring, smiling broadly as she got her bag and placed the ring in her coat pocket.

As they arrived at her mother's house, Alex suddenly felt overcome with nerves, worried about what her mother's reaction would be, as she took the presents out of the boot. Hope walked behind her, equally perturbed about the day ahead, wondering how Eve would react to their exciting news.

Alex opened and entered the house, to be greeted happily by Emily, who took some of the parcels.

'Hi, Hope, Merry Christmas,' Emily said, kissing her on the left cheek.

'Merry Christmas to you also,' Hope replied, jubilant, walking into the kitchen, seeing Eve.

Eve glared at Hope, wishing her Happy Christmas, proceeding to stir the gravy over and over. Hope reciprocated as she stood in the middle of the kitchen, feeling her heart beating through her jumper. Eve continued to stir while Hope left the kitchen, finding Alex in the lounge with her aunt and uncle. Kath immediately stood up, cuddling Hope, sensing her unease, hoping to quash this feeling. Hope smiled, uptight, sitting down next to Emily.

'So what did you get, then?' Emily asked Hope.

Hope looked at Alex for a few seconds and opened her mouth about to speak. Alex nodded in approval, making Hope feel better as she began describing the clothes and make-up she received. Alex went into the dining room, shouting at Hope to come and view the magnificent table decoration.

'Wow, I know you said that it was fantastic but this surpasses my expectations. It's better than anything I've seen in all my magazines,' she joked as Eve entered the room, smiling at her flattering comment, gazing at her red and pink theme.

'Can I get you a drink, Hope?' she asked.

Alex stepped in, 'Well, not just yet, Mum; come into the lounge and we can all do a toast.'

Eve glanced at her but did as she wished, going out of the dining room and into the lounge, where the rest of the family waited. Alex entered the room behind her mother and Hope, pausing as she stood there proudly, but nervously, waiting to speak.

'I have an announcement to make,' she blurted, smiling at Hope as she took centre stage in the middle of the room, finding her knees shaking as she glanced at Emily out of the corner of her eye, seeking reassurance. Emily gave a discreet look of approval, improving Alex's confidence. Hope stood timidly, waiting for her declaration, her palms sweating. Alex had already told Emily, allowing her to leave the room briefly and arrange the pink champagne that sat in the fridge for the toast.

'Well, then …' Kath said.

'I have asked Hope to marry me and she has said yes,' Alex spoke quickly.

'Marriage? I didn't think that gay people could get married,' her uncle announced sarcastically.

Hope stared at Ron, bravely taking Alex's hand as she stood there quivering.

'It's called a civil ceremony, and we are very happy. I love Alex so much, and why shouldn't we show our love as other people can, and do,' Hope said in a heartfelt tone, peering at Eve. Eve scowled for a second before taking note of her daughter's happiness, accentuating a smile, knowing that they were very much in love, making her stand up and embrace her daughter, and then Hope. Emily and Kath also expressed their gladness at the announcement, forcing Ron to accept it too. Emily rushed into the kitchen to fetch the chilled pink champagne, bringing it into the lounge, popping the corks in celebration.

Alex took her champagne and walked towards the doorway, watching her family, happily toasting their happiness on this white Christmas Day, her body glowing, exhilarated at how she was finally happy beyond her wildest dreams. She stood thinking of her beloved father, feeling his presence in the room, evidenced by the warm glow that suddenly entered her heart. She gazed at Hope, besotted, as Hope stood conversing with her family, struck by her beauty, almost like an onlooker at a family gathering, filling her heart with joy.

Suddenly Hope glanced at Alex from the other side of the room.

Love struck, Alex whispered, 'You complete me!'